REUNITED...
WITH BABY

SARA ORWIG

WRONG BROTHER,
RIGHT MAN

KAT CANTRELL

MILLS & BOON

First Published in Great Britain 2018
by Mills & Boon, an imprint of HarperCollinsPublishers,
1 London Bridge Street, London, SE1 9GF

Reunited... With Baby © 2018 Harlequin Books S.A.
Wrong Brother, Right Man © 2018 Kat Cantrell

Special thanks and acknowledgement are given to Sara Orwig for her contribution to the Texas Cattleman's Club: The Impostor series.

ISBN: 978-0-263-93602-5

51-0518

MIX
Paper from
responsible sources
FSC C007454

Printed and bound in Spain
by CPI, Barcelona

REUNITED...
WITH BABY

SARA ORWIG

One

On a Wednesday, the first of August, Luke Weston gazed out the window of his Gulfstream jet as his pilot flew east to Royal, Texas. Looking down at the wide-open, mesquite-tree-covered landscape, it struck him that he was flying directly over the Double U. The ranch that he had grown up on and was now returning home to save.

As he stared out the window, he wondered if he should let the Texas ranch go once and for all. It was no longer home to him. Ever since graduating from Stanford six years ago, he'd been living in Silicon Valley, where he'd been working tirelessly to build his company into the tech-world juggernaut that it was today. He had no desire to live anywhere else.

Even so, he couldn't bear the thought of the Texas

family ranch being auctioned off because his drunken father had mortgaged the Double U again and then couldn't keep up with the payments. Thank heavens, he wasn't like his dad. But when he was young, his dad hadn't been a drunk—a scary fact that was impossible to forget. And his grandfather on his dad's side had been a drunk later in life, too. A drunk who was killed in a bar fight. Bad blood.

Luke's thoughts shifted to his hometown friends, especially Will Sanders. Unable to attend Will's funeral because he had been in Europe, Luke had heard about Will crashing his own funeral in Royal and all hell breaking loose. Who had been impersonating Will? That had been the big question, but answers were pointing in one direction.

This morning, before Luke left California, Will had phoned to inform him that his lifelong friend Richard Lowell had been the one passing himself off as Will. But then Rich had disappeared and no one had a clue where he was now. Another friend had also gone missing—Jason Phillips. At present, only the police and those close to Will knew about Rich, and they were still keeping it quiet while they tried to piece together all that had happened. Will had confided in Luke that Rich had tried to kill him on their annual fishing trip, pushing Will overboard and leaving him to drown. Will was rescued and survived to come home to his own funeral. The body had been cremated, so all they had left were ashes and bones to try to identify.

Adding to the mystery, Will told Luke that funds had been pilfered from the Texas Cattleman's Club in

Royal and they believed Lowell was the responsible party. Upon hearing that, Luke told Will he thought he could help him find the missing imposter via the antifraud software that he and his team at his company, West-Tech, recently created that could aid in following money trails. Will had been interested in learning more, and they agreed to discuss it in person once Luke arrived in Royal.

Once again, Luke reviewed his three purposes in going back to Texas. First, he felt compelled to save the ranch that had been in his family for more than a century. He wondered in what condition he would find the family ranch. How were the animals faring, and how many cowboys still worked on the ranch? Did his dad owe them back pay?

Second, he wanted to do everything he could to help Will find Rich Lowell. The first order of business was to contact the PI who had been hired to aid in the investigation.

And the third reason for returning to Texas was that he felt duty-bound to go visit his dad in the assisted-living home where he had been residing ever since he had been diagnosed a year earlier with cirrhosis of the liver, a debilitating disease. As always, when he ticked off his plans, he had a deep awareness of another Royal resident, Scarlett McKittrick.

Scarlett was one resident he should avoid at all costs, but he suspected that wasn't going to happen. She was the best vet in Royal, Texas, so he would most likely need her professional expertise.

As he pictured her in his mind, the memories assailed him. Memories of holding a naked Scarlett in his arms, kissing her, her intense, instant response to his every caress. Luke drew a deep breath. He was *not* the man for her, and when they parted, she had been furious with him for walking out on her instead of marrying her. Even so, what he wouldn't give for one blissful night with Scarlett before he returned to his carefree, no-strings-attached existence in Silicon Valley.

But he couldn't afford to be distracted with thoughts of his ex. He had to pour all his time and attention into trying to salvage the Double U. Luke still felt a low-burning anger at his dad because he had long ago paid off the ranch and owned it outright, but Luke had made the mistake of letting his father keep everything in his name. Luke hadn't realized what was going on and that his father was pawning things off, selling livestock, mortgaging the ranch to the hilt. Luke felt partially responsible for turning a blind eye and not coming home the moment his dad had been moved to the assisted-care facility. But he'd put on a good show, and Luke had believed him when he'd said that everything was fine.

However, when Luke hadn't been able to contact anybody at the ranch, his internal alarm bells had gone off. Then he got a call from Nathan Battle, sheriff in Royal, who broke the news that he was going to have to put the ranch up for auction.

Luke told Nathan he would be there in two days to pay off the ranch and take care of all the outstanding bills. As soon as he ended the call with the sheriff, Luke had made arrangements with his pilot to fly to Texas the next day.

He just hoped and prayed he would be able to clean up the mess his father had left in his wake.

After landing in Royal, Luke called Cole Sullivan, the PI, as he'd told Will he would do, and made an appointment to talk to Cole tomorrow afternoon in Brinkly, Texas, a small town near Royal. He then phoned Will to tell him he had arrived, and the two men made arrangements to meet tomorrow before Luke met with the PI.

As soon as Luke left the airport in the new black pickup he had purchased by phone, he headed to his family ranch. As he reached the Double U and drove up the ranch road toward the house, he gazed out at the front pasture. It was worse than he had imagined. The first two horses he came across were so severely malnourished their ribs were showing, and they stood listlessly with their heads hanging down. Luke feared they would not live one more night.

He drove on to the house, passing fences that were down and a stock tank shot full of holes. Nearing the homestead, he saw a large part of the exterior wall had been ripped away, and it felt as if a knife had plunged into his gut.

Swearing harshly, he realized he'd had no concept of the full extent of the disaster at the ranch. After taking several deep breaths to help himself calm down, he placed a call to Scarlett McKittrick's veterinary clinic and felt his frustration rise yet again when he learned she was out of the office.

Luke turned his pickup around and sped toward the McKittrick place. When he crossed the cattle guard, he slowed down. As he drove up the McKittrick's ranch road, and drank in the familiar surroundings, it finally felt as if he was coming home.

Bombarded by memories, Luke gazed at the gravel road, but all that he could see were Scarlett McKittrick's thickly lashed hazel eyes. It had been a decade since he had last seen his high school sweetheart, and his life had changed beyond his wildest imaginings. Yet, no matter how much time had passed, there was no way to ever forget her.

He swore under his breath, every part of him aching with bittersweet longing for Scarlett. He had felt certain he had gotten over her, but if he had, why were memories rushing at him like floodwaters from an open dam?

A sudden wave of nostalgia crashed through him as he thought about all that had transpired between them. Back in high school, Scarlett had said she was in love with him. And for a while during his junior year, he had allowed himself to get swept up in dating her and had returned her love fully. But then, in his senior year, reality had set in.

He had a rotten background, while Scarlett had a good, solid one. Her father died when she was young and her brother, Toby, stepped up and filled in as much as he could, while Scarlett's mother quietly took over and ran the ranch with Toby's help. Luke didn't want to mess up Scarlett's life. He was afraid of the bad blood in his family showing up in him.

As his high school graduation approached, Scarlett knew he was leaving for college, but she didn't want him to go. And even though she made it clear she wanted them to have a future together, he never expected her to tell him she wanted them to marry right after he graduated. As far as he was concerned, she was too young and inexperienced to know what she wanted for the rest of her life. She could set him on fire with a kiss, but he still saw her as a kid at sixteen. She seemed far younger than his eighteen years.

He didn't want to marry for years, if ever. His parents' marriage had been unhappy all his life. At first, they fought. Later, they drank and fought. He didn't think either one had been faithful to the other. He didn't want to pass his genes on or marry someone like Scarlett and ruin her life. Only sixteen and hopelessly in love, she didn't understand. Consequently, they didn't part on good terms—something which he deeply regretted to this day.

They'd both moved on. After graduation from Stanford, Luke built his West-Tech company and he struck it rich when he invented a revolutionary—and affordable for the masses—smartphone that left his competitors in the dust.

Meanwhile, Scarlett had pursued a career in veterinary medicine. Which didn't surprise him in the least. A real softie for animals, she always tried to help any creature that needed it, loving little kids and animals as much as he loved electronics and the challenges in the tech world. As she'd been building up her vet business, she had apparently gotten engaged but was now estranged from her fiancé, Tanner Dupree, some oil heir who'd left her stranded at the altar. In Luke's eyes, no one would ever be good enough for Scarlett—definitely not himself. The oily scumbag who had deserted her didn't deserve her, either. Walking out on her on her wedding day—the guy had to be selfish and rotten to the core.

Sighing, Luke knew he was hardly one to throw stones since he'd left her, too. He still believed that was the right thing to do because, given his tainted family history, he would never be good enough for her. But honorable intentions aside, if he was being completely honest with himself, Scarlett was still by far the sexiest woman he had ever known. Even after all this time, he could get hot just thinking about her.

He had been the first guy she'd ever been with, when they were still in their teens. He remembered holding her close, her slender body melting against his. While he was here, could he entice her back into his arms for a night down memory lane...? Groaning, he quickly squelched those illicit thoughts. When he had gone to California, he'd spent too many sleepless nights in college lying awake wanting her, fantasizing about her, fighting the urge to call her because he didn't feel worthy of her because of his family background. He didn't want to mess up Scarlett with his bad genes. He finally had put that behind him, and he didn't want to stir all those feelings up again.

It wouldn't be fair...to either of them.

With a shift of his shoulders, he forced his thoughts back to the present, determined to focus on the here and now.

As Luke approached the McKittrick house, dogs of all sizes ran toward the car. He knew they had to be strays taken in by Scarlett, and he couldn't keep from smiling while he felt a twist in his heart. He stepped out, speaking softly to the barking dogs that quieted down, the friendliest ones already wagging their tails and letting him scratch their heads.

Scarlett walked out onto the porch and stopped at the top step. His heart thudded. For an instant he couldn't speak or breathe and felt as if he was in a dream, except he knew she was real and only a few feet away. He had to curb the impulse to close the distance between them, sweep her into his arms and kiss her endlessly. She was absolutely breathtaking. When he looked into her wide, hazel eyes, he had the impact of a punch to his gut, and it was obvious she, too, drew a deep breath. As she inhaled, her blue blouse grew taut over her figure that had filled out into lush, gorgeous curves. He remembered a kid, a naive, fun young girl, but this was a woman who made his blood hot and fanned desire into flames.

While his gaze locked with hers, he lost his breath again. The urge to crush her against him was overwhelming, and he knotted his fists and focused on staying where he was. His heart pounded as his gaze swept from her head to her toes. She was wearing a blue cotton short-sleeved shirt, tight jeans and boots, and her pixie hairdo complemented her high cheekbones and big hazel eyes. Eyes that were now filled with fury.

He was dazed, stunned by the reaction she stirred in him. He had thought he was over her long ago. If he was, what was going on right now to his heart, his breathing and his lower extremities? And it was obvious from her irate expression that she also was having some kind of reaction.

Except not the kind he particularly wanted.

"You get off the McKittrick property, Luke Weston," she snapped. "And you can just go straight to hell."

"Scarlett, I need your help," he said, talking fast before she cut him off. "My dad is in an assisted-living facility and he's let the ranch go. The animals are dying and need attention—"

He knew when he mentioned the dying animals he had her. The anger left her expression, replaced by worry. She never could hide her emotions, and she was a sucker for any animal in trouble. The yard filled with dogs was proof of that.

She clamped her lips together and stared at him.

"I saw a few horses, and they look so severely malnourished that they can't even hold up their heads."

She closed her eyes for an instant as if in pain. When she opened them, he knew he had gotten through to her. "I took an oath to help animals. I'll get my instruments."

"You can ride with me, and I'll bring you back when you're through. Just save some of the horses or let's put them out of their misery. I don't know which ones to put down," he said, only half meaning it because he was certain that would convince her to help.

"You don't put any down. I'll take care of them."

"There's no feed in the vicinity. I need to get some. I'll take you with me to get supplies."

"This place is the same as it was when you lived here, and you know where to find feed and hay. Go load your pickup with whatever you need for your livestock tonight. While you do that, I'll get my things and then I'll join you," she said.

"Thanks, Scarlett. I appreciate it because I need a good vet. Those horses are in dire shape. You'll see."

Nodding, she turned away. He drove to the barn and hurried inside. One glance at the loft and memories bombarded him. The most persistent memory was of making love with Scarlett, but he had to stop torturing himself because they had no future. He wasn't the man for Scarlett. He had done well in business, but that wasn't all there was to life. Always, he came back to thinking about his parents. His dad did well enough in business for years even after the alcohol began to cloud his judgment.

Damn, Scarlett looked good. As angry as she had looked when she first saw him, he didn't think he would have any choice except to remain cool and impersonal if he wanted her help. But that was easier said than done. He better do that for his own good. He went through hell leaving her before. Now they were adults and the stakes were higher. He didn't want to get involved and have to go through another goodbye and that's all he could hope for with her.

When they reached his family ranch, was he really going to be able to keep his hands off her?

Scarlett went inside to speak to her mother, who was bathing little Carl. For an instant worries fled as she smiled at her precious, adopted baby boy. Her heart squeezed when Carl smiled at her and held out his little arms. "I can't take him, Mom. Luke Weston is here. He's in town and said his dad let the ranch go and the animals are sick, maybe dying now. He came to ask for help. Mom, I have to help those animals."

Her mother frowned and shook her head. "I know you're not going to ignore the livestock, so do what you have to and then come home. You don't need to get involved with Luke Weston again. He broke your heart, Scarlett. Don't let him come back and hurt you again."

"I won't. He lives in a different world now and he'll go right back to it," she said, thinking about the big, strapping man standing in her yard, instead of the young boy she remembered from their high school days. He was wickedly handsome, and her heart had pounded to such an extent that there was no way to ignore what she felt.

As Scarlett talked to her mother, she cut up apples from a bowl her mom kept on the counter. She bagged the apples and smiled at Carl.

Kissing her little boy's chubby cheek, she dodged when he grabbed for her hair. She and her mother both laughed, but she saw the worry in her mother's eyes as she left.

Scarlett fought the urge to tell Luke she couldn't go, but when she thought about the horses that might be hurt or hungry, she knew she had to help. She didn't want Luke putting any animal down unless it was hopelessly suffering and she couldn't save it.

She felt a tangle of emotions—shock because her pulse had raced at the sight of Luke when she had convinced herself that she was completely over him.

And then there was the anger. It was always churning beneath the surface when she thought of him. Of how he'd left her behind. She didn't want to react to him or remind herself that he was more handsome than ever. He was a man now, not a boy, and so incredibly hot.

Scarlett closed her eyes and shook her head. "No, no, no," she whispered. She didn't want to find him better looking than ever, more appealing. Breathtakingly sexy. She didn't want her heartbeat to race. All of that manifested itself, leaving her gasping as if she were sixteen again, lusting like a starry-eyed schoolgirl over the most irresistible boy in Texas.

Little reminders of Luke still popped up in her life, but for all these years since he'd left Royal, she had ignored them. So she had *thought* she was totally over him, but how wrong that was. All he had to do was step out of his pickup and stride up to the porch, and she was ready to either melt into a quivering mess, or run and throw herself into his arms.

She didn't want him to come back to town and cause that kind of reaction simply by laying eyes on him. When he looked at her, he felt something, too. She knew him well enough to know he'd had a reaction to seeing her, which just compounded her desire for him.

Could she work a few hours with him on his ranch and keep a wall around her feelings? She never wanted to suffer through another heartbreak over Luke like she had when he'd left Texas all those years ago. She had cried herself to sleep every night for more than a month.

Scarlett hurried to the closet to grab her new jeans

and a shirt she liked, and then she looked down at
the clothes in her hands. Whoa...what had gotten into
her? Dressing better because of Luke was just asking
for trouble.

"Nope, not happening," she said aloud and shoved
the jeans and blouse back in the closet. She couldn't
resist looking at herself in the mirror, though, and running a comb through her short hair. She guessed there
weren't any women he took out in California who
had freckles and pixie haircuts. She sighed because it
wouldn't matter how she looked, she wasn't the woman
for Luke. She wasn't risking her heart a second time
because he would never make her a permanent part of
his life. She had little Carl to think of now and how
what she did would affect him.

Hurrying to her office, she tried to focus on what
she might need at his ranch as she grabbed her bag.

Before she left she paused, pressing her forehead
against the wall. "Don't let him break your heart again.
Take care of the animals and then come home. Treat
him as if you're with a stranger," she whispered and
then shook her head as she hurried out of her room.
Who was she kidding? She knew she couldn't heed her
own advice, but if she could just remember he was totally off-limits and keep her guard up, she might avoid
more heartache. He hadn't loved her before—now he
definitely never would since he was completely out of
her league. She knew he was the newest addition to
Forbes's billionaire list. Luke could have any woman
he wanted, she was sure. In fact, she had seen his occasional picture in magazines or the news and knew

he dated gorgeous celebrities and some very beautiful socialites.

Holding her bag of instruments, medications and ointments, she rushed out. Luke leaned against his pickup and was looking down at his phone. She couldn't keep from stealing a glance down the length of him, admiring his broad shoulders, his narrow waist and his long legs. When he saw her, he jammed his phone into a back pocket. He straightened and his gaze drifted slowly over her as she approached him, and all her advice to herself to pay little attention to him evaporated.

Everywhere his gaze drifted over her, she tingled. Part of her wanted to turn around and go right back to the house and lock the door. Part of her wanted to yell at him to get off their property and go straight to hell because he had hurt her badly. Yet another, more urgent, part of her just wanted to rush into Luke's arms, pull his head down and kiss him senselessly. She sucked in a breath, and her hand tightened on the handle of her bag while she struggled to think about something besides Luke, his hands and mouth and her pounding heart.

He opened the door to the truck for her, and when she came close, he reached to take the black bag from her. When his big, warm hand closed on hers, she thought her knees would buckle. It was the first time in years—since he'd left for college—that he touched her, and the slight contact sent a sizzling current racing to settle low inside her. Longing rocked her, and she had to take a deep breath and clench her fists.

"I'll put your things in back," he said, his voice raspy, which happened when he was aroused. She couldn't answer him and merely nodded. They knew each other so well. He knew she was having a reaction to being with him, and she knew he was having his own reaction to her. That made the moment hotter and more intense, and kept dredging up memories of their lovemaking when he had lived in Texas.

Again, he took her arm to help her into the pickup—help she didn't want or need. Help that made her quiver and have to fight more memories of his hands on her. When he closed the door and walked around to the driver's side, she inhaled deeply and watched him. A breeze tousled his dark blond hair over his forehead. He looked sexy, more handsome than ever—something she didn't want to acknowledge. Luke was tall, with scruffy stubble on his jaw, and he had gorgeous blue-green eyes, broad, powerful shoulders and well-shaped hands. Hands that could carry her to paradise. In short, Luke was a fantasy come to life.

He slid behind the wheel, closed the door and started the pickup, glancing at her. He sat too close, looked too enticing. "Thanks, Scarlett," he said in a husky voice that still wasn't his normal speaking voice and she knew it.

She nodded. "Let's get this over with," she said curtly, staring out the front window, fighting to ignore him as much as possible. What was happening to her? She was over him, over the hurt he caused when he left for California and said goodbye without a second thought. The old familiar anger and pain made her sit up straight and look out the window as he drove away from the house.

"Stop at the barn, and we can get some bales of hay," she said.

"I did. They're in the back of the truck. I loaded up hay and feed, and then drove back to your house to wait for you." He spared her a quick glance. "I'll reimburse you for everything. I appreciate not having to go back to town to get supplies. I'm guessing there's nothing at the ranch—just on the drive in, the place looked abandoned. There were signs of vandals, and the animals have been left to die," he said gruffly. "I was just there a few minutes, but it's clear I have a catastrophe on my hands. I want to save what animals we can."

Scarlett knew Luke so well that she could tell he was angry with his father. When they drove past the barn on her family ranch, she stared ahead, sitting stiffly, fighting yet another wave of memories.

"You still have the big barn," he rasped.

"We're not going down memory lane," she snapped without looking at him. But she was already down it. Her fingers knotted and she fought the urge to glance again at the barn she saw every day of her life, yet it held special memories of an unforgettable night.

Her whole family had been away for a barn dance. Early in the evening, Luke had coaxed her to leave with him. They had gone back to her place because everyone had gone to the party. Instead of driving to the house, Luke had stopped at the barn. The minute they stepped inside, he pulled her into his arms to kiss her. Later, he spread a blanket on the hayloft and drew her to him again to make love to her, her first time.

Looking away from the barn, she tried to think of something else and forget that night so long ago, forget memories of his slow, sweet kisses that made her want him with her whole being, memories of his strong arms around her, his mouth on her, his seductive hands all over her body.

"How are your mom, and Toby and his wife?"

"They're fine," she answered, glancing at him. "Toby and Naomi have a little girl, Ava." While Luke watched the road, her gaze swept over him, once again taking in the short stubble that covered his jaw, his tousled, dark blond hair that she could remember running her fingers through too many times to count. His shoulders were broader now, thicker. Desire rocked her and she took a deep breath. Realizing once again where her thoughts were going, she turned swiftly to stare out the window, not really seeing the landmarks they passed, but remembering being held in his arms, her head back against his shoulder.

She gave a tiny shake and struggled to get her attention off of her ex. He would leave as suddenly as he had come, and she didn't want one tiny bit more hurt in her life because of Luke Weston, especially now that she had a son to care for.

She looked at familiar land, places she had grown up, and in seconds Luke dominated her thoughts yet again.

She had to resist his appeal. In no time he would be back in his private plane, headed to California, back to his ritzy life, back to glamorous models, celebs and rich socialites, eventually marrying one who could give him the children he'd want.

"You've done well in California. You did the right thing to move out there. It suits you as much as all this suits me," she said, knowing the Silicon Valley world was his world.

"I guess you're right, Scarlett. It's my real home," he said without looking at her. He sounded casual, but his hand was tight on the steering wheel, so obviously he felt something, too. "Common sense says to sell the ranch and forget it. I won't live in Texas again. But... I can't sell it. I just can't let the family place go. It's been in our family since the 1800s." He blew out a frustrated breath. "I paid the house off three years ago, and damned if he didn't go out and mortgage it to the hilt again. He hasn't kept up his payments—no surprise there. He's let the help go. I just found that out before I came."

"Sorry, Luke," she said, again without looking at him. How polite and cool they were being with each other. "So you're going to keep the ranch, even though you'll go back to California? You think you'll come back to the ranch someday?" she asked, watching him and curious about his answer even though she knew she shouldn't care at all. They would never again mean anything to each other. Unfortunately, the jump in her pulse today showed she still had to work at getting him out of her system.

"No, I never will, but at this point in my life, I just

don't want to let it go. I know that doesn't make sense, because California is absolutely my forever home."

"You don't need to be in a hurry. Your dad is still around. It may mean something to him."

"Booze is the only thing that means anything to him," Luke said, and she heard the anger and bitterness in his reply. "He'll never be able to live alone again."

After they left the McKittrick ranch, they rode quietly. Her thoughts were in turmoil because she couldn't lose that intense awareness she had of Luke. She never had been able to ignore him, and she definitely couldn't now. Why couldn't she ever see him as just another guy? She had to get over him or get hurt again. She could never be the woman for him because of her fertility problems. One man who loved her enough to ask her to marry him had already walked out on her. Luke hadn't been interested when he had never been out of Texas and was getting ready to leave the family ranch. Now, he wouldn't have any permanent interest in a small-town female vet who couldn't bear his children. If she got involved with him, he would love her and leave her and in doing that he would get to know her baby. If she let Luke in her life again, when he said goodbye, he would not only break her heart again, he would break little Carl's heart. That could be a lifetime hurt for her and her baby.

Scarlett tried to avoid remembering Luke's kisses, but whenever she glanced at his handsome profile or his sexy mouth, the memory was vivid, tantalizing, still painful after all this time. She looked at his big, masculine hands on the steering wheel, but shifted her attention swiftly because she could remember those hands on her body, working their magic. An undercurrent of longing taunted her.

She released a quavering breath. Why did her heart race when he had merely brushed her fingers with his? She remembered how much she'd hurt when he left when she was sixteen. She didn't want a bigger hurt now.

She couldn't understand her own reactions to him. She wasn't in love with him—she barely liked him because of the bitter fight before he left for California. How could he set her pulse pounding just by reappearing? She had to get over him. She didn't want to spend years longing for a guy she knew as a boy in high school. A guy who didn't want her.

They rode in silence until he turned and headed up the road toward the house where he had spent his boyhood.

The first sign of neglect was a rusty pickup smashed against a tree. She saw bullet holes where kids had probably placed bottles on it or just shot out the windows and used the truck for a target. The wheels were gone. Weeds grew up in the road that was barely visible in spots.

"Evidently, after Dad let the hands go, he sold some of the horses to subsidize his alcohol addiction." Luke scowled. "I used to send money home, but he just bought liquor with it, so I stopped. I'll get a crew out here as fast as I can, but right now I wanted you to see if we can't save some of these horses. But honestly? I don't know how the horses I saw can last through the night. No one works here. The damn ranch is deserted—the animals left to starve and die."

She could hear the anger and pain in his voice and couldn't blame him for his reaction. She was equally shocked by the terrible conditions.

In minutes, Luke approached a pasture with half a dozen horses standing near a stock tank that needed water. The windmill had broken boards and wasn't working. She gasped. "Oh, no," she whispered without knowing she had spoken when she saw the horses with ribs painfully revealed and two with their heads hanging. All the horses looked severely malnourished. The stock tank had holes in the side.

"Sorry to pull you into this because I know it'll tear you up, but I need your help here," Luke said.

"Oh, my heavens. Look at the horses," she lamented. "It breaks my heart. You know I'll help these animals," she said, horrified to look at the condition of the horses. She felt sympathy for Luke, even though she didn't want to get caught up in his problems. But what he had come home to was ghastly, and he had tried to help his dad to keep the ranch in good shape.

She could certainly understand his anger and disappointment, and gave a silent prayer of thanks for her own family. They helped each other and did the best they could and always could be counted on. "Oh, Luke, this is unbelievable. I had no idea this ranch had just been abandoned. We're neighbors. Our ranch adjoins yours, and nobody in the area has said a word about it. Why didn't someone speak up? The last hands that left here—why didn't one of them contact you? How could your dad neglect everything so badly?"

"Because he's a sick old drunk who doesn't care about anybody or anything except his next drink," Luke bit out, and she was sorry for saying anything because Luke was obviously suffering over finding his home in shambles.

"I'll get the pasture gate," Luke said, getting out to drag open a sagging, battered gate made with barbed wire. He returned to drive the pickup in and close the gate.

"Sorry, Luke," she said stiffly when he was behind the wheel again. She spoke without looking at him, trying to avoid thinking about what he was going through. "We'll start. Let's get to work."

"I'll patch those holes enough to get water in that tank so they can drink. I sent Dad money to get fiberglass tanks and look what we've got—the old corrugated metal the cows have pushed against and bent years ago. Damn, I wasn't sure what I'd find here, but I didn't expect it to be this bad. Every dime I sent home must have gone for booze."

She looked around and saw three horse carcasses. The live horses had moved away from them and they were decomposing, probably torn by predators and birds.

"You have dead animals."

He sighed. "Damn. I can get a temporary crew out here to help." He parked near the horses and a few watched them while two slowly moved toward them. Luke was already on his phone, calling someone who worked for him to start trying to hire a crew of cow-boys to do temp work.

When she approached the horses, her sympathy shifted to the animals, and she could hardly blame Luke for being so upset at his father for letting this hap-pen. When Luke was a kid, the Double U had been a fine ranch. His dad was a good rancher, and he knew what he was doing to his livestock when he neglected them. At least he had to have known when he was sober. She spoke softly and got her bag of apples, but the horses couldn't raise their heads. She knelt to open her bag and get a needle to give shots that would help more than anything else.

"I'll get these horses to the pasture by the barn. There's water there. I'll get halters on them and lead them back, and you drive the pickup. You can follow the road here to the house," he said. "If there are any horses we can't move, we'll try to take care of them here."

It was almost an hour later when they climbed back into his pickup and drove toward the house.

"I came home every year for the first three years while I was in college, and it was never like this. Things were messy at the house, but otherwise, he kept things in relatively good shape." He scrubbed a hand over his jaw. "We had some good hands and a good foreman. I never stayed more than a night or two, so he must have pulled himself together.

"Several years ago at Christmas, I sent a plane for him and brought him to California. He said everything here was fine. He couldn't wait to get back here and cut short his stay. Gradually, we've grown more apart than ever, and I haven't been home. If I did make contact with him, he always said everything was going okay." Luke worked his jaw back and forth. "I should have kept up with him better and maybe I could have prevented some of this. I could have hired someone to come out here and run the ranch."

"You didn't know."

"I *should've* known. He always could carry on a decent conversation when he was dead drunk. I should have guessed what was going on."

"Luke, I'm sorry. This is a disaster."

"We'll just have to hunt for the animals. I doubt if there are any cattle left. I'm sure they've all been stolen. The horses probably were passed over at first for cattle. By the time anyone turned attention to the horses, they may have been in such bad shape no one wanted them. I just barely glanced at the house, but I'll walk through in case there are any animals in it."

Scarlett cringed when the house came into view. One wall was shattered, as if someone had tried to drive through it. Windows were smashed. Steps to the porch had collapsed. The front door was missing. Bullet holes dotted the walls, and boards had been ripped from the porch floor. Someone had thrown black paint at the house, and a big splash of paint had spilled down a wall. A living room chair was upside down in the yard, one leg broken, another leg missing.

"Oh, my heavens, Luke…" she commiserated softly. Certainly it gutted him to look at his childhood home so badly damaged.

"While neglect did a lot to the house and barn and outbuildings, vandals and thieves caused the rest," he said grimly. "My dad, because of his damned drinking, has just let our home—a damn fine ranch—go to hell."

Knowing how she would feel if it had been her home, she ached for him. "I'm sorry, Luke. How awful for you to come home to this." Impulsively, she squeezed his wrist and Luke turned, his blue-green eyes intent on her, causing a chemical reaction. The minute she touched him, the moment changed. Sympathy vanished, replaced by sizzling desire. But she didn't want to be swept off her feet by him again. She'd been through too much heartache because of Luke to go through more.

When his gaze locked with hers, she drew a deep breath, conscious of Luke and nothing else. Worse, she was absolutely certain he felt something, too.

"I'm sorry for you, and I'm sorry for your dad. Have you seen him yet?" she asked, her words tumbling out too fast as she tried to get back to anything less intimate. But that slight touch of his wrist brought a truckload of memories pouring over her, and she felt her anger with Luke lose a bit of its intensity.

She felt sympathy for him. It would be devastating if she came home to find the McKittrick ranch in ruin. She tried to pay attention to what he was saying about seeing his dad.

"No, that's on my list of things to do while I'm here. What he's done—or more accurately, *not* done—is going to make seeing him again even more difficult than I expected. He must be in terrible shape to let all this happen."

"Well, let's look for the horses or whatever livestock that's still here," she said, struggling to get back to business.

He nodded. "I stopped here briefly before coming to get you. I want the house torn down. I can't stand to see it in ruin. The memories from there weren't all that great anyway," he said, and her heart lurched at the bitterness in his voice. She curbed the impulse to reach out and squeeze his wrist again. It was obvious he hurt badly.

"There's a half bath in the barn, so at least we have a little in the way of facilities for us. There may be running water and electricity in the bathrooms in the house. Right now, however, we better find what animals we can while it's daylight. I'll try to get them back to the pasture by the barn, where you can do what you have to do and I can feed and water them. Can you stay longer?" he asked.

"Yes, I'll stay. I want to save as many horses as I can," she said.

"We'll take the pickup now. Later, I'll probably have to search on horseback because there are places on the ranch where I can't drive. I may have to go buy a horse because none of these can carry me on its back." He released a breath. "But for now, I've got rope in the back of the truck, some feed and a saddle if I need it, all sorts of supplies."

"All right," he said, "let's get started." He turned his truck and as he drove she looked for any livestock. They hadn't driven a half mile when she gasped. "Luke, stop. There's an animal. It's a dog, and it's dead. I think it looks like it might be Mutt." With a pang, she remembered the dog that followed Luke around when he was home.

They got out of the pickup and walked closer. Luke knelt and ran his hand over the dog's head. "Oh, dammit to hell. That's Mutt. He was old and weak, and I guess coyotes got him."

She knelt to look over the carcass more closely, and she hurt even more for Luke because this was the ranch dog that he claimed as his.

"I left him here when I went to California because the ranch was up and running and in good shape," he said, his voice raspy with regret.

"The ranch was in good shape because you were here," she said quietly, still looking at the dog.

"The guys liked him and he was happy here. I thought he'd be better off. He looks starved. He was old and weak, but something's really torn him up."

"Luke, he's been shot. Someone shot him, and they may have done it because he was old and he may have been sick. There's one shot and it's a killing shot, so this wasn't random or someone being mean. I think he was torn up by buzzards and coyotes after he was shot."

Luke leaned closer to look as she pointed to the wound. "I hope he didn't suffer. I loved the old mutt. He was a good dog." He released a shaky breath. "I'm going to bury him. I have a shovel, and I'll wrap him in a tarp and bury him back at the house."

She heard the catch in Luke's voice, and a lump rose

to her own throat. They both stood, and she looked up at him. Without thinking about it, she touched his wrist again. "I'm sorry. I know you loved him." The minute her hand rested on his, she knew she shouldn't have touched him, even though it was obvious he was hurting badly. His wrist was twice the size of hers, warm, his wrist bone hard. Something flickered in the depths of his eyes, and he gazed at her intently.

"I haven't loved much in my life, but I loved him," he said roughly, his voice grating and a muscle working in his jaw. She couldn't get her breath, and she couldn't understand the intensity of his gaze or his remark that he hadn't loved much in his life. Was he just talking about a dog—or was there more to his statement?

She wanted his arms around her so badly it frightened her, and she stepped away quickly, going back to the truck. "Tell me if I can help," she called over her shoulder.

She was breathing hard as he walked to the back of his pickup. Pulling work gloves from his pocket, he got a tarp to wrap the dog. In minutes, he slid behind the steering wheel and drove on in silence.

Why did it feel as if Luke had been away only days instead of years? Those empty years had vanished in too many ways. The worst part was the realization that she had never really gotten over him, something she had struggled desperately to do.

She had never felt this way for Tanner, and she had been engaged to him. Was it because Luke had been the first love in her life? Or did it go deeper than that?

They rode together in silence, only a couple of feet

of space separating them in the pickup, but there was still a permanent, deep chasm dividing them.

He hadn't loved her and he never would, so why couldn't she forget him? She clearly meant nothing to him—that alone should stop the volatile reaction she had to him and the desire that still steadily simmered through her veins.

They bounced over the rough ground, and she looked around carefully, trying to see any sign of livestock. In another twenty minutes she spotted horses to the east. "Luke, over there."

"Yeah, I see. They're in a fenced pasture, so let's keep looking and see if we can find some more and get them back with these. They may be in bad shape, but hopefully we can get them to the barn." He continued to drive, and she gazed around, looking for any more signs of life.

"Luke, I see horses through the trees," she said a few minutes later, and he swung the pickup in the direction she pointed.

For the next six hours they worked—rounding up horses, finding a few cattle, getting them back to the barn—trying to do it all while it was still daylight. When the horses were finally in the corral by the barn, the cattle in a pasture, Luke closed the corral gate and turned to her.

"You start checking the horses while I get feed to them. They've got water now in that tank. Shortly, it'll be dark, so I'll get lanterns out now and have them ready, and we can keep working if you can stay. If not, I'll take you home. I'd appreciate your help if you can."

"I can stay."

He looked at her and reached out to hug her. "Thanks, Scarlett," he said.

As his arms wrapped around her and pulled her against his solid, hard body, her heart thudded. His strong embrace made her tremble and want to wrap her arms around him and hold him tightly against her heart. How was she going to work with him into the night without stirring all those old feelings she had for him?

Two

He released her abruptly. "I better get busy," he said. His words were casual and indifferent. His voice was that hoarse tone he had when he was aroused, so she knew he felt something, too—knowledge which made her heart beat faster. What did Luke feel now? She shouldn't care or even think about what he was feeling.

Why, oh, why, couldn't she get Luke out of her system? When he left Texas, he had hurt her terribly, and she shouldn't feel any kind of desire for him, but she did. How could she ever trust him again? She had to guard her heart and not let sympathy for his problems make her forget their past.

"Luke, I have to call home and then I'll get busy," she said, walking away from him.

She talked briefly with her mother, making certain

all was well with Carl. While Carl was fine, her mother had warnings about Luke and how he had broken her heart before. The brief conversation just reminded her again how much Luke had hurt her before and made her conscious that she hadn't gotten over him at all. She had been fooling herself all these years—easy to do when he was in Silicon Valley and she was in Royal.

It was a hot August night in Texas. Luke had lanterns going, and she looked around once just as he yanked his shirt off and tossed it aside. Her mouth went dry and her heartbeat sped up as she looked at his muscles, highlighted by the lamplight. A sheen of sweat glistened on his bulging biceps while he scooped up more hay with a pitchfork. She could remember being in his arms, held tightly against his body. Longing shook her to the core, and she couldn't stop looking at him while memories sparked more flames inside her. Only now this was a grown man with a man's broad shoulders, a man's muscled chest, a still flat, narrow waist and a hard, rippled stomach that disappeared below his belt.

He looked up, catching her staring at him. She boldly met his gaze, wondering if he could guess her thoughts and feelings. After several long, tension-fraught moments, she finally turned away. Heat burned in her cheeks. She didn't want him to see how easily he could captivate her attention, yet it was evident he knew the effect he had on her, just as she knew when she affected him.

Five minutes later she found her eyes drawn to him once again. She couldn't resist watching him when she thought he wasn't aware of it. He must work out in Silicon Valley because he was all muscle, his back and arms shiny with sweat. He'd rolled and tied a bandanna around his forehead to keep sweat out of his eyes as he worked. In the light of the lanterns, he looked incredibly male, appealing and sexy. He also looked fit and strong.

She couldn't stop glancing at him, desire making her heart pound. She tried to focus on the horses, working hard and fast, and shut Luke out of her mind and stop gawking at him.

Suddenly one of the horses collapsed, and she raced to it, kneeling and giving it a shot as quickly as she could.

It was breathing hard, making gasping noises with each breath. It was bleeding from gashes on its belly and neck.

"Scarlett, I'm going to put him down. You're fighting a losing battle. Go on to the next one."

Startled, she glanced up to see Luke standing with a pistol in hand. A cold chill ran down her spine. Instantly on her feet, she faced him as she placed her hands on her hips.

"No, you're not! I can save him. Put that pistol, away, Luke Weston, and don't get it out again around the horses unless I ask you to."

He blinked and then pressed his lips together. She didn't know whether he was biting back a laugh or was angry at her for telling him what to do with his own horse.

She was earnest, and there was no way she was

going to let him shoot his livestock. "This horse will be on its feet tomorrow." She ground out the words. "I've given him a shot that will help. Give him time. Don't you put any animal down without my permission, you hear me?"

"I won't, Scarlett, but look at him. He doesn't have the strength to stand. He's all bones and he can't breathe."

"He can breathe, and I'm going to take care of him. He'll be on his feet when morning comes. I know what I'm doing, Luke, so you go back to work and leave this horse to me." She glared at him and met his unfathomable gaze. Without a word, he tucked the pistol in the back of his waistband and stalked away.

She watched him go for a few seconds and then turned her attention to the horse and forgot Luke for the next hour. She paused briefly once for another call to her mother to check about Carl and once again, he was fine and all was well at home.

She went from one horse to another, trying to tend to each one, and she thought of the carcasses they had found, of horses that hadn't survived. During the afternoon Luke had grown silent, and she knew he was furious with his dad and his fury grew with each dead animal they found. She knew he was still devastated over the dog because, as a kid, he had loved that dog.

Occasionally, as she moved around, she saw Luke working, repairing the corral fence. There were so many places where the fence was down or damaged that she hoped he could get it fixed before some of the horses wandered away. The feed he had put out held the attention of those that were able to stand to eat or drink.

Luke had rounded up some cattle, less than a dozen head. She thought of the big herds they'd had when Luke was in high school. She heard a twig snap and looked around to see him approaching again.

"Unless you've changed a lot, I know you love hamburgers more than steaks. I'm having dinner brought out here."

She tilted her head to look up at him. "How on earth did you get dinner delivered to this ranch? There isn't a café for twenty miles."

He grinned and shrugged. "My money's good for some things. I should've asked you who to call, but I remember Rusty's. They're still in business. We'll take a break and eat. Okay?"

She smiled. "Okay. If I'd known you were going to do that, I would have asked you to get more apples for the horses."

"If we're still here, I'll try at breakfast. A couple of the horses are back on their feet already. You're a miracle worker, Scarlett, and I can't tell you how grateful I am that you're helping. I'd hate like hell to have to put all these horses down. That would be about my last straw."

"You're not going to have to put any down, so forget that. I don't care how bad they are, we're going to save them, but if you'd come much later—"

"I already lost some before I got here," he said, frowning as he glanced at the horses. "I better get back to work." He turned to leave. "I'll call you when dinner arrives."

She barely heard him because she had already turned back to a gash she was stitching. The smaller white horse stood patiently, but she wondered if it would collapse any minute. It didn't seem to care what she did or that she was even there.

By midnight there were still horses that needed tending to, and Luke was still fixing a stock tank. She wanted to keep working but, mindful of little Carl and her mother, she walked into the shadows, trying to get out of Luke's earshot before calling home.

As expected, her mother began to argue for her to come home, reminding her again that being with Luke was going to dredge up all kinds of pain.

"Do you really want to go through all that again?" her mother asked.

"Mom, I'm taking care of very sick horses and some of the cattle need attention. They're in dire shape, and I'm not abandoning them to die when I can save most of them."

"My heavens! How awful. I haven't heard anything bad like that about the Double U. Even so, Scarlett, I'm worried about you."

"Mom, this is my job, to save animals. This is why I became a vet. I'm needed here and we can already see a difference in some horses."

"Scarlett, Luke is going to hurt you again. Maybe even worse this time because you're not kids anymore. Please get out of there and come home. Baby Carl and all the family need you. You don't want to go through all that loss and hurt again, and that's what will happen if you stay."

"No, I won't. I won't let it happen." There was a long pause, and she knew her mother was giving up and could not continue arguing.

"Take care of yourself, then. We love you," her mom said. "And before you start to get caught up in old feelings with that man, just remember that Luke will go home to Silicon Valley in a few days and you won't hear from him until the next time he pays a visit here."

She sighed. "I love you, Mom, and I love my family. Luke's dad has done a terrible thing, and bearing witness to it makes me so thankful for all of you. I'll take care of myself, I promise," she said, wondering if she really could keep that promise, or if she would just cave if Luke wanted to hug or kiss her. She almost laughed aloud as she ended her call. Her amusement fled when she looked back and saw the lights, the weak horses, the cows in another pasture. Was she being foolish and risking her heart to try to save horses that might not survive no matter what she did?

But she felt she had to stay. She had taken an oath to help animals, and she took that oath seriously.

She just hoped she could resist Luke, but then again, she might not have any reason to worry about resisting him. He probably had a woman waiting in Silicon Valley for his return.

Her attention was taken again by the ailing horses. She suspected Luke was right about the cattle. There were few left that he had found, and she imagined nearly all the Double U cattle had been rustled long ago. Luke said he would continue searching for more when daylight came, but so far he hadn't found any. She continued to nurse the horses, wondering if she would have to work through daybreak. Dinner had given her another spurt of energy, but that was beginning to fade. She glanced at Luke as he repaired holes in the water tank, going over them a second time.

He was the golden boy from Royal who had gone west and made a fortune in Silicon Valley. He hadn't been interested enough in her in high school to want to continue their relationship, to want her with him or to want to return to Royal to be with her. How many times did she have to remind herself that he really had no lasting interest in her? He had liked to kiss and make love, but he could turn around, walk out the door and forget all about her without a moment's regret. Walking out on her didn't make her blood run cold, but thinking Luke would do that to Carl did. She couldn't bear that kind of hurt. She glanced at him again. Flickering lantern lights spilled over him, turning his skin golden and highlighting his firm, muscular back and chest, his powerful shoulders and biceps, his flat stomach. She tingled as her gaze ran over him. Her mouth had gone dry, and her heart thumped swiftly. She wanted his arms around her, his mouth on hers. She could remember his kisses. Absolutely. Too well, she could recall his mouth on hers, making her quiver with eagerness, with steaming lust, with hunger for his hands and his body.

He turned to look at her. Startled, she realized how she stared as his gaze narrowed. She spun away and bent over a horse to cleanse and patch a wound while her cheeks burned with embarrassment.

She lost track of time until she glanced at her watch

and saw it was after two a.m. About ten minutes later, Luke appeared and caught her wrist, lifting it as she was about to give a horse a shot.

"I think you should call it a night."

"Luke, there are still horses here I haven't treated. I don't want to stop."

"Aren't you tired?"

"Yes, but I can keep going and I want to."

He studied her and nodded. "Okay, a little while longer."

When he turned and left, she went back to work. The next time he appeared, he placed his hand on her shoulder. "Scarlett, it's late," he said. His voice was husky, his hand lightly squeezing her shoulder.

She turned to look up at him. He stood close, and her heart beat faster as she shook her head. "I can't quit."

"Yes, you can, for a little while. Come on. Let's get a couple of hours of sleep before the sun comes up. I've got a blanket in the back of the pickup."

Luke was bare chested, too appealing, too sexy, too damned handsome. His looks had only gotten better over time. Her gaze drifted to his mouth, to scorching-hot memories of his mouth on her body.

"You remember just as much as I do," he said in a deep, husky voice that played over her like a caress.

She drew a breath and met his gaze, her cheeks burning. "I may remember, but that's all. It won't go any further than that," she whispered.

"Scared to kiss me, Scarlett? After all this time, it won't mean anything."

"Don't try to goad me into doing something in anger

that I wouldn't do otherwise," she said, annoyed with him, and with herself, because she wanted to wrap her arms around him and kiss him until he would wish he hadn't pushed her into it. But she knew better than to do that.

"Okay, Scarlett, go back to work. So will I. I'll come back in half an hour or so. If you want to quit before then, just let me know."

"Of course I will," she said sweetly, running her hands lightly over a horse, feeling its bones and wondering how it could even stand. She forgot about Luke as she went back to work. She finally began to feel tired, but she still didn't want to stop. As she worked, Luke appeared again. He reached out, and his hand closed on her wrist. "C'mon. Let's get a little sleep. The sun will be over the horizon in a couple of hours. We'll get back to this when the sun comes up."

Nodding, she didn't argue. She left him, hurrying to the barn and the tiny room with minimal facilities. Even so, she felt refreshed when she stepped out. She was so tired it shouldn't matter if they both slept in the back of his pickup, except she knew it would.

"Luke, we can't both sleep in the back of your pickup."

"Why the hell not? There's nowhere else—all of West Texas has rattlers, so the ground is out. The front seat isn't big enough. You can keep your hands to yourself, and so can I. Don't tell me you find me that irresistible?"

She knew the last part was said in jest, but she was tired and frustrated because she didn't want to end up handing him her heart again, and, if they made love, she was afraid that was exactly what would happen.

Annoyed, she stepped close to stab his chest with her forefinger. "You know you're attractive. You know I feel something, and I know you feel something, too. If we get in the back of your pickup, we won't sleep. I'm realistic enough to know that and honest enough to admit it. I can sleep inside on the front seat, and that's where I'll be. The sun will wake me."

"You sleep where you want, but after that little speech you just made, there's no way in hell I can resist," he growled, drawing her into his arms and leaning down, looking directly into her eyes. Her heart thudded. He intended to kiss her and she couldn't resist him, either. Especially when he was holding her in his arms and his mouth was only inches away, his blue-green eyes glimmering with raw, unsuppressed desire.

"Luke," she whispered, wanting him, knowing she was crossing a line she would regret, yet still unable to say no to him. The look in his eyes made it crystal clear that he, too, wanted her with all his being. Then his mouth was on hers, opening hers, and his tongue slipped inside, going deep, stroking and making her tremble, sending lightning streaking through her.

Desire shook her, and she wrapped her arms around his neck, pressing against him and kissing him in return, pouring all the pent-up longing and aching need that she felt for him into that kiss. She wanted him to remember kissing her, to want her the way she had wanted him. She hoped her kiss haunted him, caused him to lie awake at night to deal with the desire and the memories. And she wanted to relish this moment in his arms, being kissed by him, a dream fulfilled if only for a few precious minutes. His erection pressed against her, urgent, hard, ready, and she wanted him with all her being. But then she remembered her tears, her heartbreak, her longing—he had walked away without a qualm. She wasn't going back to that.

She tore her mouth from his and then stepped away. "I'll be up with the sun," she whispered and turned to climb into the front seat of his pickup, lock the door and lean back against the seat.

She fought the urge to turn to see what he was doing. She fought an even greater urge to go back and join him, but she wasn't climbing into the back of his pickup this first night he was in town and sleeping with him. Scarlett released a shuddering breath. Was she ever going to really get over him? She thought she had— she told herself she had when Tanner Dupree entered her life, but after Luke's mind-blowing kiss tonight, she knew that Tanner had never held the appeal that Luke did.

It didn't matter. She wasn't the woman for Tanner. She wasn't the woman for Luke. Once again, she faced the fact that Luke was a billionaire businessman now, young, successful and handsome. He would not want to tie his life to a small-town vet.

Deep inside she hurt, but she also felt resigned. She had faced reality about Luke a long time ago. Now, being the newest billionaire on *Forbes*'s list, he lived in a whole different world. Particularly when he returned to Silicon Valley. She had seen pictures of his mansion and read about all the fancy electronic conveniences he had. He would go back to his world once he got his family ranch taken care of, and she wouldn't see him again, maybe ever. Worse, someday he might bring one of those gorgeous women to the ranch. Scarlett knew she should keep that prospect in mind.

And as much as it pained her, she had always known deep down that he had moved on and she would never be part of his life.

Luke gazed up at the twinkling stars. One of the things he had always loved about being on the ranch— no city lights to hide the beauty of the night sky. He saw the stars, but his thoughts were on Scarlett. He wanted her in his arms and was disappointed she wouldn't sleep beside him. If she had, they would have had more kisses.

His pulse quickened. Remembering the feel of her lips pressed so sweetly against his was going to keep him awake, which sucked since he was totally exhausted. What a way to kill his slight chance for some sleep here.

He had forgotten what a force she could be. When he had drawn his pistol, he was just thinking of putting down a suffering, hopelessly injured horse. He never thought about Scarlett jumping up and confronting him, standing right in front of a pointed gun. Fortunately, he had the safety on, but for a split second, she had surprised him. And then he remembered it was Scarlett and he should have known better. She was fiercely protective of her animals—he didn't have to be around her since she became a vet to realize that. She had been that way when she was fifteen years old. Probably when she was four years old, too.

He smiled in the darkness and placed his hands behind his head. He'd been lucky in business and done well. He had gotten accustomed to people being at his beck and call and doing his bidding, and that especially held true for his female companions. His life was filled with his pick of pretty, flirtatious women saying yes to whatever he wanted. But now he was back at his childhood home, and right away Scarlett told him to get off her property and go to hell. His smile grew. If she didn't agree with him, she would let him know in no uncertain terms. And it would be not only "no," but "hell, no." Clearly she didn't have a qualm about telling him what to do and what he *wasn't* going to do.

His smile faded. He knew it was all kinds of wrong, but he wanted to go out with her. He wanted to take her to bed and make love for hours. She was as off-limits to him as much as if she had married that oil jerk who walked out on her, but his heart obviously hadn't gotten the memo.

Luke thought of the three women he'd seen the most this past year—gorgeous women who were fun to be with, sexy in bed, with dream bodies. They would never give him trouble or tell him to go to hell. He had to forget Scarlett, and as soon as he returned to California, he would look these women up and go out with whichever one he enjoyed the most.

Luke groaned. He had about an hour and a half and then the sun would be up. But now that he had a chance to get some shut-eye, Scarlett still filled his every thought. She was like a powder keg with a short, lighted fuse. At the same time, she was hot, luscious, sexy enough to make his blood boil. Her kiss should send steam out his ears.

He ached to hold her, to make love to her, to ravish her from head to toe. But as much as he wanted her, he knew he couldn't seduce her. He'd hurt her when he left before, and he didn't want to do that again.

That thought moved sleep further away. Thoughts of making love to her conjured up images that would keep him up another hour, he was sure. He might as well just get up and go back to work.

"Damn, woman, either get out of my thoughts or into my bed so I can get over you one way or another," he ground out, all the while knowing neither were going to happen.

With a muttered curse, he got up, trying to be quiet and move carefully so he didn't shake the pickup as he crawled out and went to work.

It was almost 9:00 a.m. when he returned to the pasture where he had parked and he saw Scarlett. She picked up her bag and approached him. Just watching her walk toward him turned him on. She had a sexy sway to her hips and an enticing walk. Wind caught locks of her hair and blew them across her forehead. He pushed his brown Resistol to the back of his head and waited.

"I've looked over all the livestock. You really are a miracle worker—the horses are on their feet. It may be my imagination, but they all look better, too." He grinned down at her. "How're you doing this morning with less than two hours' sleep?"

"I'm fine," she said, turning her back on him as she stepped up to a black horse to run her hands over it.

"When you're ready, I'll drive you home, Scarlett. You've been a fantastic help, and you've saved these horses. Whenever you have it ready, give me the bill."

"Sure." She peered up at him, her brow furrowed with concern. "You didn't get much sleep either. You were already up and gone when I got up."

"Yeah," he said, not wanting to tell her that he hadn't slept a wink after their smoking-hot kiss.

"I'll work for about an hour more, and then I think you'll be able to take care of them with no problem."

With a sigh, he moved on, going back to his truck to start making some calls now that it was morning. He needed to hire all sorts of people as quickly as possible to start getting the ranch up and running again.

An hour later he looked up to see Scarlett approaching.

"I think you can take me home now," she said. "At least until you find some more animals. Here's my bill."

He took the bill without even looking at it, his fingers brushing hers. He saw the flicker in her eyes, felt his own pulse jump in return. How could she do that to him? Even after all these years, she caused a chemical reaction in him from just barely having contact with her.

"I've been making calls and have already got someone hired to get a crew out here to start working. This afternoon I have an appointment to talk to a highly recommended Dallas contractor about the house. But those are my problems…nothing you need to concern yourself with." He squeezed her shoulder. "Come on, how about I take you to breakfast before dropping you at your place?"

"Thanks, but I just want to go home. Mom will have breakfast for me. I want a hot bath, and then I'm going to get some sleep."

"Okay, home it is," he said, taking her arm and smiling at her. "I need to check into the Bellamy Resort. After a night in the back of my truck, I'm ready for a five-star resort."

She drew a deep breath, and the moment he touched her, he was aware of another sizzle that ignited desire. He released her arm and turned away. Scarlett was off-limits, and he couldn't even touch her in the most casual way without having a physical reaction.

He held the door of his pickup, and when she climbed in, his gaze swept over her long legs clad in tight jeans. As he drove, he thought again about what an amazing job she had done with the animals and his chest swelled with appreciation.

"Everyone says you're the best vet in this part of the state," he praised. "And now I can see why."

"Thanks, Luke." She smiled and then turned to look out the window. They rode in companionable silence for several minutes before she glanced back toward him and asked, "So when are you planning on seeing your dad?"

"I think I need to wait a day or two until I won't lose

it over the way he abandoned the ranch without telling me. If he had just clued me in, things would not have gotten so bad." He blew out an angry breath. "And I still don't know why none of the men who worked for him didn't let me know what was going on. He must have really ticked them off."

"He might have told them you were coming to take over, and they figured you knew."

"I hadn't thought of that." He hesitated. "I'm here not only to see about the ranch, but I have other matters to take care of, too. I'm going to see Will today."

She gave him a startled look. "Really? I have to say, I'm surprised to hear that. You're pretty removed from Royal and all that goes on here."

"Will and I've always stayed in touch and he's been out to see me a couple of times."

"I guess when I stop to think about it, you two were good friends."

"It's the damnedest thing about Will coming home to his own funeral. Quite a shock, right?"

She nodded. "You've got that right. This deal with Will—some of us know a few things, but not much. He is staying pretty hush-hush about the whole thing. But if you're seeing Will, I'm sure he'll bring you up to date on what's happened. Will's close friends apparently know some things. Like my brother, Toby."

"People in certain professions hear more secrets— people like hairstylists, bartenders—how about veterinarians?"

She laughed softly, and it was a sound that made him smile and he wanted to hear that beautiful laugh again.

"I don't think so. My furry, four-legged regulars have very little to say to me, except to convince me they're glad to see me. I don't have to have any proof of that."

"I'll bet you've never been bitten by one of your patients."

"No, I haven't," she said. "They kind of melt when they come to the hospital. The ones that come to board go to a different section, and they're happy campers. We're happy to see them, too."

"You like your job, don't you?" he asked, but he already knew her answer.

"I love my job," she said, and he could hear the enthusiasm in her voice and knew that she felt the same about her work that he did about his.

"Lots of changes for me to come back to."

"I'm sorry about the Double U. I know that was a shock yesterday. I still can't believe your family place got so bad that the animals were just left to starve and die." She sighed. "I think it probably went downhill fast after your dad had to go to the hospital and then the assisted-living facility."

"Our family attorney helped with all that. You know Fred Sweeney?"

"Mr. Sweeney...sure. So how is your dad?"

"They're trying to get him dried out, and he's resisting. Nothing new there." He grimaced. "We've been down that road before."

"Sorry, Luke."

"Just be thankful for your family, Scarlett."

"I am," she murmured quietly. "If you find more horses and need my help, let me know."

"You were great last night. You passed on breakfast, but let me take you to Dallas to dinner Friday night. I owe you that much," he said, suddenly wanting a night with her and knowing he did owe her big-time for what she did last night.

She glanced at him and looked away, drawing a deep breath that made him glance down as her shirt hugged her curves. "Thanks, Luke, but you don't need to do that, and I have plans."

He didn't think she really had plans, but suspected she didn't want to go out with him. He nodded. "Sure, Scarlett. I owe you, though. You saved horses for me."

"That's my job."

He slowed and stopped in front of her house and came around to open her door, but she had already stepped out and gathered her things. She looked amused. "You don't need to walk me to the door. This isn't a date. I'll see you, Luke. Call if you have sick animals."

"Scarlett, you saved those horses. Your bill doesn't cover half of what you did. Let me do something to repay you. Can I make a donation to your business to help with abandoned animals?"

She nodded. "I'll take you up on that one. I'm on the web, so you can get my address and send a check. We take in dogs, cats, horses, occasionally other animals, even birds. We can always use more money to feed and care for them and advertise to get them placed in good homes."

"You're a softie for anything furry and four-footed."

They looked at each other, and for an instant he

wanted to draw her into his arms. This was another goodbye between, them and he didn't like it. It shouldn't make any difference at all, but it did. That was just one more shock since he had returned to Royal. He should be able to walk away from Scarlett without batting an eye after all this time, so why was this simple goodbye so damned difficult?

"Bye, Scarlett. Thanks again."

She nodded. "Sure." She turned and went up her porch steps, and he headed back to climb into his pickup to leave. He looked in the rearview mirror and saw her standing in the doorway. She glanced over her shoulder at him and then went inside and closed the door.

He wondered whether he would see her again while he was in Royal. They had no future together and no reason to cross paths again. His parents' bad genes haunted him and because of that, he wasn't the man for Scarlett.

He drove to the new elegant five-star resort and was relieved to be in luxurious surroundings with instant service. Even before he showered, he made an appointment for his own PI from Dallas to come check the suite for bugs or hidden cameras because of the ongoing investigation of the attempt on Will's life, the funeral supposedly for Will, the disappearance of Rich Lowell and Jason Phillips, as well as the disappearance of money. He intended to work with Will's PI, but he didn't want Will's PI seen at the Bellamy where he was staying.

When the Dallas PI finished, Luke gave him instructions and had him check into a room in his name in the nearby small town of Brinkly. The PI was to leave the key with the concierge for Luke to pick up when he arrived later to meet with Will's PI, Cole Sullivan.

Luke ordered breakfast sent up and headed for his shower. This afternoon he would meet with Cole Sullivan. If they could find where the money went, they might begin to get some answers to the disappearance of Rich Lowell and Jason Phillips. As the hot water sluiced over him, washing away the dirt and grime of the last several hours, he released a frustrated breath... Whose ashes did they have when they had the funeral for Will? Ashes that were supposed to be Will's until he showed up alive and well at his own funeral.

Questions came to mind that Luke wanted answered. Questions for Cole Sullivan, questions for Will. And though it shouldn't be, the biggest question hovering in his thoughts was, would he see Scarlett again?

Three

Luke had time before the meeting with Cole. He dressed in jeans, a brown-and-red-plaid Western-style shirt, brown boots and a Stetson. He wanted to blend with the other men in Royal, and this Western attire would do the trick unless someone was specifically looking for him.

After climbing into his pickup, he drove a few short blocks to the bank where he kept an account. The bank president, Jeff Kline, had been a friend since high school, although he was two years older than Luke. Having grown up in Royal, Luke knew most people, which made doing business with them easier. When his meeting at the bank was over, Luke headed down to City Hall to meet with Sheriff Nathan Battle.

Luke had grown up knowing Nathan. They shook

hands, and Nathan motioned for Luke to have a seat. Luke pulled a check out of his pocket and extended it. "This is for the Double U, the back taxes, everything. If you need more, let me know, but this is what you wrote to me that Dad owed. I've been to the bank, and Double U is now in my name, and my father is no longer an official part of it. I hate to do that, but you've seen how he left it."

Nathan looked at the check, wrote a receipt and got out a file. "This is the right amount, and I'll give you that lien and auction notice, and this should ensure you keep the Double U. It was a fine ranch the years you were growing up. I'm glad to know you'll stay connected with us in Royal, and I hope we see you at the Texas Cattleman's Club sometime."

"I don't know how much I'll be back. I'm hiring good people to run the Double U, and if you have any suggestions, please let me know. Here's a list of the men I'm talking to. Do you know any of them?"

Nathan took the list and scanned it. "I do. I know all of them except this Chet Younger. I can look him up if you want."

"Thanks, but I can check him out."

Nathan laughed, crinkles forming at the corners of his dark brown eyes. "I guess you can. And you'll probably get better info than the Royal Police Department can dredge up. Well, I hope you come back here to live."

"I won't do that any time soon. I have West-Tech, and I love my work." He smiled amicably at the other man. "Nathan, thanks for your call. Scarlett McKit-

trick came out and tended to the animals that had survived until I got home. She's a miracle worker because
I didn't expect her to save half of them, but I think
they'll all make it."

"She's good and she's another one who loves her
job. I'm sorry, Luke, about your dad."

"Well, he drank himself into it." Luke stood and
folded the papers, putting them in his shirt pocket. "I'm
damn glad to have the ranch out of debt. I just couldn't
bear to see it go to auction. What a hell of a thing."

"It won't now. It's your ranch, free and clear, and it
looks as if you'll get it back in great shape."

"I hope. It's good to be home in a lot of ways."

Nathan walked Luke to the door. "When you have
time, maybe we can meet at the diner and have lunch."

"Sure. Thanks again, Nathan. You saved the Double
U by your call."

Luke left, feeling better. The Double U was his
again, and he felt he had taken the first step toward
salvaging the ranch and eventually making it one of
the best in Texas.

Moreover, his father's bills at the assisted-living center had been paid and arrangements made for Luke to
take care of his father's bills from this point forward.

He returned to the Bellamy where he changed into a
pale blue dress shirt and navy slacks. Promptly at 11:00
a.m., Will Sanders stepped into Luke's suite, and the
two shook hands. Luke gazed into his friend's green
eyes and smiled as he closed the door behind him. "I'm
glad to see you alive and well."

"Just one more big shock in my life. Thanks for

coming, Luke. If you can help follow the money trail, I think we might unravel a lot of the mystery."

"I'll do my best, Will. I'll meet with Cole Sullivan this afternoon and get started."

Luke listened to Will talk briefly about all that had happened to him, and how one thing after another pointed to Rich Lowell passing himself off as Will.

"To avoid compromising the investigation, not many people know all the details of what I've told you. I'm cooperating every way I can with the police, and I've informed them I have my own PI to help move things along."

Luke nodded. "You can count on me to keep your confidence, Will. I know how much is at stake for you."

"Thanks for getting involved in my problems, which touch a lot of lives here. In addition to trying to track Rich down, I'm also concerned about Jason Phillips's disappearance. It isn't like him to just vanish, and it really isn't like him to lose contact with his daughter, Savannah. His brother, Aaron, is filling in to help take care of little Savannah, who's only six. Jason's sister, Megan, is helping, too. She and Aaron take turns." He blew out a breath. "They're worried, and rightfully so, about Jason. The more we find out about Rich, the worse it looks."

"I'm still trying to wrap my brain around this, so I can only imagine how his loved ones must be feeling."

Will nodded grimly. "And you might as well know— Megan received the urn with the ashes, presumably *my* ashes, because she was supposedly my wife. There was a note about how I died. They've sent the note for handwriting analysis, so we should get an answer any time now on that. They are also testing the ashes' DNA." His mouth hardened into a tight line. "We'll get answers sooner or later. I just don't want anyone else hurt." He ran his hand over his short black hair. "Everyone is reeling from Rich's deceit. As you know, he and I grew up together."

"That's part of why he could get away with impersonating you. He knows everything about you,"

"I feel such a sense of betrayal. Rich wasn't poor. He was well-off. What would cause him to go to such extremes?"

"Greed. He wasn't as wealthy, and he wasn't the golden boy that you've always been," Luke said. "Most friends are happy for your wealth and success. Rich must have envied it beyond anything any of us could imagine."

"I suppose," Will said, shaking his head. "It's still shocking."

"Yeah. Life is filled with shocks."

Will nodded. "Sorry. I've just been thinking about my problems. I hear you have plenty of your own."

"I'm working on them. I paid off the ranch today, and I own it free and clear now. I can't believe how my dad left it. Rich Lowell was after money. My dad was after booze. It's pitiful, Will. I'm scared someday I'll be like him."

"You'll never be like your dad, Luke. Not ever," Will said, shaking his head and smiling. "You can relax on that one. You're a straight arrow filled with brilliant ideas and a great ability. Stop worrying about following in your dad's footsteps."

"I hope to hell you're right. Well, I'll talk to your PI and I'll see what I can come up with. If we can get proof of Rich taking some of that stolen money, then you can nail the bastard."

"Thanks again, Luke. I'll let you know if I learn anything, and you do the same for me. I'm telling you, watch your back. Rich tried to murder me."

"Even though I've know that, it still shocks me. I'll be careful."

"If we can pick up the money trail, that will be amazing." Will reached out and clapped his friend on the shoulder. "By the way, congratulations on making the *Forbes*'s list. Their newest billionaire—that's great."

"Thanks, buddy. But to be honest, I came home to a passel of trouble, and Silicon Valley and that list seem far removed from Royal, Texas. If I can help here, though, I'll be very happy. Money is paper, and it does leave a trail. And if Lowell took TCC money, we ought to be able to get some information about it."

"Rich has to have bank accounts, has to have places he keeps money and gets money."

Luke nodded in agreement. "My days will be pretty much filled with ranch business, but I can work on this at night if you or Cole can provide me with whatever information you have about the thefts."

"Thanks again, buddy. I know you already have a lot on your plate. I can't tell you how much I just want to look Rich in the eye and ask how he could do such a thing. Hurting so many people the way he did." He blew out an angry breath. "I shouldn't even have survived when he pushed me overboard off the yacht, but fortunately, I was rescued. I still have blocks of time I don't remember."

"We'll catch him, Will. We just have to."

After they said their goodbyes, Luke closed the door behind Will and made some calls. About thirty minutes later, he went downstairs and climbed into his pickup, driving south out of Royal to the scheduled rendezvous in Brinkly with the PI.

Promptly at one, Luke opened the door to the hotel suite, and Cole Sullivan stepped inside, introducing himself. Luke shook hands with the blue-eyed investigator who had once been a Texas Ranger.

"Thanks for driving to Brinkly," Luke said. "I felt we would have a lot better chance of having a private meeting here instead of Royal."

"I agree. I know you met with Will before lunch, and that's good."

"I'm all set up. Come pull up a chair and let me show you this new antifraud software we have."

"My business changes by the day, and I have the feeling I'm going to learn something new now."

"I hope I can help you catch Rich. We've all grown up together, and we know each other well. We know habits, sayings, mannerisms."

Cole nodded. "If we can pick up the money trail, you should be able to find Rich."

"It can't be a minute too soon."

As they talked, Luke had already set up his things,

getting ready to look at what figures and information Cole had unearthed. The two men worked together for an hour, making arrangements for Cole to get information to Luke and set up how and when they would keep in touch.

When Cole left, Luke packed up his things to go back to Royal. He had three interviews already set up to hire a man to run the ranch. He also had two interviews to hire a contractor to build another ranch house. As soon as he reached Royal, he bought a black sports car and had it delivered to his hotel.

That night back in Royal, over a solitary dinner in his hotel room, for a moment he was lost in a vivid memory of holding Scarlett in his arms and kissing her. She had kissed him back, a fiery kiss that was a challenge and an invitation at the same time. He wanted her in his arms again. He shouldn't kiss her or even see her again, but he couldn't shake her out of his thoughts. Why did it seem so damn good to be with her?

He wanted to call her, ask her out, go have a fun evening, bring her back to his hotel and make love all night long. That was a dream and about as likely to happen as Rich Lowell appearing in Royal and surrendering to the police for his misdeeds.

Scarlett was probably back to not speaking to him and would tell him again to get off the McKittrick ranch. Luke blew out an exasperated breath. He needed to put Scarlett out of his thoughts, get done what he came to do and go home to California where he really fit in better. With his family, his genes, he would never be the man for Scarlett. Why was it so impossible to forget her?

* * *

He woke shortly before 6:00 a.m. the following morning. His phone was buzzing. He picked up and heard Will.

"We need a clandestine emergency meeting at my ranch today. Can you get out here by eleven?"

"I'll be there."

"Thanks. I want you here so I can fill you in on what's going on. We have to keep this meeting quiet, so don't breathe a word of it to anyone, okay?"

"Will do, and I'll see you." Putting aside his phone, Luke stretched and sat up. He'd slept in because he usually was up by 5:00 a.m., maybe a carryover from living on a ranch a lot of his life and getting up early. His schedule was blown to hell anyway after staying up all night at the Double U.

He wondered what had happened to cause Will to call a meeting. Well, he would know soon enough, he supposed. He also wondered how the animals were doing. He needed to get out to the Double U. He had talked several times to the man in charge of the crew of cowboys who were working on the ranch temporarily. Also, he had a contractor with a crew that would start work today. They would demolish the house he had grown up in, and he had seen this done before to homes in Silicon Valley. The house and any trace of it would be gone in hours. He'd have a vacant lot.

Did he want to rebuild in the same spot? He thought about the big trees on the property. There was a live oak that he suspected was well over one hundred years old. He thought it would be best to just rebuild where the original house had stood.

He wasn't in a hurry, but the sooner he could get good people hired, the sooner he could let go and let someone else take charge of the Double U and get back to the home he loved in Silicon Valley.

Once again his thoughts drifted back to Scarlett. No matter how hard he tried to concentrate on other things, she was always first and foremost in his mind. A grin spread across his face. He would drive out and check on the livestock, and if he had any sick animals he was calling her. First, because he wanted to see her. Second, she was a miracle worker where his livestock were concerned.

She'd always had a way with animals and had never been afraid of any of them. He remembered seeing her as a kid walk up to a snarling, growling, injured dog that was in pain and had its teeth bared. Smiling, he remembered how he kept telling her to get back, but she just went ahead and knelt by the dog, speaking softly, holding out her hand with a treat. She started singing, and the dog stopped growling and looked at the treat and took it. When he did, Scarlett gave him a shot so fast that Luke could barely believe his eyes. In seconds, the dog calmed, and she picked it up, put it in a carrier and off she went.

Later, he asked where she got the painkiller and when she learned how to give animals shots. She gave him one of her smug looks and said that she was studying to be a veterinarian and she had learned how and where to give a dog a shot for pain. Scarlett worked one day a week when she was fifteen for the local vet, and she obviously was a quick learner.

Still smiling over the memory, Luke shook his head, thoughts of her still prevalent in his mind as he carried on with his morning routine.

At 11:00 on the dot, he drove up to Will's house at the Ace in the Hole Ranch, one of the finest spreads in Texas—which made Luke think about the ruin his father had brought to the Double U.

Other cars were parked in the drive, and he wondered how many knew the truth about what was happening. A butler showed Luke where everyone was gathering. With a firm handshake and friendly green eyes, Will welcomed Luke.

"It's good that you're here, buddy. I talked to Cole, and he's here, as well. He thinks this money trail is going to really help."

"I hope so. As I said before, I'll do my best."

Will gave him a crooked smile as he shook his head. "Thanks. I can't ask for better than that."

"I hope this meeting helps shed some more light on the case."

"Yeah, me, too. Thanks for coming on such short notice."

"No problem. I'll go say hello to the others."

"Sounds good. We'll start in just a minute."

It was easy to spot Aaron Phillips's dark hair and broad shoulders on the other side of the room, so Luke began to head that way, saying hello to others as he went. Toby McKittrick was present, standing across the room, and if looks could kill, Luke was certain he'd be a dead man. He nodded at Scarlett's big brother, seeing ice in Toby's aqua eyes before Toby turned away.

Luke couldn't be angry with Toby for being rude because Toby was protective of his family. Luke would always be sorry for hurting Scarlett but the alternative—if he had proposed to her when she was sixteen—would probably have brought Toby after him with a shotgun and dire warnings to get out of her life. Luke couldn't regret not getting engaged to Scarlett back then. He hadn't been ready for marriage at eighteen, and he didn't think Scarlett was at sixteen, even though she thought she was.

He moved around the room, greeting friends from his high school days and earlier. Nearly all the men in the room were members of the Texas Cattleman's Club, and Nathan Battle was among those present.

"Nathan, thanks again. If I'd lost the ranch at an auction, that would have been a horrible blow."

"Forget it. You own the Double U now, and it's in your name, so that takes care of losing the ranch. Good luck with the restoration. If anybody can get it done, you can."

"Thanks." Luke smiled and moved on to greet Aaron, Jason's brother.

"I'm sorry your brother is missing, Aaron."

"Thanks, Luke," he said, turning worry-filled eyes on Luke. "That's why this meeting has been called. They've turned up some new information. You'll hear about it in just a minute. I guess the only good news here is now we know a little more and we have an answer."

"I've come home to all kinds of problems, my own with my dad and all this with Will walking into his own funeral."

"Yeah. Welcome home," Aaron remarked drily. "I'm sorry about your dad being sick."

"Thanks. We won't start on what all my dad has done. Take care, Aaron."

He moved on to greet Rand Gibson, second in command to Will at Spark Energy Solutions, an oil, gas and solar energy company that Luke knew had been extremely successful.

"Congratulations on making *Forbes*'s list," Rand said, shaking hands with Luke.

"Thanks. I'm doing what I love, and I suppose you are, too."

Before Rand could answer, Will spoke above the sounds of everyone talking. "I think we better call this meeting to order. Thank you for coming on such short notice.

"I'd like to get this meeting started because it was called suddenly and I know I've interrupted plans and schedules. It won't take long," Will said. "Well, for starters, Cole Sullivan, the PI I hired, has discovered that Jason has actually been kidnapped and may be in grave danger. He encourages anyone with information regarding the case to step forward so they can work to bring Jason home." He looked around the room. "If there is anyone here who has information, please talk to the police or Nathan. Even if it seems insignificant, if you know something about Rich or Jason, please let the authorities know."

Nathan waved his hand. "Right now, all we can do is hope and pray that Jason is still alive out there," he added.

Luke thought of the urn of ashes at Will's fake funeral. It was beginning to look as if those ashes might belong to Jason.

How could Rich Lowell, who had grown up with all the men in the room, betray those friendships in such a terrible way? No one could answer that question.

When the meeting adjourned, Luke left to go to the Double U ranch to meet with Abe Ellingson, his new builder, and Reuben Lindner, the man he had hired to run the ranch, so the three of them could go over what needed to be done and what Luke wanted.

He spent the next three hours talking to the builder about the house and the outbuildings. Reuben left to go back to Royal to set up interviews to hire cowboys to work at the Double U.

When his meeting with the builder was finished, Luke fed and checked the livestock. In less than an hour he found a sick calf. He knew it was a case for Scarlett, so he sent her a text. Luke felt an uncustomary sense of loss, albeit a feeling he'd had several times since returning to Texas. How could his father let everything go to hell like this—starving animals, a rising debt—all to drink himself senseless? Luke thought of Scarlett. If he was the last man on earth, he didn't deserve her and shouldn't get entangled in her life. Suppose he turned out like his father someday?

When Luke got no text answer and couldn't get

Scarlett by phone, he climbed into his pickup to drive to the McKittrick ranch. As he approached the house, he spotted two women rocking on the porch. When he stepped out of his pickup and headed toward the house, the dogs came running, so he paused to pet some of them and let them calm down. The dogs followed as he walked toward the porch. His gaze flitted over Mrs. McKittrick and then swept more slowly over Scarlett, and he was startled by what he saw. Seated in a rocker facing her mother, Scarlett held a baby in her arms.

Waving to him, Joyce McKittrick went inside the house. He climbed the steps and walked to Scarlett, his pulse beating faster. Why did she always look so good to him? Dressed in a red T-shirt that fit her gorgeous curves and snug jeans, Scarlett rocked the little baby.

Knowing nothing about babies, Luke looked at a little boy with thick, curly black hair, big, long-lashed, soulful brown eyes and beautiful, golden-brown skin. Luke gave the bigger dogs a cursory pat and walked up to Scarlett. "Are you babysitting?" He'd heard Toby and Naomi had a little girl, so it wasn't her niece.

As she gave him a level look, Scarlett raised her chin. "No, I'm not babysitting. This is my baby boy, Carl."

Flabbergasted, Luke looked at the infant again. "He's yours?"

"He's my adopted baby. I can't have children of my own, Luke."

Stunned, he looked at the baby and then at her. Why hadn't someone mentioned Scarlett's baby when he'd been told that she had been engaged until the guy walked out on her?

"Why a baby, Scarlett?" he blurted, still staring at the little guy.

"I thought I was going to get married and we wanted a baby, so we started adoption proceedings. It takes time to adopt a baby, just as it takes time to have a baby. Tanner walked out and the marriage was off, but then Carl came up for adoption shortly after he left. I think Tanner went to Chicago. I lost track of him." She tenderly stroked her baby boy's head. "It just seemed like it was meant to be. The agency approved the adoption, I went through the legal process and I'm now a single mom."

He heard the note of challenge in her voice and stopped staring at the baby to look at Scarlett. "Congratulations seems inadequate. That fits you, Scarlett. You collect animals to care for. Why not a baby?" he remarked, his surprise diminishing fast after her explanation. It was so like Scarlett to adopt a baby if she could. She was a caregiver deluxe, and it spilled over in all aspects of her life.

"Why are you here, Luke?" she asked, a cold note in her tone.

"Oh, damn, I forgot. I've got a really sick calf and I can't help him—"

Instantly, Scarlett stood and handed the baby to Luke. "I'll get my things. Hold Carl for a minute," she said. "Watch him until I get back."

Luke couldn't recall holding a baby in his life. "Scarlett, I can't—"

"Sure, you can. He doesn't bite. He only has one tooth," she flung over her shoulder as she disappeared through the door, and he was certain she was laughing.

He blinked and looked down at the little baby she had thrust into his arms. He was holding Carl underneath each arm. Realizing that wasn't any way to hold a baby, Luke sat and put the little boy in his lap.

"Hi, Carl," he said, smiling, his heart pounding with fear that he would frighten the little fellow. "Dammit, Scarlett—whoops, sorry, Carl. Thank goodness, you're too little to repeat words. Your mama would be unhappy with me. I'm glad I don't scare you." He smiled at Carl again, and when the baby smiled back at him, a dimple showing in his cheek. Luke felt as if his heart melted.

"Hey, Carl, you're a cute kid," he praised, suddenly feeling at ease with the little guy. "You're not screaming or crying or making angry faces. You must not even care that I don't know zip about babies."

Carl giggled and Luke laughed, making Carl giggle again. Scarlett stepped back outside.

"Well, look at you, Mister Doesn't-Know-Anything-About-Babies. You've got him giggling and laughing and happy as all-get-out."

"He doesn't know he's with a terrified man who has never held a baby before."

"Then it is time you did, and Carl is a good one to practice with. You're doing fine. You get an A for amazingly okay." She smiled at him, and, as he smiled in return, Luke's heart thudded.

He remembered the fun moments with Scarlett when they dated in high school, the laughter that came so easily. He felt an ache in his gut. This moment, laughing with Scarlett, holding her baby on his lap, felt so right—which was ridiculous. He was *not* interested in babies, families, getting tied down, and it could never work with Scarlett. Even if he wanted it, she didn't. She was barely civil to him unless it involved animals and now her baby, Carl.

"I always figure babies and animals sense when someone is afraid of them or doesn't know what to do. He doesn't seem to care."

"He likes you," she said, laughing again. "You're good daddy material, Luke. Who would've guessed?"

"Scarlett," he snarled, teasing her because she was teasing him. "I'm not daddy material in any way, shape or form. Forget that."

She leaned closer, batting her eyes at him, teasing and flirting with him as her voice thickened, "I'm not about to forget that very appealing aspect of your personality."

He drew a deep breath. "Scarlett, you're just asking for trouble."

Laughing, she took Carl from him and stepped away."

"Let me give Carl to Mom, and then we can head out. I can drive and you won't—"

"Forget it. I'm here. I'll take you to the ranch and bring you back."

She nodded and left to hand Carl off to her mother. Once again, he remembered old times with her, fun times when she was carefree, flirty and oh, so sexy. He wiped his brow. She had too easily fanned flames between them.

He was still amazed that Scarlett had a baby. He was a cute kid and a happy little baby, which made life easier. It had actually been a fun few minutes, and that surprised him. He couldn't recall holding a baby, and he wouldn't have thought he could keep one happy five seconds.

In minutes, Scarlett reappeared. "Ready to go?"

"Sure am. And thank you, Scarlett. You're coming to my rescue again. I really need you this time, too. This little calf is so dang sick. I don't know whether it'll be alive when we get there, but I had to try," he said.

"I'll do everything I can to help him, Luke. I promise you that."

"I never doubted that for a moment." He smiled at her. "Scarlett, pick out two of the reliable big mutts that we can take with us for watchdogs tonight. Unless you have to be back here for your baby, I have a feeling you may be sitting up all night. You and I will be on the ranch alone, and Milt Dawson, the man in charge of the cowboys, said last night there were vandals who just messed stuff up. He's bringing lights and part of the crew will start staying at night after tonight. If you're scared, I'll bring you home, but he said it's only vandalism, so it's probably kids. Nothing big. I can run anyone off."

"I don't doubt that and I'm not scared. I may be up with the calf."

"If we can, I want to sleep in peace and not have to keep one eye open for someone sneaking up. Do you have two big dogs we can take with us?"

"Oh, my, yes."

She whistled and more than a dozen came on the run. She picked out four and got them in the back of the pickup with minimal effort. "We're ready. It was that easy, and you can trust that you have four watchdogs."

He laughed. "You could be an animal trainer, too. Very talented woman."

"I just know them, and they know me. They're smart and they do what I want."

"I would, too, if you'd scratch my belly and pet me," he said, leering at her, and she had to laugh.

"You can't resist, can you? Some things never change."

"You bring out my wicked side," he drawled, and reached out to give her a quick, impersonal hug.

It should have been impersonal, but it wasn't for him at all. He held the pickup door for her. As she passed him to climb in, he caught a scent of perfume, something exotic, making him think of holding her and kissing her. His gaze slid down the length of her, the tight jeans over her trim ass, her long legs. For a long, heated moment, he wanted her with all his being. Common sense reminded him that was not going to happen. She slid onto the seat, and he closed the door, drawing a deep breath, wishing he could at least kiss her once more. Only he would want more than once. Right now, he wanted a night of endless kisses.

"I'm glad you're trying to save the calf," she told him when he was in the pickup and headed toward the county road.

"I found a small herd in that canyon on the far west side of the ranch. This calf looks about a week old. The mother isn't in great shape, but both of them and a dozen others have survived. For once, mama isn't trying to run me off. She either senses I'm trying to help her baby, or she's too sick and weak herself to try to chase me away."

"Oh, my. She's really sick. We'll do what we can."

"Thanks for coming on such short notice," he murmured, thinking how polite they were with each other. She hadn't been cautious and polite when he'd kissed her the other night, however. His pulse jumped at the thought, and he wondered if he would get the chance to kiss her this time. He had a feeling she would stay the night to sit with the calf if need be.

"No problem."

"I own the ranch now," Luke added. "I paid off Dad's debts, the mortgages, the loans and the incredible bills. I'll bet guys left here without their pay. Some of them may have taken livestock to make up for missing pay, and I hope they did. It bothers me that Dad might not have paid guys that worked for him. We used to have good guys that did a fine job.

"I've already hired a man to run the place. Reuben Lindner. He came with all kinds of good qualifications. Do you know him?"

She shook her head. "No, but that doesn't mean much. I'm not a rancher."

"I've got a builder, too, Abe Ellison."

"That one I do know. He built my clinic. He's good at ranch buildings, barns and houses, too. You have an excellent builder, but that's no surprise. I think he does a lot of business in Dallas as well as in Royal."

"Soon they'll finish demolishing the house so they can start building a new one."

"One like you have in Silicon Valley?" she asked.

Surprised, he glanced at her. "How do you know about my Silicon Valley home?"

"It's been in magazines, and I've read about all the electronic gadgetry and amazing things for houses of the future."

"So you read about me?" he asked, surprised. Her cheeks flooded with pink and he wanted to reach out and put his arm around her.

"Sure, when I see something in a magazine or the paper about a former schoolmate, I usually read it," she said, looking out the window. "Thank you for the chance to save the calf. I'm glad you didn't just put it down."

"Maybe you can work some more of your magic."

"I'll try."

"You have a cute kid, Scarlett."

Her eyes sparkled with joy. "He's my whole world now. Mom adores him, too. All of us do. So does Toby. Carl's too little now, but eventually he and my brother's little girl, Ava, will play together."

"Your ex-fiancé didn't want kids?"

"Just the opposite. He comes from old money and was under a lot of pressure from his family to have a baby, an heir. When he found out I couldn't get pregnant, he almost broke up with me. So then we decided to adopt. But then the adoption proceedings began to drag out, and Tanner left. I debated with myself about taking my name off the list, and while I was thinking it over, the agency called. I've told you the rest."

"That must have been a difficult decision, deciding to raise a baby on your own."

"It was, but it was the best decision I ever made. Even though I'm a single mom, because of living with Mom and having Toby and Naomi close, they approved the adoption without Tanner. I'm so glad I went ahead. I love little Carl so much, and he's such a sweet blessing. I don't expect to have any more children."

"He's cute, all right." He winked at her. "It's just a shock to see you with a baby."

"I'm happy. Carl and my job are everything to me, Luke. I think I was meant to care for others and for animals. It's what I've done all my life."

"It's a good thing there are people like you in the world. The world needs your help."

"I have a good life," she said.

"We both do. You're doing your thing and love it, and I'm doing mine and I love it, as well."

"And never the twain shall meet—isn't that how an old saying goes?"

"I don't know about that old saying. My job is pretty much my whole life. Dad and I have grown apart through the years, which is sad, but that's the truth. He's the only one of my family left. I have no relatives."

"I'm sorry," she said, giving his wrist a squeeze. The minute she touched him, he felt a current buzz through him, and he took a deep breath. She released his wrist instantly, and her cheeks were pink again. She didn't glance his way, but her breathing was deeper and she had a reaction just as much as he did, which made him want her in his arms more than ever.

"Good or bad, no matter what you have, family is important. I feel like I should have done more but all

I can do is go from here and try to make things better. I want to save the ranch and you're helping save the animals. That's a start."

Coming home isn't turning out to be what I expected. It's worse, but with your help, we've saved the surviving animals. I may lose this calf, but the rest seem mostly okay. None of the other animals are as sick as this calf."

"As I said, I'll do what I can."

He smiled. "You always do more than anyone could expect. While you're here, I'll check the livestock we've found and see if any others need your attention."

He turned in the familiar road that used to lead to his home. When they drove to the barn and parked to get out, he could hear the mother cow bawling. She stood in the corral by the barn. "She wants her baby," he said.

"I'll check her over and give her something to calm her. Let's look at the calf first, though. He may be critical."

The dogs stood in the back of the pickup, and she walked around to tell them to get down.

"They'll stay in whatever area I'm in," she told Luke. He smiled.

"I guarantee you, I would, too," he said and she shook her head, but she returned his smile.

Luke took her arm to lead her to the barn. He didn't need to hold her arm, but he couldn't resist reaching out to touch her. He ached to pull her into his arms and kiss her again. It was good to be with her and had seemed natural and right to be with her and baby Carl.

He knew it was ridiculous for him to feel that way, but he couldn't help it.

He scowled. Scarlett hadn't even wanted him on their property, and she was only with him because she was such a softie for animals in trouble. She still felt something though, because she reacted slightly each time he touched her. He needed to think about the tasks he had to get done, but this darn woman was in his system and he had no clue how to stem these feelings.

His hand was clasped lightly on Scarlett's upper arm, sending waves of longing within him to turn her around, haul her against him and kiss her again. Another one of her bone-melting kisses that could make him shake with longing, almost explode into flames, and want to make out with her for hours.

"Luke, where's the calf?" Scarlett looked up at him, speaking loudly, and he realized she had asked him more than once.

"Sorry, I was lost in thought and memories about you and me and this barn," which he hadn't been, but he was now. He saw her faint blush.

"Keep your mind on today and the problems here. That was a long, long time ago. Forget it."

He leaned closer. "There's no way in hell I can forget a single moment I spent with you, especially if I was kissing you, and when we were in this barn, we were definitely kissing. If you don't remember, I can tell you exactly—"

"Don't you dare bring that up, Luke Weston!" She glared up at him. "Where's that sick calf?"

When Luke led her to a stall, she pushed ahead of

him and knelt in the hay, opening her bag and bending over the calf.

"Text if you need me," Luke said. "I'm going to look and see if there are other animals I want you to check before you leave here."

"Sure," she said without looking up, and he wondered if she really even heard what he said.

He walked through the barn and remembered years earlier how they had made love several times in this very barn. He could remember it so clearly, and he guessed that she could, too.

For several long moments, he just stood motionless inside the barn, staring into space, thinking about Scarlett and lost in memories of making love. With a groan, he tried to get her out of his thoughts, focus on the animals that needed looking after. But it was impossible to shake taunting images and memories of times when he had held Scarlett in his arms, both of them naked while he had run his hands all over her, kissed her and spent hours making love to her.

Right or wrong, he wanted one night with her now. Was there a chance in hell of that happening?

Four

Scarlett worked swiftly. The calf was malnourished, ill and, like some of the other sick, weaker horses and steers, wild animals had tried to bring it down. It was dinner to them. She hoped she could save the calf. She left to find the mama cow, and it didn't take long to get something to quiet her. The cow had cuts, too. Every weak or injured animal was prey for wild animals, but Scarlett suspected the mama cow had gotten attacked when she was trying to protect her baby or fend off predators that were after the calf.

Luke ordered dinner again, and they ate hamburgers about ten that night.

"I think the calf will make it through the night, but I've sent Toby a text to come get the calf in the morning first thing and get it to the Royal Veterinary Hospital. It's been attacked, probably by coyotes, and I'm surprised it survived."

"That was probably its mama's doing. Even a pack of coyotes would think twice before taking her on in a fight." He met her gaze, and a smile flickered on his lips "I've said it before—you're a miracle worker with animals. I mailed you another check. You should get it tomorrow."

"You paid your bill."

"This is extra. Take it and use it to save some animals. You said that you take in the big animals, horses and cattle."

"Yes. I'll take any animal that's abandoned and needs help."

"Then you consider this check a donation and you cash it and use it to help the animals."

She smiled at him "Thanks, Luke. That's nice." He had a lantern that ran on batteries hanging from a rafter, and it shed a soft, golden glow over the stall. The calf was in the next stall, and they had moved to the adjoining one when they ate their burgers. She could hear the calf breathing and could tell what was happening from where she was.

A golden light spilled over Luke, and she couldn't resist reaching out to take his hand. "Thanks," she said softly. "Whatever you sent, it's welcome and will help some animals."

She released his hand just as quickly and knew she shouldn't touch him. However, the moment she started to take her hand off his, he placed his other hand over hers to keep her from pulling away. His hot, hungry gaze held her transfixed more than his hand, and her heart pounded with excitement. Too swiftly, she remembered being in his arms, recalled his kisses that could make her pulse race and set her ablaze with desire.

He was all she wanted, and he had hurt her so badly before. She never wanted to go through that kind of hurt again and she couldn't bear even a tiny bit of hurt for Carl, but it was Luke, and he was holding her hand, looking at her as if she were the only woman on earth, desire glimmering in his eyes. He stood and pulled her to her feet.

Common sense said to pull away, to move, to say no to him. She couldn't. She wanted him. Her gaze lowered to his mouth, and then she looked up to meet his eyes again.

"A kiss isn't going to hurt, Scarlett," he said in a husky, coaxing voice that was as sexy as a caress. Her heart throbbed as she looked at him, and, hard as she tried, she couldn't say no and couldn't move away.

"If we kiss, we won't be able to stop," she whispered. "I don't want to get hurt."

Something flickered in the depths of his eyes. "A kiss—that's all. Just a kiss between old friends. You'll forget all about it," he said, drawing her to him.

And then she was in Luke's embrace, devoured by blue-green eyes, his delicious mouth hovering above hers. She wanted his kiss, wanted to kiss him in return. Common sense was a small voice of protest that faded fast beneath the hungry look he gave her. There was no mistaking his intention. When he leaned closer, her heart pounded until she thought he would hear it. She wound her arms around his neck, turned her face up and closed her eyes as his mouth brushed ever so lightly against hers.

Scarlett moaned, spinning in a swirl of desire, wanting him and wanting him to remember kissing her. She wanted to kiss him until he was as hot, as eager, as consumed with desire as she was. Holding her tightly against his hard, muscled body, he ran his hand down her back and over her bottom, pulling her up against him while he spread his legs and pressed her intimately against his thick erection.

He leaned over her, his tongue stroking hers, his kiss making her want to kiss him ravenously in return, until he wanted her more than he could remember ever wanting anyone. She wanted him to remember their kisses when he was back in Silicon Valley in his glitzy, high-tech world. She didn't want him to walk away without remembering or looking back or realizing he might have shaken up his own world when he kissed her.

She ran her fingers through his hair while she thrust her tongue over his and shifted her hips slightly, moving against him, hearing him groan. Luke had taken her heart when she was sixteen years old. She thought she had gotten over him, but when he kissed her like this, she realized she had never gotten over him completely. He could walk back into her life, make her melt, set her on fire with longing and lust. She wanted to ravish every inch of him, and she wanted him to ravish every inch of her.

Scarlett knew the magic he could cause when he

had been a kid in high school, and her heart thudded faster at the thought of making love with him now that he was a man. But if she did, she ran the risk of really falling in love with him. The deep, real kind of love that she couldn't get over. What mattered even more now—she didn't want Carl hurt. If Luke was really in her life, he would be in her baby's life, too. And Carl could so easily love Luke. She couldn't bear for Luke to break Carl's heart.

She had barely shed tears over Tanner walking out and had chalked it up to being grown and not a high school kid.

But now she knew she hadn't cried over Tanner, because she hadn't really been in love with him. Sure, he was fun and exciting and they were compatible, but something had always been missing. That spark, that flame of passion that she was feeling right now in Luke's arms.

The thoughts spun through her mind as she kissed Luke, and then thoughts were gone and feelings took over completely. Desire overwhelmed her. Luke was holding her, kissing her until she couldn't think of anything except wanting more of him, of his hands, his mouth, his strong, muscular body, his thick, hard cock. She and Luke didn't belong together—there could never be marriage or anything lasting. There couldn't even be anything, except maybe tonight. How much would she get hurt if they made love once? How much would she get hurt if they *didn't*?

She didn't want to look back with longing or regret. Life was meant to be lived.

She moved her hips against him slightly again, rubbing his thick erection, sliding her hands down his back, down over his butt. He raised his head to look at her.

Desire darkened his blue-green eyes and made her heart race. He wanted her, and she knew it when she looked into his eyes.

"Luke," she whispered just his name, but she meant more than that. In that whispered plea, she was telling him she wanted to make love tonight, to do all the things she had dreamed about. She slid her fingers around to unbutton the top buttons of his shirt and pull his shirt out of his jeans.

He already had the hem of her shirt in his hands, and he drew the shirt over her head and tossed it aside. She heard his gasp of pleasure as he looked down at her and unfastened her lacy bra to push it away. He cupped her breasts in his hands and groaned, a guttural sound of longing and approval.

"Beautiful," he whispered, running his thumbs lightly over her nipples. "Scarlett, you're so beautiful, so soft. I want you."

She reached up to slip her hand behind his head and pull him down to kiss him, running her tongue over his lower lip first, then darting it up to touch the corners of his mouth, before plunging deep inside when she pressed her mouth against his and kissed him passionately.

Her hands fluttered over his muscled chest, unfastening the buttons to push open his shirt, then drifted down to undo his big belt buckle and pull off his belt.

While they kissed, she unbuttoned his jeans. As she pushed them away, he returned the favor and peeled off her jeans. She stepped back to hook her fingers in her lacy panties, drawing them down slowly while he watched her.

Scarlett stepped out of them, moving her hips in a slow circle as she took his thick rod in her hands to rub against her legs before she knelt to take him in her mouth, her tongue stroking him.

His fingers laced in her short hair, and he groaned as she slowly licked his hard erection, drawing her tongue over him while she held him with one hand and caressed him between his legs with her other.

She heard the sharp intake of his breath, which excited and satisfied her because she wanted to steal his breath, make him lose control, cause him to remember this night, to stir him up as he did her. He pulled her up to look into her eyes. She leaned forward placing her mouth on his to kiss him, her tongue thrusting slowly in and out of his mouth again. He held her tightly with one arm, his other hand caressing her, running reverently over her bottom.

He bent lower to circle her nipple with his tongue while he stroked her other breast, his hand a feathery caress that made her quiver as he brushed a taut peak.

She gasped, closing her eyes, shutting away everything except his hands, his mouth and his tongue on her, working magic. Or was it magic because it was Luke holding her and kissing her?

He walked away, rustling hay with each step, to reach up and pull down a horse blanket that he spread on the hay-covered dirt floor. He picked her up and knelt to place her on it, and then, as he stretched out beside her, he drew her into his arms and kissed her, another long, heated kiss that shut out the world and left only the two of them.

While they kissed, he caressed her, running his hands over her until he shifted and moved between her legs to trail his lips up the inside of her thighs, planting slow, wet kisses. His tongue slid over her, hot and wet, moving up, causing her to arch and spread her legs for him. Kneeling between them, he propped her legs on his shoulders, to give him access to her as his hands fluttered over her in light caresses, his fingers drifting on her thighs, stroking between her legs, making her writhe with desire.

As he ravished her, his tongue thrusting, going over her intimately, she arched her back with pure, wanton need, craving more of him. She wanted him inside her, but if they were going to make love, she didn't want to rush it, not after waiting all this time. The moment felt dreamlike because she had thought about it, imagined it, longed for it so many lonely, aching nights. But his hands and his mouth and his thick erection, his muscled body and strong arms weren't a dream. They were real for her to touch, caress, kiss, memorize and pleasure herself with.

Shifting away, he kissed her ankles, running his tongue over her, caressing her long legs, watching her shift as he touched her and her need heightened. He drifted higher and she could run her fingers in his hair, gasp with pleasure as his hands and then his tongue moved up her inner thigh, first one leg and then the other.

"Such long, long, gorgeous legs," he rasped, showering more caresses and wet kisses along her inner legs, inching higher, now a thrilling torment that made her want to spread her legs and draw him into her softness. He had moved up where she could kiss and caress him, stroking his manhood.

While his hands and tongue heightened desire and need, she closed her eyes, lost in sensations. She had yielded herself totally to him. She cried out, grasping his strong arms as he used his hands and his tongue to drive her wild.

"Luke, love me," she whispered. "I want you now."

"Wait, wait for more," he whispered while his fingers continued to rub, building her need, carrying her toward a climax.

As she kissed and ran her hands lightly over him, she relished the moment. It was Luke in her arms, Luke kissing her, Luke taking her to paradise.

She tensed and clung to him, moving her hips furiously. "Luke, I need you now," she gasped, wanting him inside her, holding her, consuming her.

"It's too soon, Scarlett," he said, picking her up and putting her astride his lap, so she sat facing him with her legs spread apart to give him access to her.

"We're going to have some sexy fun. Hot, steamy, fun," he said, trailing kisses lower along her throat, down to her breast, to take it in his mouth and tease and run his tongue over her nipple.

He paused to look up at her as he cupped each breast in his hands. "You're breathtaking."

He toyed with her, with one hand between her legs and his other hand caressing her breast, while he kissed her and she stroked his erection.

With his arm around her neck, Luke pulled her close to kiss her passionately, his tongue exploring her mouth. She kissed him in return just as feverishly, hungry for more of him, wanting him more than ever.

He kissed her again, pulling her into his lap while he ran his hands languorously over her. "You're gorgeous. You're perfect."

"I'm not, but I want you to continue to think that way. You won't need a condom. They said I can't get pregnant."

"We won't take chances," he answered. "We have a lot of catching up to do," he said, putting on the condom and moving between her legs. His gaze swept over her. "Tonight you're mine," he whispered with a hoarse, grating whisper.

He kissed away her answer and came down between her legs to enter her. She gasped with pleasure, crying out and holding him. His mouth covered hers as he entered her, filling her completely.

She clung to him, desire driving her now with all reasoning gone. She ran one hand down his back, over his firm bottom, moving her hips against him, while they rocked hard and fast. Everything about him felt powerful and masculine and potently sexy. And then she was lost and couldn't think about anything. Sensations swirled through her, and they moved faster, pumping wildly as she gyrated against him.

Suddenly, she climaxed. Waves of release and rapture washed over her when she moved with him, and then, dimly, she heard his low, guttural groan while he climaxed.

Still thrusting hard and fast, they moved together as ecstasy and joy swamped her. They both gasped for breath, their bodies glistening with sweat.

She clung to him as they slowed and began to breathe normally. Closing her eyes, she held him tightly. For this night, this hour, Luke was in her arms, loving her and letting her love him. This was her dream for so many lonely nights as a teen. When he left for California, she thought he had gone out of her life forever, and, in truth, he had. But for a few precious minutes tonight, her wishes had been partially fulfilled.

Realistically, she knew that this loving wouldn't last, and it was meaningless for both of them. There was no way he would ever truly love her or want her in his life on a permanent basis. She wasn't the woman for him in too many ways. But for tonight, she could forget the yesterdays and the tomorrows and just hold him and have hot, lusty rapturous sex with him.

"There's no woman on earth like you, Scarlett," he whispered and turned his head to kiss her lightly on her forehead.

"I could say the same about you. We're good together in bed."

"Damn good. I think you melted my bones."

She flashed him a coy smile. "I know one way to help you recuperate. I can see to that."

"I hope you do, but not quite yet. Let me catch my breath. This has to be the best night in my life in a long, long time. I hope the little calf survives—that would really make it the best night ever. It won't be quite the same if the calf doesn't make it."

She rolled over to pull out her phone. "Toby will be here at 6:30 a.m. to transport the calf to the Royal Veterinary Hospital."

Luke shifted to his side, still holding her close, showering light kisses on her temple, her cheek, her ear, her throat. "You're marvelous, Scarlett. Marvelous, sexy, hot. I've melted."

"I hope so," she said sweetly and smiled up at him. "This is crazy, Luke, and we'll both be sorry. *I'll* be sorry. You know I can't take sex lightly the way you do."

"Who said I do?"

"Give me credit for an ounce of sense," she scoffed. "This will be a roll in the hay, literally, for you and soon forgotten."

"If you think I'm going to forget the past hour for a long, long, long time, if ever, you are sorely mistaken."

"Time will tell." They grew silent, and she was content, trying to avoid thinking beyond the present moment. She was in Luke's arms, and it felt right, and it finally chased away the memories of the sad and angry moments between them. The euphoria, the closeness, their making love—none of it would last, but she would relish this night with him and, right now, she didn't want to think beyond it. She would be hurt again, but there was no way she could have said no to him tonight.

He held her close against him and she felt wrapped in euphoria and guessed that he did, too.

" You're an adorable mom," he said, turning his head to kiss her.

She wrapped her arm around his neck to hold him as she kissed him in return. Tonight was all about them, not the past, or what would happen in the future. Luke was once again in her arms, kissing her, loving her, and she had already crossed a line, so there was no going back now. She snuggled closer and pressed against him, feeling his hard erection thrust against her. He was ready for love again, and so was she.

Saturday morning, Luke opened his eyes to see Scarlett gathering her clothes. He closed his hand around her ankle, and she turned to look at him.

"Good morning, gorgeous," he said, smiling at her. "Come down here. And toss the clothes. I really like you naked."

She smiled in return as she gave a reluctant shake of her head. "You forget—we have a sick calf, and Toby will appear before you know it. He's up before the sun."

Luke groaned. "Your brother. I'm glad he's coming to get the calf, but he could give us a little time here."

"I doubt if my brother views us being together as good news."

"I'm lucky if he doesn't slug me."

"Toby would do no such thing," she insisted. "Well,

at least not unless he's provoked by you. You're smart enough to avoid that."

He grimaced. "I hope to hell I am. How's the calf?"

"Still pretty sick. I hate to take it from its mama, but we have to. Right now I'm going to the house where I hope the water still works and I can take a shower."

Luke sat up and rubbed the back of his neck, stretching out his arms.

"Can I come with you? It'll save time if we shower together."

"I don't know how you can even say that with a straight face. If we get in a shower together, it isn't going to save time."

"Might," Luke said, standing and grabbing his clothes. "Let me show you," he drawled.

She pulled her shirt over her head, stepped into her jeans and pulled on her boots. "I'm dressing to get from here to the house. You better do the same, in case Toby drives up."

Luke nodded because she was right. He didn't want to leave the barn naked with her and run into her brother. In minutes they walked through the house that was almost devoid of furniture and had graffiti on some walls, broken windows—a standing trash heap was all he could call it. Luke tried to avoid thinking about what used to be and the years when he was young and very happy here.

Scarlett took his hand. "Luke, I'm sorry. I can't imagine how I would feel if this happened to our place."

"You don't ever have to spend one second imagining this in connection with your place. You have a super family. Toby's a fine guy and a good brother. Your mom is a rock for her whole family. You can always count on her, and she constantly showers all of you with love and affection. Your place is one of those oases in the world where it's a haven of love for the family."

"I have to agree. I just hope I can give that to Carl the way Mom gave us so much. But I'm sorry for what you're going through."

"Thanks. I'll go home to California and get on with life, and this will just be a bad memory I'll try to forget. Last night is what I'll remember. That makes up for a lot of hurt."

She was silent, and he wondered if he had hurt her again. He didn't feel he had because she was mature enough now to see his tainted family history for what it was. If he asked her to take him back, he was certain she would say no immediately. They weren't in love, and she wouldn't want to be any part of a family that let a ranch go to ruin like the Double U and abandoned the animals they owned.

To Scarlett, Luke knew he could never mean anything more than a fun night in bed with an old friend. She would never want to be seriously connected with a man like him. He really didn't blame her. He wished he could disconnect himself. He wouldn't ask her for a binding relationship because of the possibility he would turn into a man like his dad.

"It's good for everyone in this area that you're going to keep the ranch and rebuild. It'll thrive with you in charge, and you'll have a fine working ranch again."

She patted his shoulder. "Just think about what will be, and try to let the past go."

"If I can keep my dad from wrecking it again. I don't really think he'll be back on the ranch, anyway. I'll get him a house in Royal if he wants one, but from the reports I'm getting, I don't think he'll ever be able to leave the facility where he is now, unless it's straight to the hospital." He told her all this because it was obvious she was trying to be sympathetic and thought he was quiet, lost in thoughts about his dad and the ranch. He didn't think he would get sympathy if she knew he had been thinking about the two of them.

Only there really wasn't any "two of them." He could never really be a part of Scarlett's life, and if he ever started thinking he could, all he had to do was remember the condition his dad had let the ranch sink into because of his drinking addiction.

"I have a beer, especially on hot days or out partying. I probably should cut the alcohol and view it like poison before I end up like my dad."

"You're not going to do that," she said. They had reached a bathroom with a working shower, and she turned to put her index finger against his chest.

"I get to shower first so I'll be ready to meet Toby."

Luke smiled at her and put his hand on the wall over her head to lean closer to her. "As I told you before, we can cut the time in half if we shower together. If I promise to stick to just getting a shower, everything should be fine. C'mon, Scarlett, we're wasting time." He stepped closer, reached past her and turned on the shower.

"Luke, I mean it, Toby will be here—"

He turned to catch the hem of her T-shirt and pull it over her head.

"Luke—" Her muffled protest stopped as he pulled the shirt away and unbuttoned his shirt to pull it off.

"Skin out of those clothes, sweetie. Let's hurry it up. I don't want Toby finding me in here with you." Luke stripped as he talked and stepped into the shower, turning the water temperature down to try to cool himself down, because he was saying one thing, but he was feeling another. Scarlett was naked, gorgeous, sexy and enticing. He was instantly aroused, ready to make love and wanting her.

"Don't you dare touch me," she admonished. Her hazel eyes flashed fire, and he knew he'd better shower fast and dress, but it would be the worst kind of torture. Scarlett just made him want to pull her into his arms and kiss her from head to toe.

"I'm hurrying," he said in a husky voice, "but we're coming back here to do this again later and do it right."

He washed, stepped out, dried and started dressing, watching her intently. She was breathtaking, and he was rock hard with desire. He needed to dress and get away from her and cool down fast, because he knew Toby McKittrick well enough to know he was protective of Scarlett and unhappy with Luke from his earlier years.

Reluctantly, Luke walked outside to wait for Scarlett. Images of her in the shower tormented him, and he promised himself he would coax her into showering with him again. He kicked a rock with the toe of his boot. He might not be with Scarlett much again after Toby picked up the sick calf.

"I'm ready," she said, coming outside and joining him. They walked back to the barn, and she knelt to check the calf over. Her jeans tightened across her trim, sexy butt, and once again he wanted her in his bed.

"I'll get our things packed up," he said, stepping into the next stall and gathering her things to get them stowed first. It took only minutes because they hadn't brought much. He closed the stall and carried their things to his pickup to place them in the back.

He heard a motor and saw dust stirred by an approaching car that was hidden by trees. "Your brother's coming up the road," he told Scarlett. "Our things are in my pickup, and we better get our stories straight."

"I slept with the calf. You slept—"

"Next stall. Stay as close to the truth as we can." He left to meet Toby.

Toby was big and tough, a great guy and they had been friends until Luke left for college and abandoned Scarlett. His relationship with Toby haad been cold since that time. Since that time Toby hadn't wanted him around his sister and Luke couldn't blame him.

Toby parked beside Luke's pickup, walked around the back of it and paused a second to look at it. He picked up Scarlett's things and carried them back to put them in his pickup.

He returned. "Scarlett's inside with a calf, isn't she?" Toby asked as he approached Luke.

"Good morning to you. Thanks for coming, and,

yes, she is. She has saved my horses and some of the cattle, and she's kept this little calf alive."

Toby stepped closer. "Weston, I don't give a damn that you're on *Forbes*'s list or what you've done in Silicon Valley. If you hurt Scarlett again, the way you did before, I promise you Royal will have another missing person's case on its hands. You stay away from my sister. You broke her heart."

"I've never meant to hurt your sister," he said, knowing Toby was just a protective brother. He waved his hand and glanced toward the wreckage that had been his home. "Look at the house and the ranch and see the results of the family I come from. I don't think you want me to propose to her. Not then, not now."

"No, I don't. I want you to get the hell out of Texas and away from her." Toby brushed past him, and Luke stepped aside. Toby looked back. "You come from bad blood, bad people. You hurt my sister badly before. Stay the hell away from her."

Luke watched him disappear into the barn. He didn't blame Toby for tearing into him and still respected and liked the guy. When he'd said goodbye to Scarlett when they were high school kids, he'd done the right thing, and, contrary to what she'd thought at the time, it had been for her own good.

Toby had nothing to worry about where he was concerned. His sister wouldn't want a serious relationship with Luke ever again because of the family he came from. Toby just said it—Luke had bad blood—and that point would be driven home once Toby got a good look at some of the disaster Luke's dad had caused at the

Double U. Luke knew for certain that what he had accomplished in Silicon Valley wouldn't ever matter to any McKittrick. At one time, his dad had one of the finest ranches in the area, but Scarlett knew all about his parents' drinking and the results, and wouldn't ever want to tie her life to his. All she had to do was to compare his family to her family.

Luke turned to go into the barn, and Toby looked up as he approached. "Can I help get him into the pickup?" Luke asked.

"Yes, you can," Scarlett said quickly, probably cutting off Toby telling Luke to go to hell again. She began giving directions.

He knew Toby didn't want his help, but with Scarlett directing and both of them working together, they had the calf lifted into the back of Toby's pickup in seconds, with a minimum of jostling to the calf.

"Scarlett, I put your things in my pickup," Toby said. "I told them I was bringing you and the calf to the vet hospital, and they're ready for you. Thanks for your help, Weston."

"Glad to. Thanks, Scarlett. I know you'll save him."

"The hospital will," she said. "Take care of the mama."

Before he could answer, Toby started the ignition and drove off. Luke went to his pickup and got out his phone to make the calls he planned for the day. He felt a loss with Scarlett gone, and he knew that was ridiculous. Scarlett wasn't really any part of his life. The sooner he got that through his thick head, the better.

He looked at the list before him and tried to get Scarlett out of his thoughts.

Will was one of the first calls he wanted to make, but as he started to dial, he received a text and saw it was the PI, Cole Sullivan. What had happened to cause Cole Sullivan to text him so early in the morning?

Five

He read Cole's text and saw that the PI wanted to meet with him, but not at his hotel. Cole suggested a private room in the Cattleman's Club at 9:00 a.m. Luke sent a text back that he would be there.

About fifteen minutes before the designated meeting time, Luke walked into the Cattleman's Club. It brought back memories of eating there with his dad, who had been a member. Later, when he was home visiting his dad, he joined. By then he was out of college and working in Silicon Valley and had started West-Tech.

He parked and headed toward the front door of the large dark stone-and-wood rambling building. New rooms had been added on through the years, but it still retained some of the rooms built in 1910. Sunshine spilled over the tall slate roof. Inside, the high ceilings left room for hunting trophies and historical artifacts that adorned the paneled walls.

He went to one of the private meeting rooms, and in minutes Cole stepped inside and closed the door. "Thanks for coming on short notice. Meeting here seems better because, if anyone is following either of us, there's no assurance we're here to see each other. You might watch to see if you're followed."

"I will, but I go see all sorts of people in Royal. I don't think Rich will have any interest in me."

"He may be a thousand miles from Texas, but it pays to be careful. No one has found Jason Phillips yet." Cole placed a briefcase on the table, opened it to reveal papers, tablets and envelopes. He waved his hand.

"I have all this for you to sort through. Some of it, Sheriff Battle has gotten and let me copy. Some of it, I've found. The Club has been cooperative and given us some information. Actually, the big banks here have cooperated, too. They always want to catch anyone who has taken as much as a nickel from the bank. They don't give up."

Luke smiled. "Probably not good for business to let anyone get away with theft."

"This is all for you—it's copies, but this holds information that hopefully you can use in your new programs and come up with something."

"Good deal," Luke said, moving the papers, receipts and folders from Cole's briefcase to his own.

"That's it. If you want to leave, I'll go have a cup of coffee and stick around. Or vice versa. I just don't want to walk out of here with you."

"Nope. I can sit right here and start looking at this stuff, and you can go."

"Okay. Thanks. Good luck with it. We need to nail the bastard because one man may be dead and Will was lucky he survived."

"Thanks, Cole. We can get a locker here, share the combination and you can just put info in it, and I can get it out,. And then we don't have to be here even close to the same time."

"Fine. I'll go now and get the locker, text you the combination."

"Can't beat that."

Luke shook hands with him, and Cole left. Luke put everything away and left to go back to his hotel, where he put the briefcase in the safe.

He had an appointment with the builder again and left for that.

Midmorning he saw he had a text from Scarlett telling him the calf was doing better. He smiled, thinking about this amazing woman and her way with animals. She was doing what she did best, caring for animals, being mother to little Carl. Luke always felt he was doing what he did best by working in Silicon Valley and devoting his efforts to electronics. However, now that he was in Royal, he didn't feel the urgency to get back to California that he had expected to feel.

Maybe it was just because he was needed here to straighten out the mess made by his dad. Once he got the ranch up and running and bills paid, saw his dad, helped Will get some proof about Rich Lowell, then he would probably feel that itch to get home to California.

But right now, he wanted to see Scarlett. He sent her a text inviting her to dinner. She had turned him down before, and she would probably turn him down again, but maybe she would accept.

Thirty minutes later when he heard a slight ping that indicated he had an answer, he picked up his phone. She'd accepted this time. His pulse jumped, and the whole day looked better. It was foolish to feel this way. He couldn't ever mean anything serious to her or be a permanent part of her life, but she was going to have dinner with him, and he wanted it to be as special as possible.

Luke left, stepping outside to text details to her. In minutes he got a brief answer back from her that made him smile. She would be ready at five today, and she should get home by noon tomorrow. Her mother would keep Carl.

Luke's heart thudded with anticipation. She would be with him tonight. He started making arrangements, finished up his appointments, then went back to his hotel suite to get ready for their evening. He had a limo driver in his employ who was also a pilot and had flown out the day after Luke's arrival. Luke couldn't wait to see Scarlett. They'd been apart only hours, but it had been way too long. Scarlett was special. She always had been, and that hadn't changed.

Scarlett changed clothes four times before she decided on a simple, sleeveless red dress. It had a straight skirt, a belted middle and a scoop neck. Excitement made her eager for the evening. She would be with

Luke, and he would see to it that they had a good time. She wanted this night with him. She'd had too many empty nights, too many tears shed long ago over him. This was a special moment, a night to share with him and she wanted it.

She opened a drawer to look at jewelry, which she didn't wear often. She touched a gold bracelet and picked it up to look at it. Luke had given it to her after they had made love the first time.

She couldn't ever get rid of it. She never wore it— she had worn it when they dated, but once he left her, she dropped it into a bottom drawer and didn't see it often for a long time. Now it looked sort of like a kid bracelet. She just had never wanted to part with it.

When she was ready, she stepped into high-heeled red pumps. Her hair was short, easy to run a comb through. She checked her reflection in the mirror one last time and then went to find Carl and her mother. Joyce had just finished feeding him.

"Mom, I would take him, but he has little bits of food on him."

"Don't pick him up. He could easily spit up. You look pretty, Scarlett."

"Thanks, Mom. Now stop worrying. Luke is taking me to dinner to repay me for taking care of his animals and saving this little calf."

"I just don't want him to hurt you again."

"I'm not sixteen, and I'm not going to get hurt," she said, hoping she could live up to that promise.

She looked at her baby and he smiled, his dimple showing, and she had to laugh. She leaned closer to him. "You're trying to get me to come close and then you'll get part of your dinner on my dress. You'll probably think it's prettier that way." He laughed, and she did, too. "You are sneaky, Carl McKittrick," she cooed, and they both laughed again. "Mom, isn't he adorable? I think he is," she said, without waiting for her mother's answer.

"He has the best disposition of any baby I've ever seen. I thought you did, but he's even jollier than you were. Scarlett, are you sure you want to go to Dallas with Luke tonight?"

"I'll be careful. Stop fretting, Mom."

"Never," her mom said with a beleaguered sigh. "Oh...you have mail that came this afternoon. I didn't get out to the box until late. It's in the dining room. You have something from Luke."

"He paid his bill, but he said he sent something extra and to use it to help the strays I take in," she said, hurrying to get the mail. She moved slowly as she returned. "Mom, he said he sent this because he knows I help strays and all that. He said just to put it in my business however it will help," Scarlett said, staring at the check in her hand in Luke's bold scrawl.

"What's wrong with it? You sound worried," her mother said.

Scarlett stared at the check and then looked up at her mom. "I can't take this. He said use it to help animals. I still can't do it."

"Why not?" Joyce asked, frowning. She crossed the room to look at the check. "My heavens! That's half a million dollars, Scarlett. You could build a whole second facility with that."

"I could do all sorts of things, including buy TV spots where I could show the dogs that are up for adoption. Half a million, Mom. I could do so many helpful things for the rescue animals with that much money."

"No, I don't think you should. You don't want to owe Luke Weston anything. Half a *million*. Scarlett, he wants you. He's trying to buy you."

She shook her head. "Luke knows me well enough to know that if he gave me five million, I wouldn't feel obligated. It's a gift. He can afford it, and I can use it to help stray and injured animals. I can add on so we can take in more homeless animals. I have to give this one some thought."

"Just don't let his money get you carried away."

She looked at her mother. "Mom, don't worry about it. Whatever I do, the money won't make one bit of difference about how I view Luke. He broke my heart once. It won't happen again, especially not because Carl will be involved. I'm not going to do anything to let Luke hurt Carl."

"If you weren't my daughter, I wouldn't believe that. But you *are* my daughter, and I know you, and I think you mean every word you just said."

"Honestly, he may just be that grateful. You can't imagine how pitiful his horses and some of the cattle were. They were just hours away from dying, Mom. If I hadn't been there, he would have had to put them down. You've lived on this ranch long enough to know what that's like and how much it hurts when it's just one animal. When it is a lot of livestock, it's excruciating. I saved him a lot of money, too." She smiled. "Not half a million, mind you. But, in any event, I'll think about this. I can save so many animals if I cash this check. I won't have this chance again."

"Just as long as it doesn't come with strings."

"Luke knows me better than that."

"Your brother will blow his lid."

Scarlett laughed. "Yes, he will. Toby will be suspicious of Luke's motives. I'm sure of that."

"Your brother is just protective."

"I know it. He's a good brother. A little overbearing sometimes, but good. Just wait until that cutie daughter of his grows up and starts dating. I feel sorry for the boys that go home with her."

Her mother smiled. "His daughter may have enough of Toby in her that she'll be a match for her dad."

Scarlett laughed as the doorbell rang. "There's Luke. Bring Carl and come say hello. I don't dare carry Carl in there in this dress."

Her mother wiped Carl's face, unbuckled him and picked him up to follow Scarlett toward the front door. As Scarlett went to the door, Joyce carried Carl into the living room.

When Scarlett opened the door, her heart skipped a beat as she looked up at Luke. He wore a navy suit, a white dress shirt with gold cuff links, a navy tie and black boots. He had on a white Stetson, and he took her breath away. She didn't think she had ever seen a man look as handsome as Luke did at that moment.

"Hi. Come in and say hello to Mom and Carl."

"Hi, yourself. You look gorgeous," he said and she smiled.

"Thank you." She led him into the big living room where Joyce was holding Carl and turned to face them, smiling at Luke.

"Hello, Luke."

"Hi, Mrs. McKittrick." He walked closer. "Hi, Carl." Carl gave him another dimpled grin. "He is one friendly kid."

"He gets smiles all day," Scarlett said, "so he's friendly in return. He's a happy baby. Don't stand too close. He just had dinner, and he might have some food stored in those little fat cheeks. Food that he could blow out all over you. That would give him a laugh."

Luke grinned. "Thanks for the warning. He looks delightfully harmless. So he has a sneaky side."

"He just thinks it's funny." She leaned over to kiss Carl's cheek and moved away quickly. "Bye-bye, sweetie. Mom, I have my phone and I'll keep in touch."

"Both of you have a nice evening," Joyce said politely.

Scarlett knew her mother didn't want her to go out with Luke and hadn't forgiven him for the hurt he caused when she was a teenager. But Scarlett always wondered if Luke had wanted her to drop out of school at sixteen, marry him and go off to California with him, if her mother wouldn't have fought that to a bitter end. She had a feeling that her mother and her brother both would have been adamantly against her marrying Luke. Scarlett shoved aside the speculation on the past. It hadn't played out that way, and her mother and her brother were both still angry with Luke. Either way, he had lost their friendship.

Luke took her arm, and they walked to the waiting limo.

When they were settled in the back seat of the limo, she smiled at Luke. "Thank you for your so very generous check to me for my vet services."

"I'm really grateful for all you've done, Scarlett."

"Your check goes way beyond what I did."

"Not to my way of thinking. No other vet would have given me the time and attention that night that you did, and you know it. No one else would have worked straight through the night. No other vet would have saved as many animals as you did. Not only that, I can afford what I paid you, and you can use it to save a whole bunch more mutts." He sighed heavily. "Too bad you didn't come along in time to save old Mutt. I did love that dog, and I should have taken him with me to California. There are a lot of things I should have done."

"You need to stop blaming yourself for all your dad's shortcomings, Luke. You had no idea."

"You're right. I need to leave that all in the past and just fix things as fast as I can."

"You've really stepped up, Luke." She met his gaze. "And, yes, I'll use your generous check to help the rescue animals and get some up-to-date equipment for my clinic, and I'll give part of the money to the Royal Veterinary Hospital."

"Save your money there. I've already sent them a check because of my calf."

"You get what you want in life now, don't you?" she said, smiling at him.

He looked at her without smiling. "Not really. There are some things all the money in the world won't buy," he answered, his blue-green gaze holding her mesmerized. Was he talking about her? She drew a deep breath and told herself that was ridiculous. She didn't mean anything to Luke beyond a quick romp in the hay. He had proven that a long time ago.

"I suppose, Luke."

"You're lucky, Scarlett, to have little Carl. I never thought I'd feel that way about a baby, but he's a cute little kid and I'll bet he brings you and your family all kinds of joy."

"Yes, he does. Toby and Naomi's daughter is a little doll, as well. It's fun to have the little kids in the family. You'll have a family someday, Luke," she said, thinking of that half million.

He shook his head and looked out the window. "I don't think so. I never want a marriage like my folks had. That's strike one. I have bad genes. That's strike two. I don't want to settle down. Strike three. Three strikes, and you're out," he said, and she heard the bitter note in his voice.

She took his hand. "Luke, you don't have bad genes," she whispered. She shouldn't be holding his hand. She shouldn't be caught up in sympathy for a man who was handsome, sexy and one of the richest men in the country. Why did it hurt to hear him say he had bad genes and he didn't want to marry? Luke had walked out on her years earlier, and he hadn't really changed in all the time between. He liked making love. He was lusty, sexy and energetic. But his heart was so locked away, she wasn't certain he could find it.

Scarlett swallowed a lump in her throat. She shouldn't care, but no matter how hard she tried, she *did* care. So very much. And now, she was going with him to Dallas for a night—a night that would bind her heart to him more than ever. She was on the verge of falling in love with him all over again, despite knowing how badly she was going to get hurt again What was important was keeping Luke away from Carl. She intended to keep her baby from being hurt. She didn't want Luke in her life again because if he was, Carl would love him and get hurt, too, when Luke went back to California.

She should tell him to turn the limo around and go back to her safe, quiet life that she had before he came back to Royal and melted her with fiery kisses, taking her to paradise with his lovemaking. She was going to spend the next twenty-or-so hours with him and fall all the way in love with him. And in the end she would end up burned even worse than the last time.

She had read about him, seen the pictures of the celebrities he was involved with in California. They could give him babies that were his own bloodline, and they were gorgeous women with dazzling careers. If she thought he would ever fall in love with her, she had lost her grip on reality.

"You're quiet, Scarlett," he said, taking her hand in his. "A penny for your thoughts. That's a silly old saying."

"Just thinking about the evening."

"I've been thinking about it all day—since the shower this morning. We can do that over tonight or in the morning and do it right," he said in a husky voice.

But if, by some miracle, he fell in love with her and asked her to marry him, she would have to say no. She couldn't give him babies. She couldn't have his children. A man like Luke would want babies that had his blood in their veins. She felt certain of that, in spite of his spiel about bad genes. He couldn't really think that he had bad blood after all the gizmos he had patented and the fortune he had made from his inventions, the company he had built and the success he had. He was smart, strong, healthy, and he definitely had good genes.

She couldn't trust him to stay. She couldn't let Carl think of him as dad only to have him walk away. She looked out the window of the limo and felt as if she were riding straight into a disaster of the heart.

"You are way too solemn. Something's worrying you."

She smiled. "Sorry. Sometimes I worry about my patients after I leave them. I need to stop stressing about them, but sometimes it's impossible."

As the limo slowed, she glanced out to see a plane waiting on the Royal airport runway. In minutes they were aboard, and she gazed out the window as they taxied down the runway to take off.

"Your limo driver is up front with the pilot?"

"There are two of them. Jake also has a pilot's license, so he's up there, where he can fly if necessary.

I don't like to take chances." He flashed a grin. "You ought to come out and see me, Scarlett. See where I live and let me show you around. California has everything your heart could ever desire. I'm partial to my part of it."

Amused, she smiled back at him. "I can't ever get far from my vet practice."

"Sure you can. If you don't have someone now who can take over when you're gone, you need to get somebody."

"Maybe someday, Luke," she said, doubting if she ever would.

In Dallas they were met by another waiting limo and another driver who worked for Luke. He had whatever he wanted, when he wanted it. And witnessing it up close made her realize how she would never fit in his grandiose world with her dogs and vet business, with little Carl and a far simpler life. She would take tonight, and maybe another night or two, but he would go back to Silicon Valley before long and would never look back. She needed to face what was ahead and not have any illusions.

In no time, he opened the door to his penthouse suite and held it for her to enter.

"Luke, this is gorgeous," she said, looking at a large, elegant living area with mirrors, oil paintings, huge bouquets of fresh flowers, statues and comfortable fruitwood furniture. The lighting was soft, and he pressed a switch for music. A table was set, and Luke lit two candles. "I've ordered dinner, and I let them know at the airport we had landed, so they should be here with our—"

The bell rang and Luke turned. "There's dinner," he said, opening the door and ushering in two waiters who wheeled a cart with covered dishes.

While they put dinner on the table, Scarlett walked to the floor-to-ceiling glass window and gazed beyond the balcony at the twinkling lights of Dallas that spread for miles in all directions. As they uncovered steaming dishes, enticing aromas of hot bread, coffee, thick steaks filled the room. Soon, the waiters were gone.

When Luke dimmed the lights, she glanced around to see him shed his jacket and tie and unbutton the top button of his shirt. As he crossed the room to her, her heart drummed, and she couldn't catch her breath. She forgot the view and the dinner. All she could see was the handsome man approaching her, the man she loved. The man who was never going to fall in love with her. At least she could face the true situation this time and wasn't in a dream world, as she had been at sixteen.

"You're all I can think about. I've wanted this moment since we stepped into the shower together this morning. You're beautiful, Scarlett. I can't tell you how you excite me." He leaned closer, wrapping his arms around her and kissing away any reply she had.

She closed her eyes and clung to him, her heart pounding while she kissed him as if it were the last kiss between them. In every way possible, she wanted to make love to him, to kiss, caress and arouse him to the point that he wouldn't be able to forget her and walk away easily. All that about bad genes—she knew he didn't have bad genes, and he had to be smart enough to know it, too. He just didn't want to be tied down.

"Scarlett, I want you. I thought about you all day today and couldn't wait for this moment. I can't wait. Dinner can."

She kissed him, stopping his conversation, relishing his strong arms holding her tightly against his hard body. His arousal pressed against her. He was ready to love, kissing her with a desperation as if tonight were their last night together. At any point in time, it could be her last night with Luke. She intended to make the most of her moments with him.

Leaning away slightly, her hands slipped between them to unbutton his shirt and push it away. It dropped to the floor. She ran her hands across his muscled chest, tangling her fingers in the scattering of chest hairs across the center of his chest.

Eagerness made her fingers shake. She wanted all barriers between them removed. Wiggling out of his embrace, she stepped back and watched him as she began to remove her clothing. She heard his sharp intake of breath when she reached behind her and pulled the zipper down the back of her dress, turning her back to him as she shrugged out of it, shimmying slightly so it fell off her shoulders and dropped just below her waist, resting on her hips. She held it and watching him over her shoulder. She slipped it down over her bottom and then let it pool around her ankles. When she stepped out of it, she turned to face him. She still wore a scrap of lacy bikini and a matching bra, and her red high heels.

While he watched her, she walked a few steps closer. As she did, he stripped away the rest of his clothes.

He wrapped his arms around her, crushing her against his chest, leaning over her. "Damn, you're beautiful, and I want you."

She rubbed against him and wound one long leg around him. He caught her leg instantly and held it, caressing her from her knee to her bottom, letting his fingers slide over her intimately. She gasped and arched her back.

"I can't wait, love," he whispered as he let her stand while he got a condom and put it on. Drawing her to him, he kissed her while he picked her up and lowered her onto his thick manhood, easing into her.

She whimpered with pleasure and need, moving on him, locking her limbs around him while she put her arms around his neck. She wanted him, needed him to be part of her life. He was driving her wild, teasing her, a tempting torment as he held her on his thick erection.

He eased slowly out of her, lifting her off and then entering her again while she gasped and clung to him. "I want you," she whispered fiercely, desire overwhelming her. And then he began to pump, and she moved with him, holding him tightly and kissing him. Lights burst behind her closed eyes. Her pulse drummed in her ears. Bracing himself, he held her with one arm while his other hand toyed with her bottom.

Her climax burst and she moved frantically, crying out and then sinking on his shoulder as he pounded in her, reaching his own climax. She didn't know how much time passed as they gulped for breath, trying to calm their racing heartbeats. She slowly lowered her legs, and he withdrew. Then he pulled her into his embrace, and they stood holding each other. He ran his hand lightly up and down her back, over her bottom and up to caress her nape.

"I've wanted you naked in my arms since we left the shower," he said. "I couldn't keep my mind on anything else for thinking about you all day," he said.

She turned her head to gaze up at him. "I'm glad. I want you to want me. I've always wanted you, Luke. I hope I'm in your dreams at night and in your thoughts during the day." She trailed her fingers over his chest and ran her tongue along his throat, his ear, back to his shoulder, letting her fingers glide suggestively down his hip.

Still holding her tightly, he scooped her up and carried her to the shower. "We can shower and eat in bed if you want."

She pursed her lips. "We're not taking any food to bed. It would end up spilled, and we'd be making love in the gravy."

He grinned. "Scarlett, oh, baby, how I like being with you," he whispered and drew her close against him to hug her. He turned the water on, got it warm and began to run his hands over her wet body.

"Here goes dinner," she said, doing the same to him, gliding her hands over his hard muscles, bulging biceps and flat belly. When he ran his hands between her legs and began to toy with her, stroking her, his other hand caressing her breast, she gasped and closed her eyes, clinging to him as she moved her hips.

"You can't be ready again."

"I've got two hands," he whispered. "I can take you

to a climax with my fingers," he said, rubbing her intimately.

She writhed against him as he started another storm of desire. He turned her, sliding his thick cock between her legs, holding her close as he rubbed against her, and she cried out, all the while using her hands to try to excite him as much as possible. And then she was lost in sensation as tension grew and she felt as if she would burst with need.

"See what you do to me," he said, his words husky, claiming her lips with his before he picked her up and thrust his hard rod inside her. She gasped and cried out, holding him tightly, wrapping her legs around him and moving on him until an orgasm burst through her and release came.

He shuddered with his climax, pumping in her, emitting a throaty growl as he shifted his hips, and then he finally slowed and held her tightly.

"I think that might have been able to go in Ripley's list. I didn't think that was possible so soon after I reached a climax."

"You don't know your own possibilities," she whispered, kissing his shoulder.

"One of us has been working more than the other of us," he said. "Give me a break."

She smiled. "You're saying you don't want me to kiss you, or caress you, or rub against you—"

"For the next ten minutes—no, fifteen minutes—Scarlett. Then you can do whatever you want to do."

"Whatever I want to do?" she said, smiling mischievously at him. She turned to let the water run over her, washing and then stepping out to grab a huge, fluffy bath towel. When she began to dry, Luke took the towel from her and dried her, rubbing her lightly, watching her as he ever so slowly dried first one breast and then the other.

"You're beautiful," he whispered, leaning forward, bending to run his tongue over her nipple. Sensations streaked from his hot, wet tongue making circles.

He walked behind her and began to dry her back, starting at her shoulders and slowly moving down. She turned to stand on tiptoe and kiss him briefly and then leaned back.

"Now I get to dry you." She ran the towel over his strong body, pausing to touch his hip. "I remember this scar—bull riding when you were eighteen."

"I was lucky I didn't break any bones. My bull riding career was short. Very short."

He tossed the towel away and grinned down her. "So far we've had a good start to the evening. Want to have a glass of wine? Beer? Eat dinner?"

"I'm ready for some dinner, except I'm not eating naked. I want clothes, and let's go sit on the balcony and look at the lights.

"Whatever the pretty lady wants, the lady gets. The one plus about wearing clothes to dinner is that I will look forward to taking them off of you *after* dinner."

She smiled at him. "Give me a few minutes on the balcony to enjoy the city lights."

He caught her hand and brushed a kiss on her knuckles as they walked back to get their clothes and dress again. "This is good, Scarlett."

"I think it is," she answered. She paused. "I'm ready to eat now. Let's get our plates filled and sit on the balcony."

"Sounds like a deal." Dressed again, Luke draped his arm casually across her shoulders. "Scarlett, it's good to be with you."

Her heart missed a beat. "I'm glad," she answered truthfully. "It feels very good to be with you like this, as well." Was he just being polite? Was it euphoria after making love? She knew better than to count on his remark having any deeper meaning, but hope took root anyhow.

"It's beautiful up here, Luke," she murmured a few minutes later, looking out at the sparkling city lights as Dallas spread out in all directions. Luke had poured wine and they had helped themselves from a spread with lobster, salmon, steak and creamed pheasant. She was more captivated by the view and the handsome man across from her than her dinner.

"Absolutely breathtaking," he said in a deep, raspy voice that caught her attention and made her turn to face him. He smiled a slow, hungry smile that held a promise of kisses to follow. Her heart thudded.

"*You're* breathtaking, Scarlett. I like being with you, and I'm glad you're here tonight."

"This is magical, Luke. I'll always remember tonight."

They sat quietly, Luke eating while she had a few bites of lobster with melted butter. "I'm glad you're keeping the Double U ranch. You'll have a fine ranch again."

"I'll have a fine new house. I'm going to have at least three houses—one for me when I come back. One for someone I'll hire to run the ranch and be responsible for it, and a third for a guest house. There might be more, but that's a start."

She wondered how much he would come back to Royal. "That's a good start, Luke."

I just have to hire the right people. Either that or come home and do it myself, and I'm not ready to turn rancher."

"You were good at it when you lived here."

"California is my home. You should come see me, Scarlett."

She smiled at him. "I wonder if I'd love it the way you do," she answered, certain she would never see his Silicon Valley home.

"I've put it off long enough and my anger over the ranch has cooled slightly... I need to go visit my dad. Would you go with me? That'll keep me from yelling at him."

"You won't yell at him. Especially now, because it sounds as if he's very ill."

"I think he is. It's sad."

"I'll go with you if I can. Just let me know when."

"Sure." They sat quietly eating. She wasn't very hungry and she enjoyed the view.

"Let's go inside," he said, standing and taking her hand. They walked into the living room. He blew out the candles and turned to face her.

"Come here," he said. Before she had taken three steps, he picked her up to carry her to the bedroom, where he stood her on her feet. He framed her face with his hands and leaned closer to kiss her. As her arms went around his neck, he wrapped his arms around her.

Scarlett's heartbeat raced. She kissed Luke, knowing with full certainty that she loved him, wondering if he even had a glimmer of a notion that she felt so deeply for him. It wouldn't matter. She wasn't the woman for him, and she never would be. Luke would have his happy, rich, wonderful California life, and she was glad. He belonged there, and she belonged here in Texas with her baby, her mother and all her family. She was needed here. Her job was important and she had saved more than a few animals. Carl was happy and she didn't want that to change. It was just unfortunate for her that they could never have anything beyond what they had tonight—a fun time making love, good company and that's all.

She held him tightly and kissed him, wanting him, wishing she could just keep holding him. It wasn't possible, and she had to take what she could and live with the beautiful memories. And she didn't want to worry her mother or get Toby all riled up and angry with Luke. She hoped this time around she could keep her feelings from all of them. But could she really hide what she felt for Luke?

Sunshine spilled into the room and across the bed. It was 8:00 the following morning, and they'd slept in each other's arms between the times they made love throughout the night. Scarlett had to get back to Royal. As sweet as Carl was and as capable as her mother was, she didn't want to leave her mother to deal with her son for too long. She told Luke she needed to get home, and he agreed because he was getting information from Will about the missing Texas Cattleman's Club money.

"Okay, Scarlett, the jet's fueled and ready to take us home."

"When we get there, I'd love for you to come in and see Mom and Carl. Mom will want to hear about the Double UΔ and Carl will just want some attention. I bought him a toy downstairs in the gift shop."

"I should get him one, too. Come help me because I have no idea what's safe to give him or what he would like or what is appropriate for his age." He grimaced. "Scarlett, I know absolutely nothing about babies."

"You did fine with him. He liked you, and you made him happy. You don't need to get him anything. He's happy whether or not he has a toy. And he does have plenty. I just can't resist taking him something."

"I suspect he likes everyone he meets and he's happy all the time."

She smiled. "That's true. You did quite well with him, and I'm sure he'll be happy to see you again."

They started to go to the door, and Luke caught her arm, pulling gently. Surprised, she turned to look at him.

"I don't want to leave yet."

"Luke, we can't hole up here—"

"One more kiss," he whispered and slipped his arms around her to draw her closer as he leaned forward and placed his mouth on hers. The minute his lips touched hers, her arguments vanished. She dropped her things and put her arms around him, holding him tightly, feeling each time they were going to part that it was probably the last time she would see him before he left for California.

When he ran his hand over her breast and then reached for the zipper to her dress, she caught his hand and stepped away.

"You're headed for another hour in bed, and we can't. Let's go, Luke. We both have things to do and places to be."

For a moment she thought he was going to argue with her, but then he nodded and reached around her to open the door. As they walked out, she felt as if she was walking out of his life for the final time. Would she feel that way each time she left him?

Six

Luke returned to the Bellamy to his suite. He'd had his computer set up where he could work. Cole was getting information to him about the stolen money with dates and what little records on withdrawals the PI had unearthed. Luke worked at night, going to the Double U in the day to see what progress they were making and to go over plans for the new ranch house.

On Monday, Luke asked the architect for a copy of the plans so he could review them back in Royal. That afternoon, he called Scarlett and told her he'd like her to look at the plans for the new ranch house and see if she had any suggestions. "I need a woman's perspective."

She laughed. "Sure. Come have dinner with us. Mom is cooking her chicken and dumplings, and they're good."

"I remember and they are good, and you don't have to ask me twice. What can I bring for Carl?"

"Like I said the other day, you don't need to bring him anything. He'll be happy to see you. Just smile at him."

Luke laughed. "It's easy to smile at him because that's all he does. Does he ever cry?"

"Of course, he cries. He can get grumpy when he's tired. But most of the time, he's happy."

"He gets that from being around you."

"I hope so. I try to be happy around him. So far, he's a sweetie."

"I never knew a little kid could be fun, but yours is," Luke said.

"It's good that you like him," she said, but her voice had a wistful quality, and he wondered if he had said the wrong thing.

That night when the doorbell rang, Scarlett opened it to welcome Luke. She took a deep breath as her heartbeat sped up. He wore a white shirt, navy slacks and his black boots. Taking off his black Stetson when he entered the house, he filled the room with his masculine presence, and she couldn't help noting that he looked more handsome each time she saw him.

"You look great," he said softly, his gaze sweeping over her and making her tingle. They wouldn't be alone until maybe late this evening before he went home. She just wanted to walk into his arms and kiss him.

"Thanks," she said, wondering how many outfits she had pulled out before she decided on her blue sleeveless dress and sandals. "Come into the kitchen. Mom's cooking and Carl is playing with his toys."

"I brought the house plans. I'll leave them with you—these are copies. Look at them when you can, and we'll get together to discuss them. I want your input."

"Sure," she said, thinking with a pang that she would never live in this house she was going to help him plan. Would he ever marry, or was he just going to avoid marriage because of his parents' disastrous marriage?

Her mother came from the kitchen to greet Luke. She wore a bright red apron over her gray slacks and white blouse. Her honey-blond hair grazed her shoulders, and her vivid blue eyes sparkled with warmth. Scarlett knew how angry she had been with Luke in the past, but that was gone tonight and she was her usual friendly self. "It's good to have you here with us, Luke. It seems like old times."

"It smells wonderful in here. Thanks for having me for dinner. The Bellamy food is good, but I remember yours, and there's no comparison."

She laughed. "I remember you used to like the chicken and dumplings."

"Yes, I did, and I imagine that I still do." Scarlett walked to Carl, who sat in a little bouncy chair. Scarlett picked him up and handed him to Luke.

"Hi, Carl," he said, smiling.

Carl smiled back and patted Luke with a chubby little hand. "Ahh, those dimpled smiles of his. Let's look at the toys." Luke glanced at Joyce. "Mrs. McKittrick, can I help you in any way?"

"No, thanks. We'll be ready to eat in about half an hour. I'm going to check on the dumplings. I'll join you two again in a few minutes."

"Sure, Mom. When you're ready, I'll help get dinner on the table." She turned to Luke, who was playing with Carl, swinging one of his toys back and forth.

"What would you like to drink? Beer, red wine, white wine, margarita, old fashioned, whatever. Mom has a well-stocked bar."

"I'll just have a glass of water, thank you. Scarlett, I've been drinking beer since I was about sixteen or sooner. My folks didn't care. Now when I look at alcohol, I just think about the ranch and Dad, and I don't want a drop." He exhaled roughly. "I know that will pass, but that's the way I feel right now. I just keep seeing the sick livestock and the dead carcasses."

"I can understand. That was a shock."

"Does your brother know I'm here tonight?"

She shook her head. "No, I don't think Mom said anything about it."

"I'm glad. Keep peace in the family. Your mom's cooking is fabulous. This is going to be a real treat. This and maybe a few other things," he said, winking at her and she felt her cheeks grow warm and knew she blushed.

During dinner Luke entertained them and he also fit in and Scarlett was sorry Toby couldn't accept Luke.

At one point Luke smiled at her mother. "Dinner is delicious and this is great. I feel at home here," he said, looking at Scarlett and she was startled that he felt totally welcome and at home during dinner. Her mother had a way of making company feel part of the family.

After dinner, Luke said he would clear and for Joyce to join Scarlett and Carl and put her feet up. After a polite argument, which Scarlett ruled, she and her mother cleaned the kitchen, leaving Luke with Carl.

When Joyce and Scarlett joined him, all of them had to smile at Carl's antics.

Scarlett smiled with the others, but she felt a pang. It was wonderful to have Luke with them, but soon he would go back to California, and she really didn't expect to ever be with him like this again. Luke would marry some wealthy woman, and his life would move on.

At one point, Luke picked up Carl and held him on his lap, making faces and funny noises at the baby, and when Carl laughed, all of them laughed. Scarlett got her phone and took a picture of Luke and Carl, both laughing up a storm. She couldn't resist—she shifted and took a picture of Luke.

"A baby's laughter is contagious," Scarlett said, loving having Luke play with Carl, yet wanting to avoid times like this too often where Carl would get attached to Luke.

"He sounds so damn happy," Luke said. "Whoops. I better watch my language around him. At least he won't copy me tonight."

Finally, Joyce picked him up. "I'll take him up to bed. Kiss Mommy goodnight, Carl," she said, handing him to Scarlett, who hugged him and kissed his cheek.

"Mrs. McKittrick, that was a wonderful dinner. Thanks for including me. You have a cute grandchild."

"Thanks, Luke. He keeps me young. I have so much fun with him. And as he grows, he just gets to be more fun."

"Well, he's the first baby I've ever been around. He's set the bar pretty high."

"He's special. Come back and see us, Luke," she said. "You're always welcome."

"Thank you. That means a lot," he replied. Scarlett knew from her mother's tone of voice that she had meant what she said to Luke, which had surprised her. And she thought Luke was also sincere in his answer. His answer didn't surprise her, but she intended to ask her mother about her remark.

He smiled as Joyce left with Carl in her arms.

"She sounds as if she means that," he said to Scarlett.

"She does or she wouldn't say it, believe me. I think you mended some fences with her tonight. You said and did all the right things, and you took a second helping of her chicken and dumplings, which she loves to see someone do."

"You've got a great family, Scarlett. I've always thought that. Is your mom coming back?"

"No. She'll read to Carl and then rock him, and when he finally goes to sleep, she'll go to bed to read. We've seen the last of her tonight. Want to go to my place? It's next to this house."

"Sure. Carl sleeps here, and you sleep there?"

She shook her head. "Nope. I still have my suite here, and Carl's nursery is here because Mom keeps him so much of the time while I work. I just stay over here since I got Carl. I don't mind. There's no husband—just Carl and me—so we might as well stay here. And, besides, Mom is here and she loves taking care of him."

Luke put his arm around Scarlett's shoulders. "Scarlett, I hope you say, 'Thank you, God,' every day in your prayers for your family. You are so blessed to have them. My dad can be mean as a snake."

"Believe me, I do." She gazed up at him. "Your dad wasn't that mean when you were growing up, was he?"

"Not to me. He and Mom fought like a mountain lion and a rattlesnake. They had big fights—verbal, not physical—but then they'd drink themselves into not caring, and life was bearable. Actually, I just got out of the house as often as I could—worked on the ranch, hung out with the cowboys, went into Royal to see my friends. Later, went out with you."

"You didn't complain."

"It was just a fact of life and when I was away from it, I didn't want to talk about it."

As they talked, Scarlett took him next door to her house. "I've had this all redone," she said. "I used to have my office downstairs and I lived upstairs. I had my clinic and everything out here, but later, I built in Royal and then changed this from an office downstairs turning all of it into a house for me. I didn't think about becoming a mom then. I don't spend much time over here now," she admitted, stepping inside and switching on one light. "Come look around." She led him into a living room that was rustic with framed paintings of horses and ranch scenes on the walls.

Luke turned her to face him. "It feels good, Scarlett. Being with you just feels so damn good. Tonight was just like I'd come home, only my home was never as filled with love as this one is," he said and pulled her to him to kiss her.

Her heart thudded and she wrapped her arms around his neck as their lips met. She pressed against him, desire sweeping over her. "Luke," she whispered and then kissed him again, tightening her hold on him. He shifted, his hands moving to the buttons on her dress to unfasten it.

"Do you have a bedroom in this place?" he rasped against her lips, kissing her between each word.

"Oh, yes," she answered breathlessly. "I'd hoped we'd end up here. The bed is ready."

Scarlett pushed against him, turning so she could walk backwards while they kissed. He continued to kiss her as he followed her from the living room to her bedroom.

She had unbuttoned his shirt and pushed it off him, pulling it out of his slacks to toss it away. While she peeled away more of his clothes, he began to remove hers. She stepped back from him to unfasten her bra and take it off, watching him as he yanked off briefs. Her breath caught in her throat and her pulse pounded. He looked magnificent with his muscled body, his broad shoulders and trim waist, his narrow hips. Just looking at him made her throb and want to reach for him, to feel his hard body pressed against hers.

"You look like one of the California stars," she whispered, running her hands over his shoulders, his biceps and his chest.

"You're the one who's gorgeous, Scarlett. You take my breath away and keep me awake at night. You're beautiful. Your body is stunning, and the sight of your legs can have me ready for love in seconds."

His hard erection sure was ready, and she slid her fingers over the smooth tip, leaning down to run her mouth over him, curling her tongue around him and stroking his rod while she toyed with him between his legs. She peeled off her panties and reached out again to caress his erection, leaning close to run her tongue over him again, and then turning to rub her bottom slowly against him.

He reached around her, fondling her breasts, circling her nipples with his thumbs so lightly that she gasped with pleasure.

With a groan deep in his throat, he wound his fingers in her hair as she knelt to kiss and fondle him.

She heard his sharp intake of breath and then, in seconds, he swept her up into his arms, carrying her to bed, where he stretched out and pulled her on top of him. His body was marvelous, masculine and strong, and hard-muscled, his arousal big and erect. She wanted him with all her heart, wanted to hold him and not let go, but that was impossible and she knew it.

She was astride him as he positioned her over his hard cock and then pulled her down to enter her, thrusting inside, filling her and beginning to move.

Closing her eyes, she cried out, feeling him hold her hips as he moved with her, pumping into her, each thrust and withdrawal heightening the tension that gripped her. She rode him hard and fast until release burst and she cried out in ecstasy, falling over him and gasping for breath.

"I can't move," she whispered.

"You're fabulous," he said, trailing his hands over her back and down over her bottom. "So beautiful, so sexy. This is paradise," he whispered. One hand stroked her bottom while the other fondled her breast. "Scarlett, I'd like to touch you all night long."

"You can't. We have to go back. I sleep in the room next to Carl, and I get up with him at night so Mom doesn't have to. He doesn't always wake up, but I can't stay out here tonight."

"Okay, I'll get up and go home soon, but let's take one more hour, maybe one more round before I go."

She smiled as she sprawled over him, her fingers running through the hair on his chest. "I might be talked into that," she purred.

"If I have to talk you into it—"

"Surely you can think of something persuasive," she teased. "But not yet. For right now, just hold me against your heart and let me hold you and pretend you're not going to leave me."

"It's good to be together. It feels right, doesn't it?" His voice was a lazy drawl as if he might be on the verge of sleep. She suspected it might just be euphoria, him rambling without really thinking about what he was saying. She wished he meant it, but she was certain he didn't. In any case, it felt right to *her*. She loved him and had loved him since she was fifteen years old. Sadness gripped her. She wasn't the woman for Luke, and she knew it. He didn't think he was the man for her, but he was being ridiculous. He would never be like his parents. Luke had too much drive, self-discipline, control. He didn't have bad genes. She couldn't argue much, however, because she knew she could never be his wife. He needed a woman who could have his babies. She thought of precious little Carl. How lucky she had been to get him. She couldn't get a more wonderful child.

She kissed Luke. If only—"if onlys" were impossible. She had to take life like it really was, but she was thankful for what she had, thankful for Luke in her arms tonight, that they could have memories. So thankful for little Carl, the joy of her life. Thankful for Toby, Naomi, her little niece, Ava, her precious Mom. They had a wonderful family, and when she was with Luke and he talked about his family, she knew how lucky she was. It was a good thing Luke wouldn't be around a lot because they would never marry, but Carl would love Luke so easily. Luke was great with Carl. She could spend a bit of time with him while he was in Royal, but it was just as well that he would go back to California soon.

She showered light kisses on Luke's throat, shoulders, chest and then snuggled against him. She loved him and there was no way to keep from loving him. She would get hurt again, but this was worth some hurt.

"Some terrible things brought you home to Texas, but we have this, and, to me, this is marvelous," she whispered. "I know it can't last, but, Luke, it's so good. In your arms is the best place to be."

"At least I can help right some of the terrible things,

and you've already helped me make it right. You saved so much of my livestock."

"The little calf is getting stronger each day. I hope you took care of the mama."

"I did," he assured her. "There are cowboys out there now taking care of the animals. I don't even need to go every day, but I have been. When I go back to the hotel, I'll go back to work. I hope we can nail Rich on the money. Cole is bringing me all sorts of info. That, my love, is absolutely for your ears only."

"So your antifraud software is working?"

"We haven't found anything so far, but we're just getting started and putting in the info we have. I think we'll find something eventually."

Running his fingers lightly over her breasts, he sighed. "Ah, Scarlett, this is even better than my memories of us. I didn't know that was possible."

"I quite agree," she said, caressing him, thinking she could never get enough of touching him, kissing him, being with him. Too soon he would be gone forever. At the thought, she tightened her arms around him and held him close.

It was two in the morning when he stepped out of bed. "I think I better go back to my hotel now. I don't want to impose on your mom's hospitality. Her cooking improves with age. She's a fabulous cook, while you, my darling, are a fabulous sexpot. You're wonderful in bed."

"Stop that, Luke Weston!"

He laughed. "You love me to tell you how sexy you

are, and you know it. Scarlett, you have to be the sexiest woman in all of Texas."

"Now, that is such a stretch that it's absurd. You
better stop your exaggerations about me being sexy,
or I'll stop doing all those sexy things to you that you
love to have done—like this," she said, stroking him.

"You convinced me," he said, drawing a deep
breath. "You'll be in town tomorrow. Call me when
you can have lunch, and I'll buy you a burger at the
Royal Diner, and it'll be like old times. Afterward, let's
go up to my hotel, and let me introduce you to my bedroom and my shower."

She grinned. "I might take you up on that offer, although a bedroom and a shower? Nothing new there."

"I might have some new tricks to show you in the
bedroom."

"Now that does catch my interest." They both
laughed and kissed, and she held him, looking up at
him and smiling. "We can have fun still, Luke. We
used to have a lot of fun together."

He gazed at her and he suddenly looked solemn.
"We sure did, Scarlett."

"I don't know about old times, but I'll take you up
on that lunch. I'll call you." She dressed as he did, but
she watched him and drew a deep breath. She wished
she could go right back to bed and spend the whole
day making love with him. He was the most handsome
man she knew, and she still had the best time with him
of anyone ever.

As she reached for the door to leave, he caught her
wrist. Surprised, she turned, and when she saw his

face, her breath caught. His arm went around her waist, and he drew her to him, leaning down to kiss her. He covered her mouth possessively, kissing her thoroughly, with hot, fiery passion. Finally, he stepped back. His blue-green eyes were dark and stormy as he gazed intently at her.

"I better go, Scarlett," he said gruffly, turning to hurry out into the darkness. Outside lights burned and in seconds he was on the path back to the main house, where she caught up to walk beside him.

"It's been fun, Luke."

"It's been perfect. I'll see you tomorrow at lunch." At his pickup, he turned, hugging her tightly, and bent down to give her one last mind-blowing kiss. When he released her and climbed into his pickup, she watched, dazed, her lips tingling while she wished once again that he wouldn't ever leave her.

She stood there until his pickup's red taillights faded from sight. She was hopelessly in love with him, but he hadn't given her any indication that he wanted her for keeps. She sighed. For Carl's sake, it was for the best. She might end up with a broken heart, but at least her son's heart was safe. Still, how much hurt was she going to have when Luke left Texas?

Later that morning, Luke got a text from Will to meet him at the Texas Cattleman's Club. Once again, Luke went to a private room, where this time he found Will waiting.

"Thanks for coming. News has come back from the handwriting analysis of the note Megan Phillips received, the note that her brother was supposed to have written. Jason Phillips has been excluded by a margin of 99.9% of being the note's author. Consequently, Richard Lowell has not been excluded as the person responsible for Jason's disappearance. In fact, now he's the prime suspect."

"Wow. We're beginning to get proof. Oh, damn. It's great you're alive, but I'm sorry because it isn't looking good for Jason."

"No. We won't have a positive answer until we get the DNA report on the bone fragments in the ashes in the urn. Ashes that were supposed to have been mine. If you can find some ties to the stolen money and Rich, we will have absolute proof that he's responsible."

Luke scoffed. "He may be far, far away on some island, enjoying his ill-gotten gains and planning his next crime."

"We'll get him. We have to. I wanted to tell you in person. Also, even though no one knows where Richard is, we're all beginning to learn what he's capable of doing, so be careful."

"I will. I'll let you know what I find about the money."

"I want proof so he can't ever wiggle out of facing the consequences for what he did. Especially if those are Jason's ashes, and right now it's not looking good. Poor little Savannah. She's only six years old, and I know she misses her daddy terribly. At least she has her aunt Megan and her uncle Aaron." He shook his head. "I'd better take off, but let's keep in touch."

Luke followed his friend to the door. "You can count on it, Will."

As soon as Will departed, Luke went back to his computer to work on following Richard's money trail.

The next day, with more information from Cole, Luke was able to trace some of the money taken from the Texas Cattleman's Club back to the accounts Richard Lowell had used when he'd been pretending to be Will. He sent a text to Will to inform him to let him know that now they had proof.

In the afternoon Luke drove to the Double U to meet with his new builder. Scarlett had looked at the house plans with him Tuesday night, and he'd had another dinner at her house. Why did it feel so right to be with her, to be at her family home? And it amazed him how much fun he had with her little baby. Every time he was there, it also made him wish things were different, that his family legacy wasn't one of destruction.

It made him feel better to go to the Double U now because the animals were looking a degree better. When he drove up where the house once stood, the land had been cleared. Since the house was in such terrible shape, he was relieved he didn't have to keep looking at the wreckage.

On Thursday, when he drove back out to the Double U, Reuben Lindner had hired cowboys. Again, Luke was amazed how much better the animals looked each time he drove to the ranch. He felt another stab of gratitude to Scarlett and admiration for her dedication and ability. He thought of the moments of passion, of holding her in his arms after making love, of her sexy, soft, beautiful body that set him on fire. If only he didn't come from the family he had. There was no way he could tie his life to hers. Scarlett was absolutely off limits for him forever.

He didn't know why he was even thinking about marriage. He would go back to Silicon Valley, and everyone in this town, including Scarlett, would all fade from his life once again. He had asked her to go with him to see his dad, something he dreaded, but felt it was his duty to do. He had gifts to take—chocolates, a basket of fruit, a new shirt, two books he thought his dad would like. He wondered how his dad was because he couldn't count on what he said on the phone.

The following morning, Luke held Scarlett's arm lightly as they walked into the assisted-living facility. People sat in the lounge in groups, some playing cards, others just talking or watching TV. Luke stepped to the desk to sign in, and then they headed to his father's apartment.

Scarlett went with him as they rode the elevator to the second floor, and they walked down a long hall before Luke stopped and knocked on a door.

"I haven't seen your dad since your graduation," Scarlett confided.

"Your mom doesn't look that different since I graduated. I suspect my dad is going to look very different because of the liver disease. I'm going to have to tell him about putting everything in my name."

"He should be relieved that you saved the ranch," Scarlett said.

"Knowing my dad, he won't view it that way. He always wanted control, even when he was the reason he lost control."

Even though it had been two years since he'd seen his dad, Luke wasn't prepared for the man he faced when the door opened. His father's gray hair had thinned, and Bruce Weston looked shorter. Luke guessed his dad had lost sixty or seventy pounds from the way his clothes hung on him. Instead of the ruddy complexion he always had from working outside, his skin was wrinkled, yellowed and pale. Shocked, Luke had another stab of guilt for not coming home more often and keeping up with things.

"Dad?" Luke said, reaching out to shake his father's hand.

"So you really did come home."

"There wasn't much home left to come back to, Dad. You remember Scarlett McKittrick."

"Joyce McKittrick's girl. You're all grown up now, Scarlett. I heard you're a vet. Imagine that, a woman vet. Y'all come in and have a seat. Sorry the place is not cleaned up for you."

"I brought you some things," Luke said, setting them on a table.

"I don't suppose a bottle of whiskey is in there?"

"No, Dad, there's not," Luke said, knowing his dad had not been kidding. They walked into an apartment that had papers on the sofa and dishes on tables. "Dad, don't they clean your apartment for you?"

"Yes, someone comes. I tell them to leave things alone. I don't want them messin' with my stuff."

"I think you should let them clean. You'll be in a swamp before long if you don't."

"My friend, Charlie, his girl works for the city and saw the papers. I heard from Charlie that you put the Double U in your name. You took my ranch away from me."

Luke drew a deep breath, wondering when his dad had gotten so quarrelsome. "The sheriff's office was going to auction the ranch, and we wouldn't have owned it any longer. It's been the Westons' land since the early days of Texas settlement. I thought it should stay in the family, and, yes, it's in my name now. Which means I'll take care of the bills for the ranch and your bills here. You won't have to worry about any of it."

"Well, I can't stop you from taking it away from me. I'm not surprised. You've gone out to California and become a rich, successful hotshot. You're going to live life your way, and you've got the money and the means to take the ranch from me. I'll get out of here someday, but I guess I won't go home to the ranch. Or are you going to let me go back to the Double U?"

"If you get well and move out of here, you know you can go back to the ranch," Luke said, hanging on to his temper because his dad was old, ill and not thinking clearly. And sober, he was mean and bitter now. With some drinks, he became jolly.

"Do you feel better? I talked to Dr. Gaines, and he said you don't want the rehab nurse to help you get a little exercise."

"That quack. What I'd like is for you to bring me one bottle of whiskey. One bottle wouldn't hurt, and it would be the one and only bottle in almost a whole year. Now, that is long enough for anyone to go without a drink. If you want to be nice to your dad, come back by while you're here and bring me a bottle."

"I don't think that's good for you, Dad. You don't want to end up back in the hospital."

"Indeed, I don't. Get a bottle and bring it by. That isn't going to put me back in the hospital."

Bruce turned to look at Scarlett. "You've joined the Texas Cattleman's Club, haven't you, missy?"

"Yes, sir, I did. They've included women for some time now."

"Oh, I know they have. They have a nursery for screaming kids and a playground. The minute the females got in, they took it over, which I figured they would. The Club has been going to hell since they let women like you into the club, greedy single mothers, too hard and unwomanly to keep a man."

"Dad, that's uncalled for and absolutely unfitting for Scarlett, who has spent hours saving Double U livestock that you didn't take care of and left to starve to death. I think we've paid our visit, and we're not doing any good here, so we'll say goodbye," Luke said, standing, trying to hang on to his temper.

"Let's go, Scarlett." He took her hand and led her toward the door. "We'll let ourselves out. You just keep your seat."

"Luke, you come back by and bring me a bottle of whiskey. That's the least you can do when you've got the ranch now."

"Sorry, Dad. Not until Dr. Gaines tells me to bring

you a bottle." He opened the door, and they stepped out, then he closed the door behind him. A moment later, he heard something smash against the door and fall. Luke shook his head.

"The last few years, he'd get meaner when he was sober, but that happened so seldom when I was around that I didn't give it much thought. He wasn't ever *this* mean. He must have run the men that worked for him off the place. Sorry, Scarlett, that he tore into you. He doesn't know what he's talking about."

She reached up and gently cupped his jaw. "I'm sorry for you. He doesn't bother me. I haven't seen him in years and probably won't see him again. The active members of the Texas Cattleman's Club don't seem to share his views. There are two or three who still object to women belonging, but otherwise everyone seems okay with it."

"I'm definitely okay with you belonging," he said and smiled, but his smile faded. "Seriously, you see what I mean about bad genes running in my family."

"Luke, you don't have bad genes, and you're not like your dad, and you're not an alcoholic. I haven't seen you drink anything. You don't inherit being mean, either."

"I have the same blood in my veins, and it worries me. And despite what you think, I know deep down that I've been a terrible son to him. I neglected him and the Double U and failed to do what I should have done."

She blew out an exasperated breath. "Luke, I will keep telling you this until it gets through your thick skull! You *can't* blame yourself for what your dad did, and besides he told you over and over again that everything was all right."

"I hear you, Scarlett, I do. It's just a bitter pill to swallow." He took her hand again, and they headed back down the hallway to the elevator. "He had no business to call you greedy and talk about single moms ruining things. Too hard and unwomanly—that doesn't fit you and never will. I shouldn't have taken you with me to see him."

"Stop worrying about it. It doesn't mean anything to me. You got here in time to save the ranch and you own it now and you're getting it back in shape. That's all that matters to me."

He sighed as they stepped into the elevator and headed back down to the lobby. "Ahh, Scarlett, you're so forgiving."

"About some things."

"Why do I think that remark is directed at me?"

"No. You're wrestling with a guilty conscience, so things just strike you that way." She squeezed his hand. "Let's go to my house and talk to Mom and see Carl. My little boy will cheer you up."

"I'll bet he will," Luke said, smiling as they left the elevator, headed to the exit and then climbed into the back of the waiting limo. "Before we do that, let's have a stop at my suite in Royal. That will cheer me beyond measure," he whispered, brushing a light kiss on her lips and then looking into her big, hazel eyes. "Okay?"

"Of course," she whispered back, sliding her arm

around his neck. He picked up the phone to tell Jake to take them to the hotel in Royal and later they would go to Scarlett's ranch.

He turned to wrap his arms around her to kiss her. She *would* cheer him up. So would going to the McKittrick ranch and seeing little Carl. Why did being with Scarlett seem so right? He was missing work in Silicon Valley, missing making megadeals that he had loved to do. He felt drawn to this Texas town and to hanging with Scarlett and her baby. Was it the near loss of his family legacy that had upended his world and changed his priorities? Or something else far more personal? He sighed, once again reminding himself that he couldn't start dreaming of a future with Scarlett and her little baby because he might wreck both their lives. All he had to do was look at his dad and what his dad had done. And was still doing. He had been terrible to Scarlett.

He had bad genes, and Scarlett and her eternal optimism couldn't convince him differently. She saw the world through rose-colored glasses, and she didn't see the reality in his life at all. Not even after his dad criticized her so much.

"Luke, you're quiet, and I know what's worrying you. You'll never ever be like your father, and it is just absurd for you to worry you will."

He gave her shoulders a slight squeeze as he forced a smile. "I hope you're right," he said, but he wasn't feeling particularly optimistic right now.

As soon as they were in his suite, he drew her into his arms. "I don't know much right now but I *do* know

I want you in my arms now more than I could want anything else on this earth."

He meant what he said, and, as he kissed her, he wondered how important she was becoming to him? Was he falling in love? He'd better not because it wouldn't have a happy ending. It was just so good to be with her. So fantastic to make love to her. She sent him up in flames, and he knew he would never forget these nights with her. Before he could walk away from the ranch and leave Royal behind once and for all, he wanted to make more memories with Scarlett, memories he would never forget.

He had the life he wanted in Silicon Valley. Constant deals, chances to develop new ideas, new electronic gadgetry, money beyond his wildest dreams and his pick of beautiful women. It was a fun, carefree world with no strings attached, so why did that sound empty and no longer hold the same attraction and pull that it once had?

"Scarlett, have dinner with me in Dallas. I'll get you home early in the morning."

She knew Luke was unhappy, worried he would end up like his dad and incredibly hurt to find him in such a bad shape. She also knew he was angry with his father for what he said to her, but she wasn't disturbed by the ramblings of an old, sick and bitter man who was probably suffering from a guilty conscience for his misdeeds as much as from his booze consumption.

She nodded, agreeing to go with Luke because time was running out for them, and she also might be able to cheer him up. "Thanks, Luke. I will. Mom's good about keeping Carl. I'll send her a text."

The minute they closed the door on his hotel suite in Dallas, Luke turned to draw her into his arms and kiss her. He paused, raising his head to look into her eyes. "You make the world better for me, Scarlett. When I'm with you, my problems seem to fall away and all seems right with the world."

Luke carried Scarlett to his bedroom, where he stood her on her feet by the bed and kissed her again. His fingers unfastened her buttons and soon all clothes were gone, and he held her in his arms in bed while he caressed and kissed her.

She trailed her fingers over him while he did the same for her. He made love with a sense of desperation, taking her fast and hard. Afterward, he turned on his side, cradling her close, wanting to hold her and never let go.

"You've saved me again, Scarlett. I needed you tonight."

"Luke, I'm sorry. I know it hurt today to see your dad that way."

Luke tenderly combed her hair away from her face with his fingers. "You're good, my love. So good. When you're in my arms, it's the best feeling in the world. That's as good as it gets."

"Ahh, if only you really meant that," she said softly.

He held her, running his hands over her, finding solace and comfort in just having her close. Even so, he still couldn't get the visit with his father out of his thoughts. Seeing his dad just convinced him more than ever that their paradise couldn't last. If he truly was his father's son, he had no business promising Scarlett and little Carl forever.

He cuddled Scarlett against his side while he ran his finger up and down her slender arm. Her skin was smooth and warm. "Scarlett, this is a dream come true, but I don't want to mess up your life."

"You're not going to mess up my life. I like having you in it—or haven't you noticed? Why do you think I'm here in your arms?"

"We're good together in a physical way, but I'm not the man for you. I don't have to tell you why. You were aghast at the condition of the Double U. You can't just shrug that off. That blood runs in my veins, too. You've seen my dad. Is that going to be me years from now?"

"No, you'll never be like him." She brushed a kiss on Luke's cheek. "Maybe we weren't ever meant to be, Luke. It isn't just you. I'm not the woman for you. You should have children who have your blood in their veins, your talents. I can't give the man in my life children who are blood kin. That's what it should be for someone exceptional like you."

"That is just ridiculous. You have an adorable son. You shouldn't ever worry. You couldn't have a cuter little baby. You clearly can adopt a baby, and the blood in my veins could get a kid in a hell of a lot of trouble. Bad genes, remember?"

"You have good genes, but you leave. Your life is California, not Texas. I can't risk loving and saying goodbye again. I'm a mom now and I don't want my baby to love you and then you walk out. I have to think about Carl."

He took a deep breath while he frowned. "We just weren't meant to be. I don't plan to stay in Texas. I'm a workaholic, and no woman likes that."

She smiled and got a twinkle in her hazel eyes that made his breath catch. She ran her finger over his chest. "The right woman might get you to come home at night and quit work early in the evening," she said in a sultry voice.

"You think?" he asked, his voice getting deeper as he slipped his hand behind her head and pulled her to him to kiss her. He rolled her over and moved on top of her, keeping the bulk of his weight off her.

Gazing up at him, she wrapped her arms around his neck. "You don't have bad genes. You have wicked, fun genes," she whispered. "And ooh, la, la, what a body." She pulled his head down to kiss him.

Luke's heart pounded and he was hard again, wanting her. Scarlett was unlike any other woman he'd ever had. He'd been with some breathtaking women who were sexy, enticing and eager, but no one could excite him as quickly or to the extent Scarlett did. She had freckles, an adorable pixie cut, a gorgeous body with lush curves and long, long legs—every man's fantasy woman come true. But even more importantly, she had her own view of life, and his money didn't mean beans to her. Neither did his job or the power he had to do things. Scarlett was very much her own person, and he could warn her about bad genes until the sun fell out of the sky, but she would draw her own conclusions and stick by them.

"You're a puzzle in a lot of ways," he whispered, trailing kisses over her throat and ear. "You're not impressed by things that impress other people. You put a high priority on helping others and animals, but you don't have a qualm about telling me to go to hell when I annoy you."

She looked into his eyes. "Luke, you worry too much. And you'll never figure me out." She kissed away his answer, and he forgot their conversation as he deepened the kiss and ran his hands over her tempting body. He rolled on his side, taking her with him and thrusting his leg between hers to move them apart so he could caress and fondle her. He heard her gasp and felt her arch against his hand as he stroked her. He wanted her in his bed, in his arms for the entire weekend if he could talk her into it.

On Saturday, Scarlett sat in her office in her veterinary clinic in Royal right off the downtown area. Luke had brought her to work that morning from his hotel, and he was going to see Will and Cole Sullivan. He had asked her to have lunch with him afterward. They were together constantly now, and when he left Royal and went back to Silicon Valley, she was going to miss him terribly. She knew he would go back without her and without even thinking about asking her to go with him. He understood that she had a life here and would never leave it. Just as she knew he had a life in Silicon Valley and was certain he would never want to leave it, either. They just weren't meant to be as they had agreed. He thought he had bad genes, and she knew she couldn't trust him to stay.

If he got the Double U running efficiently, would he even come back to Royal again? He and his dad were obviously not compatible. His dad was being taken care of. The ranch should run smoothly. There was nothing to bring Luke back, and she suspected, the next good-bye would be permanent. Tears pricked her eyelids. She'd loved him all her life, and the thought of never seeing him again hurt deep inside, but she couldn't turn back time or change the future.

Her intercom buzzed, and the receptionist spoke up. "Scarlett, there's a man to see you. He said he knows the way and wants to see you in your office. His name is Tanner Dupree."

Seven

Surprised, her first inclination was to say she was unavailable and refuse to see him. Instead, she said to send Tanner back to her office because she felt obligated to hear him out since they had a history together. She was shocked her ex had returned.

A few moments later, he knocked lightly and entered. "Good morning. I should have sent a text or called, but I didn't want you to say no."

"I wouldn't say no, and I'm surprised. Please have a seat." Nodding, he sat in a leather chair on the other side of her desk facing her.

"You look great, Scarlett."

"Thank you. So do you, Tanner," she said and meant it. He had thick brown hair that had a slight wave and thickly lashed pale brown eyes, and was several inches over six feet tall. As usual, he was well dressed in a dark brown suit and tan tie. Although he was undeniably handsome, he had never made her heart race the way Luke did. She sighed despite herself. Luke, with his blue-green eyes, dark blond hair and mouth that she loved, could make her heart pound even when she was angry with him and she didn't want to feel anything.

Tanner looked at the picture of Carl on her desk and picked it up. "This is a new picture. It's not your brother's baby, is it?"

"No, Tanner. That's my son, Carl. Remember, I started adoption proceedings because you wanted me to have a baby. There was a lot of pressure from your family. Well, after you left, a newborn became available, so I adopted him."

"I'll be damned. You're a mother," Tanner said. "I'm shocked you went through the adoption alone. They contacted me and I had no interest in adopting at that point. I assumed you didn't either. I hope in the future you can at least try fertility treatments to conceive a biological child. I can overlook that you went ahead without me," he said, staring intently at the picture of Carl.

"They needed a home for this baby, so when they called I said yes. End of story."

"I'll tell my family. That will make them very happy. I've heard of women who adopt suddenly getting pregnant without fertility treatments. Scarlett, I regret leaving and now, with you having a baby, this is better than I expected."

She listened to him without even really hearing what he was saying, and knew with full certainty she would never marry him. The truth was, she had never really been in love with him the way she was with Luke. If she ever needed proof she loved Luke, here it was. She felt nothing for Tanner even though she had almost become his wife.

"Tanner, thank you."

He looked startled. "For what?"

"For walking out. We weren't really in love, and I realize that now."

"Scarlett, how can you say that? We were almost married. I just made a terrible mistake. I had pressure from my parents because they wanted an heir and you couldn't get pregnant, but now you're a mother and you can see a doctor about getting pregnant."

"Tanner, I—"

He held up a hand. "No, please, Scarlett, let me finish. You see, I've got it all worked out. I went to Chicago and thought I'd go back into sports, being an agent, but I've given up being a sports agent. I'm going into the family oil business, and I'll take over for my dad when he's ready to retire. After you and I marry, we can live in Dallas where I'll work, or we can reside in Royal where your clinic is. It's your call."

"Tanner, can you hear me?" she said, trying to be patient. "We're through. You walked out, and that was that. We're not getting back together. Thank you, but no thanks. We're finished forever."

"Give me one more chance."

"There's just no point, Tanner," she said. "I'm not

in love with you, and I know it. I don't think we were ever really in love. You wouldn't have walked out if you'd truly been in love with me."

"Is there another man in your life?"

"No, there's not," she said because she knew any day now Luke would go back to Silicon Valley and she might not see him for years, if ever.

"I've heard your old boyfriend, Luke Weston, is back in town and you two have been together a lot."

"Yes, we have," she admitted. "His father left the family ranch in shambles, with the livestock starving and dying. Luke needed my help."

"Are you two a couple?"

"Not at all. I saved some of his livestock, and he was grateful. Mom has had him out for dinner because he was a family friend, but he has never asked me to commit to him. He has his Silicon Valley life, and I have my vet life in Royal, Texas. We have no future plans. Luke is a long ways from getting married, and so am I...and definitely not to each other."

"I'm glad to hear that. So I don't have any big competition?"

"Tanner, have you not heard a word I've said? You and I are *not* in love. I don't know why you left. I don't know why you're back. I have my baby, Carl, and he's adorable. I don't want to marry, and even if I did, it would not be to you."

"I can't believe you're saying that. Please, let me take you to dinner. I'd like to see your son. My parents will be so happy to hear that you have a baby. A baby we both could have had. I'm so sorry I walked out. I got scared about such a big commitment. I have huge regrets."

"It worked out for the best. Find the right person. Someone you want to spend the rest of your life with. Someone you love who loves you back, with her whole heart and soul."

His eyes turned hard and angry. "Are you sure this isn't because of Luke Weston? You were in love with him once."

"No, Tanner, Luke isn't the reason why. You and I are finished."

"At least just go to dinner with me and tell me what you've been doing. Tell me about this little boy. You surely will give me that much, won't you?"

She smiled politely and shook her head. "I'm sorry, but the answer is no. You made your choices. I'm making mine. Going to dinner won't change anything."

"I made a terrible mistake."

"Actually, Tanner, the way it all worked out, I have my little boy now, so, in my eyes, what you did was never a mistake.

She walked around her desk and toward the door, hoping he get the hint. She breathed a sigh of relief when he followed her. "I've missed you," he said.

She shook her head. "My life has changed a lot, and we can't go back and undo our pasts."

"We did have fun, Scarlett."

"Yes, we did, but it's over now." She stepped into the hall, and, when he followed, she stepped back into her doorway. "You know the way out."

Tanner clamped his jaw closed, nodded tersely and

strode away. She knew he was angry, but he had made his choices earlier and now he was living with the results. He had just walked out on her when they were ready for the wedding and then disappeared without a word. Looking back, she realized that Toby hadn't been nearly as angry over Tanner practically leaving her stranded at the altar as he had been with Luke when he broke up with her all those years ago. For the first time it dawned on her that Toby might have been happy to see Tanner go out of her life.

As she walked back to her desk, she thought of the few times Toby had been around Tanner, and he had been cool and not quite his usual friendly self. She smiled because Toby had never said an unkind word to her about Tanner until he bailed on her, but now she realized Toby never had liked him in the first place.

When she had dated Luke in high school, Toby had liked him. This anger with Luke had come about after Luke left for California and hurt her so badly.

She closed the office door and crossed the room to pick up Carl's picture. Love filled her and she smiled. This was why Tanner had been good in her life. Because of his insistence on a baby, she had started the adoption procedure, and then Tanner left and she got Carl, her own little boy. She put the picture against her heart and hugged it lightly.

Setting the picture back on the desk, she looked at her calendar, called her assistant and told her she was going home for a couple of hours, something had come up. She called her mom to tell her that she wanted to come home to get something and she would see her shortly. She had called just to make sure her mom and Carl would be home.

Smiling, she grabbed her purse and left through the back to hurry to her car and head home to the ranch.

She passed the hotel where Luke was staying and thought of him naked in bed, a thought that made her draw a deep breath. At this hour he would either be poring over the information Cole Sullivan had provided, or out working on something else. He wouldn't be in bed by himself at this hour.

She couldn't wait to get home and hold Carl in her arms. Her son was the only reason she could think kindly about Tanner and be glad that he was in her life briefly. There was only one man who was the love of her life, but he wouldn't return her love, and she couldn't trust him not to break her little boy's heart.

Even so, she loved Luke Weston with every fiber of her being, and it was going to hurt even worse than before when he left.

Luke sat in the Royal Diner over coffee. He had met with Abe Ellingson yesterday afternoon, and they had pored over the house plans and everything was set. He had an appointment today with Reuben, who had already hired three men to help. Reuben had wanted Luke to come to the final interviews on the first men he hired because Reuben wanted one of them for the foreman job. He wanted the other two because they could take charge in the foreman's absence. In a few more days, everything should be moving smoothly along, but Luke hadn't felt any rush to return to California.

That shocked him because Silicon Valley had been his world for a lot of years now. It was Scarlett that held him here, and he knew it. It didn't do any good to know the reason because he couldn't do one thing about it. He was not messing up Scarlett's life and little Carl's. His visit with his dad had brought back how terrible things had been at his home when he was growing up with two drunks for parents. He was going to see to it that that never happened to him, but the best way was to stay single. He had been supremely happy with his no-strings life in Silicon Valley. Why did it seem so empty now?

"Luke Weston?" a deep voice said, and Luke glanced up to see a tall man facing him, and he recognized him from pictures.

"You're Tanner Dupree," Luke said, but he didn't stand and he didn't offer his hand.

"May I join you?"

Luke wanted to tell Tanner to go to hell and wondered if Scarlett had—or had it gone the other way? Had she been happy to see Tanner again? If Tanner was in town, he felt certain the man had already seen Scarlett.

"Sure. Have a seat. Want coffee?"

"No, thanks. I've been with Scarlett this morning. Actually, mending our relationship. I made a colossal mistake leaving her. Especially when we had started adoption proceedings. I got jittery—a wife, a baby and all." He cleared his throat. "Anyway, I've been to see Scarlett, and she showed me the picture of our baby. We're getting back together so our baby will have a mom and dad. She said there's nothing between the two of you."

"No, there's not," Luke said, suddenly hurting badly, feeling as if he had been stabbed in the gut. He thought about the hours he had spent with Scarlett. Was Tanner lying to him? He didn't know if Tanner was telling the truth—it didn't matter. He realized he loved Scarlett. Forever love with all his being even though she could never be his. He couldn't be a dad for Carl, a husband for Scarlett. He loved her with all his heart and he thought her baby was adorable.

He was losing Scarlett again—except she had never, ever really been his to lose. He realized Tanner was still talking.

"I'm taking her out tonight to celebrate. We'll have the wedding soon because all plans had already been made before. She said you were an old friend, nothing serious between you."

"No, there's not," Luke said stiffly, knowing that was the damn truth. There wasn't anything binding between them, and there never could be. Damn his heritage. He had always known that she couldn't be his. He wasn't the man for Scarlett. He wasn't the man to be part of her family. They were the family he always wished he had as a kid. Still did, for that matter. Mrs. McKittrick would never be mean to a friend of Scarlett's, the way his dad had been to Scarlett. Toby was a good guy and a reliable one.

He couldn't even hear what Tanner was saying, but he gritted his teeth and tried to focus on him.

"Good luck, Weston, although you don't need it. I saw the *Forbes*'s list. Impressive. Congratulations."

"Thanks," Luke stated without thinking about it.

Luke didn't believe Dupree. He just wanted him to move on and out of his life.

"Goodbye, Weston."

Luke nodded and swirled his coffee. The minute Tanner was out of sight, Luke paid and left. He'd finally acknowledged that it was Scarlett keeping him here, even though he should have ended things already. But now, it had to be over. It was time for him go back to Silicon Valley.

He made arrangements to fly back to California late in the afternoon. Next, he phoned Cole and scheduled an appointment to meet with him at 1:00. Afterwards, he called Abe and Reuben and filled the two men in on his travel plans. By the time he had finished all the calls, it was time to meet with Cole. Luke missed lunch, but he didn't feel like eating anyway. While he and Cole talked in Luke's hotel room, Will joined them.

"We can tie some of the stolen money from the Texas Cattleman's Club directly to the accounts Richard Lowell used while he was assuming Will's identity," Luke said. "I have more information from Cole, and he's learning this program, so I can work from California and he'll work here. We'll coordinate with conference calls."

Cole looked up from the computer screen and ran his hand through his tangled, short, dark blond hair. "This is fantastic. It's the more recent transactions. Rich is getting a little careless, and he isn't trying to pass himself off as you now. He's got his own name on some transactions he's made."

"Thank heavens for that one. I have some other good news," Will said. His green eyes sparkled, and he had a faint smile. "At least, it was something that needed to be done and I think it's going to be good. Brent Smith, an attorney from Dallas, showed up at Aaron's house. It's official now—Aaron Phillips has been appointed guardian of Jason's daughter, Savannah. She loves her uncle Aaron. Megan has been alternating with Aaron to care for Savannah, but Megan agrees it's best to have an official guardian. Legally, it is definitely best. I'm still shocked by the terrible things Rich has done."

"Well, with the handwriting analysis, a bit of the stolen money actually traced from the Club to him, and soon we should have the DNA report on the bone fragments in the ashes, probably Jason's—there's going to be a solid case to nail this bastard," Luke said.

"Catching him can't come too soon. How soon are you leaving, Luke?"

"Late today. I've been away too long. I need to get back to work and to my business."

"Sure," Will said, offering his hand. "It's been great to have you here, and thank you for all your help. Seems sort of like old times."

"'Sort of' is right," Luke said, with a crooked grin. "No fake funerals back then."

"Hell, no. I do hope there are no more surprises like that. Go back to your golden world where everything comes up smelling like roses, to drag out an old cliché. Mrs. Hodge, our old English teacher would shudder." They both smiled, but Luke hurt and was trying to hide it.

When he was finally through and went back to the hotel to throw his things into a suitcase, all he could think about was leaving Scarlett and little Carl. How could he get so damned attached when he'd gone into this knowing he shouldn't?

His heart was telling him to stay and fight for Scarlett because he loved her, but he thought about his bad genes, and the last thing he wanted to do was cause Scarlett to end up with a family like the one he had. Maybe after seeing his dad so sick and mean, she would understand his decision. Maybe she really was going to marry that Dupree guy.

He was going back to the life he had wanted. He'd vowed to never allow himself to be tied down. He excelled at building smartphones and software programs, not relationships. But could he return to his lush Silicon Valley life as if these past couple of weeks—the best of his life—with Scarlett and her adorable kid had never happened?

Luke threw things into his suitcase, hurrying as fast as possible. He wanted away from Texas, back to the life he had in Silicon Valley, where he wasn't torn to pieces loving a woman he couldn't have, loving a little baby he wouldn't be able to watch grow up, loving Scarlett's whole damn family because they were the family he never had.

But most of all, loving her. Scarlett was everything—gorgeous, smart, fun, sexy, kind—and he'd loved her all his life. She was the only woman he had ever truly loved. "Dammit," he muttered. Glancing at his watch, he rushed out of the room, taking the stairs two at a time and racing to his car to drive to her clinic.

"I need to see Scarlett as soon as possible," he told Tracie, her receptionist. "It's private, so I'd like to see her in her office."

Tracie smiled at him. "I'll tell her, Mr. Weston." He wanted to go on back to her office and not wait, but he tried to be patient.

"She said to come to—"

He was gone, letting the door close behind him as he rushed down the hall and into her office. "I'm leaving, Scarlett. I wanted to see you before I go."

As her big, hazel eyes widened, she stood up. She had a white medical coat over a pale blue cotton blouse and a pair of jeans, and she'd never looked more beautiful. "You're going back to Silicon Valley," she said.

"I just wanted to tell you goodbye. I don't expect to see you again for a long time. I don't think I'll be back this way."

She blinked, and all the color drained from her face. She raised her chin. "My second goodbye to you. This one is probably permanent."

Luke crossed the room and swept her into his arms to kiss her, crushing her against his chest, kissing her as if it was the last kiss of his life.

Shocked, hurting, Scarlett clung to him until he swung her up, gave her a look that made her tremble. She started to reach for him, but then he was gone, slamming her office door behind him.

Stunned, Scarlett stared at the door. That had not

been the kiss of a man who wanted to tell a woman goodbye. She touched her tingling lips with her fingertips. That had been the kiss of desperate man. One would have thought he'd left to face a firing squad.

She stood blinking, trying to figure out what had just happened besides Luke saying goodbye—a goodbye that sounded permanent—and then rushing out of her office as if he were chased by demons. What was going on with him?

Her intercom buzzed, and she rushed to answer in case he was coming back. Instead, it was Tracie reminding her of an appointment. She had dog surgery, and she had to stop thinking about Luke and his kiss and focus on her patient, which she did.

For almost the next two hours, she was busy with her patient. Once the surgery was over, one of the assistants would take over for the night to check regularly on the dog and make sure everything was all right and that the dog wasn't in pain.

Scarlett glanced at a wall clock. She tried to call Luke, but his phone was turned off, and she knew he was airborne, heading back to his California life and flying out of her life, maybe forever. One question kept niggling away at her, over and over again. Why had he been so desperate to get out of town? Luke set his own schedules, so if he hadn't really wanted to go back to California yet, he wouldn't have done so. Was he trying to get away before he broke down and proposed? She might think that, except he could get very iron-willed when he felt strongly about something, and he felt strongly that his "bad genes" would ruin not only her life, but Carl's also.

And if he really felt they had no future together, why such a frantic, possessive, final kiss that conveyed so much desire it made her knees weak and her heart race? For the first time since she was a teen, she felt that Luke loved her. That kiss had been filled with love. What upheaval had happened in his life to send him running for California, but first to come kiss her goodbye?

She ran a comb through her short hair and headed out to her car to drive home. Tanner was waiting for her in the parking lot. "You don't look as if you've been working all day. It's wonderful to see you again, Scarlett."

"Tanner, what are you doing here? This seems a waste of your time and mine."

"Not at all. Give me a chance. I know you're angry with me, but what we had at one time was good, and we planned a wedding together."

"A wedding you walked out on. You act like that never happened. It happened. Live with the consequences. We all live with consequences."

Her cell phone rang and she saw it was Toby. "Excuse me, Tanner. This is Toby," she said and walked a few steps away, wondering what was happening.

"Is everything okay?" she asked him.

"That's why I called and what I was going to ask you. I saw Tanner today. He's back, and I just want to make sure you're all right."

She smiled. "Tanner isn't the violent type, Toby. Go play with Ava or hug Naomi. I'm fine."

"Okay. I know I'm butting in, but he was sneaky before, and I just wanted to make sure everything was all right. He said you've gotten back together."

She frowned. "He told you that?" she asked, stunned that Tanner would lie about their relationship. Who else had he told that to?

"That's what I thought. I didn't think you'd go back with him the minute he showed up again. I just wanted to make sure he wasn't up to something. He obviously wants back in your life."

"You're a very good, considerate protective brother, Toby. Thank you. I'm fine. Don't worry about me, and I'll talk to you later."

"I heard Luke went back to California, and I thought maybe that was why you went back with Tanner."

"Oh, no. I haven't gone back with him and I won't."

"Frankly, Scarlett, I'm glad. That's a crummy guy who will walk out and leave you stranded at the last minute before a big wedding. I've been angry with Luke for hurting you, but you two were teens. Luke was up front with you about everything. He didn't blindside you when he left and then come try to take you back. Okay. I'll stop being nosy big brother."

"You did good, bro. I love you for it. Thanks." She ended the call and hurried back to find Tanner still leaning against her car. "Tanner, have you been telling people today that we're getting back together?"

"It may have been premature or presumptuous, but, yes, I have, because I think we will. I want to, and if you'll give me half a chance, I think you'll want to, too."

"Listen closely. No, I don't want to—now or ever. Sorry, Tanner. Best wishes for a happy life." She unlocked her car door and pulled it open.

"Scarlett, don't go."

"There's just one man for me. I'm going to try to save a Texas cowboy from himself," she said, smiling and driving away, trying to avoid speeding.

Now she knew the reason Luke had kissed her as if life was going to end. He loved her, bad genes or not.

Maybe this time he'd be willing to stay.

Eight

The next morning, Luke walked through his Silicon Valley mansion. It was quiet, filled with all kinds of electronic conveniences. The house was mostly glass, giving spectacular views of the California countryside. It was contemporary, with large expensive modern oil paintings by famous names and unique, one-of-a-kind furniture. He had enjoyed it, felt at home in it, loved the contrast to the old-fashioned ranch home he grew up in.

He had a huge-screen television, streaming shows that he liked, a gym. Why did it seem so empty and cold since his return? He had a cook who did an excellent job, with two assistants to help in the kitchen if necessary.

Luke didn't feel like eating. He missed Scarlett. Hell, he missed Carl, he missed Royal and his friends.

What had happened to him on his trip home? It wasn't as if he didn't have friends here. He called one of the women he enjoyed the most and talked about twenty minutes and ended the call without asking her out. He didn't want to go out with her. She was a beautiful blonde singer who was hitting the top of the charts and he'd had fun with her. But his mind wandered while he talked to her, and he knew he couldn't get through an evening with her.

"Scarlett," he said, talking to an empty room. "What have you done to me? What have you done to my life?" All the years growing up, he dreamed of the life he had found in Silicon Valley. Now it felt empty and not what he wanted at all. He felt alone and restless, and when it got right down to it, he missed Texas, Royal and his life there.

He groaned and stared out a window. He had been a workaholic, billionaire bachelor, but from his sterile, modern marvel of a home in Silicon Valley, his care-free, no-strings existence was beginning to feel like a whole lot of lonely. And his heart was far from free. It was very solidly in the possession of a stunning, take-no-prisoners Texas cowgirl.

Was he tossing aside a wonderful family and life because he was scared he couldn't control himself enough to avoid becoming a drunk like his father?

Luke hadn't ever stopped to think about whether he could have enough self-control, but he'd spent all his life using self-control one way or another. Why had he let his parents' addiction change and govern his life?

He sat in his silent house and then went out by his pool and sat watching a waterfall and a fountain in his pool, thinking about his future. With Scarlett as his wife and little Carl his son, he would never turn to drink. He loved them too much.

Why the hell had he thought he couldn't have enough control to avoid losing them because of drink?

He had been through college, built a company, developed a successful smartphone, developed programs. He'd had deadlines, stress, tests in college—why did he think he would just buckle and become a drunkard, dependent on booze like his dad? All his life his mom and dad had fought. Maybe that had driven them to use alcohol excessively. He didn't know, but maybe he was all wrong in assuming he would be like them. He was in his thirties and had no problem dropping alcohol altogether. He ran four miles a day. That took self-discipline. He worked out an hour a day besides the running. More self-discipline.

Had he lost Scarlett and little Carl all because of wrong assumptions about himself, unfounded fears that he had let control his life?

Could he go back in time to fight for Scarlett's love? He didn't think she was in love with Tanner. She hadn't sounded like she was.

He got out his phone and called her and didn't get an answer. He made arrangements with his pilot to fly back to Royal in the morning.

He sent Scarlett a text message, but didn't get a response.

Was he going to ask Scarlett to move to California

and settle in Silicon Valley and give up her thriving vet practice? She might be willing to. Or would he like to open a West-Tech office in Dallas?

That appealed to him. He would be near Royal and friends, Scarlett would be near home and her family. She could keep her practice, while he would have the challenge of starting up another West-Tech branch in a city he loved in a state he loved while he lived with a woman and baby he loved. Damn, but he'd been blind.

He was going back to Texas to fight for her love.

He couldn't wait for morning, so he called and asked his pilot to get ready to leave at four in the afternoon.

He remembered some of his mother's jewelry that had been passed down from his grandmother and got a box out of his safe and carried it to a table to search through necklaces, lockets, bracelets. It didn't take long to find the necklace of small diamonds and a golden heart covered in larger diamonds. Scarlett didn't wear a ton of jewelry, but she did wear some.

The necklace was in a box lined with black velvet. He'd had the jewelry appraised, insured and then put in boxes. He put the others away, carrying the velvet box with him. He wanted a present for Carl, too. He went to a storage closet and rummaged through boxes until he found the one he wanted. It was a little teddy bear that sat on a shelf in his room. His grandmother had given it to him, and his mother never would let him play with it because she was afraid he would tear it up, so it was in good shape.

He took both presents and put them in gift bags, then

tried to call Scarlett again but still got no answer. He didn't want to think about her with Tanner.

Luke got his travel bag to pack, when he heard the bell to the security gate. Surprised, he went to see who was at the gate. He looked at the picture on the monitor, and his heart thudded.

The two most important faces on earth were smiling out at him. Scarlett held Carl as she rang again.

"I'll open the gate. Come on in."

He raced downstairs and to the door to open it as Scarlett walked to the door. She held Carl in her arms, and she had a small, shaggy black dog on a leash. Carl held out his arms.

Luke wrapped them both in his embrace and kissed Scarlett while his heart pounded.

"I feel as if I'm dreaming," he said, looking down at her and then at Carl, who gave him a dimpled grin. "Scarlett, why are you here? You and Carl and a dog?"

"I was trying to figure out that kiss—why you rushed into my office, kissed me like it was your last hour on earth and then rushed out for California. That isn't exactly like you. While I was thinking, Toby called me to ask if I was going back to Tanner."

"Yeah, Tanner came by my office to tell me you are, but you didn't fly out here to tell me that," Luke said, looking intently at her. "Not with a baby and a dog. I didn't believe him."

"I'm glad you didn't because of course I'm not going back with him, I couldn't figure out why you rushed in to kiss me like that until I learned what Tanner had said. Your kiss was the kiss of a man who wanted to stay. A man in love."

"Thank heavens for your brother."

"You kissed me as if it might be the last kiss of your life. To my way of thinking, that was the kiss of a man in love. Am I not right?"

"You figured that out just like that." His smile vanished.

"Yes, I did. That kiss meant you love me. I flew out here to fight for that love. I'm not sixteen and giving up when you pack and leave Texas."

"That's awesome. Tanner shocked me and when I hurt so badly, I really thought about my life. I realized I love you with all my being, a love I'll feel for the rest of our lives. When I realized that I truly love you, I also faced another truth about myself. Instead of giving you up, I can give up the notion of having bad genes because of my parents."

"Luke, thank goodness."

"I realized that I won't become a drunkard like my parents. I have self-control—enough for a lot of things, including resisting alcohol all the time. Mostly though, Tanner gave me such a jolt when he said you were getting back together—that was like having my heart ripped out. That's when I realized that I was deeply, seriously in love with you."

"Ah, Luke," she said.

"That's why I went to your office and kissed you goodbye, but flying back here, I had time to really think things through and get rid of old fears."

"Luke, I'm so glad that you've let go that idea of

being like your parents. There's one problem that's mine—I can't have your children. That problem isn't going away."

"Carl is a super baby and I love his mom with all my heart. Scarlett, if little Carl needs a sibling, we can adopt."

"You really mean that, don't you?"

"With all my heart. I'm not doing this right, but I can't wait a minute longer. Scarlett, will you marry me?"

"Yes, I will. I thought you'd never ask, so I came to California to ask you."

"I have a plane getting ready to take me back to Texas. I'm glad we didn't pass each other. I was coming back for you and Carl."

"You were coming back for me and Carl," she repeated. "You weren't going to leave me this time."

"Never, Scarlett."

He kissed her briefly. When he released her, he looked down at her and took Carl from her and set the bag she carried on the floor. "Hi, little guy. How do you like Silicon Valley? Scarlett, what is this little black dog?"

"It's a little black rescue dog. He's almost a year old, well-trained, sweet, and he's to make up for your old Mutt."

Luke laughed and shook his head. "Come inside, my darling. Are you hungry? Did you eat?"

"I'm too excited to eat, and Carl was getting sleepy, but I think that's gone now. Oh, my goodness, look at your house. Luke, we've got to get a pen for Carl or something. This is the most un-childproof house I've ever seen. Mercy. I'm not sure we can stay here. It's perfect for the dog, though. Mutt Two can stay here."

"Oh, yes, you'll stay here, right in my arms tonight and Carl can stay if I have to get someone to bring new furniture out here this afternoon. Or empty one of these rooms. Matter of fact, I'll get on it right now and get us a baby bed or whatever he can sleep in. Scarlett, I don't know much about babies."

"You'll learn," she said, still looking around.

"You're really going to marry me?" he asked and he looked at his phone.

"Yes, I am. I don't know if we'll have to see each other on weekends. I'd like to stay in Royal and keep my practice, so this may be a long-distance marriage."

He slipped his arm around her waist. "No way, my sweet. I'm ahead of you because I've been thinking about it."

"How about this," he said, wrapping his arms around her waist while Carl sat on the floor playing with a toy Scarlett had given him. "We live on my ranch and we'll have a house in Dallas, too. I'll open a West-Tech office—"

She threw her arms around his neck and hugged him. "Yes, yes, yes. You'd do that for me? I love you, Luke. I've loved you all my life."

"I love you, Scarlett, and I've loved you all my life, too."

"We have a lot of lovin' to make up for."

"That we do." He winked. "And I'll get a baby bed in the next hour."

"You can't get a baby bed in an hour."

He quirked a brow. "Wanna bet?"

"Okay. I'll bet you one two-hour session of hot sex that you can't have a baby bed bought, delivered, set up, and sheets washed, dried and ready in two hours from now."

"You're on. Watch what money can do. I'll get the sheets washed first." He made calls, and when he finished, he turned to her. "Now, I'll show you my big bedroom, which we can share, and we'll put Carl in the next adjoining room in my suite. And, by the way, you're the first woman to stay in this house. That makes you extra special."

Her eyes sparkled with happiness. "I am extra special. I'm marrying an incredibly wonderful man."

He grinned and tugged her into his arms. They heard Carl making little noises and looked around. He sat holding his arms up, and Scarlett laughed as Luke scooped up Carl to hold him, too, as he kissed her. "We'll be a happy family, Luke," she said, certain they would be and that there would be at least one more child in their family.

Luke took the leash off the dog and pet it. The dog leaned against Luke's knee and wagged its tail. Luke looked at Scarlett. "Mutt Two. He's a good dog, Scarlett." Luke stood and walked to her to take Carl in his arms. He held Carl with one arm and put the other around Scarlett. "C'mon, Mutt Two," he called over his shoulder and looked down at Scarlett. "I love you, and I need to make up for a lot of lost time with you. I love you with all my heart."

"I've always loved you with all my heart," she said, smiling at him. "Life will be good, Luke."

"It will now," he said, smiling back at her, and her heart pounded with joy because soon she would marry the man she had always loved.

* * * * *

WRONG BROTHER, RIGHT MAN

KAT CANTRELL

One

Soulless. The CEO's office of LeBlanc Jewelers in Chicago's Diamond District hadn't changed since the last time Val had darkened the door. Despite sharing a last name with the man behind the desk, this was the last place he'd choose to be. Which was too bad considering it was going to be Val's office for the next six months.

Val's brother Xavier sat back in his chair and eyed him. "Ready to take over?"

"Not by my choice." Val flopped into one of the seats ringing the desk, more than happy to let Xavier keep the chair on the other side. That was where his brother belonged. Val didn't. "But yeah. The sooner we get this nightmare over with, the better."

There were few things Val disliked more than the chain of jewelry stores that bore his name. His old man came in a close second, or would if he hadn't died two months ago.

If there was any justice in the world—a concept Val lost faith in the moment he'd heard the terms of the will—the LeBlanc patriarch even now was being roasted over an open flame. Which wouldn't be nearly punishment enough for forcing him to switch places with his twin brother.

LeBlanc peddled *diamonds* for God's sake—the most useless of all possessions on the planet—hawking propaganda that coerced men into spending thousands of dollars on a rock for their lady that would eventually be worth a quarter of what they'd paid for the piece. Not that it would matter overmuch in the divorce settlement.

"The nightmare is all mine," Xavier corrected.

"Please. You got the easy task." Val ran a hand through his longish hair, as he willed a brewing headache into submission. "I have to increase the profits of a company I've scarcely set foot in. If pushing LeBlanc over the billion-dollar mark in revenue for the calendar year was simple, you'd have done it already."

His brother's near-identical features mirrored none of the indignation that Val felt. Of course not. Xavier had never met an emotion he could tolerate, showing the same arrogant, coldhearted behavior as their father. No mystery why Xavier had been the favorite.

"Definitely not simple." Xavier steepled his fingers, every inch the corporate stooge he'd been groomed to be. "But doable. If I were the one doing it. Instead of being given that chance, I've been banished into the bowels of LBC."

LBC was Val's, which automatically gave it less importance in his brother's eyes. LeBlanc Charities had a noble purpose, and Val had poured his heart and soul into it since the age of fourteen. That was when he'd followed his mother through the doors of the nonprofit organization she'd founded.

Val snorted and didn't bother to cover the flash of annoyance. "You act like your test is a punishment. LBC is an amazing place, full of dedicated people who work as a team to change the world. You'll emerge a better person from your stint there."

Val, on the other hand, was being set up to fail. Deliberately.

The hot spurt of injustice wouldn't ease. Death had only been another step in Edward LeBlanc's diabolical need to ensure Val understood that he was not the favored son. If he and Xavier weren't twins, he'd wonder if he had even a drop of LeBlanc blood running through his veins.

But he'd counted on his inheritance to bolster the flagging donations at LBC. People were starving on the streets of Chicago, and Val was doing his part to feed them, one meal at a time.

Having a basic need met allowed people to feel more secure in their future. Val would never abandon those he helped.

He needed that money. The people he served needed that money. The things he could do with half a billion dollars—it was mind-boggling. Val had already poured a lot of his own personal fortune into the coffers, but LBC was a large organization that required a dizzying amount of overhead. More than seemed appropriate most days, given that it took away from money being funneled into food supplies.

And Xavier was going to be the conquering hero as he did Val's job.

"At least you have a shot at passing your test." Xavier sneered. "Raising profits over the billion mark at LeBlanc within six months was already in my plan. I have those dominoes set up. All you have to do is push them over. But I have to become a *fundraiser*."

He said the word with distaste. Likely because he had no clue what it meant to be selfless, to spend time in pursuit of something honorable as you sacrificed your time, day in and day out, to better someone else's life.

"Should be a piece of cake for someone with your connections." Val flicked his fingers. "Ten million in six months is essential. So it's not a lark that you can do or not do if you don't feel like it. The organization will collapse if you fail. It hardly matters if I pour more money into LeBlanc's coffers, but people depend on LBC for survival."

Val gave his money gladly. LBC didn't depend on it to stay afloat, but he believed in his cause and in setting an example.

Glowering at Val's casual dismissal of his responsibilities, Xavier tapped an expensive pen against his laptop. "If LBC is in such dire straits, Dad should have allowed me to write a check. But no. He specified in the will that I have to raise the money through donations as some kind of character building exercise. It's ludicrous."

On that, they agreed. But not much else.

Before Val could blast apart Xavier's assessment of LBC's current state—which was not dire—Mrs. Bryce stuck her head into the office, glancing between the two of them with eyebrows raised. "Your one o'clock is here, Mr. LeBlanc."

"Thank you," Val said at the same time as Xavier, who stared at him balefully as he processed that he'd already lost his admin to the new CEO.

"You have a one o'clock?" his brother asked and shook his head with bemusement. "Would you like my suit too?"

That straitjacket? Not even if it came with a hot redhead inside it. "That's okay. I'll take your chair. I have an interview."

No time like the present to get this crap-storm of a party started.

Xavier stood and then turned a shade of green that looked horrific. Which meant Sabrina had walked into his office. Excellent. Too bad Val had forgotten his popcorn.

Sabrina Corbin swept into the CEO's office as if she owned it, her cool smile dropping the temperature faster than an arctic front. Holy hell. Tactical error. She was far more beautiful than Val remembered and far frostier. Xavier needed to go, stat.

"I believe you two know each other?" Val flipped a hand at Xavier's ex as he skirted the desk to sink into the newly vacated seat. He locked eyes with the woman he'd only met once but desperately needed.

Sabrina had insight into the mind of LeBlanc's CEO. Who better to assist Val into a checkmark for his task than an executive coach Xavier had dated?

Suddenly, he really wanted to know what had happened between them. And how he could do better than his brother. It was a complication he hadn't seen coming, but there it was. He wanted Sabrina to choose him over Xavier, especially since Xavier had had her first.

"Sabrina." Xavier's expression smoothed out, magically eliminating a good bit of the tension. "Nice to see you. I was just leaving."

With his brother's exit, the rest of the tension should have gone with him. It didn't. Sabrina turned in Val's direction, and he resisted the urge to check under his seat for icicles.

"Shall I call you Valentino or Mr. LeBlanc?" she inquired as she slid gracefully into the spot Val had just vacated, crossing a mile of leg under the pencil skirt she wore like a second skin.

Even her stilettos looked like she kept them in the freezer. What would it take to warm her up? Instantly, his body got in on that action, every nerve poised to figure that out. Did she like slow and romantic? Fast and blistering hot? Both, spread out over a long weekend?

"You should definitely call me Valentino but not under these circumstances," he told her with a lazy smile.

Sabrina lifted a brow. "Mr. LeBlanc then."

Ouch. His grin widened. That had *Interesting Challenge* written all over it, and he did enjoy besting his brother or he wouldn't have contacted Sabrina in the first place. "Thanks for coming by on short notice. You up for the job?"

"My last client succeeded in her goals three months before our deadline. If your check clears, I'm up for whatever you throw at me."

Well, now. That perked Val up considerably. "Like I told you in the email, I have to run this joint for six months. I'm not corporate in the first place, but the terms of my father's will say I have to move the needle from 921 million to a billion dollars in revenue by the end of the fourth quarter. I need you to be my ace in the hole."

To her credit, she didn't blink at the sums of money being thrown around. "You have to raise profits eight percent in six months?"

"You did that math in your head?"

Coolly, she took his measure, clearly amused. "Anyone can do that math in their head. It's the easiest math problem in the world."

He could do all sorts of things in his head, but math wasn't one of them when the majority of his thoughts for the last five minutes had been more of the carnal variety. For example, he could imagine what Sabrina would look like spread out on his desk, cinnamon hair flowing as he pleasured her. And once he'd got that stuck in his head, there was no going back.

She'd be gorgeous as she came. Of course she would. Xavier didn't do second class.

"You're hired," he said.

Smart did it for him in so many more ways than sexy. Combine the two, and he was going to have a very difficult time keeping his hands off Sabrina Corbin for the next six months.

Of course, no one said he had to.

"We haven't even discussed the contract yet." Her expression had that not-so-fast feel that raised his hackles. "You should know that I'm very difficult to work with if you don't take this seriously. I don't deal well with less than one-hundred-percent focus from my clients."

As subtle digs went, that one was a doozy. She was essentially saying *Don't flirt with me*.

"I can guarantee I will be focused," he assured her, his smile slipping not at all, and it wasn't even a lie. He was great at multitasking and, when Sabrina was the subject, focus wasn't going to be a problem. "I can't—I *won't*—fail at this."

And with that, his throat tightened, and he did not like the wave of vulnerability that washed over him. But this was so far out of the realm of what he'd expected from his father's will. *Prove you have what it takes, Val*, his mother had insisted when he'd railed at her for accepting this insanity.

But why did he have to prove anything? Val had always spun gold out of straw when it came to feeding hungry people. Corporate politics bored him to tears, and Edward LeBlanc had never fully appreciated that Val had taken after his mother instead of him, which was at least half the problem.

"Oh, you will not fail. Not on my watch," Sabrina promised, her hazel eyes glittering with something mesmerizing. A heat that Val would never have associated with her, if he hadn't seen it personally. "I thrive when others give up. You might even say it becomes personal."

A jab at Xavier? Now he had to know. "Because you have a score to settle with my brother?"

She didn't so much as blink, but recrossed her legs, which was as telling a gesture as anything else she could have done. "Xavier is irrelevant to this discussion. I take my work seriously. I don't have anyone else to rely on, and I like it that way. I'm a consulting firm of one, and that's served me well."

Oh, so she was one of those. Ms. Independent, with no need for a man. "So you dumped him."

"Are you going to constantly read between the lines when I speak?"

"Only when you force me to."

They stared at each other until she nodded once. "I can appreciate the need to clear this up prior to working together. For your information, I broke up with Xavier, if you can call it that. We didn't date that long and were never serious."

Long enough for Xavier to introduce her to his brother. Of course, thinking over it, Val had run into them at Harlow House, while he'd been on a date of his own, earlier in the summer. Or it might have been May-ish. He'd been seeing Miranda then, who had some wicked moves between the sheets, so Val could be forgiven for failing to precisely recall the circumstances of his first meeting with Sabrina.

"So, you're in the market for a real man this go around, are you?"

That fell so flat he started looking for a spatula to scrape himself off the carpet.

"If you're flirting with me, you can stop," she informed him, and that did not help the temperature.

She didn't like having to spell it out, that much was clear from her expression. What, she didn't look in the mirror in the morning? Sabrina was a beautiful woman, dressed to the nines in mouthwatering nylons that begged to be peeled from her body by a man's teeth. Val could no more stop being turned on by the challenges she threw down than he could stop the sun.

"If there's a question about that, I'm doing something wrong," he muttered. "But okay. I'll reel back the charm. For now."

She hiked an eyebrow nearly to her cinnamon-colored hairline. "This was charming?"

There was no way to hold back the laugh, so he didn't bother. Sabrina was a piece of work all right, and he was starting to see why things hadn't gone so well with Xavier. But Val wasn't his brother, who bled dollar signs and slept with his bottom line. "Touché. I'll work on my delivery."

"You should work on your CEO costume first. You can try on your Romeo act on your own time. After we get you that inheritance."

Ms. Corbin had a touch of pit bull, which Val appreciated in someone paid to help him succeed. And maybe in a woman he was planning to get naked eventually too. Jury was still out on that one.

All at once, a fair bit of curiosity surfaced about her goal for this gig. "Are you hoping I'll share?"

"Not on my radar. Winning is."

And that told him enough to know that he liked her on his side, not his brother's. If winning was what turned her on, then he was game. He had something to prove to everyone, even if one of the people who most deserved to eat crow was dead. "Great. Where do we start?"

The look she slid over the length of his torso put a little fire in his belly, a total paradox given the chill still weighing down the air. Even that was more of a turn-on than it should have been, and he was sorry the desk was in the way of her line of sight. He'd be happy to let her stare at him if she wanted to.

"For one, you need a makeover," she announced with zero fanfare.

Speaking of things not being on the radar... He glanced at his untucked button-down, sleeves rolled up the forearms. Which was comfortable and necessary attire when transferring boxes of macaroni and cheese from the stock room to the kitchen. "What's wrong with the current me?"

"Dress the part," she advised, "and you're halfway there. Act the part and you're at ninety."

That sounded suspiciously like business-school rhetoric, something he could do without. Val had never faked anything in his life. "What's the other ten percent?"

"Show up."

"Got that locked. I work hard." He sat back in his chair—*Xavier's* chair. LeBlanc Jewelers would never feel like home, and he didn't intend for it to. "But I play harder. Have dinner with me tonight and find out which one I'm better at showing up for."

Two

There was something fundamentally wrong with Sabrina because a *yes* had formed on her tongue before she could catch it. Fortunately, she didn't actually say it. "We're working together, Mr. LeBlanc. We may eat within shouting distance of each other at some point during our association because food is a necessary part of survival, but it will not be a date, and there will be no playing."

She kept her face composed through sheer force of will and years of practice. Men of his ilk didn't take a woman seriously unless she had an iron backbone and an immunity to all forms of flirting. Sabrina had both. Valentino LeBlanc had started testing out her weaknesses sooner than she'd expected, but she'd get through to him. Eventually.

Lazily, he spun his chair as he contemplated her, his dark blue eyes a startling warm contrast to Xavier's. She only vaguely recalled meeting Val a few months ago, and before she'd walked into the CEO's office, she'd have said he was the boring brother, the one everyone forgot about.

She'd have been wrong. Shocking, uncomfortable awareness of him had ambushed her from the first.

Because Val was now sitting behind the desk? It was no secret that she'd always been attracted to powerful men. Xavier had checked all her boxes. He was a good-looking man who commanded people's respect by virtue of his presence alone. You could tell he helmed a vast corporation the moment you looked at him. Authoritative and decisive, he ate weaker people for breakfast, and he was perfect for someone who liked her men unemotional.

Emotions ruined everything, especially when they were hers.

Xavier was exactly her type: a man who could provide plus-one services, interesting conversation, and the occasional sleepover without either one getting the wrong idea. Though she hadn't gotten that far with Xavier. Instead, she'd lost interest in him almost immediately. Case in point: the moment he'd walked out of the CEO's office a few minutes ago, she'd forgotten about him.

Valentino LeBlanc checked none of her boxes. Sensuality wafted from him in a long wave that caught her in places it shouldn't. His hair was too long, his lips too full and his eyes—they had a depth that she'd have never considered attractive. Vulnerability was for losers. But he carried himself in a way that promised there was more to him than the ability to feel things.

Val tilted his chin, and long, inky strands of hair fell against his cheeks. Her fingers itched to sweep it away.

"And you should get a haircut," she told him decisively. Back on track. Finally.

"Eating is more than a basic need, by the way," he said, deliberately not letting her change the subject. "I know a lot about food. How it can control you. How the lack of it can cause you to do things you'd never contemplate under normal circumstances. But, in the right scenario, it can become a form of expression. Art. Let me cook for you."

Oh, not a chance. He was likely a savant in the kitchen, turning spaghetti sauce into a seduction and, next thing she knew, he'd boost her to the counter, thighs spread and dinner forgotten as he made love to her.

That did not sound appealing in the slightest. It didn't. Except for maybe the spaghetti sauce, the seduction and the part where a man would be between her legs. She sighed. It had been too long since she'd had a date. Clearly. But, even so, she'd never been a sex-on-the-counter type. It was too…passionate.

She worked hard not to inspire that kind of abandon in a man. Hell, she didn't even know if that was in her own makeup, nor did she want to find out.

"I'm here to do a job, Mr. LeBlanc."

She needed clients, not a man she'd have to shed sooner rather than later. They all cheated eventually, and she enjoyed men enough to date them but not to hang around for the eventual evisceration. Her father should have been enough of a warning, with his multiple affairs that had hurt her mother over and over. She scarcely spoke to her father anymore and she was still too mad at her mother for putting up with it to have much of a relationship with her either.

And then her ex, John…well, he was a man, wasn't he? Suffice to say she wasn't repeating *that* mistake.

"Food is my job," he told her and waved a hand to encompass the whole of the office. "This is temporary. A speed bump on the way to my inheritance."

"Which you will not get if we don't shift things into your favor," she reminded him and stood. "Perhaps we should take a tour of the company. Learn some people's names."

Get out of this office, where it's far too easy to imagine non-work-related things happening.

He didn't move. "I know where accounting is and how to find the bathroom. So I'm good. If we're going to work together, I should probably know more things about *you*, not LeBlanc Jewelers. I can read a shareholder report later."

Fair enough. And she'd practiced her intro enough times to do it while half-asleep. "I've been an executive coach for five years, and I worked as a corporate trainer for a Fortune 500 company before that. I've worked with the CEO of Evermore and the CFO of DGM Enterprises. I like to knit, and my uncle collects antique cars, so sometimes I go to shows with him on weekends."

"That's funny. That's exactly what the bio on your website says." Val's smile had a tinge of smirk in it. Too much of one. "Curious. Did you stick knitting in there because it's in vogue?"

What was he implying, that she only put that in her bio to make her seem like less of a workaholic? If so, how the hell had he figured that out so quickly? No one had ever questioned that before.

"I can knit. I *like* to knit." When she remembered where she'd put her needles. And to buy yarn. Neither of which had happened in about five years.

"No one likes to knit. Knitting is something grandmas do because they can't handle much excitement. I think you can. And you should."

That was not a test she had any intention of passing. "I'm sensing that you are not in the frame of mind to start with our coaching sessions today. I'll come back tomorrow."

She spun to go find her sanity, but Val beat her to the door. Somehow. It had been a mistake to try to leave, obviously. He leaned on the door in front of her, holding it shut with his body. Forcing her to acknowledge that he had one. The scent of male permeated everything, digging into her marrow.

Suddenly, she could think of nothing but how close he was, how easily she could reach out and touch him. Her skin tingled as his gaze swept her with an almost physical weight, and the awareness she'd been fighting dropped over them both like a heavy cloak.

What was *wrong* with her that she couldn't get her brain out of the gutter?

He was a sexy man, no doubt. But not so different from a hundred other men within a stone's throw, right down to the womanizing bent of his rhetoric. Normally it was easy to keep her distance. Men got the message pretty fast when she froze them out, but she was having the hardest time making ice around a man with so much natural heat.

"Leaving so soon?" he drawled. "We've got six months. I'd like to make the most of them. Please stay."

She crossed her arms over her racing heart, trying to pretend it was because he'd blocked the door and thus her exit. Not because he excited her. He didn't. Or rather he *shouldn't*, which wasn't the same at all, sadly. "I'm willing to stay if you'll start taking my skills seriously."

"I take every inch of you seriously."

How he managed to turn that into something that sounded like a promise of the carnal variety she'd never know. Probably it was a testament to her state of mind, not his. A guy like Val flirted without conscious thought, almost as a reflex. *Woman* equaled *conquest* in his world, so the better course of action would be to ignore his innuendos, get him on a professional footing with her and go on.

"Great," she said smoothly and wiped her clammy hands as surreptitiously as she could on her skirt. "Then let's get serious. If you don't want to take a tour of the building, where would you like to start?"

His gaze drifted along her face to land on her lips, lingering there with such intensity that she felt it way down low in her core, the same way she might if he'd actually traced her mouth with his fingertip. It was ridiculous. Phantom caresses were not on the agenda.

"How do you usually start with clients?" he asked.

Good. Okay. He was in the realm of appropriate work-related conversation. She was the one veering off into things she had no business imagining, like what it would feel like to be kissed by a man who knew his way around a woman. Val did, she could tell.

Sabrina cleared her throat. "Where do you feel your deficiencies are?"

His brows raised. "Who says I have any?"

Ugh. That hadn't been so smoothly done. Might as well announce that he'd thrown her off-kilter. "What I meant was…you hired me for a reason. You clearly think you have some areas needing improvement. What is the number one thing that you'd like to be different in one month?"

The wicked smile that tore through his expression did not bode well. "I'd like to say that you'd unbend enough to have dinner with me. But I assume you meant related to my position as temporary CEO of LeBlanc. Then I would say I'd like to have command of how the staff expects decisions to be made. In the nonprofit world, we do it as a team. I'm the tie breaker. Is that how it works here?"

"But that's easy, Val," she said without thinking. Without even consciously realizing that she'd switched to call-ing him Val in her head. She rushed on before he could comment or she could stumble over it. "You make the de-cisions, period, end of story. The rest of the staff doesn't get a say. That's the beauty of the corporate world."

"That doesn't sound beautiful at all," Val muttered. "It sounds like a recipe for getting it wrong."

Speechless, she stared at him, grappling for the right words to explain that, in the corporate world, it was ex-pected that the CEO be domineering and opinionated. But maybe it didn't have to be that way for Val, not in this case since he was only temporarily the CEO. Xavier was domineering enough for both of them, and he'd be back in the saddle throwing his weight around soon enough.

"I'm not sure how to advise you, then," she said cau-tiously. "But we'll get there."

She'd only worked with a handful of CEOs, which was part of the reason she'd accepted Val as a client. More ex-ecutive clients on her résumé could never be a bad thing and, as she'd told him, there was no backup income if she didn't have a continual stream of customers.

"How will we get there?"

"Together," she promised with only slightly more con-fidence than she felt. "I've never failed to deliver on a client's expectations. I'll work up a plan for the next few weeks, and we can go over that tomorrow."

"So, essentially you're saying that the one thing I'm unsure about is something you can't advise me on. But you'll have a plan put together tomorrow." His gaze burned into her, scoring her insides with his particular brand. "Not today."

Something inside snapped. "What are you implying? That I might not be good at what I do because I haven't got a list of trite strategies to hand you? My coaching is personalized to each client. I have to evaluate where you are in relation to the corporate culture. That takes more than five minutes."

"Then, I'm making your job harder by refusing to engage with the rest of the team," he surmised quietly. "I'm sorry. I didn't mean to do that."

She blinked. Had he just apologized because he hadn't taken her suggestion to tour the building? "You shouldn't apologize. Ever."

His brief smile shouldn't have smacked her as hard as it did. She hadn't expected to like Valentino LeBlanc. What was she supposed to do with that?

"Because you're the forgiving sort?"

"No, because they're going to eat you alive, Val."

She pinched the bridge of her nose to cover the swirl that had started up in her stomach, a merry-go-round of confusion and awareness and sheer terror. What had she signed up for with this gig? LeBlanc was poised to become a billion-dollar-a-year company. It needed Xavier, not a man who seemed better suited to be drinking wine at an outdoor trattoria in Venice with a lush Italian film star.

Deep breath. He was paying her to fix that. Quite well.

Val needed her. More than she'd ever have assumed. Executive material he was not, and the odds were stacked against him almost unfairly. It dug under her skin in a wholly different way than the erotic promise that dripped from his pores. The sensual vibe that wound between them needed to go, or she was going to botch this. She couldn't. Consulting was going to get her to the next level. Specifically, having a nameplate on the door with her name and the title *CEO* stamped on it. The more she gleaned from experiences with her clients, the easier that would be.

Except Val was watching her with those bedroom eyes that said he was imagining her naked and liked it a whole lot. Men generally weren't allowed to look at her like that. She shouldn't let him do it either but, just as she was about to say so, he tilted his head and she got distracted by the way his midnight-colored hair fell into his eyes.

"You don't think I can do this, do you?" he murmured without a shred of guile. He was genuinely asking.

She nearly groaned. Boy, she had really inspired his confidence, hadn't she? "I do. I have absolute faith in you. And myself. The problem is…"

Brain-dead all at once, she scouted around for a plausible reason why she'd bobbled their interaction thus far that didn't sound like he'd come on to her inappropriately when, in reality, he'd mentioned dinner one time. She'd shot him down, he'd ruefully suggested it would be nice if she'd reconsider and they'd moved on. *He'd* moved on. She was the one stuck on how to haul the frosty distance back between them, an atmosphere that she usually created so easily.

"The problem is," she repeated, "that I haven't properly assessed your strengths."

Yes. That was exactly it. Brain engaged! If they focused on his strengths first instead of the areas for improvement, there'd be less opportunity for her to stick her foot in her mouth again. And it would help her get a handle on him professionally.

"That's not true." A smile climbed across his face, and it was fascinating to watch it take over his whole body. What kind of man smiled with every fiber of his being? "You know I can cook."

Okay. If that's what he was giving her to work with, fine. "Then tell me how you can use that to succeed here."

"Aren't you supposed to tell me?"

She shook her head. "That's not how coaching works. Does the coach pull the quarterback off the field and start throwing the passes himself? No. He guides the player according to his knowledge of strategy, honing it to the specific needs of that athlete. That's what I do."

"Sounds like I'm expected to do all the work," he suggested with a wink that should have been smarmy. It wasn't.

He was far more charming than she'd ever admit. "There's absolutely no question about that, Mr. LeBlanc. You have a very long battle ahead of you, especially given that you've had no exposure to the corporate world. Most men in your position have had years to become…"

"Hard?" he supplied handily. "And I liked it better when you called me Val."

Brittle was the word that had sprung to mind. But from where, she had no idea. CEOs were resilient, resourceful and, above all, in charge. "To become acclimated. It's a different world than the one you're probably used to."

At that point, he crossed his arms, and it was as telling a gesture as anything he'd done thus far. "What do you think I'm used to?"

The defensive posture put her on edge. She was stumbling again, with few handrails to grasp. He wasn't a typical client who wanted to leapfrog over the men ahead of him in line to the corner office and had hired her to give him an edge. Val was clearly sensitive, with land mines and trip wires in odd places. Things she had little experience with.

But she couldn't tell him that.

"You're used to an environment where people are working toward common good." She assumed so anyway. All she knew about his charity was that it fed homeless people, an admirable cause, but likely had nothing in common with the corporate world. "LeBlanc is for-profit, and that makes it instantly more treacherous. If you want to succeed, you're going to have to listen to me and do exactly as I say."

His brows lifted. "Now that's the best proposition I've had all day. By all means, Ms. Corbin, I'm at your complete command. Tell me what you'd like me to do."

Her brain automatically added *to you* to the end of the sentence, and she flushed. He hadn't meant *that*. Had he? "Call in your c-suite, and let's get the lay of the land."

With a nod, he levered his hips away from the door, grazing her in all the right places—*wrong* places—as he reached behind him to open the door. Scrambling backward, she landed in the center of his spacious office. Her pulse raced as if she'd recently lapped the building, but why she couldn't fathom. He was just a man.

He called out through the open door to his admin, asked her to gather together the staff that reported to him and swung the door wide. The cloak of awareness eased a bit, and she dragged air into her lungs. Val strode past her to take a seat at the desk again.

As people began to file into the room, his expression hardened into something more suited to a CEO. Where had that come from? Fascinated, she edged toward the back wall as LeBlanc's vice-presidents ringed the desk.

"Thanks for joining me on short notice," Val told the eight men and women who had answered the summons, meeting each one's gaze in exactly the same manner that she would have advised him to if he'd asked. "We're in for an interesting ride over the next few months. I'm not Xavier, nor do I pretend to be, but I will keep this company afloat. I hope you'll all stick around to see how it plays out. If not, there's the door."

As Val jerked his head toward it, Sabrina's pulse faltered for an entirely different reason. Val had morphed before her eyes into a force to be reckoned with.

He'd been toying with her. Throat tight, she watched him lay down his authority with the people he needed most to have his back, struggling to rearrange everything she'd learned about him today.

Valentino LeBlanc's middle name might well be *chameleon*. Which made him dangerous in more ways than one. She could not trust him, that much was clear and, come hell or high water, she had to stop letting him blindside her.

Three

The next morning, Val arrived at LeBlanc shortly after six. No one else had arrived yet, which had been his goal. Gave him time to acclimate, which had been the number one necessity he'd gleaned from Sabrina yesterday.

As he settled into the CEO's chair with a cup of coffee—which he'd bet half his inheritance was not Fair Trade or even very good—from the executive suite's breakroom, he had to hand it to Ms. Corbin. Acclimation was indeed a great first step.

Now, if only she could keep up a string of next steps, he'd be golden.

The office was still soulless, which he'd long attributed to the fact that his father didn't have one, but Xavier seemed to have followed in Edward LeBlanc's footsteps in more ways than one. Now that Val was firmly in the CEO's chair, he'd started to wonder if it wasn't the other way around: the corporation had sucked the heart from both father and brother, as opposed to the corporation being a reflection of the men.

That wasn't going to happen to Val. He still felt like crap for his dictatorial throwdown to the executive staff yesterday. It had been easier to channel his father than he'd liked to admit. All he'd had to do was envision the hundreds of times he'd been called to appear before Edward LeBlanc to explain whatever debacle his father had caught wind of and been disappointed by this time.

So that was the trick? Just act like a conscienceless jerk and profits flowed? Totally not worth the gutting. It weighed on him that he'd conformed, falling into the mold that seemed to be what everyone expected from him, including Sabrina. That wasn't how he wanted to do things nor the kind of man he was. But what if that was the point of the will—to show Val once and for all that he didn't belong in the LeBlanc family?

If so, Val hoped his father had a front-row seat in hell for the fireworks.

He'd brought in a sweet potato plant from home that he'd grown himself, and the green spade-shaped leaves made him smile. The potato had rolled from a bulk bag at LBC and, by the time he'd found it behind a pallet of dried fruit, it had already sprouted. It was a crime to waste food in Val's book, so now it had new life as his one and only office decoration.

For about an hour, Val fought with his laptop, eventually managing to figure out how to log in and set up email without breaking anything, all while resisting the urge to check in on LBC. Then Xavier blew through the door.

He stopped short when he spied Val ensconced in his chair. "Wasn't expecting to see you here so early."

"Surprise," Val said mildly. "I could say the same,

only with an *at all* at the end. Don't you have a food bank to run?"

His brother's expression left little doubt as to his opinion about the switch. "I left in a rush yesterday and forgot some paperwork."

Xavier stood inside the door of his office, running a hand over his unshaven jaw, halfway between his old world and the portal to his new one. It was the first time in Val's recent memory that his brother had let his appearance go. They didn't see each other all that often—by design—but Val would bet that Xavier always shaved before coming to LeBlanc. What did it say that he'd change his habits to take Val's place?

"I'll take care of any paperwork that has to do with LeBlanc," Val advised him. "Just point it out. My job now."

Xavier frowned. "Temporarily. Besides, the will didn't say it was against the rules to check in."

Check in equaled *checking up on Val*, no doubt.

"No. And I'm not arguing that point." Easing back in his chair, Val tamped down his rising temper. "But this is mine, for better or worse, for the next six months. If you have an issue, why not let me handle it?"

Thank you, Sabrina. She was going to be far more valuable than he'd dreamed and, as his first act toward conquering the task laid out in the will, hiring her had been a good one.

"Fine." Xavier strode to the bookcase along the south wall and pulled open the glass door, extracted a binder that was a good four inches thick and dropped it onto the desk with a thud. "These are printed copies of contracts we're—*you're*—negotiating with the government of Botswana to purchase interests in diamond exploration. Good luck."

Val's head immediately began to swim. "You purchase *interests* in exploration?"

"You do," Xavier emphasized, heavy on the sarcasm. "Baptism by fire, my brother."

"Wait." Val quelled the urge to massage his temples as he sorted through how helpless it would sound if he admitted that he couldn't handle this. "Can you tell me who's the best person on your staff to advise me about negotiating with an African government?"

"That would be me." Xavier's gaze glittered as he crossed his arms and stared at Val. "I always handle the African government because it requires delicacy. And experience. The politics there are beyond anything I've seen anywhere else in the world, especially if you want to keep LeBlanc far away from the blood-diamond regions. Hint—you do."

Great. So Val's initial thought about being set up for failure had been dead-on. Not only did it extend from beyond the grave but his brother was planning to perpetuate what their old man had started. "No problem. I'm not above a little research. Are there other contracts of a similar nature in that bookcase?"

Xavier nodded once, a curt move that said he didn't like giving up information but liked the idea of Val taking LeBlanc down even less. "Anything I need to know about LBC before I go?"

"Just that you can't treat my people like you do the ones here," Val said easily, not that he was worried about anyone on his staff getting bent out of shape. He'd debriefed them all a few days ago, begged them to give Xavier a chance and told them if it seemed like he wasn't getting it to carry on in Val's stead until he could return to the fold.

LBC had stellar, committed people on board, who cared about making life better for those who needed help. They'd keep on doing that whether or not they had the necessary donations to fund the operation, albeit on a much smaller scale if Xavier failed to complete his task. The tenure of the CEO of LeBlanc Jewelers there would be but a blip.

But Val couldn't resist the opportunity to make things a little more difficult for his brother. "Remember, a lot of the people involved with LBC are volunteers."

"What's that supposed to mean?" Xavier's scowl could have peeled paint from the walls if there'd been any. Instead, they were covered with this odd wood-grain paneling that always reminded Val of his father's lawyer's office. "Are you implying that I might drive them off?"

"Yeah, that's not even a remote possibility, is it?" The sarcasm might have been a little thick, but come on. Xavier had to realize how he came across. "We do a lot of compromising at LBC. Some months are leaner than others. We try to maintain an even influx of capital but, when you're dependent on donations, you can't plan as well. Remember that flexibility is your friend."

"I'll keep that in mind. Try not to make more of a mess than I can conceivably clean up, all right?"

"Well, there go all my plans to flush my inheritance down the toilet." Val shrugged as if he didn't care, which was how he'd long played it with those in his family who saw him as nothing but a dreamer, who couldn't cut it in the corporate world. Which might be less of a stretch than he'd have credited before today. "Hey, if I screw up, you're still good. Just do your thing, and you'll have half a billion dollars to play with."

"Yeah, that's comforting." Xavier pulled a pen from the holder at the corner of the desk and pocketed it. "That was a gift from the daughter of a Russian ambassador. I wouldn't want to lose track of it."

Val snorted. As if stealing pens from LeBlanc was

one of his top priorities. "Sabrina's due any minute, FYI. Make yourself scarce unless you want to say hello."

"You think it bothers me if you sleep with her?"

"I didn't until now," Val lied. "Do tell."

"She's frigid, man. You'll have better luck with the president of Botswana than you will with her."

"Wanna bet?" Val asked pleasantly because, while Sabrina dripped ice cubes as a matter of course, the glimpses of heat between them had kept him awake far longer last night than it probably should have.

And the stakes had gone up. Xavier was still pissed about Sabrina dumping him, which meant Val was doubly interested in rubbing it in his brother's face when he did score.

His brother shook his head. "We've got enough on the line already, don't you think? Besides, if you do bag her, it can only help you."

"And perhaps you should consider that the reason she dumped you is because you're an ass. I'm not," Val shot back, a little more hotly than he'd intended, but the sentiment was warranted. Sabrina was a lot of things but not a faceless notch on the bed post. No woman in Val's rearview was. He loved being with all the women he'd slept with, loved learning their bodies, their laughs. Quantity did not preclude quality. The more the merrier.

"Which is going to bite you," Xavier informed him. "Bleeding hearts aren't her type. They don't increase profits eight percent, even in six years, let alone six months."

"We'll see about that." Val's confidence might be a little misplaced, given that his one foray into The Buck Stops Here mentality had made him sick to his stomach. "Maybe some heart is what this company needs."

"And maybe a solid hand is what LBC needs." Xavier smirked.

Val's stomach turned over again. His staff would be fine. They knew not to fold under his brother's dictatorial style. Somehow, reminding himself of that didn't make him feel any better. "You'd do well to leave your Tom Ford suits at home and dig into LBC's mission statement with an open mind."

His brother flipped him a smartass salute and strode out of the office without a backward glance. Good riddance. Val scrubbed at his face with his hands and trashed the unpalatable coffee without taking a second sip. Maybe he could duck out for twenty minutes and make it to Fuel for Humans Coffee near LBC's main facility before anyone else showed up.

"Ahh, I see we're taking our CEO position seriously today."

Sabrina strolled through the door Xavier had vacated mere minutes before, looking far too fresh and untouchable given the hour. A temperature drop accompanied her as if she'd tucked the Snow Queen into her clutch in order to unleash winter upon the hapless souls in her wake.

Of course, the logical explanation lay with the pronounced hum of the air conditioner. But he liked his version better. What fun was life if you couldn't see the fanciful in the everyday?

Speaking of his overactive imagination, if she'd been in Val's bed last night—which he'd envisioned more times than he could count—they'd still be there, and her hair would be tousled from his fingers instead of wound up in that severe bun thing. Seeing her in the flesh doubled his resolve to get to that point. Soon.

"Good morning to you too," he greeted her gallantly. "I was about to go get some coffee around the corner. Come with me."

"We can't leave."

She crossed her arms over the kelly-green knit top she wore under a classy white suit, the skirt of which hit just above her knees. It shouldn't have been as sexy as it was, but Sabrina was one of those rare women who had such an arresting vibe that you scarcely noticed what she was wearing. Her appeal came from somewhere beneath, and his mouth wanted to uncover her secrets.

After Xavier's welcome to LeBlanc, Sabrina's frost needed to go.

"On the contrary, I'm the CEO. I can do whatever I want. Right?"

"Have coffee delivered, then," she said with raised eyebrows. "We have a four-week plan to go over."

Lazily, he spun his chair as he contemplated her, the coaching plan suddenly very far down his list of things to do today. "Only four weeks?"

"We have to start somewhere. At the end of four weeks, I can make some assessments about where we are in your progress, then make adjustments. I have no idea how well you're going to take suggestions or what you'll do with my feedback. It will do me no good to have spent time on a six-month plan if you ignore everything I say."

"So far, you haven't said much," he countered. "And if you truly wanted to know how well I respond to suggestion, you should have had dinner with me last night."

Her expression didn't change, but her gaze flicked over his face. "Because you expect me to spit out commands of a sexual variety on a first date?"

Oh, man. She was far more charmed by him than she knew what to do with. Excellent. He grinned. "Because I had planned to ask you what you wanted me to cook for you. But I like the direction of your thoughts so much better. Now that we've opened that Pandora's box, what commands would you give?"

"Oh, no." She shook her head, the hard cross of her arms tightening over her midsection. She must not have realized that action had pulled her blouse down a half inch, displaying a very lovely section of her breasts. "We're not going there today, Val."

"You started it, not me." He held up his hands in mock surrender to distract from the sharp little number this whole exchange was doing on his lower half. Didn't work. But, then, he was starting to think nothing would, except the obvious.

"We have a professional relationship. If we can't stick to that, then you can find another executive coach."

Her expression had none of the heat from yesterday. He was failing with her today, for some unknown reason.

With that warning ringing in his ears, Val sobered. Those contacts with the Botswana government still lay prominently in the center of his desk and, as reminders went of how he'd go down in flames without her, that was a stark one. "I take this very seriously. Please forgive me. Let's go over your plan."

She rolled her eyes. "And stop being so conciliatory. Men in the corporate world take no prisoners. Don't ask for forgiveness, and do not look at me with those puppy-dog eyes."

He had to laugh. "Is that what I was doing?"

"We're going to have a problem if you don't take accountability for the changes you need to make. That's why you hired me, right?"

No, he'd hired her because she liked to win. And because he had a score to settle with his father but, in lieu of being able to do that, he'd settle for taking a few chunks out of Xavier's hide. Sabrina was his ticket to that. "I hired you because I need my inheritance. You have a proven track record working with executives to better their ability to lead. Nowhere did I agree to change."

Sabrina blinked. "Then you've already decided that we've lost."

No. That was not happening. If nothing else, he needed that money to undo all the damage Xavier would likely do to LBC without Val there to fix it.

"Sit," he told her with a head jerk at one of the chairs as his temper started simmering again. Or maybe it hadn't fully cooled from Xavier's drive-by earlier.

To her credit, she didn't argue and just did as he said, which wasn't going to work either. He wanted a partner, not a lackey. "I'm a team player. Always. I don't boss people around for the sake of getting my way. If your four-week plan includes strategies to turn me into a corporate shark, you can trash it. I need you on my side. To work with me to use my strengths and gloss over what you perceive to be my weaknesses. Can you do that?"

Sabrina let her spine relax against the back of the chair and shook her head. "I don't know."

"You promised me yesterday that we'd do this together. You moved me with that speech. Figure out a way," he said. "And that's as tyrannical as I'm going to get."

There was no way in hell he'd let this job-switch mandate turn him into his father. Or, worse, into Xavier. But he was going to use his stint at LeBlanc to show everyone that, while his brother might have been their father's favorite, Val could and would pass whatever test the old man posthumously threw down in his path—as long as he had Sabrina to help him avoid becoming the soulless corporate type his father had likely hoped this task would shape him into.

Four

Together.

That was not a coaching strategy, not the way Val meant it. He was essentially asking her to get into the game with him, to be his Cyrano de Bergerac behind the scenes as he took the spotlight. Be in lockstep next to him, figuring out how to guide him on the fly.

Sabrina didn't work that way. She needed to analyze. Study. Contemplate. Caution was her default for more reasons than one, and having a well-thought-out plan helped. *Together* in her mind meant supporting him as he followed the plan. Not that she'd be part of a *team*.

Sabrina was and always had been a team of one. She'd never disappointed herself, never cheated on herself, never broken her own heart. The only way to avoid all that was to stay far away from anyone who could possibly wield that type of power.

She glanced at the printed pages in her hand, the ones

she'd worked on until midnight because she'd needed the distraction first and foremost, but also because she'd said she'd deliver her initial four-week plan today. None of which she could actually use if Val was serious about trashing anything that resembled either change or modeling him into a corporate executive.

Instead, he wanted her to storm the gates of the CEO office alongside him. The concept scared the bejesus out of her. But, at the same time, it felt like an unparalleled opportunity. What better way for her to glean the skills she needed to remake herself into a CEO? She'd been on the sidelines for many, many long years, parroting strategy to her clients in clinical one-off sessions that were more personal growth than nitty-gritty.

She couldn't tell him *no*. Neither did she think *yes* made a lick of sense.

"Watching the gears turn in your head is fascinating."

Sabrina made the mistake of glancing at Val. He hadn't moved from his chair, but it didn't matter. His presence filled the room, winnowing into corners with ease, and not all of those corners were in the room. He'd found plenty of her nooks and crannies too, even the ones that she'd have said were quite hidden beneath her layer of frost.

She hadn't slept well last night, that was the problem. Too busy trying to banish Val's sensual edge from her consciousness to sleep, but she'd finally given up, realizing far too late that she'd have had better luck willing her skin to change color.

"Really?" she commented mildly. "You should get out more if watching me think is the slightest bit interesting."

"If you were just thinking, I might agree." He tipped the chair a bit, peering at her from behind strands of his ridiculously long dark hair. The tips grazed his cheekbones for crying out loud. "You were doing far more than that. Come on. Spill. I want to know what you were so furiously working out in your head."

She stared at him while scrambling to put parameters around a rapidly shifting dynamic. What was she supposed to do, admit that he was pushing her out of her comfort zone? Worse than that, he was pushing her, and she wasn't pushing back. "Nowhere in our agreement does it say I have to share my thought process with you."

The grin that flashed across his face shouldn't have been so affecting. "That's the whole basis of our agreement, Sabrina."

And he should stop saying her name like that, as if they were intimate and he had a right to color his tone so richly when he spoke to her. Val at full throttle was throwing her off. They had to get out of this private office before he pushed her beyond what she could handle.

"Fine. I was thinking that I have to start from square one with you. That none of the strategies in this plan are going to work, since you're being so stubborn."

His chair swiveled as he contemplated her. "Good. Then that means I'm getting through to you. Dump that whole thing in the trash, and let's start over. Figure out step one together."

There was that word again. *Together*. As a team. She had the wildest urge to see what that felt like.

Blinking her eyes for a beat, strictly for fortification that did not come, she did as he suggested, sliding the entire file into the trash. Oh, God. She'd thrown away her game plan, her link to sanity. What was she *doing*? Without structure, she'd crumple. Wouldn't she?

"You're much braver than I was expecting," Val told her quietly, and her gaze flew to his. He caught it easily and held on, letting so many nonverbal things tumble between them that she almost couldn't breathe.

The compliment shouldn't mean so much, but it did. It was bar none the most affecting thing anyone had ever said to her, and the greedy part of her soul that craved recognition gathered it up tight before it slipped away.

But Val wasn't done slicing her open.

"What did you see in Xavier, anyway?"

She flushed, heat climbing across her cheeks. "That's not relevant."

She'd seen a powerful man who came with guarantees: she'd never trust him, never fall for him and never allow him to hurt her. None of which she'd admit to anyone, let alone her client. Why was Val so fixated on her relationship with Xavier? This wasn't the first time he'd brought it up, and she had a sneaking suspicion it wouldn't be the last.

Val shrugged. "It's relevant to me because I don't see you two together. You're far too deep for him."

That was a new one on her.

Most men called her *icy* or, at least, that's what they said to her face. She didn't have any illusions about what they called her behind her back, and that bothered her not at all since she purposefully cultivated a reputation for being remote and frigid.

Never had she been called *deep*. It intrigued her against her will.

"*Deep*?" she repeated with just the right amount of nonchalance that she could play it off as lack of interest if he went a direction she didn't like.

"You have these layers," he explained, shaping the air with his fingers as he mimed filtering through them. "They're fascinating. One minute I think I have you pegged, and then you do something so shocking that I can't get a handle on it. Have dinner with me. I can't wait to see what happens on a date."

She had to laugh at his one-track mind. "You say that as if a woman who veers between extremes is a draw. After you painted such a flattering picture of me as a crazy person, I hope you won't find this next part shocking. *No.*"

He watched her with this fine edge, his gaze digging into her layers right here and now, and his slight smile clearly conveyed his anticipation of finding something juicy. What he'd do with it she had no idea, nor did she want to find out. Her frost barrier stayed firmly in place to prevent exactly that. Or, at least, it did with everyone else on the planet. Val acted like it didn't exist, and she had no idea how to get him on the right page—she didn't do his brand of passion. Sabrina had tasteful, quiet affairs with even-keeled men who could help her achieve personal goals. That was it.

"The *no* wasn't the shocking part."

"Do tell," she suggested blandly.

"It's that you seem to think you're one-dimensional and that veering between extremes is a bad thing. Life is extreme. We experience so many highs and lows as humans. Why try to stuff that into a box? Let it out, and really feel what's happening to you."

What was this conversation they were having? Willingly open yourself up to feel things, like pain and betrayal and suffering? No, thanks. "Um, why would I want to do that, again?"

His dark blue eyes danced. "Because that's when you get to the amazing part."

There was no doubt in her mind they'd veered firmly into intimate territory and that Val unleashed *would* be amazing. Amazingly dangerous, sensual, driving her to extremes, as promised. That sounded like the worst idea in history. She concentrated on avoiding those types of emotions, and any man who spent that much energy indulging in hedonism did not stick with one woman. The signs were all there, in neon. He practically bled erotic suggestion, even in the way his full lips formed words. She'd never believe he'd be satisfied with monogamy.

Which mattered not at all since she wasn't asking him to apply for the nonexistent position of her lover. They had a professional relationship, and that was the full extent of it.

Speaking of which…there was very little coaching going on thus far this morning, and she needed to get it together. Step in and guide him toward the end goal since he'd made it clear he either couldn't or wouldn't rein himself in.

"Val." She held up a finger as he cocked a brow. "No. Back to business. I threw away the plan because it's useless at this point. But you're still my client, and I promised you that we'd get your inheritance. We're going to concentrate on that. There's nothing else between us."

"Right now, yes," he agreed readily. "But not forever."

So sure, are you? She shook her head. "We need to focus here, Val. I'm treading on some shaky ground without the proven strategies that I just abandoned. I need you to be on my side if I'm going to be on yours."

He let another indulgent smile spill onto his face. "Are you admitting you have vulnerabilities? And here I thought you weren't embracing your highs and lows."

"I'm not admitting anything of the sort," she shot back primly. "I'm saying this is uncharted water. If I'm not reshaping you into a CEO, what am I doing?"

"Winning," he said succinctly. "Just as soon as you figure out if we're on shaky ground or in uncharted water."

The man was going to unglue her. "Are you deliberately trying to sabotage this?"

He abruptly extricated himself from behind his desk and sidled around it to end up on her side of it, leaning against the edge as he towered over her. This close, his masculine scent couldn't be ignored, and her needy, treacherous insides sniffed it out instantly, inhaling him in one gulp.

Mayday! Val was not for her. She had rules about dating clients, rules about men like him, rules about her rules. Why was all of that so hard to remember when he pursed his perfect lips and watched her with undisguised wickedness sparking in his expression?

"I'm deliberately trying to get you out from behind your walls so we can work together. You've got more land mines ringing you than a military outpost in Iraq. I get that I'm asking you to do this gig differently than you're used to, and that there's no tried and true formula that fits me. I trust that we're going to figure it out. Together," he stressed.

Trust. That was a word that didn't get thrown around in her world very often. But if she'd engendered his, great. That was a fantastic first step. Unfortunately, it was the first in a long line of them.

"Then you have to trust me when I say that the first step is that makeover." *Please, God, get him the hell out of this office, and make him go somewhere else.* "You need a wardrobe that tells people that you're the one who makes the decisions. Then you don't have be a shark because people already recognize your power even before you open your mouth."

He nodded once and extended his hand. "You have to come with me. That's part of the deal."

"What? No. I'm not going with you." She needed

decompression time, best done miles and miles away from Val.

"Yes," he said simply and wiggled his fingers. "We're a team. I need your critical eye. What if the suits I get give people the wrong message? Come on. We can talk about next steps at the same time."

Yeah, no, that was not happening. She did not take men shopping for suits. Or anything else. That was entirely too intimate an activity. "That's what the tailor is for. You explain what you're looking for, and he creates it. When you're spending five grand on a suit, they tend to be a little better than average at customer service."

"This is why you have to come," he returned without blinking an eye and pushed his hand further into her space. "Because there is no way I can actually hand someone my credit card to purchase suits that cost five thousand dollars. You're going to have to do it for me."

She rolled her eyes. "Seriously?"

Judging by the mulish glint in his gaze, she had two choices. She could test out which one of them could hold out the longest or give up now since he didn't intend to concede. He'd spent the better part of fifteen minutes laying out how this coaching assignment needed to work differently than her other ones, and either she could climb on board his crazy train now or keep fighting him—and losing.

"Fine," she spit out for the second time this morning, and it wasn't even nine o'clock yet. "But I can stand on my own."

He didn't move his hand. "The offer to help you out of your chair has nothing to do with your abilities and everything to do with my character. The faster you learn that, the easier this is going to go."

That sank in much more quickly than she would have

credited and, for God knew what reason, she believed him. Or, rather, she accepted that he thought it was true. She'd expended an enormous amount of energy trying to be accepted into a man's world, and letting one treat her like a woman didn't get her anywhere but frustrated. Val was in a class by himself and probably really didn't get the dynamic, nor would he if she explained it. So she opted to skip the lecture about sexual politics in the c-suite and clasped his hand.

The shock of it swept over them, and he didn't even bother to hide the result. Awareness swamped her, heightened by the decidedly carnal edge to his smile as he pulled her to her feet, which didn't diminish the snap, crackle and pop in the least. He still leaned on the desk, only now she had him boxed in against it, and the delicious position put her in a reckless frame of mind.

How else could she explain the sudden urge to step into his space and pin him to the desk as she kissed him?

She didn't do either. Yanking her hand free through an enormous burst of will that she hoped never to have to muster again, she stepped away.

The tension should have been severed instantly. But no. Her skin prickled with a strange, shivery sort of heat that made her restless. She could not stop her muscles from flexing. Rationally she recognized it as a fight-or-flight adrenaline response pumping through her body, but that didn't make the experience any easier.

Nor did she believe for a moment that, if Val closed that distance, fighting him would be her first instinct.

"If we're going shopping, we should leave," she told him hoarsely and cleared her throat. "The faster we get that done, the faster we can move on."

"I'll drive," he offered, and it was so not fair that he had the capacity to sound normal when her insides were a quivering mess. Over a touch of their hands that lasted less than a half a second, no less.

She had to pretend everything was kosher. "Whatever. That's fine."

It turned out that being wedged into Val's SUV gave her none of the reprieve she'd been hoping for. The vehicle was roomy enough, but he drove with his elbow on the center console and, when he turned corners, his arm drifted over into her space. She spent the entire drive trying to make herself smaller so he didn't accidentally graze her, which was enough of an indicator that she should have been adamant about not going on this shopping trip.

The exclusive shopping center he'd selected near Grant Park had the right qualifications for the type of look she'd envisioned for him. They walked into the suit shop, which had maybe five of its wares on display, and her brain had just enough functional cells left to figure out that he'd brought her to a place that custom-made suits, as opposed to selling ready-to-wear. Of course, that was what a man built like Val needed. He was tall, with a wiry frame that matched his brother's pretty well, and that was literally the last thing she needed to focus on at this inopportune moment.

The sales clerk or tailor or whatever title people held in a place she had no business being in rushed over to start working his magic on Val. Sabrina hung back, seriously thinking about slinking to the car. What value would she have at this point, anyway? Her job was to ensure he crossed the finish line, which was way off in the distance.

That's when Val motioned her forward to introduce her to the clerk. "This is my companion. She's going to make sure I'm dressed appropriately."

So that was it then. She'd been dragged into the entire process, bless him. "I thought I was just here to pay."

A giggle almost burst free of its own free will. How was that for a nice reversal? The clerk probably thought he was the gold digger and she'd brought him here to get him clothed for her world. In that scenario, he'd definitely be trading sexual favors for the privilege.

"You're also here for moral support," he told her, and the clerk whisked him away to a fitting area to take his measurements, which no one seemed to expect her to participate in, thank God.

She took the reprieve and sank into one of the plush couches near the bay windows, phone in hand so she could read the slew of emails that had stormed her inbox in the hour since she'd last checked it. The joys of being a team of one. There was no assistant to take care of the minutiae, which normally she enjoyed since it meant she was the only person accountable for ensuring her success.

The reprieve lasted all of five minutes, a blessing because she hadn't read one single email. Her brain was still stuck on Val and what sort of sexual favors he might perform under the fictional circumstances that she'd invented.

The man she'd been objectifying reappeared, draped in suit pieces that did little to hide that he'd shed his button-down shirt, revealing a soft white undershirt that fit him like a second skin. She swallowed and peeled her eyes from the abs she could just see through the thin white material. "I'd hoped you'd be wearing the suit."

"Which color?" he asked and held out both arms, where the clerk had pulled on one sleeve jacket the color of charcoal and another in a blue so dark that it would match his eyes perfectly.

Either one would look amazing on him.

"Both," she said automatically. "And another one in a dark gray. Also don't forget that you need to think about formal wear."

Val's face screwed up. "I generally try to not think about formal wear. I have a suit I wear to fundraisers. Can't I use that?"

"Uh, no, you cannot." *Dear God.* "The CEO of LeBlanc Jewelers wears black tie to formal events. And arrives in a limo."

His eyebrows lifted. "To where?"

Obviously he was testing her professional capacity, both her ability to remain so without losing her temper and her skill set. "I don't know. That's your job to figure out. Everything is about business, all the time, even things that masquerade as social."

Xavier had taken her to a couple of events, a random society thing where he'd wanted to be seen and maybe an industry dinner. She hadn't really paid a lot of attention to the reason for the events, only that she couldn't wait to leave. But Val had absolutely no need to know that.

Val made another face. "So three suits is enough?"

"How many days are there in a week?" *Not rocket science.* She took a deep breath and smiled, hoping it looked less like a grimace than it felt like. "You need at least seven. Maybe more. It's your wallet."

"You realize I could feed a small country for what this is going to cost."

"You realize that you can feed a lot bigger country if you get your inheritance." Neither of them blinked. "I'm here, as instructed, to provide advice. Take it."

He grumbled about it but, in the end, became the reluctant owner of seven suits that the clerk informed him would be ready in a week, which frankly seemed like a pretty quick turnaround to Sabrina. That gave them plenty of time to work on the rest of the strategy before Val would be fully launched as the CEO.

Since they were almost done, thank God, she wandered over to the counter while Val finished up in the dressing room. The final bill did end up crossing the line into staggering, but Val handed over his credit card like a good boy and managed to do it without turning green.

Once they exited the shop, Val didn't immediately head for his SUV. "I need something to wash the taste of capitalism from my mouth."

Oh, no. She did not like the look on his face. "We have a lot of work to do, Val."

Not only that: she needed to vanish inside her job, where things made sense. Nothing with Val made her comfortable and, while she'd objectively agreed that chucking her plan had been the right decision, that didn't make it any easier to be winging it. She *had* to find her feet here. More importantly, she had to find the upper hand. Val unsettled her, to the point of being so unhinged she couldn't think. That stopped now.

"I can't go to LeBlanc like this, where the sole order of business is to sell colorless rocks that do nothing other than sit on fingers and ears. Besides, the other execs have day to day operations under control. LeBlanc can do without me for another thirty minutes." He scouted around until he spied something over her shoulder that made his face brighten. "Perfect. Come on."

Five

Sabrina whirled on one stiletto heel to follow the direction of Val's line of sight.

"There's nothing there but Grant Park," she said, her tone firmly in the realm of *Stop wasting my time*.

"Exactly." Before she could figure a way to protest, he linked fingers with her hand and tugged, forcing her to follow him across the street once the light changed. Spending a small fortune on suits that he'd wear for six months and then donate to a shelter topped his list of time-wasters, but taking a stroll near the waterfront—that was more his cup of tea.

Besides, Sabrina would just slip into Snow Queen mode if they returned to LeBlanc, and that would be a shame. He had her off-balance enough to make it interesting, and he deserved something for sacrificing his morning to the gods of fashion. In lieu of what he really wanted from Sabrina, he'd take an hour doing something—anything—that wasn't work related.

He needed a partner, not a by-the-book professional who couldn't relax.

They couldn't be an effective team if she wasn't comfortable around him. And she wasn't. Diving straight into a new and improved 947-step plan for turning him into a carbon copy of Xavier wouldn't help. Snow cones might.

Sabrina figured out pretty fast that they were holding hands and jerked hers free. "Val—"

"If the words *no* or *work* come out of your mouth, I will be forced to find a way to stop you from talking," he advised her silkily. "If you're feeling lucky, roll the dice. Otherwise, humor me."

She clamped her lips together, a minor miracle, though a part of him was disappointed she didn't take the gamble. Sabrina had brains to spare. She knew exactly how he'd shut her up and had opted not to push him into kissing her. Too bad. Now he had to come up with a different way to cross that line. Ever since that moment at the office, when he'd pulled her to her feet and she'd been almost close enough to taste, that's all he'd thought about—how to get her into a repeat situation, where pulling her into his arms would take scarcely any effort at all.

"What are we doing?" she asked as they entered the park at the top of a concrete loop that edged a wide swath of green.

"You suck at the quiet game." The snow-cone cart sat off the left fork and had no customers in line, a plus. "I'm buying you a snow cone as my way of saying thanks for taking me shopping. I genuinely appreciate your advice, and this is how I intend to show it. What flavor floats your boat?"

She eyed the white cart, taking in the giant palm tree painted across the front. "I don't even know how to answer that."

The noise of disgust that emanated from Val's throat really couldn't be helped.

"That's a crime. We'll mix, then. Two please," he told the smiling guy behind the glass and handed him a folded twenty, with a nod indicating that he could keep the change. Working a small business like a snow-cone kiosk came with meager financial rewards, and Val liked to spread the wealth where he could. "Come on. You pour your own syrup over here."

She peered over his shoulder as Val stuck the mound of shaved ice under a spigot and pushed the handle to dispense the thick, bright red liquid in loopy swirls across the width of the cup. His true skill was displayed in how he didn't spill a drop, despite Sabrina's firm press against his arm. He bet she didn't realize that was happening, or she'd jerk away like a scalded cat.

So he let the syrup drain through the ice and enjoyed the warmth of a woman against him.

"How do you know all of this?" she demanded.

"I'm assuming you're looking for a different answer than *because I've eaten snow cones before*?" he asked blithely and handed her the cup. "That's half tiger's blood and half blue raspberry. My money is on you liking both equally, but if you skew one way, it's going to be toward the blue raspberry."

Mouth slightly open, she stared at the concoction he'd shoved into her hand. "This is something you eat?"

"Geez, woman. This is not a complex math problem that requires a slide rule and NASA scientists to unravel. It's a snow cone." Her expression was so dubious that he did a double take. "You've really never had a snow cone before?"

"Not once. It looks…sticky."

Val checked his eye roll. What did she do on dates

anyway? Something boring like the opera, no doubt, or, worse, wine tastings in a highbrow, exclusive restaurant, where it cost ten dollars to sneeze. "It is sticky. So don't spill it on that beautiful white skirt. Here's your spoon, Coach. Dig in."

Instead of concentrating on his own half watermelon–half black cherry like he should, he watched her take a tiny bite from the blue side and didn't bother to hide a smile when she flinched.

"It's cold," she explained unnecessarily. A woman in the midst of brain freeze was not hard to recognize.

"But good," he threw in and managed to stop himself from offering to warm her up. This dance had to be taken slowly. "You like it. Admit it."

She shrugged. "I haven't made up my mind yet."

"Take a bigger bite."

"That's your philosophy for everything, I'm assuming?" she shot back with raised brows. "Jump in with both feet, and let the splash fall where it may?"

"As it happens, you're not far off." What a great segue into the conversation he'd rather be having.

"Is that why you're avoiding LeBlanc? So you can make a big splash later?"

How had she seen through the snow cones so effortlessly? She was shrewd, no doubt, but they were having fun, and there was nothing wrong with that.

"Who said I was avoiding the office?" he returned easily. "This is a thank-you. Like I said. You've never had snow cones before, and *voilà*! You've got one in your hand. Valentino LeBlanc, at your service."

"I'm not really a snow-cone kind of girl."

"You don't say." Curious now, he eyed her. "What kind of girl are you, then?"

"This is not a date. We're not feeling each other out to

see whether or not we're going to end up in bed together later. I'm humoring you as asked, but only because you mustered up the courage to buy the suits."

Well, now. Guess that answered his question about what she did on dates—she spent the evening letting her companion audition for the part of her lover. Now Val had an insatiable desire to know what landed a guy the role. Sure, he'd started out interested in her solely because Xavier had had her first, and that was still a really important box to check, but the woman had begun to intrigue him along the way. The heat between them couldn't be denied, yet she continued to pretend she could. It was fascinating. And way too much of a challenge to ignore.

"You might not have ever had a snow cone before, but you're definitely that kind of girl."

She rolled her eyes. "Why does everything sound slightly dirty the way you say it?"

"Does it?" He tucked his tongue in his cheek and pounced on that extremely provocative statement. "I don't know. I've never been told that before. Are you sure it's not you who has the dirty mind? You're obviously thinking about sex. You are the one who brought up the very excellent point that our time could also be spent figuring out whether or not we're going to end up in bed together later. The answer is *yes*, by the way."

Her long, low laugh had a touch of silk in it, surprising him with its richness. And the fact that he'd gotten her to laugh.

"I don't sleep with my clients," she informed him without a shred of emotion on her face, which only whetted his appetite to get her good and hot.

"See, that's my point. You drip icicles when you walk." No reason not to call a Snow Queen a Snow Queen. And if he did this right, he could get her to loosen up and lose the frosty routine. "Something made entirely of ice is right up your alley."

"Too sweet."

"Told you, you're not eating it right." Fully engaged with this game, he set his cup on a nearby park bench and stole hers, taking up her spoon to scoop up a big mound of red ice. "Let me show you. Open up."

Dubiously, she eyed the spoon. "I'm not three years old. I can eat on my own."

"Yet you aren't. Open," he instructed and nearly had a heart attack when she obeyed. Quickly he pressed the advantage, moving in to get good and close as he levered the spoon into her mouth, letting the ice melt across her tongue before fully transferring the cold treat.

Her gaze toyed with his as he withdrew the spoon, dancing with something he liked a whole hell of a lot. Part pleasure, part intrigue.

"That's the red side?" she murmured. "It's…different."

"Tiger's blood," he informed her. "No real tigers were harmed in the making of it."

That made her laugh again, and he couldn't for the life of him figure out how he'd slid into this spot with her, where she was letting him feed her shaved ice on the heels of talking about sex.

"I like it." She opened her mouth again, prompting him to scramble for another spoonful even as his body caught the faint scent of something womanly and exotic from her cleavage.

His pulse quickened. "As advertised."

The second spoonful went down easier than the first, and she watched him the entire time as he pulled the spoon from her lips. She didn't let up, sucking every last drop from the plastic, her mouth conforming to the shape with shocking ease, which of course elicited images that were more appropriate for the two of them tangled up in his bedsheets.

"What flavor do you have?" she asked huskily.

"Uh…" He had completely lost track of his snow cone and, frankly, did not care to retrieve it. "I don't know. Black cherry. And something else."

She blinked up at him guilelessly, and he fell into her hazel eyes, letting them wash through him as his body woke up in a hurry, hungrily sniffing around for more advantages to press because he wanted to kiss her. Badly. She'd taste like the best combination of sweetness and a cold-and hot-tongued woman.

"How am I doing?" she asked.

Awesome. So much better than he'd have expected. Or hoped. Sabrina had layers he couldn't wait to unveil— and not just because she'd been Xavier's first. "You're a snow-cone natural. Not that I had any doubt."

"So we're at a place where we can be honest with each other?"

So honest. Especially if the next words out of her mouth had something to do with how much she wanted him to kiss her. Because that was coming. The wild spark between them only got hotter the longer they danced around each other. This was definitely one of those times when it made so much more sense to jump in with both feet. "Of course."

"Good," she murmured. "Then, I need you to tell me what scares you so much about taking that corner office at LeBlanc. I can't effectively coach you if you're not being honest with me."

He blinked. And blinked again. "Scared? I'm not scared. What are you talking about?"

"I thought you were just being stubborn and diffi-cult, but snow cones put this problem in a much different perspective for me." She reached out and covered his hand with hers, effectively retrieving her cup at the same time as she pulled it from his suddenly nerveless fingers. "Anyone who uses snow cones as a distraction has some deeper issues that need to be addressed. Tell me what they are so I can help you."

Reluctant admiration spiked through him, and the only thing he could do with her semiaccurate statement was laugh. "Can't just take it as a thank-you, can you?"

"No. Because that's not what this is." She shrugged delicately. "Maybe it's a combo deal, avoidance dressed up as a seduction scene. I have a feeling you use your charm to distract women on a regular basis."

"Now, hold on."

This would be a good time for that snow cone to make an appearance, strictly to cool his suddenly hot throat, courtesy of the temper he'd had to clamp down on lest he unleash a few choice words. Accusing him of seducing women to avoid unpleasantness in life rankled. He seduced women to *attain* pleasantness in life. Didn't everyone?

"That's not judgment, Val," she said quietly. "We all use something to avoid unpleasantness. The method is not the issue. You want us to be a team? Tell me how to help you. What's got you spooked about being LeBlanc's CEO?"

She had him *all* figured out, did she? Except she didn't. She had no clue how much Val hated LeBlanc for any number of reasons, not the least of which had to do with the fact that he shared a last name with the corporation. This inheritance test stank to high heaven of his father's manipulative nature, and Val was *not* okay with it.

"I'm not my father, all right?" he burst out and flinched. Too late to take that back, but then he wasn't the dark-secrets type. Might as well confess the whole kit and caboodle on the off chance that she might actually be able to use his demons to keep this train moving. "Xavier got the corporate gene, and I've spent the years I've worked at LBC thanking my lucky stars for that too. They're both soulless money-making machines, and I will not become that strictly to get my inheritance."

"That's completely understandable," she said, confusion marring her arresting face. "Why would acting as the CEO for the next six months turn you into your father?"

"Because that's what this task is designed to do," he informed her grimly. "My old man didn't have an altruistic bone in his body. You can rest assured that he chose this switcheroo to punish me for what he perceives as the sin of following in my mother's footsteps. If he can do that and get me to be more like him at the same time? Bonus points."

Of course, that meant the old man was punishing Xavier for something too, and Val hadn't quite worked out what. Probably because it wasn't a punishment for Xavier—their father had thought he walked on water, which meant his brother would thrive no matter. Val was the one in trouble.

She processed that for a long moment. "That's the real reason you asked me to trash the plan, isn't it? You're worried that my coaching strategy will interfere with your need to do the opposite of what your father wants."

"I'm worried that I'll spend six months in the CEO chair and fail," he told her harshly. "That's the danger here. I will never be like my father, could never be. Refuse to be. That means I already have a ninety percent probability of not hitting that billion-dollar mark. It's not rocket science. I can either become a jackass, in the mold of the last two LeBlancs who have steered this ship, or lose my inheritance. Do you blame me for avoiding that reality for a paltry hour?"

"But Val, you're forgetting a critical piece of this," she said. "I'm here. You're not in this alone, and I'm going to help you. I already agreed to use a different strategy. Why not wait to see what I can do before bemoaning your chances?"

"Because." Bleakly, he tossed the rest of his uneaten snow cone in the trash. "I'm asking you to do something outside your realm of expertise. You excel when your client already has a shark mentality. You're honing what's already there. This situation isn't like that, and the odds are already stacked against us both."

"Stop it, Val," she said so fiercely that he did a double take. "The only thing in this scenario that is outside my skill set is your fatalistic attitude. We're in this together and, if nothing else, you've done as I've asked. You've been honest with me about your weaknesses, and I can use that. No, I've never coached someone like you. But that doesn't mean that I have nothing to offer. It means we're going to do this thing together. I am firmly on board. Even more so now. Give me a chance to prove to you that I can be the asset you sorely need."

There was not one ounce of frost in Sabrina's voice, and it climbed on top of his taut nerves, leveling him out somehow. Who would have thought she'd be the one soothing him through a freak-out? "Sorry. I do believe in you. It's the suits. Even trying on small pieces of one made me insane."

Of all things, that made her smile. "I'm sorry too, but that was a necessity. We'll skip the haircut though. Your best strategy is going to be embracing who you are. Heightening it to the nth degree. You're clearly missing a really important point in all of this. Xavier has been the

CEO of LeBlanc for almost five years. He hasn't hit the billion-dollar mark, and I can guarantee you that's been on his radar. So why hasn't he done it?"

Xavier *had* said as much. Val shrugged, impressed that she'd picked up on that. "I don't know, timing? He told me he has dominoes set up."

"Of course he did. He wants to be able to slide into his office later and tell the board that he had as much as or more than you did to do with hitting that goal, or else he might be out of a job in the future." Sabrina got so animated with making her point that her half-melted snow cone came perilously close to sloshing out of the cup. "The point here is that maybe what LeBlanc needs to propel it forward is *you*, Val. That's what's been missing all this time. Instead of some diabolical manipulation scheme, maybe your father hoped you'd find the magic button."

Something unfurled inside Val's chest as he drank in Sabrina's sincere expression. There was no chance in hell what she'd described had graced his father's thought process for even a quarter of a second. But the fact that she'd made so many out-of-the-box connections encouraged him nevertheless. Sabrina would be that magic button if for no other reason than because she'd proven exactly what she'd said she would—that she could be an asset.

And it didn't escape his notice that instead of Val relaxing Sabrina so they could work together, she'd done that for him. With style. She might be a far more effective coach than he'd ever dreamed.

Which only increased the complexity of the dynamic here. If they were a team, truly working together toward this goal of attaining his inheritance, how smart would it be to introduce a personal element to their relationship? Sabrina wasn't a woman he could romance and then move on when things fizzled. They had to be tight, like gears on a clock, until this inheritance test was done. Sex might complicate that.

He cursed. There was no *might* in that statement. His perverse need to push women away before they did it to him could easily bite him with Sabrina. The best thing to do would be to maintain professional boundaries and set his sights elsewhere.

"So, are we good here?" she asked and licked the last spoonful of snow cone into her gorgeous mouth. It was so provocative that he had a physical reaction, way down deep in his gut, where all of the instincts that he fully trusted lived.

The only way to know for sure what kinds of complications would come from romancing his coach would be to take that next step.

"Not yet." Since her hands were occupied with the cup, he took the opportunity to sate his curiosity. He tipped up her chin and laid his mouth on hers before she could open it in protest.

The second their lips touched, the ever-present spark between them exploded, and he was instantly sorry he'd initiated this kiss while so many variables weren't in his favor.

And, worst of all, her mouth opened under his, inviting him in, and she made a noise in her chest that heated his blood beyond anything he'd ever experienced before. Sabrina was *kissing him back*, and the significance of it carried implications he hadn't prepared for.

The kiss deepened almost automatically, sweeping him away in the power and beauty of it. He wished he could start over, draw out this kiss differently with a level of anticipation that would heighten it. There was only one first kiss with a new woman, and he wanted to savor Sabrina's.

Except she broke it off irrevocably by wrenching away and stepping back, her eyes huge and limpid, snow-cone cup listing in her hand as if she'd forgotten how her grip worked. She was so beautiful with her lips plumped and red from the syrup that he had to seriously check his urge to drag her into his arms.

"Why did you do that?" she whispered. "I told you I don't sleep with clients."

"Kissing is not sex," he informed her raggedly, his chest so tight he couldn't seem to get enough air in his lungs. "Though I'll consider it a win that your brain jumped straight to that after a simple kiss."

"There was nothing simple about that." The frost had climbed back into her voice. At least he knew now how to melt it. "You shouldn't have done it. I dated your brother, for God's sake. That alone should make me off-limits."

But it didn't. She'd thrown that out as a shield and, if anything, the fact that she could compare him to Xavier meant that Val had more incentive to come out on top. Figuratively, literally and every other way because he was *not* the LeBlanc who would end up cast in a bad light when he got her between the sheets.

"You can't deny that there's something between us, Sabrina. You felt it in that kiss as much as I did."

"That's irrelevant. We're working together, and we need to maintain a level of professionalism."

Which wasn't a denial. He couldn't help but take a perverse sense of satisfaction from that. And that the complications between them seemed to fade when he was kissing her. Everything else stripped away, leaving only the barest level of basic human desire.

Yeah, the only way he'd stop wanting Sabrina would be if he stopped breathing. He could hardly fathom how she'd found the will to end that perfection, and all he could think about was getting her into his arms again.

"*Now* we're good," he told her.

Six

Fortified by Sabrina's timely reminder, Val spent a hellacious week jumping feetfirst into LeBlanc. Endless board meetings blended into marathon sessions with the chief accounting officer, who first had to educate the interim CEO on how to read jewel industry financial reports, then scarcely concealed his impatience with the nineteen billion follow-up questions Val had for the man.

Did these people want him to succeed, or what? He'd read some financial reports in his day. The nonprofit he ran did have to appropriately account for donations and expenses, or they risked losing their 501(c) tax-exempt status. But the accounting for a corporation was different. Not Val's fault.

Regardless, he had to get this or die trying.

After a round of field trips to nearby retail outlets to monitor the sales end of the spectrum, Val wished dying was higher on the option list. The only reason he even registered how long it had been since the last time he looked up was because the suit shop had called to say his order was ready.

Had it been a whole week since he'd dragged Sabrina to the tailors and then bared his soul over snow cones? Blearily, he glanced at the date on his computer screen and had to concede that time did in fact fly even when you were not having fun.

The only bright spot came at 7:00 a.m. when his coach popped by for their daily debrief. She'd put their dynamic into stark perspective by acting as if that kiss hadn't happened, and he'd let her, strictly because he'd needed the step back too, or his concentration would be shot. It would be too easy to fall into a place where all he could think about was a repeat.

Instead he let her energy galvanize him. Seeing Sabrina first thing in the morning put him in the right frame of mind to tackle the rest of his packed schedule. Unfortunately, that had been hours ago, and he needed a hit of Sabrina now. Fortunately, he had a good excuse to call her, as well.

He picked up his cell phone and dialed.

"Sabrina Corbin."

Val grinned and tipped his chair so he could put his feet on the corner of Xavier's desk, a guilty pleasure he indulged in as often as he could. "I know. I called you. If you really wanted to throw me off, you should answer *Hal's Mortuary*."

"'You stab 'em, we slab 'em'?" Sabrina's eye roll came through the line loud and clear.

He laughed, the first time he'd felt like doing that all day. God, she was something else. "You have my number in your contacts. There's this handy thing that your phone has. Caller ID. When it rings, it tells you it's me."

"Did you specifically dial me up to school me on phone etiquette, Val?"

No, he'd called specifically to hear her voice. It still did a number on him, soothing the savage beast of capitalism that ran rampant in this building. And sometimes her voice took on this ragged edge that had all of these interesting nuances in it. Especially when she said his name. "Depends. If I ask you to dinner, are you going to shoot me down again?"

"Most definitely."

Great, then he could skip that for today and move right in with something guaranteed he'd get a *yes*. "Then I called to tell you that you can just say *Hi* when you answer the phone. You don't have to be formal with me. Except for tonight. Be formal with me tonight."

"What's different about tonight?"

"I have a thing. An event. I need a plus-one—"

"No."

"Come on, you didn't even let me get the whole sentence out."

"I didn't even have to," she informed him with the slightest tinge of amusement coloring her tone. "I've already told you I don't date clients."

"Oh, this isn't a date." Not if her knee-jerk reaction was *no* anytime he so much as breathed the word *date*. That's what made this whole setup perfect. "It's a meet and greet for local artisans, and I have intel that says all the hot up-and-coming designers will be there. LeBlanc needs both hot and upcoming. This is me playing to my strengths, being myself, and me, myself and I need to be at that event."

He could have the best of both worlds—business and pleasure. If Sabrina gave him the slightest sign that mixing the two would cause problems, he'd reel back the pleasure side and focus on business. He still needed his coach by his side to gloss over deficiencies Val might have considering he'd never wooed talent before.

"Great. Have a good time."

That sounded like a woman about to hang up the phone. "I can't do this without you."

"You not only can, you will," she informed him frostily.

Wow. They'd gotten through the first week together, and she'd been true to her word thus far, playing for the team without blinking an eye. Try to throw in the slightest curve ball and she flips out. Interesting.

"Sabrina. Think for a sec. I'm asking you to go with me to an artisan event. These people are looking for sponsors. It's the whole reason the organizers do it, so those looking can find. I have an opportunity to be the highest bidder, so to speak, but I need you to make sure I don't screw it up."

He had absolutely no intention of screwing up, but he also had no intention of attending this event without a plus-one. It would look bad. And he didn't want to spend the evening alone.

"Please," he threw in. "I can't bring a date. I need to focus on business, which will be much easier with you on my arm."

Ha. How he got that out without being fried by lightning bolts he'd never know. But he could feel her wavering, hear it in the slight hesitation on her end of the line.

"I'll drive my own car."

"The hell you will," he growled. "The CEO of LeBlanc arrives at events in a limo, and his companion does too. Humor me."

She sighed. "You say that a lot."

"Because you need a lot of convincing to do things

that normal people just nod their head at and agree to without coercion. What can I do to seal the deal? Offer to lend you a necklace from LeBlanc's private collection?"

"Val, please." But the noise she made in her throat clued him in that she wasn't necessarily opposed to the idea.

He sat up. "Really? That would be something you'd like?"

Geez. That was the key? Jewelry? At last—a use for the rocks his family peddled. He'd have draped Sabrina in ropes of diamonds days ago if he'd known that would hold some kind of magic to get her on his arm for a dress-up event.

"I didn't say that."

"You didn't have to," he informed her blithely, his tongue firmly in cheek. "Stop protesting. Pick you up at seven. Oh—text me the color of your dress."

"Why?" she asked somewhat faintly.

"It's a surprise." He ended the call, totally giddy over how that had gone and not the slightest bit ashamed about it.

Val had a date with Sabrina Corbin. Before the end of the night, he'd either have made some headway with her on a personal front or determined a new game plan. He might not have all the skills he needed to run LeBlanc—not yet anyway—but he sure as hell could seduce a woman, especially one who intrigued him as much as Sabrina did. All he needed was the right opportunity and a clear sign that doing so wouldn't jeopardize his end goal with his inheritance.

His phone lit up with a one-word text message from Sabrina: Red.

His favorite color. Coincidence? Or fate? Oh, yes, tonight was going to be interesting.

* * *

Valentino LeBlanc in a tuxedo should be illegal. Barring that, Sabrina was pretty sure it was the missing eighth deadly sin because the wicked, sensual edge to her companion had the definite potential to kill her before the night ended.

She should have slammed the door in his face and climbed into bed with a book. Instead, she'd taken his offered arm and let him escort her to the long, black car at her curb. She should have her head checked. If nothing else, maybe a psychologist could explain why she couldn't get that kiss out of her blood. The memory of it heated her at odd moments, when she should be focused on work.

Like now.

Being crammed into a limo with him? Torture. Never mind that the vehicle could seat ten and there was a good foot of space between their thighs. Didn't matter. Val's presence was so dominating and so impossible to ignore that they could be on opposite ends of a football stadium and she'd still have this heightened sense of awareness prickling her skin.

He felt it too. There was no way he'd missed the snap, crackle and pop that had made the atmosphere of the limo come alive. Probably she shouldn't have worn this dress. It was too…backless. Too bold. Provocative. She had a much more appropriate beige dress that covered everything and made her invisible.

But the moment she'd flipped that switch in her head that meant she'd rationalized going to this event with Val, she knew she'd wear this one. The artistic crowd had a different set of rules when it came to style. Blending in wasn't a goal, and she'd had a perverse need to keep up with the other women who'd be in attendance and surely dressed to the hilt.

The driver pulled away from the curb, and Val hit the button to raise the tinted dividing panel, the one that plunged the back of the limo into complete and utter privacy. She swallowed and opened her mouth to protest when Val pulled a wide, flat box from a hidden compartment on his other side.

"For you," he said silkily and popped the hinged lid.

Fire and ice tumbled over the length of velvet. She gasped at the intricacy of the necklace, the delicate lines of filigreed platinum that held what had to be hundreds of diamonds and rubies. It wasn't a necklace but a celebration of what extreme, stark beauty the earth and humans could create together. "Val, I can't wear this."

But she wanted to. How bad was that? She'd never been impressed by expensive things, but the necklace could hardly be described as merely a bauble purchased by someone with more money than sense. The design flowed almost as if it was alive, and it commanded attention. She'd have every eye in the place on her.

"You not only can, you are," he corrected and pulled the ends loose from their moorings. "You'll be on the arm of the CEO of LeBlanc Jewelers. There are certain expectations. You do want everyone to believe LeBlanc is the industry leader in diamonds, don't you? The necklace is a walking advertisement."

Without any fanfare, he looped the priceless jewels around her neck and fastened the clasp, letting the stones settle around her neck, cool and beautiful.

She hadn't even had to move her hair. "You've done that before."

Of course he had. His last name was LeBlanc and the parade of women in his rearview was probably too long a line to quantify. He'd likely learned at his father's knee about giving women jewelry and had perfected the art before he'd turned eighteen. She shouldn't have to keep reminding herself that he wasn't worth her time because she'd surely not get much of his before he waved *adios*.

But she forgot regularly. In the park. When he'd asked her to attend this event. A minute ago.

"I've never done this before with this necklace or with you," he said quietly. "Don't distract me while I'm busy worshipping you in that dress. You're exquisite. The necklace can hardly keep up."

The appreciation in his expression warmed her. There was no mistaking that he liked what he saw when he looked at *her*. That was all 100 percent about Sabrina. It was heady to have a man like Val aim his sights in her direction, and she couldn't stop herself from reacting.

She shouldn't react. He'd practiced complimenting women before hitting adulthood too. This wasn't a date. Every aspect of tonight was an elaborate setup to ensure Val succeeded at finding new talent for LeBlanc and, as his coach, she'd do well to remember that, especially since there was zero chance Val had forgotten.

"This old thing?" She laughed it off. "I just threw on the first dress I ran across in my closet."

"Don't diminish your effect on me." All at once, he reached out to clasp her hand, drawing it into his. His thumb traced a pattern over her knuckles, setting off fireworks under her skin. "Or vice versa."

Flustered, she shook her head and jerked her hand free. "I'm not diminishing it. I'm ignoring it. There's a difference."

"Then don't ignore it." His voice draped over her, imploring her to settle into the recesses of the limo and let him have his way with her. He hadn't so much as suggested anything of the sort, but the implication was clear.

He wanted her. Intimately.

"I have to," she told him through gritted teeth. "You're a client, and this is an event for work. Period."

After a long, very tense pause, he said, "I don't think that's the reason."

Sabrina bit back the urge to scream. "I'm not asking you to think. I'm asking you to respect the fact that, while I realize flirting is your default, you don't have to do it with me because I'm…immune."

Hardly the word she'd intended to pick, but it worked and was a far sight better than what she should have said: *I'm too professional*. But she hadn't because he'd likely stomp all over that claim, and rightly so. She'd long abandoned *professional* with Val, from the moment she'd agreed to take him shopping and then let him push a snow cone into her hand. It had been a deliberate shift, because he'd needed something different from her, something deeper than a surface-level coaching arrangement.

And then he'd kissed her, shattering everything she thought she knew about herself and her ability to work with a man she couldn't control her attraction to. She'd put them on even ground through sheer force of will, but there was little doubt Val could tilt her world again without breaking a sweat.

Val raised his eyebrows. "Shall we put that to the test?"

"You've been testing me since moment one," she countered primly. "And since I've yet to fall for your charm, I'd say my actions speak louder than words."

"On that we agree."

The tension stretched to the point of snapping, and she had the worst feeling that she'd challenged him to something that she would be sorry for later.

The limo joined the long line of similar vehicles snaking to the entrance of the performing arts center where the event was being held. The impressive building had long been one of Sabrina's favorites along the downtown skyline, but a sudden bout of nerves had gripped her, and she couldn't seem to shake off the jitters skittering through her stomach.

"Hey." Val's quiet voice cut through the tension, and she glanced at him.

That was a mistake. The lights from the street illuminated his gorgeous face and, with all that inky hair falling into his eyes, coupled with the black tie he'd donned in deference to the evening, he was pretty much the most devastatingly handsome man she'd ever basked in the presence of.

She couldn't breathe. Silly. He was just a man, one she shouldn't even be attracted to. He wasn't her type. Or, rather, he wasn't the kind of man she normally considered, but there was something about him that constantly drew her attention. A depth that she'd never sensed in Xavier—and that's why she should be giving Val a wide berth.

But she couldn't for the same reason. In all actuality, as attracted as she was to him, she shouldn't even be working with him as a client. She'd broken all sorts of ethical rules and then smashed them to smithereens by agreeing to come with him to this event as his plus-one. She'd excused it because he'd made such a pretty plea about how much he needed her, and she'd let herself be seduced by that alone.

"What?" she murmured because she'd been staring at him too long already.

"You're shaking." One of his warm palms landed on her bare shoulder. "All over. If we need to skip this event and go kayaking in the river instead, say the word."

"Kayaking?" For some reason that made her laugh,

despite the heavy tension that had only gotten worse the moment he'd touched her. She should shrug him off, but they were almost to the front of the line, and she was nothing if not aware that they were about to be thrust in the spotlight at an industry event. She'd agreed to be here, ostensibly to help him navigate, which would be made difficult if she kept being standoffish. "Please tell me what gave away my strong desire to go do something athletic."

His quick smile kicked her in the stomach, setting loose the butterflies that had started fluttering when she'd first realized how close they were to the building. Yeah, she had no immunity against him. None. And the longer she kept *that* gem of a fact from him, the better.

"Your sarcasm is showing. Maybe not kayaking then. But something. You pick."

Unexpectedly grateful for the offered reprieve, she shook her head. "That's sweet of you, but I'll be fine. I'm just…" *What was she?* "…aware of how important this event is for you. I want to help you succeed."

Bottom line, she had no clue how to do that. If she had no value as a coach in this scenario, then she had no business being here. What on earth had possessed her to say yes?

Val's hand smoothed along her arm, and his touch was so electric, she shivered.

That's what had possessed her, and it indeed felt like someone else had taken over her body. She could lie to him but not to herself. This was her one chance to spend an evening with Val without agreeing to a date. It was the only way she could have broken her own rules and lived with it.

The nerves were pure adrenaline and expectation. She might have insisted to him that it wasn't a date, but there was no escaping that this event had all the trappings. Labels didn't matter to a man like Val, who could turn a simple phone call into a seduction if he so chose.

"If you're truly concerned about how the night will go for LeBlanc, don't be." He withdrew his hand as the limo pulled to a stop at the curb, and the driver rounded the car to open the door for them. "This is only the first in a laundry list of things that I have to try. No one item will push LeBlanc over the billion-dollar mark, so relax. Your job is to keep me out of trouble. I'll take care of the rest."

For whatever reason, that was the exact right thing to say. The butterflies settled and, with them no longer swarming her stomach, she found the will to smile. "I think I can do that."

Seven

Val led his date into the top-floor loft with a skyline view of downtown Chicago, acutely aware that Sabrina's bare back was mere inches away. That *dress*. It fit her like a second skin. He clasped her hand tighter, strictly so his fingers wouldn't wander, which was a very real danger. Her luminous skin begged for his touch and every nerve was poised to do so in a split second if she gave the slightest sign she'd welcome it.

She hadn't yet. It was maddening. Why would she have worn a dress with no back if she didn't want a man's hands on her?

But this was Sabrina, not a woman he'd invited to a shindig with the sole intent of using the evening as a long seduction until he finally got her behind closed doors, where he'd strip her out of that dress. Sure, he'd fantasized about doing exactly that for pretty much every second of that limo ride from her house. The privacy panel had been up. There had been plenty of opportunity to slide that dress right off Sabrina's body and plunge them both into something of the carnal variety.

She wasn't ready for that, no matter how much he wanted that to not be true. Even he could see that she had 100 percent of her focus on the job, so much so that she'd had a minor freak-out in the limo over her upcoming performance. What had he expected when he'd proposed her attendance at this event as his coach? That she'd magically transform into a warm and willing date just because she'd worn a sexy red dress that was calling his name?

He needed to get a grip—and not on her clothes. He had a job to focus on too. He'd do well to take a lesson from Sabrina, as ironic as it was to have her fill the made-up role he'd laid out for her strictly to get her on this date.

"Hungry?" he murmured to her as they threaded through the crowd toward the buffet tables. He nodded to a couple of LeBlanc executives who were standing at a high table with martini glasses in hand.

"Not especially." Sabrina's gaze cut through the room, evaluating everything in her path.

"Tell me what you see," he said, fascinated by the way her mind worked. He saw nothing in the room except her. But she'd scarcely glanced at him, and it was as intriguing as it was crushing to be categorically dismissed when he was wearing a tux like she'd instructed him to.

"Opportunity," she responded instantly.

That made two of them. "What would you recommend I do as my first move, Coach?"

She slid him a sidelong glance. "Stop calling me *Coach*, for one."

Grinning, he released her hand to guide her through a knot of people and couldn't even find a shred of shame that it gave him the perfect excuse to lay his palm flat on the small of her back. Her warm skin made his hand tingle. He should get a medal for resisting the urge to take liberties, now that he'd moved into the perfect position to feel even more of her.

"After that?" he prompted when they'd cleared the crowd.

"Smile at that blonde."

She tilted her head toward a woman near the bar clad in a hot pink kimono-style dress that had a two-tiered skirt, short in the front and long in the back, with a train that dragged on the floor. Two chopsticks in a shade that matched her dress held a twist of her hair on her crown, but part of it spilled out artfully in a messy drip of curls meant to make a man think of a long roll between the sheets. A pretty face and impressive cleavage rounded out the package and, on any normal day, Val would be all over the suggestion that she might be someone he'd like to get to know.

Given that Sabrina had been the one to mention it set him back a step. "Are you trying to ditch me?"

Sabrina laughed as if he'd been kidding. "That's Jada Ness. She's the hottest designer of the season, according to the organizer's website." She did a double take when she caught Val's expression. "What? I do my research."

"Clearly," he murmured. Not that he was shocked at her thoroughness. It was more that he'd never been shuffled off onto another woman by his current date. "Should I ask her to dance?"

"The sooner the better." Sabrina shooed him away with a chop-chop kind of motion.

More bemused than he'd like to admit, Val drifted away from Sabrina of the Red Dress toward Jada Ness, who was indeed the very person he'd targeted as a potential coup for LeBlanc. He'd recognized her, of course, but the closer he got to the hot pink–clad woman, the slower his steps.

He was moving in the wrong direction, also known as not toward Sabrina. Worse, she'd been the one to send him off. It shouldn't be stuck under his skin like a splinter. But it was.

What was *wrong* with him? Sabrina had offered advice, exactly as he'd requested, and her recommendation had been solid, aligning with his own already-formed opinion. He and Sabrina weren't involved, not really, so there was no reason he should feel weird about asking another woman to dance. Especially one he hoped to extend a business offer to.

He still felt weird.

And he still had the expectation of a billion dollars in sales looming over him. That much-needed reminder got him moving again.

A plethora of Val's competition ringed Ms. Ness, and she did her level best to give the impression the whole event was boring her, and that included the four men trying to woo her. Val didn't recognize any of them but they all had that corporate look about them, as if they'd been born with two-hundred-dollar haircuts.

The lady in pink noticed Val a millisecond after he came into her line of sight, and she let her gaze slide all the way down his body so suggestively that he thought about charging her for it. Something was definitely off for him because normally he welcomed bold women, but Ms. Ness somehow made him feel a bit like a side of beef. Eventually her wandering eyes lit on his face, and she smiled, beckoning him over.

Val wasn't bothered by usurping industry rivals in the slightest and stepped directly in front of the suit who'd been talking her up. Ms. Ness had been ignoring the guy anyway and, thankfully, all of her admirers took the hint and made themselves scarce.

Taking her extended hand, Val held it two deliberate beats too long, his gaze on her. Never hurt to stack the deck. "Pleasure to meet you. I'm Valentino LeBlanc."

"I know who you are." Her sultry voice dripped with magnolias and sweet tea, underpinning her Georgia roots. "Since you and your brother have different hair. And I must say I'm thrilled to see you here instead of Xavier."

Well, that was an interesting and very provocative statement. Either his brother's reputation preceded Val or Ms. Ness had a personal bone to pick with Xavier. *Please, God, let it be the latter.* "Xavier is taking a hiatus from his position as the CEO. I'm filling in."

"Lucky me," she murmured as she moved in a little closer, letting her kimono skirt brush up against Val. Subtle, she was not. "Just when I was starting to think I'd have to leave empty-handed, fate dropped you right into my lap. Let's find you a drink and talk in an uncrowded corner, shall we?"

His marching orders had the dance floor written on them but, in the name of LeBlanc, he'd have to compromise. Odd how this whole scenario had a slight distaste to it that he couldn't quite shake. It had all the usual elements of something he should embrace: beautiful woman, social scenario, clear interest. So he'd embrace it. "My treat. What can I get you?"

Ms. Ness fluttered her lashes. "Whiskey sour."

Yeah, she didn't seem like the cosmopolitan type. Val signaled the bartender and ordered Ms. Ness's revolting concoction, as well as a beer for himself. That he could sip for an eternity and keep his wits about him. He grabbed both drinks and guided his pink admirer to a table near the edge of the room.

"Whiskey sour, as requested, Ms. Ness." He slid the glass across the table.

"I'm Jada," she purred. "To my friends, that is."

"I wasn't sure you counted LeBlanc among your friends." He sipped his beer, watching her over the rim. She had that look about her as if you didn't want to take your eyes off her for too long in case you needed to see something coming. "Since you're anti-Xavier, I mean."

Jada pouted prettily, which she'd no doubt practiced in front of an actual mirror more than once. "I can't help it that he doesn't turn me on. You, however, do."

Funny how much of that seemed to be going around. First Sabrina and now Jada had both drifted away from Xavier out of sheer lack of interest. Shame that his brother's game had fallen off. This was the part where a caring sibling might mention it to the wounded party, strictly to help him get better. It was the right thing to do. Val smiled, the first genuine one he'd mustered since leaving Sabrina's company.

"I'm definitely not my brother," he told her smoothly. "I'd love to talk to you about showcasing your work at LeBlanc."

She sipped her drink with a deliberate pause as if weighing what he'd said. "I like the sound of a showcase. What would you do with my pieces?"

Poor choice of words. It implied a marketing strategy at the very least that he had not worked out yet. Scrambling, he spit out the first thing that came to mind. "I envision a collection of unique, exclusive designs that travels well. We could make a big splash with press if your pieces were on display for a limited time in some of our flagship stores."

Her upper lip curled slightly and not in a good way.

"What, like you'd schlepp my jewelry from store to store and tout it as a sideshow?"

"No," he corrected easily. "As the star attraction. We could limit viewing to invitation only. Very exclusive."

Somehow he'd hit on the magic words. Jada nodded slowly, a crafty glint climbing into her expression. "You'd pay me a premium for the display. Since they wouldn't be pieces for sale."

Uh, no. That hadn't been on his radar *at all*. There was little point in a display that didn't have revenue tied to it. Such a thing would benefit Jada, not LeBlanc. Holding in a groan, Val picked up the pieces of his idea and tried to reassemble them into something that would be mutually beneficial. "We could agree to that. If you signed a contract with LeBlanc to allow us exclusive distribution rights to your jewelry."

"I'm not big on contracts." Her nose wrinkled up at the concept. "Especially not when they include the word *exclusive*. That's a little tight of a handcuff."

What Jada Ness lacked in subtly, she more than made up for in shrewdness.

"Perhaps. But LeBlanc is hardly a small player in the industry. We have hundreds of retail outlets and a robust online business. LeBlanc's team would be poised to help you launch your career to the next level."

Val had no idea if his executive team would agree to any of this. He was unilaterally binding the company to this one designer in the course of a five-minute conversation. But Val had always been an all-in kind of guy, and Sabrina had coached him many times on this precise scenario. The CEO steered the ship, made the decisions and never apologized. Even when the ship hit an iceberg.

So he wouldn't hit one.

But it still felt like a huge gamble, and he'd prefer to

have a team of people making these moves. That way, no one could blame it on him if the thing went south. Of course, he wouldn't get credit in the event of a success either, but that hardly bothered him.

Jada's dark gaze found his and clung. "I might be interested in discussing contracts in a little deeper detail. Over breakfast."

"I'm free now," Val returned smoothly. "Let me get you another drink."

She reached out and snagged his arm before he could move, her fingers curling around his wrist in an approximation of the very handcuffs she'd mentioned she'd like to avoid. "I don't usually have such a difficult time getting my point across. Talk to me about contracts at breakfast. After we've spent the hours between now and then talking about everything else."

Blatantly, she dragged her tongue across her upper lip in case Val had missed the come-on. Problem was, he hadn't missed it the first time. Or the second. He'd been politely avoiding the subject because…he didn't know why. This was his wheelhouse. Take a sexy, willing woman to bed, rock her world and emerge the next morning ready to get down to business. What could possibly go wrong with this scenario?

Tell her Fine. *Say* Okay, *and tuck her into the limo.* This was a no-brainer.

"I'm otherwise engaged tonight," he spit out instead. "Any handcuffs we discuss should come without complications."

Her eyebrows rose. "Handcuffs always come with complications. It's just a matter of finding the ones you can manage. Let me know when you're ready to talk contracts. My door is always open."

All at once, Val grew weary of dancing around.

Was there something wrong with saying what you really meant? "To be clear, you're not interested in talking about an agreement with LeBlanc unless that discussion happens on the heels of me taking you to bed. No room for negotiation."

She blinked. "I wouldn't have put it so crassly. But sure. Let's lay it on the line. I'm expecting you to come along with any contacts. And that's nonnegotiable."

Wow. Okay. File that under *Be careful what you wish for.* Val was starting to get an inkling of why she'd gotten crossways with Xavier—she seemed like the type who got crossways with everyone at some point. Had she made a similar proposition to his brother and been likewise shot down?

If so, this was Val's chance to turn the tide of LeBlanc where his brother had failed. It was a unique opportunity, one he should jump on. No one would be the least bit shocked to learn he'd had to sleep his way into an exclusive contract. This woman commanded top dollar for her jewelry designs and had thus far eluded the grasp of all major players in the industry. Val could score here in more ways than one.

But the strange taste he'd had in his mouth since first coming in contact with Jada wouldn't fade. "Let me get your number. I'm here with a date tonight, and it would be bad form to leave her unescorted."

Surprisingly, Jada's expression softened. "You must be one of those good guys I've always heard about."

Yeah, that was so not Val. But if Jada wanted to think so he wouldn't correct the notion. Nodding, he took her card and walked away from the table feeling very much as if he'd narrowly escaped being sold to the highest bidder.

Sabrina wasn't hard to pick out in the crowd, despite

the fact that she'd wedged herself into a corner as if trying to hide. For God knew what reason, that made him smile. In that dress, she couldn't possibly escape the notice of a single eye in the room, least of all his.

"That looks like the face of someone who had a rousing success," she said brightly, by way of greeting when she saw him approach, and he was so blinded by her that he only nodded.

What was he supposed to do, tell her the star designer had pounced on the idea of bedding LeBlanc's CEO in exchange for exclusive rights?

This corner of the room had fewer people in it, likely because it was the farthest spot from the bar. A decorative urn stood at Sabrina's back, almost taller than she was. Val liked this spot. Dimmer lighting, fewer prying eyes. Interesting shadows. "She agreed to talk to me about an exclusive contract. I'd call that a success."

"That's great." Sabrina glanced over his shoulder and back again. "But not now? If you want my advice, you should strike while the iron is hot."

Suddenly, his date's constant insistence on removing him from her presence grated on him. That was at least half his problem tonight—the woman he wished to be bedding wasn't biting, and he'd never dealt well with rejection. "She didn't want to. I'm here with you, and I've barely said two words to you thus far. Dance with me."

"Ask Jada Ness," she insisted, apparently either clueless that his temper had started swirling, or she'd realized it and didn't care. "You should have already."

"No," he growled. "I shouldn't have. The only person I need to dance with right now is you."

Without waiting for more protests, he snaked a hand around her waist and drew her against him, settling her into the grooves of his body. Holy hell, she felt amazing. Exactly the right palate cleanser after the encounter with Jada.

"Right here?" she squeaked, but her hands had drifted into place at his hips, maybe by accident, but he didn't think so.

"I'm striking while the iron is hot," he murmured in her ear as he drew her closer, still with a firm hand at the small of her bare back. "Close your mouth and dance, Sabrina."

She did both, and he tucked away that huge concession for later, when he could fully examine it.

The jazz music was slow and sensuous and perfect for this little unpopulated corner of the room. Swaying to it effortlessly, he turned Sabrina in a circle to make it seem like dancing was really the goal when in reality, he simply wanted to be touching her. The bare skin under his palm tantalized him into wishing he could let his hand drift further south, but they were still in public, and he didn't think she'd appreciate him groping her.

Maybe later.

"So what was her temperature?" Sabrina asked.

Smoking hot. "You mean toward the contract discussion? Fine," he lied. "I got her card, and I'll call her tomorrow."

Or next week. *After* he'd done some more research into whether her conditions were worth it. And he had time to get over whatever was wrong with him that made him unable to fathom taking her up on her offer.

Eight

All at once, Sabrina felt the giant porcelain urn brush her spine. Val had guided her into the darkest part of the corner, where the urn shadowed the space, a true testament to how befuddled her senses got when he touched her because she hadn't even registered the movement.

It shouldn't have been such a shock to glance up into his dark gaze and register the stark need in his expression. Neither should she have swayed forward. But her body cried out to be closer to him, and she'd been cold for so long.

Val's lips claimed hers a beat later, warming her exactly as she'd hoped. And then the heat spread like molten molasses through her blood, sensitizing everything in its path, as the master of seduction kissed her.

She should stop him, step back. But the urn was in the way, and she let herself relax against it as the firm press of Val trapped her. Delicious. She couldn't pretend she hadn't dreamed of this, over and over. Well, not *this*. She couldn't have imagined how truly hot a kiss from Val could get, not after the way-too short introduction to his magic she'd gotten in the park.

This was something else. Bold, unapologetic. So *not* the way Xavier kissed that it threw her for a loop a second time. Why she'd even thought there might be similarities between the brothers she'd never know, but they might as well be distant cousins instead of twins for all their differences.

Val's mouth worked across hers with masterful power, and she fell into the sensation, unable to stop herself from greedily sucking up all he was offering. He spoke to her at a visceral level as if the layers of skin separating them didn't exist and he had the power to winnow his way to her core without breaking a sweat. Maybe because she'd welcomed him in.

Seeming to sense that she'd be a willing participant to more, he tilted her head with one tender hand to her jaw and took her impossibly deeper. With one long stroke of his tongue against hers, he dissolved her bones, and she would have melted to the floor if he hadn't been holding her tight. So tightly, every curve of her body nestled against his, and it was all so hot that she couldn't breathe.

That's when she knew she was in trouble. Simple desire she could handle, could easily walk away from. Val had never been simple.

She pushed on his shoulders, and it took a moment for him to register it, but then he immediately stepped back, releasing her. Val let his hands drop to his sides, and she nearly wept as his heat left her.

But that's what she'd wanted. Or, rather, what she was trying really hard to convince herself she'd wanted.

"We can't keep doing this," she stated firmly.

"I completely agree. Next time, we'll be behind closed doors." His rough voice thrilled through her, and there was no mistaking the intensity of his desire. For *her*. Not Jada Ness, the gorgeous designer who had been eating him alive with her hungry eyes.

No matter how hard she'd pushed him in that direction, he'd kept his distance from the man-eating blonde and worked his way to Sabrina in under fifteen minutes. She'd practically gift wrapped the woman, to no avail.

That alone had been enough for her to ignore the dangers of falling into his arms. She couldn't do that again. He'd show his true stripes soon enough, and then where would she be?

"There's no next time. That was nice, but we're through with that."

"We haven't started anything that we could conceivably end," he growled. "Trust me. You'd know if we had, and you wouldn't be labeling it *nice*."

Of that she had no doubt. "No, I'd call it a mistake. I shouldn't have let you kiss me."

"There was plenty of you in that kiss. You weren't *letting* me do anything."

She shrugged, praying that he'd buy her nonchalance. What *was* it about Val that pushed so many of her buttons? "I already admitted it was nice. It wasn't a chore. We're just not right for each other."

The music piping through the sound system from the live band in the corner moved from fast to sultry as he cocked a brow and crossed his arms. "You're making stuff up as you go along, aren't you? First you don't date clients, then you agree to a date that you insisted on pretending isn't one, and now we're not right for each other. Tell me, will I ever get a straight answer out of you about what your objection is to taking this thing between us to a natural conclusion?"

"Probably not," she said with false cheer that she didn't feel in the slightest. No man had ever put her as far off balance as Val, and she wasn't feeling particularly charitable about it. "I'm cycling through all my tried and true lines until I find one that works on you."

"I'll save you some time. None of them work. I've got some definite ideas about what we should be doing right now instead of hashing this out, and I refuse to believe we're not going to get there once I dismantle all of your objections. So, okay." He circled his finger in a get-on-with-this motion. "Let's have it. Give me what you've got. Both barrels."

She almost laughed, but that would only encourage him. Then she did a double take at the expression on his face. "You want all my lines up front? Is that seriously what you're asking me?"

"Yep. Start talking."

His crossed arms began to irritate her. Why? No clue, but he wore this smug smile that said he had every confidence he'd blast apart whatever challenge she laid down as if her will on the matter didn't count. Therefore, regardless of what she told him, he'd figure out how to convince her otherwise, or at least that's what he'd sold himself on.

So she didn't deflect him with one of her many and varied rules designed to keep her heart whole. She went with the cold, hard truth.

"My father cheated on my mother. Constantly." Catching his gaze, she held him fast, forcing him into her hell. He'd asked for it. She wasn't going to pull any punches. "He came home smelling like perfume, with lipstick on his collar. Unapologetically. Never even tried to hide it. I had to listen to my mother cry herself to sleep. I swore I'd never put myself in that position, swore I could find a man who would be loyal and steadfast, honoring his marriage vows. Surely it can't be that hard, I told myself."

Val shook his head, his good humor draining away instantly. "I'm sorry, Sabrina. That's a rotten thing to deal with."

"Oh, no. That was a rotten thing for my mother to deal with." The low, short laugh that escaped her throat had not one ounce of humor in it. "The part that I had to deal with was when I found out how wrong I was about not ending up in that position."

That's when she'd really learned what it felt like to be the woman on the other side of the bedroom door. When she'd learned why her mother had stayed. Your brain and your heart argued with each other so much that you couldn't sort truth from fiction. You couldn't leave because maybe you were wrong. Maybe it was all a horrible mistake, and you didn't want to make other, bigger mistakes.

And then came the point when it wasn't possible to keep lying to yourself any longer and you had to make choices with cold reason instead of hot emotion. She didn't do hot emotion anymore.

He flinched, but before he could open his mouth again, she held up a finger. "It's odd how being cheated on changes your perspective about everything. I realized my problem was that I'd been looking for a man I could trust. Instead, I should have been looking for a man I could replace."

"Ouch." The look on his face did have a bit of a pained quality to it. "Would it be redundant to say I'm sorry again?"

"And unnecessary." She lifted one shoulder. "I'm over it."

She wasn't. She'd never be over it. How did you erase the bone-deep knowledge that you'd chosen someone to love who could betray you like that? It made every decision suspect, especially when it came to men.

"Don't be cavalier," he countered fiercely. "It's not okay."

A little taken aback, she stared at him. "It is okay. It has to be. I've moved on."

"Have you?" His dark eyes glittered, more black than blue in the low light, sucking her with mesmerizing depth that she couldn't look away from all at once. "You told me that story to explain why you continually shuck me off. That's the opposite of moving on."

"That's *how* I moved on. Now I only date men I can easily get rid of." She jerked her head toward the door. "But if you want to be a man I get rid of, let's go."

He didn't move. "So, let me get this straight. You won't go on a real date with me because I might be worth keeping around. I like where this is headed."

Instead of backing off like he should have—like she'd intended for him to do—he'd gotten a whole lot closer, crowding into her space with his pretty cheekbones and hard body that was made for a woman's hands.

"Please." She rolled her eyes, but the quaver in her voice might have ruined the effect. "You're my client. That's why I can't get rid of you."

Leaning in, he brushed a strand of hair from her cheek and the rest of the partygoers over his shoulder faded away. "But you practically dared me to leave with you in the same breath as telling me you'd be looking for the easiest, fastest way to call it quits afterward. That's a risky challenge, Sabrina, especially since that might be precisely what I'm looking for."

She shook her head. "I told you that story so you'd understand that I date cautiously. I haven't been seeing anyone since I split from Xavier and neither am I looking for someone new. My job takes a lot of my time, and I like it. Men simply aren't high on my list of priorities."

Val made a noise in his throat. "Because the men you've dated are subpar. My brother included. You clearly need someone to show you what you've been missing."

"I'm not missing anything," she insisted. "I'm just not interested in dealing with the problems."

"If that's your mindset, you're definitely not doing it right." He scowled. "Wow. I had no idea Xavier was such a dud in the romance department. That's a crying shame. No worries. I'll have your thinking reset in no time at all."

Was this the part where she laughed or cried? "I wasn't worried. This is a conversation about why we're not going to be dating. So you can leave with your ego intact, and I can go on being your coach. No harm, no foul."

"Oh, no, sweetheart." He *tsked*. "That's not what we're talking about at all. This is a conversation about how you've been treated like trash by men who should be lined up and shot. I'll get all the names later. Much later." He palmed her hand and raised it to his lips, caressing the soft skin with his mouth. "For now, it's obvious to me that you have had a lack of passion in your life. I feel a distinct need to romance you so well that you have to beg me to stop."

She shivered as the things he was doing to her hand pulled on strings in places that would be impossible for him to physically touch. This was the fundamental problem with Val. He dove headfirst into everything, and she had a feeling he'd do the same with her—well enough that he'd make it difficult for her to ever surface. That kind of passion wasn't on the table. "That doesn't even make any sense. You ask someone to stop something that you *don't* like."

"Then don't ask me to stop."

There it was. Val's challenge to her. Either she lied and said she didn't like the way he spoke to her, touched her, pursued her…or she did as he suggested and closed her mouth. Or door number three.

"I have to," she whispered. "This is where I draw the line, Val. I'm trying to do a job, and anything personal will get in the way. Period."

He nodded but didn't drop her hand. Of course not. What had she expected, that he'd actually listen to her?

"That's where we're going to agree to disagree," he told her with a wicked smile. "Passion is everything. In life. In our jobs. Having it, experiencing it…that can only make you better at your job. But I'm willing to concede that tonight isn't the night to convince you of that."

Bemused, she shut her eyes against the things shooting through his expression and avoided asking questions, which he'd likely welcome. Except she didn't want any explanations as to how he'd make good on something so ludicrous as a claim that letting herself fall into the passion he'd promised would increase her coaching efficiency.

As it stood, she'd already envisioned with stark clarity how easily she could transition from telling him what to do in the boardroom to telling him what she wanted him to do in the bedroom. The problem was, she could not envision what would happen after that.

The morning after the design event, Sabrina showed up in Val's office at 7:00 a.m. as expected. What he had not expected was the hard shell that she'd erected between them.

God, no. All the work he'd done to dismantle that. Gone. Poof!

"Good morning," she called from the doorway, her tone carrying a wealth of subtle messages. All of them were of the *Back off* variety, and that was not going to work.

Somehow she'd managed to put that layer of frost between them again—after such a hot kiss, it should have melted permanently. If he wasn't so pissed off about it, he might find a way to admire her ability to move so easily into the professional zone.

Last night should have put them in a completely different place. He'd worked through her defenses, kissing her thoroughly and then—*bam!*—ran smack into that truth he'd sought. She wasn't so much opposed to sleeping with a client as she was opposed to sleeping with anyone she perceived as a threat to her carefully reconstructed emotional center that some jackass in her past had destroyed.

Val was a threat. How, he wasn't quite sure yet. But she'd been painfully clear about that. Which meant not only did he have to tread so much more carefully with her as his coach he also had to be extra vigilant about her wounds.

Never had he been so invested in a woman and yet had so many impossible roadblocks. If he was smart, he'd forget about Sabrina and worry about LeBlanc. He had an inheritance to win and a score to settle with the ghost of his father. Shouldn't that be enough for him to worry about for the foreseeable future?

Apparently it wasn't, because the odds of him backing off from what he knew would be something amazing with Sabrina were zero.

Last night had whetted his appetite to dive deeper below her surface. Only something precious would be so heavily guarded, and he ached to learn more about her, to show her that she didn't have to hide behind her frost. Not with him. She could trust him. He knew a thing or two about dealing with rejection. Abandonment. Pain.

Connection and romance and passion between two people fixed all of that. It was the antithesis. She'd never learned that. He wanted to be the one to teach her.

He watched her as she crossed the room from the door to the desk and sat back, drinking in the beautiful body that he hadn't gotten nearly enough of under his hands last night. "Good morning."

She slid into the chair on the opposite side of his desk, her all-business face on. "I thought we'd talk about the strategy for Jada Ness."

The last person he wanted to talk about. The whole concept of securing Jada Ness as a designer for LeBlanc should thrill him—it was a slam dunk. He'd rather discuss the concept of root canals. "I thought we'd talk about the strategy for Friday night. I'm cooking for you. At my place."

Sabrina didn't even crack a smile. "Jada Ness is a bit slippery. She's a brilliant designer, highly sought after. I read a couple of comments on social-media sites that led me to believe that her presence at the event last night was highly unusual. You're in a great position with her already. Capitalize on that."

"I'm thinking Thai," he mused and contemplated her. "You look like the type to order pad thai at restaurants, so I'll go with red curry shrimp. I know this great Asian market where the little old lady behind the fish counter likes me, so I get the biggest shrimp."

Leaning forward slightly, Sabrina put one hand on the desk. "Normally I'm not an advocate of carte blanche, but I would highly encourage you to give Ms. Ness whatever she wants. No price is too high to secure her for LeBlanc. I'm not a huge fan of Thai, by the way."

He nearly did a double take at how she'd tacked that information on to the end but caught himself. So that's how she wanted to play it. He probably shouldn't mention how far into his space she'd leaned either. Or she might crawl back behind her shell.

"No price, huh? Would it surprise you to learn that Ms. Ness wants a showcase at LeBlanc flagship stores in each major city? None of the pieces would be for sale, just on display. I can't get her to budge on that."

"Really? That's what she suggested?"

"No, it was my off the cuff idea, one I'd blurted out before thinking it through fully, and she jumped on it." Val shrugged. "Fortunately for you, I'm even better at Italian than I am Thai. If you bring the wine, I'll pick you up at seven."

"It's a tough sell to the board, given that there's no automatic revenue. Unless…" Sabrina cocked a brow and paused. "Give her the showcase, but stipulate that the pieces go on the block at the end."

"What, like an auction?" Intrigued against his will, Val crossed his arms and contemplated how well that would work for LeBlanc. He'd done a few auctions in his day at LBC, high-profile things that generated some buzz, but he'd had to procure the items himself by going around to local businesses and begging people for donations.

This would be totally different. The auction would be pure profit after paying the overhead and would get people excited about the idea of owning other Jada Ness pieces once LeBlanc started carrying her line.

With a nod, Sabrina let her lips curve. The last of her frost vanished. "It was a throwaway expression. I only meant that the jewelry would be for sale, but I like the way you think. Italian food always works."

"You got me thinking in that direction. We're a good team." He didn't dare upset this delicate balance they'd achieved by reaching out to touch her like he wished he could. Though, how he'd gotten her to admit what kind of food she liked in the midst of a conversation about Jada Ness, he had no idea. It worked for them though. She didn't respond well to being railroaded. Noted. "I would go with a Chianti, if I was the one picking the wine."

"We are a good team." She said it like she might be a little shocked by that realization, but he was so thrilled with the admission, he managed to hold back a smile.

Instead he pulled out the mining contracts. "Since you're on board with that idea, maybe you can help me figure out a strategy for working with the president of Botswana."

Sabrina's pretty eyes widened at the size of the binders he'd pulled from his desk drawer. "I can't recall the last time I've seen something printed out that was that large."

"Xavier didn't say, but I suspect that Botswana doesn't do a lot of online business."

After the depressing setback with Sabrina last night, sleep hadn't come easily, and the mining contracts had haunted him. He'd made almost no headway on determining how to handle them other than to read through the previous set.

Everything in the new ones seemed in order, but some of the clauses had been changed, seemingly in the favor of the client's federal government, but what did Val know? Maybe those benefits had been a verbal stipulation of the last contract.

"That's way out of my realm of expertise, Val."

Oh, he did like it when she called him Val while biting down on her lush bottom lip like that. "Mine too. But when was the last time you coached someone through how to manage a bohemian jewelry designer? Never, I'd wager. Yet you did it. You think strategically as a matter of course. If you were the CEO, what would you do?"

Something filtered through her expression that warmed him unexpectedly. He couldn't put his finger on it, but she'd lit up, as if he'd crossed the gym at the school dance to approach a row of wallflowers and she'd been his choice.

Of course she was. Hadn't he made that clear?

Or perhaps he hadn't. He'd spouted a few lines about romance last night but, thus far, he hadn't really followed through. Granted, she'd been a prickly audience this morning, but that didn't excuse him from giving her what she needed—which was romance, loads of it. The woman did nothing for fun and had little in her life that could conceivably pull her away from work, obviously.

He drank in her expression, intrigued by this button he'd unwittingly pushed.

"I'd hire an expert," she said almost immediately.

"Like I did with you."

It wasn't a bad idea. But where did one find an expert in diamond mines? You'd think the walls of this building would house the premier minds on the subject. Except Xavier had been the LeBlanc executive most well versed in these types of contracts, and he'd previously been clear about his role in handling them.

Which left Val twisting in the wind. "Give me your backup plan. What would you do if an expert wasn't available?"

After a long pause that he didn't dare interrupt because he enjoyed watching her think, she said, "I might go to Botswana. And get the lay of the land. Talk to some people, including the president of the country. Explain that you're filling in and need to meet the players personally. I've done some research into Botswanan culture and I believe they would appreciate that."

He raised his brows. "You've researched Botswanan culture?"

"I do a lot of research. It's important for me to have a wide variety of knowledge."

Since she'd just demonstrated the necessity of that, he couldn't argue. "I think that might be my new favorite thing about you."

And that solidified it in his mind. Sabrina was the most exciting woman he'd met in a long time. Maybe ever. That kind of smart appealed to him on so many levels. Never would he admit it but he didn't hate how she kept presenting him with a set of unusual challenges. Nothing worth having came easily. Why should this be any different?

Sabrina flushed under her carefully applied cosmetics. "You can't say things like that."

"Why not? I like you, and I'm not usually shy about expressing that. You're an intelligent woman who thinks before opening her mouth. It's outrageously sexy."

She blinked and stared at him. "You can't say things like that either."

There she went again, making things up as she went along to avoid feeling anything about anyone. "I can and I will. I would get used to that if I were you. Come Friday night, I'm going to say a lot of things like that."

And neither would he allow her to back out. He was onto her game of sliding agreements to dinner in between business conversations, almost as if she couldn't own the decision outright. That was okay with Val, as long as she agreed.

She shook her head. "I didn't agree to dinner. I simply mentioned that I like Italian. We're working together, and it's not a good idea to get involved."

"The hell it's not," he growled. "If you have to tell yourself all of that to make it okay in your head for us to eat a meal together, fine. But I'm setting expectations ahead of time. You're coming to dinner, and it's a date."

It was also a concession on his part. Jada wanted Val to come with her contract, but given Sabrina's history, he didn't for a second believe he could sleep with both women and come out unscathed. Neither did he want to. Sabrina was more than enough for him to handle at the moment, thanks. He'd have to find a way to finesse Jada into signing a contract *without* the corporeal benefits she'd tossed around.

How hard could it be to balance the two?

Nine

Normally, Sabrina left LeBlanc shortly after she and Val went over the things on his agenda for the day. She provided insight and advice, worked through sticky HR issues with him and left as soon as his day ramped up around eight o'clock.

As much as he was paying her, she'd have stayed all day, especially now that Val had started wearing the suits he'd bought. The tailor he'd selected must have made some sort of deal with the devil. There was no other explanation for how perfectly made the suits were or how exquisitely they encased Val's long, lean body.

She might have drooled the first time she caught sight of him in the dark blue one that matched his eyes.

But he never asked her to stay. He'd been the one to set the schedule, citing the fact that he more often than not ended up in meetings for hours on end that would bore her. Leaving worked for her because she could go to her little office and hash out pitches to other prospective clients. Answer some emails. Read Sheryl Sandberg's *Lean In* for the fifth time.

Or at least that was the theory.

Val's high-handed invitation to dinner with the promise of Italian food and seduction had crawled across her nerves, then parked at the base of her spine until it became almost like a living thing. No matter which way she sat at her ergonomic chair, it wasn't comfortable. And her shoes started pinching her toes after five minutes. Which was ludicrous, given that they were sandals with nothing more than a half-inch-wide strap of leather across her foot.

Val had finally driven her around the bend.

She hadn't agreed to a date. Val had gotten confused. What had possessed her to counter his suggestion of Thai with Italian instead of a flat out *no*? Okay, well she *knew*. She'd been fantasizing for days about what that man could do with a simmering pot of spaghetti sauce and about five feet of clear countertop that he could boost her up onto.

She couldn't go. She should call him and make it clear. No date. What in the world did she even have to wear? *Nothing*. Except…the short, kind of flimsy, filmy skirt she'd bought at Nordstrom with absolutely no purpose in mind other than she liked the way she looked in it—that could work. Maybe. If she was actually considering going, which she was not. But if she did, the skirt would bunch up around her waist easily and—

Her phone rang and Val's name flashed across it. Heat climbed into her cheeks. Had he read her mind or something? He couldn't possibly know that she'd envisioned something completely filthy happening on his kitchen counter or that she'd been cursing the lack of details since she'd never been to his house.

"Sabrina Corbin," she croaked into the phone. "I mean *Hi*."

Val laughed. "I changed my mind. I like it when you answer *Sabrina Corbin*. It's sexy."

And she liked it when he said her name, but that would be counterproductive to mention. What was wrong with her? A couple of kisses from a man shouldn't have put her brain in permanent frappé mode. Except it was Val, not some random man. He *liked* her. And had no qualms about spelling that out.

No man had ever said that to her before. Men did not like her. They liked power and ambition and dominating weaker people. Since she did her level best to play with the big dogs, she'd have said she liked those things too, except sometimes the chill she exuded was all an act.

With Val, she could do things differently. Not only could but had orders to. Maybe she could admit that sometimes it was nice to be admired. *To be wanted* for no other reason than uncomplicated desire.

Nice, but not a necessity. He was a man. She couldn't show him any weakness, or he'd exploit it.

"I'll answer my phone how I please," she informed him and cursed how breathy her voice sounded. That needed to stop, or he really would clue in that she had naughty thoughts on her mind. "No matter what you say."

"You were going to anyway," he teased. "But I didn't call to talk phone etiquette yet again."

"What is it this time?" She tilted her chair back and stretched her feet out. Oddly, her toes weren't feeling all that cramped any longer. "Spider in your office?"

"Yeah, as a matter of fact. Will you come by and take it outside for me?"

She heard the smile in his voice, and it put one on her face, as well. He couldn't see her and therefore had no idea how amusing she found him. "I kill spiders, FYI. I do not knit them blankets and find them a cozy place to spin a new web."

"I can work with that. How fast can you be here?"

"Are you seriously asking me to come by?" Her feet slipped off the desk and hit the floor. Mentally she re-arranged the rest of her afternoon as fast as she could, which pretty much meant kissing the idea of rearranging her filing cabinets goodbye. Oh well.

"I need to talk to you about a…thing."

"I'll see if I can squeeze you in."

It only took about fifteen minutes to drive from her office to LeBlanc, even with the midday traffic, but it felt like a million years. "A thing." That could be any number of problems, and she wished he'd given her some kind of clue what they were dealing with here.

When she strolled into Val's office a little before two o'clock, he'd taken off his suit jacket and draped it along the back of his chair. When he glanced up at her from under his lashes, the long sensual pull in her center was so strong it rendered her mute for a moment.

What was it about Val that was so affecting? Xavier had never plucked at her insides like this. And the two were practically identical in build and features. It was ev-erything else that marked them as vastly different men. *That* was why she couldn't go on a real date with Val; he made her feel too much, and that couldn't be good.

"What's up?" she murmured because she had to say something to break the sudden and intense tension.

"I talked to Jada." Val pushed his rolled-up sleeves higher up his forearms. "She's a no-go."

"She's a…what?" Sabrina swallowed and pushed back

all the inappropriate longings for her client. This was what happened when she lost her focus. "She didn't look like a no-go last night. What happened?"

"The auction idea happened. She doesn't have any pieces that she thinks will work for that."

His voice seemed even and sure, but she heard the slightest rasp of hesitation in his tone, as if he'd paused before blurting out something he didn't think he should. She knew that pause. It was the sound of a man with secrets.

She pounced on it, watching him carefully for other tells. They all had them. "What did she say would work then?"

There. Val's mouth twitched. "She didn't."

He was lying. She could feel it in her spine, where the greasy oil slick started to spread, leaching into her stomach lining where it would begin to eat away at her. Oh, thank *God* she had listened to her instincts and stayed far away from getting intimate with Val.

"So you called her to say you had some ideas, and she shot them all down and then hung up. Is that what happened?"

He cocked his head, and one long strand of hair fell into his eyes. "Something like that. Is that a problem?"

That's right. Turn it back on me so I don't ask too many questions that would expose your lies. Val was just like all the rest. "I don't see why you're taking all of this so calmly. This is your inheritance on the line. Seems like you're the one who should be having a problem."

"That's why I called you. It's definitely a problem."

His expression was so flat. She couldn't get a bead on what was happening here, and the uncertainty prickled across her neck. Why couldn't he be truthful? "Then tell me what we should do about it."

"I'm not sure *what* to do. I can't admit that to them." He jerked his head to the office full of people outside his door. "They're looking to me for answers, not more questions. I need to increase revenue, and Jada Ness should have been the ticket. I can't get her for the price she's asking."

His willingness to be vulnerable with her struck her sideways. What on earth was he lying about then? "Wait. I thought she gave you a flat *no*. What was her price?"

All at once, Val stood, unwinding from his chair. He came around the desk into her space, at the same time spilling his masculine vibe into places inside her. That shouldn't be a thing, but it wouldn't work to deny that she had a physical reaction when he got this close.

Watching him walk shouldn't be such a treat. He barely took three steps to get to where she stood in the center of the room. But he moved with such purpose. Lots of men did, but usually they were moving toward the next target. He moved for the sole purpose of showcasing his body and how comfortable he was in it.

He should put the jacket on. Without it, he was entirely too touchable. The bare skin on his forearms begged for her fingers, and she nearly reached out before remembering that he'd yet to answer her.

Neither did he seem in a hurry to talk about Jada Ness's price.

"I'm afraid I lied," he murmured out of the blue.

Of course he had. This was not news. He was a man, wasn't he? The real front-page story lay in the fact that he'd admitted it without her calling him on it.

Which mattered not at all. She could not deal with lies. Disappointed that her radar hadn't fizzled in the slightest, she contemplated him. "About what?"

"I didn't call you to talk about Jada. I wanted to see you."

Oh. That wasn't precisely a lie. Her ire dissolved in a hurry, and the earnestness in his expression melted her spine a little. The touch of his palm on her jaw did the rest of the trick. "You could have just told me that."

What was it about him that had her so mixed up and off-kilter? No other man had so quickly gotten back into her good graces. He wasn't a liar and a cheat, and she'd do well to remember not to paint him with the brush for other men. It wasn't fair to Val.

He laughed softly. "Yeah, because you have such a good track record of accepting it when I reach out to you on a personal level."

"Maybe you're not reaching far enough."

His brows rose, and the palm on her jaw flattened to cup it with a bit more purpose, as if he meant to draw her forward into a kiss. She stared at him, daring him to read into her statement. But this was Val, who didn't have to be goaded into anything.

His thumb brushed across her lips a moment before his mouth did, and she fell into the kiss with abandon that had no place in a busy office building. She didn't care. They were insulated here behind closed doors in this oasis of Val's domain, and everything faded away as he deepened the kiss, shifting her head with his firm hand. The noise she made in her throat was pure pleasure as Val washed through her, enlivening everything he touched—which was all of her.

Heat bloomed in her center and rushed outward, gobbling up her insides as it spread.

It was almost enough to make her forget that this expert kiss had also served to change the subject. Should she care that Val had such slick moves? She tried to. But then he levered her mouth open with his and claimed her, his tongue hot with need against hers, and she didn't protest when he swept her into his arms. The embrace aligned them perfectly, and he rubbed a thigh against hers with so much intensity that she saw stars.

A small taste of what he had in store for her if she got over herself and went to dinner like a normal person. She could handle this. There was no reason Val had to be anything special. *Get In and Get Out* could still be the order of the day, no matter how effective his seduction techniques were.

A knock on the door split them apart instantly. Val stepped back, dropping his hands from her waist, and she hated the loss of his touch so much that she almost whirled to take the interloper to task.

But of course she couldn't. Instead, she smoothed her hands over her skirt, hoping that her lipstick wasn't smeared all over her face. Fortunately, she hadn't left any of it on Val's, so that was a small win.

Val's admin poked her head in the door. "Oh, hello, Ms. Corbin. I didn't realize you were here. Sorry for the interruption. Mr. LeBlanc, Karl Bruner asked me to move the New England meeting. He's going to be out of the office next week. The only opening you have is now, so I told him I'd check. I can tell him to reschedule if you like."

"No, I'm free. Send the meeting details to my calendar."

The admin nodded and disappeared. Within seconds, Val's phone buzzed.

"Duty calls," Sabrina said wryly. She shouldn't be wishing they could pick up that kiss where they left off. Where could it lead in the middle of the day?

Asking that question led to nothing other than wondering what he could do with a Friday night with no interruption. No. She was *not* considering dinner.

"Come to the meeting with me." His dark eyes flashed. "I'd hoped to have time to talk to you about this New England situation before, but obviously the timing leaves a lot to be desired."

His tone tripped her radar. "You have a concern about it? What's the situation?"

Grimly, he shook his head. "That division is hemorrhaging money. The meeting is with division management and the CFO to talk numbers. I don't know what they're going to ultimately decide, but apparently Xavier has already approved whatever measures it takes to get the division under control."

"Guess what? He's not here. You are. You get to decide."

How many times was she going to have to explain this to him? He didn't have a domineering bone in his body. Instead, he seduced and conquered. Not a bad strategy all the way around, but it wasn't one he could use on LeBlanc's c-suite. He had to come out swinging and keep swinging until he hit the ball out of the park.

Flashing her a brief smile, he snagged her hand. "This is why you need to be in the room. To remind me that I have the gold, so I get to make the rules."

"I'm not going to speak up in the middle of a tense meeting about a failing division!"

"What if I ask you to? I'm in charge." His lips quirked. "Right? I get to decide whether you speak, and I say you do. Can't have it both ways."

"Fine."

Had that come out too quickly? Secretly, she could hardly hold in her glee. This would be an opportunity for her to experience a real, live meeting with executives. She rarely got so lucky as to see both her coaching mentee in action and an unfiltered corporate problem-solving session designed to get results.

But she couldn't walk into the room holding the CEO's hand. She pulled hers loose and followed him to the meeting room specified on his calendar, donning the most professional expression she could muster. Difficult given that she'd just been kissed by the man taking the head chair. He'd shrugged on his jacket as they left the office and, no, it was not better.

Val looked sexy as sin in a suit. Or out of one. Heat flushed through her face and her body simultaneously as she tried valiantly to erase the images that had sprung into her mind.

But that wasn't going to happen, she reminded herself. Ever. He was a client, the brother of an ex, a dangerous, passionate player who probably didn't even know how to spell *monogamy*. She had rules about all of the above for good reason.

But, all of a sudden, she couldn't remember why.

The rest of the meeting invitees filed into the boardroom, shooting her curious glances, but no one said anything. They all knew who she was and likely had guessed why she'd been asked to attend. Val had been extremely open about his coaching sessions—against her advice—but that decision worked in her favor here since she was storming into their realm unannounced.

"Karl." Val addressed the middle-aged man in a silver suit about halfway down the table. "You asked to move this meeting. I assume there's a pressing reason we need to discuss New England."

From her research, Sabrina knew Karl Bruner helmed the division as its vice-president. The grim slashes of his eyebrows told her he hadn't brought good news to the meeting. She listened as he spelled out the bleak bottom line, citing a rival chain of jewelers who were eating LeBlanc's lunch in same-store sales and had expansion plans that LeBlanc couldn't hope to match, given that their existing retail outlets weren't even turning a profit.

The whole discussion thrilled her, or it would if the direction hadn't put a crimp in Val's mouth that she didn't like. He'd probably followed the money talk well enough, but she could see in the set of his shoulders that he didn't have any good suggestions to turn the tide.

The CFO cleared his throat. "I hate to bring it up again. But we need to talk closure."

Karl Bruner steepled his fingers. "That's the easy way out. Cutting our losses will put LeBlanc in the black, sure, but it will ultimately hurt our image as a family-friendly employer."

"What are you saying?" Val interrupted, a shadow darkening his eyes. "Closing stores is an option? As in layoffs?"

He spat the word out as if it had been mixed with poison, and the vibe in the room grew teeth. The other executives glanced at each other with discomfort and uneasiness. Sabrina sat on her hands. Not her business if this meeting was about to get dirty.

It was a legit strategy, though. One she'd missed as having been on the table, since this was the first she'd heard of it. But that path had Xavier written all over it. Probably it had been his first choice.

The CFO nodded. "It's not ideal. There would be severance costs and asset liquidation. But the numbers work on paper to put us on the positive side for the year."

That was the wrong thing to say. Val stood and carefully placed his hands on the table to lean in, speaking to the room at large. "Let me give you some numbers, Alvin. Three: the average number of kids a single mother is looking to feed when she comes to my food pantry. Twelve: the number of hours between meals for most homeless people. Twenty: the average night-time low in the northeast during winter, which is fatal if you don't have a place to live. When you don't have a job, these numbers are your life in some instances. One instance is too many. If you like those numbers, I have some more."

The other executives blinked, but Sabrina had a feeling it was due to the unexpected turn the conversation had taken and not because they were fighting tears the way she was.

Passion flowed from Val as he spoke. It wound through the very atmosphere, painting a bleak picture with a small ray of hope that he personally gave people. She'd never donated to a place like LBC before, but it shot to the top of her to-do list. Val knew these stats off the top of his head because he lived it. He *cared*. LBC wasn't just a job to him, nor could he treat LeBlanc like one.

Willing him to take a step back, she sent him messages via osmosis that would likely never hit the mark, but neither did she think she should step in, not even to tell him to table the discussion for another day. She had a much greater respect for his passion now than she ever had, but making emotional decisions about corporate health wasn't the best plan. He needed to cool off.

Fortunately, the chief operations officer either caught her silent messages or had already arrived at the conclusion that nothing more would be decided today. He raised his hands, which had the effect of drawing everyone's attention away from Val. "We clearly need some more raw numbers to present to the group. I think speaking in abstracts is not the best plan. Alvin," he said to the CFO. "Get us a projection of where the sale of those assets would put us for the year. Facts speak the loudest. We'll reconvene after Karl's surgery."

"My answer will not change," Val said flatly. Clearly he had not intercepted Sabrina's subliminal messages. "I will never agree to layoffs. Period."

Val crossed his arms, looking every inch like a man who would fight these store closures with every fiber of his being, and her heart cracked, opening up and greedily sucking him in. It didn't matter what the numbers said. He'd weighed everything against his ideals and, even though it affected his inheritance directly, he'd stuck with what he knew was the right thing. That was *powerful*. Sexy. Affecting. Much more so than a man who cut a wide swath through the corporate world while seeking his own ambition.

Valentino LeBlanc was absolutely not her type. He was better.

Ten

Val canceled his sessions with Sabrina for the rest of the week in favor of diving into the numbers the CFO had provided for the New England assets. It was a toss-up whether the absence of Sabrina or being forced to review accounting reports for hours was harder to take.

The numbers sucked. No two ways about it—the division had been poorly managed for quite some time. At LBC, most of the people involved were volunteers and Val rarely had to deal with personnel issues.

How did Xavier do this on a regular basis and keep his stomach lining intact? Nerves of steel. Practice. A gift for compartmentalizing. Whatever the secret, Val didn't have it.

And there was something completely wrong with the world if Val could find even a smidge of admiration for his brother. There were no heroics involved—Xavier had a deep freeze where his heart used to be, obviously. No mystery there. The real mystery lay in how his brother would survive at LBC, where being coldhearted wasn't considered a virtue.

For the tenth or twelfth time in the last hour, Val reached for his phone to call Sabrina. And yet again didn't dial, even though hearing her voice might steady him. There was little she could coach him on at the moment and, frankly, he didn't need the distraction. New England was hard enough to handle without splitting his attention.

Though he couldn't claim to be 100 percent focused, not when he had a date tomorrow night with Ms. Corbin. No, he wasn't deluded enough to call it that to her face or even bring it up again. That gave her an opening to say no. He'd already blocked his calendar so he could leave the office early and go grocery shopping. Nothing short of a government ban on diamonds would be allowed to interfere. And even that could theoretically wait until Monday.

The desk phone beeped, then his admin's voice spilled from the speaker. "Mr. LeBlanc, you have a visitor. A Ms. Ness. She doesn't have an appointment."

The hint of disapproval in Mrs. Bryce's voice pulled a smile out of him. Ms. Ness must either be wearing something shocking, or she'd said something inappropriate. Or both, if his introduction to the woman had borne even a hint of her regular personality. "That's okay. Send her in."

What a fascinating development. He'd all but written off the idea of landing Jada Ness for LeBlanc, given that his last conversation with her hadn't gone well. She'd used the words *no* and *way* far too much for his taste. But that had only been because he'd kept their conversation about business, with great difficulty. She hadn't liked that, and he'd opted to let her cool off for a few days before darkening her door, figuratively speaking, for the next round.

Yet here she was. Unannounced. Curiosity was killing him.

The timing couldn't have been better. If he'd spent one more second looking at the tiny print on a LeBlanc balance-sheet report, he'd explode. Plus, Ms. Ness had come to him. That perked him up considerably and gave him hope where none had been.

She swept into the office in a short, sheer dress that could hardly be called that, wearing stilettos so high a swift stab could stake two hearts at once. Their last conversation had taken place by phone, so he hadn't been treated to the full effect of the woman in person. Beyond beautiful, there was no denying that Jada Ness could and did turn heads wherever she went.

While Sabrina had a warm, earthy heat underneath her frost, Jada reminded him of a china doll. Too fake to be real and far too brittle to touch.

"Ms. Ness," he called as she shut the door in his admin's face. "To what do I owe the pleasure?"

"We're all friends here," she purred. "You can call me Jada. I told you that before."

Yeah, but that had been before she'd also basically told him to take a hike. Her presence at LeBlanc shifted the playing field, and he'd yet to discover exactly how. Or who had the advantage. "*Jada*, then. Have you reconsidered the auction idea?"

She waved that off with one unmanicured hand, the rare high-maintenance type of woman who didn't have long nails, likely due to the intricate work required to craft her pieces. "I still don't like it. But I'm willing to listen to your ideas. I ran into some…unexpected expenses. So I'm in the market for opportunity."

On the heels of this New England disaster, that sounded so promising that Val nearly pulled out a pen and paper right there to get something in writing. But he didn't. This was still very much a negotiation, rife with potential pitfalls. Jada hadn't even taken a seat yet.

Val stood and skirted the desk, biting back anything that might be construed as overly eager. Also, delicacy was of the utmost importance here. "Please. Let's sit over here by the window."

He led her to the cozy area near the window where two sleek chairs faced a low, square table. The single time Val had visited his father here, he'd sat in one of these chairs to wait for Edward to finish his phone call. At ten years of age, Val hadn't had a lot of patience for the business of diamonds and had amused himself for a solid fifteen minutes by repeatedly sliding off the chair onto the floor. His father had wrapped up the phone call, yelled at Val for making thumping noises while Edward had been speaking with a lobbyist in Washington and then spent approximately eight minutes granting his son an interview for the paper Val had to write about how a corporation worked.

That had been the last time Val darkened the doors of LeBlanc. Until recently.

The chairs had long been replaced, likely by Xavier when he'd taken over. Now leather instead of cloth, Val indicated one and waited until Jada slid into it before taking the other. If there were any cards in his hand worth playing, he had to get them on the table fast before she flipped the discussion in a direction he couldn't go. Or wouldn't go. It was a fine line.

"This is a much better spot to revive a discussion about us working together," he told her with a smile, relaxing against the chair. This was a friendly conversation. The less tension, the better.

He needed to capitalize on her "unexpected expenses." Earlier that morning, Sabrina had sent him a text message reminding him that Jada could be the answer to the flagging sales in New England, like he hadn't thought of that. The problem was, he couldn't consider it unless she changed her stance on the expected benefits of working with LeBlanc.

Val's skill between the sheets wasn't a negotiation point here.

Or was it? He eyed her thoughtfully as a dangerous, highly unethical plan percolated through his mind.

Perhaps he could consider it if he changed *his* stance. There was no law that said he had to be so black and white about those benefits. Just because he gave her the *impression* he might be willing to indulge in a personal relationship with a designer under contract with LeBlanc didn't mean he actually had to follow through.

Val was nothing if not an accomplished flirt. Lots of men did that without having any intention of bedding the woman in question. He just rarely met a woman who interested him enough to flirt with that he didn't also want to get naked—and he pretty much crossed the finish line on that 100 percent of the time. But for the sake of his inheritance, he could switch it up a bit.

"I'm glad you were able to see me on short notice." Her fingers briefly grazed his arm as she spoke, sending a subliminal message that said she'd welcome a whole lot more intimate contact.

Not that he had any illusions about the reasons why. Jada likely thought of him as a challenge. Men no doubt fell at her feet, and she got what she wanted on a daily basis. Val was that one man who'd told her *no* and it had been like waving a big, red flag in her face. Odds were good she couldn't tell him the color of his eyes if he shut them, but he didn't mind being objectified if it got him closer to his goal.

"Of course," he returned smoothly. "I always have time to fit in a beautiful woman who comes to call unexpectedly. I'm pleasantly surprised that you were willing to drop by after our last conversation fell apart. Thank you for giving me another chance to discuss *opportunities*."

She did not miss the extra color he injected into the word. Her expression warmed instantly, and she leaned in, crossing her legs at the ankle while accidentally on purpose grazing his knee with hers. "I like the sound of that. Tell me more about your ideas for the auction."

"A glorious tribute to the talent and genius of Jada Ness." Val spread his hands wide as if indicating a banner that would be emblazoned with that phrase. "You'd have free rein. Design whatever you want. We'd foot the bill for all the expense to transport and then display your pieces in several of our stores in advance of the auction, but we'll keep it small. Intimate. I'm thinking New England is a no-brainer for that. Really appeal to the old, established money in Boston and New York."

Nodding, she bounced her leg as she considered what he'd laid out. The little dress she wore rode higher on her thighs, and there was no chance that had been accidental. More like deliberate advertising. He presented a scenario and finished up with the idea of exclusive pieces.

Her nose wrinkled. "Mass producing my designs? I've never been about that. My pieces are unique."

"Definitely," he cut in and fought the urge to move his knee away from her encroaching leg rub. "Just like you. So design a few new things with mass production in mind. Don't spend a lot of energy on it. Just do enough to get your stamp on it so it's still uniquely *Jada Ness* and cash the check."

Thoughtfully, she nodded. "I'm not opposed to it as long as the price points are high enough to keep buyers in the upper echelon. I don't want riffraff wearing Jada Ness."

Val bit back a groan. The whole point of mass production was to achieve lower price points so you moved a lot of volume…wherever *that* knowledge had come from. Wow, he'd absorbed more from his father and Xavier about this business than he'd thought. Or it was in his blood after all.

The thought of either one being true made him slightly nauseated. This whole scene had done a lot to contribute to that feeling, actually. No wonder LeBlanc men in the diamond business had no souls: they willingly gave them up on the altar of ambition.

Apparently Val had gotten in line to lose his too. Except he was giving his to Jada Ness.

The woman had far too many demands, but all of his sources told him it would be worth it. Jada's jewelry graced the red carpet at Hollywood award shows and regularly made appearances in top women's fashion magazines. LeBlanc could and would get major visibility from even being associated with Jada's name.

"You know what?" Val threw out with a wink. "We should discuss this over drinks. Saturday night. If you're free?"

"My calendar mysteriously cleared," she murmured and held out her hand, ostensibly to seal the deal with a handshake, but he did her one better by clasping it to pull her forward into an air kiss.

"I'll send over a draft of a contract with everything

we've discussed thus far. If you like it, you can bring a signed copy with you on Saturday."

She'd like it. He'd make sure of that. Just like he intended to make sure he had that contract signed and in his hand before the highball glasses were empty. If that didn't come to pass, he'd have to think of something else on the fly. Easy as pie. All he had to do was put his heart in the freezer, channel Xavier and then come up with the most coldhearted, callous plan imaginable.

And then figure out how to stop feeling like Sabrina would be disappointed in him if he told her what had just transpired.

The bitter taste in Val's mouth stuck until Friday night.

Grocery shopping should have cheered him up, but the sacks of potatoes reminded him of LBC, and the little basil plants wrapped in cellophane nearly put him over the edge. LBC had a central courtyard that he'd turned into a garden, cultivating rows of herbs and vegetables. When they were fully grown, he sent the staff home with fresh cut herbs, cucumbers and squash as a thank-you since the small plot couldn't produce enough to be incorporated into the food bank coffers.

Was someone watering them, as instructed? He'd texted Julie, one of the volunteers, a few times but she'd been largely uncommunicative. Which honestly stung. Val sometimes felt like a pariah, as if his staff thought of him as tainted, now that he'd crossed the threshold of the monument to consumerism that bore his name.

Most of the time, he realized that was projection on his part.

Tonight, he just wished he wasn't going to have to work some magic to get Sabrina to his house. Why couldn't she say yes to dinner without throwing out another hundred reasons against something so easy and natural as romance? It was maddening. Baffling. Challenging.

He had two hours to get the majority of the cooking done before he had to leave to pick up Sabrina, so he put that time to good use. The spaghetti sauce needed to simmer for at least an hour, and the cheesecake had to bake for as long. With some music piping through the surround-sound system, his kitchen became a place of cleansing and, by the time six forty-five rolled around, he'd started humming along with the One Republic song currently playing.

But it wasn't until he rang Sabrina's doorbell and she answered it wearing a little black dress that he completely forgot about Jada Ness.

"Wow."

Other words and phrases evaded him as he drank in the sight of Sabrina's lithe form encased in black silk. Normally, she wore suits with long skirts or tailored blouses with flowing pants, all of which looked amazing on her. The red dress from the design event had been his personal favorite. Until now.

Not seeing her for the last few days had built up the anticipation for this moment in a wholly unexpected way.

"What are you doing here?" she asked and a line appeared between her eyes.

"Picking you up for dinner." How he got that phrase out when all of his brain cells were currently circulating in his groin, he'd never know.

"I have a date."

"Yes, you do. With me."

She shook her head mulishly. "I never said yes. And I made other plans. I was expecting my...other plans, or I wouldn't have answered the door."

Oh, so it was going to be that kind of night, was it? Val had a pretty fair temper when he got riled, a by-product of letting his heart rule his head, but he couldn't help that the sudden and vivid image in his head of Sabrina on a date with some other man made his blood hot. "Cancel. Whatever your plans are, they cannot compare to what I have in store for you."

Her gaze darkened with conflicting emotions and the fact that she'd let him see that…he could scarcely take it all in. But intrigue—that was the one he liked the most. It coupled with the swirl of temper in his veins in a very interesting way, doubling his resolve to close this deal with her.

She was getting in his car so he could drive her to his house for dinner come hell or high water. He needed her tonight for a hundred reasons, many of which he'd ignored until this moment, when the outcome of the night hung in a precarious balance.

"My plans are none of your business," she informed him unceremoniously and checked her phone with fanfare, as if to make it really clear she was expecting someone who would be here any minute. Val could show himself out, leaving her to her date. Too bad if he'd mistakenly assumed that she'd come to dinner strictly because he'd already spent hours preparing for this.

Except, her other date wasn't here yet. Val was. And he was nothing if not resourceful when he wanted something, especially if there was someone else already in line. Years of practice at beating out Xavier gave him an edge he did not hesitate to capitalize on.

"Your 'other plans' is late. I'll make you a deal." He jerked his chin toward his car. "Blow him off, and have dinner with me. If, within an hour, you're not having the best date of your life, I will personally call your 'other plans' and apologize. Then I'll drive you wherever you want to go, even if it's to his house."

It was a risky proposition, sure. She might say she hated every minute of the date to be spiteful. But he didn't think so, not with that thread of intrigue running through her expression. She was wavering. He could feel it.

"Come on, Sabrina," he entreated her softly. "I made you a vanilla bean cheesecake. Guaranteed to melt in your mouth. Just have dinner with me. That's all. No agenda."

"You already cooked something?" she asked and either couldn't or didn't care to hide her shock. "You were that confident I'd be coming over?"

He shrugged. "I was that confident that I was going to do everything in my power to get you there. I want to show you how romance is supposed to work. Your 'other plans' has zero consideration for that, and it's his loss, I say."

The long pause scuttled over his nerves.

"It's a deal," she said out of nowhere, and he almost fell over in shock. "I'll cancel. But this is not a dress for dinner in. I'll just change—"

"No!" That might have come out a little too forcefully, but oh well. "It's perfect. That's the most amazing dress I've ever seen. You look fantastic."

Uncertainty pulled at her mouth, warring with the warmth his compliment had brought to her cheeks. "It's not too much for a dinner in?"

"Absolutely not," he muttered hoarsely, fighting to keep his eyes on her face instead of on the slice of cleavage revealed by the V-neck of the top. The backless red dress had been provocative, no doubt, and he'd enjoyed dancing with her since it meant he got to put his hands on her bare skin in a publicly approved activity. But this was something else. Sexy and ripe to be peeled off her delectable body. The memory of the feel of her under his hands roared to the forefront, and he couldn't have stopped himself from wanting her with bone-deep need had he been held at gunpoint.

"Leave it on," he told her in no uncertain terms.

"Okay." A smile climbed onto her face, and he caught the full force of it in his gut.

"If that's settled, then we have a dinner to get to." Val held out his arm for her to take, which she did, much to his delight. It was a struggle not to break out in a victory dance right there on her front porch.

Once he had her settled into his SUV, he dove into the driver's seat and peeled away from her curb as fast as the laws of physics would allow. He wouldn't put it past her to jump out at a red light.

"You're not going to text your date?" he asked casually. She shot him a loaded glance that he caught from the corner of his eye. "What? All's fair in love and war, but it sucks to wait on a woman's front porch. I'm not that heartless."

"I have a confession to make," she said with a bit of mirth lacing her tone. "My plans were with a girlfriend and, while you were busy sweeping me off my feet, she texted me that she'd gotten stuck at work."

"Oh." Val had no idea what to do with that information. "So I guess that means you're not going to be evaluating the fun factor of our date in anticipation of taking me up on my offer to apologize to your 'other plans.'"

"It was inventive, I'll give you that."

"Is that why you said yes?" Probably he shouldn't have asked unless he really wished to know the answer and, at this point, he couldn't imagine anything she told him would work in his favor.

"No. I said yes because I can't remember the last time someone went to so much effort to get me on a date." She lifted a shoulder. "I'm human. I like to feel special."

"You are," he murmured, and it wasn't just a line spouted off to get him further with her.

It was stone-cold truth. He couldn't remember the last time he'd gone to so much effort for a woman either. Usually they came onto him—like Jada—and he had his pick.

Enough of that. Jada Ness did not belong in his thoughts while on a date with Sabrina. A real date that they both agreed was a date. It was still enough to make his head spin that he'd somehow pulled off this coup.

"I like your house," she said as they emerged from the walkway between the detached garage and the main building. "I was expecting something a little more modern, but it fits you."

Val glanced around the hundred-year-old house that his mother had given him on his twenty-fifth birthday. Xavier had taken their father's ancestral home, naturally, but Val much preferred this one in River Forest. Traffic wasn't too bad from here to downtown and he liked the quiet.

Val had done some renovations, like adding the surround sound and updating the kitchen extensively, but the guts were largely the same, down to the exposed coffee-colored beams arching overhead.

"It does fit me. Surprisingly. It's been in the family since it was built and has a lot of history that I have grown to appreciate."

"Like what? Tell me."

Sabrina slid onto one of the stools set on the far side of the granite-topped island in the center of the kitchen. Copper pots hung from the ceiling, but he actually used his, unlike a lot of people with gourmet kitchens.

He shrugged and checked on his sauce, which was thickening nice and slow as it should. "My mother grew up here. I find things all the time that I imagine she must have enjoyed, like the shade of the oak trees along the property, or a hidey-hole in the attic where she left a book with her name scrawled across the first page."

"That's…nice. Also not what I was expecting."

He let a brief smile bloom. "I have to ask then. What were you expecting?"

Eleven

Sabrina couldn't answer Val's question without incriminating herself, and neither did she think he'd appreciate it if she hauled out the Fifth Amendment on a first date. Second date. Third?

First. The snow cones definitely didn't count, and the red-dress event probably didn't count. The fact that Val had kissed her both times notwithstanding.

"Spill, Sabrina," Val said, his voice low and silky in the candle-lit kitchen. "You said yes to dinner. That means we're going to have a very long conversation where we learn things about each other. What were you expecting?"

"I wasn't expecting anything." Did she sound as defensive to him as she did to herself? "Thirty minutes ago, I thought I was going to a wine bar with Tina, a girl I know from college. Bam! You happened, and here I am."

"Don't change the subject. Once, I could let pass, but you made it a point to tell me twice that I'm not what you expected. Since I've been trying to tell you that I'm not like the other men you've dated, I'm dying to know what finally tripped that switch in your head."

Val hadn't moved from his spot by the stove. There was a whole slab of brown and white granite between them, but the way he glanced at her over his shoulder made her achy and shivery. "I don't know. I expected a slick bachelor pad. I guess. And a man who doesn't pay attention to things like oak trees or books."

"Surprise." The pan on the stove lost his attention, and he swung around to lean on the island, his strong hands braced against the granite. "My mother and I worked together at LeBlanc Charities for almost fifteen years until she retired. We've had a lot of time to talk. Bond. She's important to me. Oak trees and books are too, but only because they are to her."

Mesmerized, she searched Val's beautiful face for clues as to why he'd say something so personal to her. Why he'd let Sabrina see love for his mother painted all over him. It was as baffling as it was affecting. "I'm starting to get an inkling why you're so sure you're not like the men I've dated before."

Honestly, she'd thought that was typical male pandering. That would have been the case with her normal type and, one of these centuries, she'd get the memo to her brain that Val wasn't her normal type.

The aromatic scent of tomatoes, garlic and basil that hung heavy in the air of his kitchen should be enough of a testament to that. No one had ever cooked for her before. That alone may have been the thing that tipped the scales, though she had a legion of reasons that she'd gotten into the car with him. The fact that Tina had canceled wasn't even in the top ten.

"Only an inkling?" His wide smile teased one out of her.

"Well, keep in mind, you do have quite a few things in common with the last guy I dated. You can see how I might get confused."

That was the wrong thing to say. Something altogether dangerous flashed through his expression as he contemplated her. "I'm nothing like the last guy you dated. We might share a last name, but that's the extent of it."

Well, that and the fact that they were twins. But she'd long stopped thinking that they looked similar. They really didn't, not to her, despite being identical. Xavier resembled the diamonds he sold: hard, glittery and indestructible. Val had the fire at the heart of a diamond, all right, but the rest? No. He was more like an active volcano with so much heat and pressure inside, it spilled over his edges, wreaking havoc all around him.

Or maybe that was just her.

"I misspoke," she allowed. "You're definitely a breed of your own. I don't think Xavier even knows where his kitchen is."

That made Val smile, but it took on a wolfish quality that didn't relax her in the slightest. "I'd wager that's not the only thing he doesn't know how to find."

True to form, everything out of his mouth had started to sound slightly dirty, and she had a feeling it wasn't an accident. She'd inadvertently tripped over her own tongue by mentioning Xavier. She wouldn't do that again, particularly since she didn't have really even the slightest interest in talking about his brother.

What she did have an interest in talking about she wasn't sure. And Val was in rare form tonight, calling her on her missteps instantly, paying far too much attention to her instead of his dinner. "Speaking of which, what are you making me?"

"Spaghetti." But he wasn't *making* anything, he was still leaning on the island, his hot, hungry gaze sliding along her shoulders and the neckline of her dress. "Italian is your favorite, right?"

The way he looked at her pulled at strings inside that she'd scarcely realized existed. It was too much and, simultaneously, not enough. She couldn't figure out what to do with her hands, so she clenched them in her lap. Had to be spaghetti, didn't it? Almost as if she'd scripted the evening ahead of time and he'd read her mind. "I don't know if I'd call it my favorite. I like it. But I don't know that I like it more than anything else."

He made a noise in his throat. "This is always the way with you, isn't it? No passion for anything. There has to be something you feel strongly about. What is it?"

"I...don't know." She swallowed at the vibes shooting from Val. They confused her. Had she angered him by not falling all over him with how much she adored spaghetti? "I have a really strong desire to be successful at coaching."

"That's not something you can feel desire for." He waved that off. "That's not something that can return your passion, feed it. Stop holding out on me. What really gets you going? What do you crave so much that you'd do anything to get it?"

You. It spilled into her head with so much force that she almost blurted it out loud. She didn't. Couldn't. It wasn't entirely true anyway. Sure, he infuriated her on occasion, and she couldn't stop thinking about how he kissed with his whole body. But that didn't mean she craved him. She hadn't ever *craved* anything. "I'm not holding out on you. I don't I have that kind of personality."

His brows rose. "Everyone has that kind of personality. Your problem is that you've had too many disappointments in your life. The fire inside you can and should be stoked as often as possible but, every time you try, someone puts it out."

"That's not—" But she couldn't even finish the sentence because her chest got tight all at once. What was going on here? She'd expected seduction, not a psychological survey. "We're talking about spaghetti. This is entirely too deep a conversation for that."

All at once, he skirted the island and crowded into her space, taking up all the oxygen in the room at the same time. He spun her stool so that she faced him. Blinking up at him, she tried to keep breathing, but her lungs had frozen.

"Sabrina." He caressed her name with his lips. "We're not talking about spaghetti. Stand up."

"What? Why?"

"Because you're going to kiss me, and you're going to want to do it standing up. Trust me."

Feigning amusement, she crossed her arms over her suddenly quaking chest. "Who said I was going to kiss you?"

"I did." His presence weighed her down, giving her no quarter. "Because you know I'm right. You know you have something inside of you that burns and you're aching to let it fly. I'm going to give you that. And you want me to."

Shuddering, she let the concepts he'd laid out winnow through her because they were that powerful. She did have passion and need that had gone unfulfilled because she deliberately sought out men who could never reach those longings. How had he guessed these things about her? Or was it more than a guess? If he *knew* she picked lovers who were guaranteed to leave her cold, what did that mean? He saw through her defenses too easily, that's what.

Or perhaps the blame lay squarely at her own feet. She'd shared far too much with him about her struggles with trust, particularly when it came to fidelity in relationships, and he'd gobbled up all that information to use to his advantage.

Except…that wasn't exactly what was happening.

The problem was she didn't know *what* was happening. Maybe that should be the first point of clarification. "Let's say I kiss you. Then what?"

His wolfish smile grew teeth, and she felt every one of them clamp on her core. Raw need—desire—radiated from his gaze and she couldn't look away. Or maybe she just didn't want to.

"That's all up to you, Sabrina. 'Then what' could be dinner. Or you could ask me to strip you naked right here in the kitchen and make you come over and over again. Your choice. The trick is for you to figure out what you crave. Food and sex are both big ticket items in that arena."

"And you're good at both," she added on his behalf.

"I assumed that was implied."

His confidence shouldn't be so sexy, nor should his teasing grin make her smile in return. She shouldn't be smiling or thinking of standing up or wondering why she couldn't crave both food and sex, especially when Valentino LeBlanc would be the delivery boy for both.

She stood. He didn't move a muscle, just let her brush up against his body until they were aligned like forks in a drawer, and the contact was so delicious that she pressed closer.

"I did have this particular fantasy," she admitted, shocking herself with her boldness.

But not Val. He took it in stride, wrapping his arms around her, and the feel of his firm hands on her body thrilled through her. The smell of male engulfed her, strong, heady and, oh, so hot. What was it about him that made her forget all her rules?

"What?" he murmured. "Tell me. I want to hear all about it."

"It has to do with that counter—" She tilted her head toward the island. "You. And some spaghetti sauce."

His eyelids fluttered shut, and he groaned, his voice scraping over the sound with a raw needy sort of rasp. "A combo deal. I cannot tell you how sexy that is."

Really? *Sexy* wasn't a word that got tossed in her direction too often. In fact, she deliberately stayed away from anything close to that.

"Try," she suggested and, when he raised his eyebrows in question, she forced herself to complete the thought. "I spend a lot of time trying to get men to see me as an equal, not enticing them. I don't do sexy well."

"I beg to differ," he growled and spun her so that her spine pressed against the counter. "You do sexy just fine. Often without realizing it, which is why it's so affecting. Now, you were about to act out your fantasy, and I was about to start enjoying it. Go ahead."

There was no way. Was he serious? A nervous titter escaped from her mouth. "I was expecting you to take the lead."

"There you go with expectations again. I'm already embracing my passion." Like silk, his hands smoothed over her buttocks, boldly making his point that *she* was in his embrace. "It's your turn."

This was the part where she was supposed to kiss him. Let it all fly, so to speak. The thought electrified her. So she did, catching his mouth with hers, and it thrummed through her, wrenching loose a hungry noise in her chest.

The kiss caught fire, mounting in urgency instantly until she'd lost all sense of time. The top of the island bit into the small of her back, and she arched to alleviate the pressure. As if reading her mind—thank God—he boosted her up onto the countertop, pushing the skirt of her dress higher on her thighs so he could step between them.

"Like this?" he whispered against her mouth. "Show me what you want me to do."

Sabrina didn't hesitate to deepen the kiss, sliding her tongue forward to find his until there was nothing but the hot skim of flesh burning her alive from the inside out. *More.* Oh, yes, she needed more and guided his palms up her thighs and kept going along her torso to her breasts. Fortunately, he took suggestion well, exploring her covered flesh, his touch searing through her until she could hardly think.

Which maybe wasn't so much of the goal here.

He shifted closer, grinding hard against her core until she saw bursts of light.

"What next, Sabrina?" he asked so impatiently that she couldn't help but respond.

I want it all.

So she showed him. Fingers flying over his buttons, she pushed his shirt open and then familiarized herself with his shape, his gorgeous skin, defined pectorals. As she skimmed his chest, he sucked in a breath, and her gaze flew to his face.

The raw need there shattered something inside. What would it be like to let go with that kind of abandon? She had to know immediately. This experience wouldn't be complete without that.

"Val," she bit out hoarsely. "I want—"

"Yeah, sweetheart? Tell me what you want."

"I want…to feel."

Oh, yes, she did. She wanted to open herself up, to heave great chunks of ice from her soul and let Val turn the rest to steam. He seemed to sense exactly what she needed, sliding his hands along her bare thighs, gathering her dress in the V of his fingers and working it off her body with swift, sure motion.

Once he bared her fully, he let his heavy lidded gaze worship her naked form for an eternity. His perusal made her achy and squirmy, and she couldn't stand this distance between them. Inching forward, she fell into him, into a gorgeously silky kiss made all the more affecting as his palms spread across her bare back.

She gasped against his mouth, thrusting her breasts forward, chafing her nipples against his hard chest until the friction nearly made her come apart. His hands skimmed to her thighs.

"Open for me," he instructed softly, and she let him push them apart, wantonly spreading herself for whatever he might decide came next.

Except she was supposed to decide. The power of that coursed through her, and she couldn't stop from blurting, "I want you to touch me."

He complied instantly without censure, his fingertips playing over her heated flesh until she cried out, unable to keep the pleasure inside. He toyed with her, slipping fingers in and out, driving her to the point of delirium.

"Let go, Sabrina," he instructed. "Feel. I'm touching you, and you like it. It's all good."

A white-hot river of sensation flowed through her body, coalescing at the center of everything, where his fingers worked their magic. Pinpricks of light and heat wheeled through her core until they finally exploded outward, rippling along conduits of her body, and even her toes felt it.

With one last burst, she went limp, sagging against the counter, elbows on the cool granite.

"Gorgeous," Val murmured as he bent to mouth a kiss along her collarbone. "You are without a doubt the most responsive, sexy woman I have ever seen."

Given that he probably had plenty of experience to draw from, she chose to take it as gospel. "I'm fairly certain the stimuli had something to do with it."

When he laughed, she let her eyelids drift open. He was leaning on the counter, his gaze heated and watchful as he openly ogled her. "More where that came from. Unless you'd like dinner first before I show you what I want."

The wicked promise curled up inside her, and she couldn't imagine anything she wanted to do less than eat. "Take me to bed, Val."

Without blinking, he gathered her up and lifted her from the granite as if she weighed no more than a sack of groceries. The real feat of strength came when he carried her up a flight of stairs without breaking a sweat. Somehow, he managed to make her feel desired and beautiful without a word. That was the true magic.

No, it was romance. As promised.

When they entered the bedroom, she wiggled from his arms and unashamedly pulled him toward the bed, stripping him as she went. His shirt hit the floor, then his pants and, when she got him completely naked, she pushed him onto the bed. Looming over him, she returned the favor by openly staring at what she'd uncovered.

To all intents and purposes, she should have been prepared for Val in all his glory. Bits and pieces of him had been pressed into her sensitive spots several times. It shouldn't have been such a shock to finally take in his sinewy, drool-inducing form, yet she managed it anyway.

Long and lithe, Valentino LeBlanc had been crafted with sex and sin in mind, wholly compliant to a woman's pleasure. She could not wait to dig in.

Amusement colored his face. "I guess this is the part where you're going to get bossy."

"It is." She arched a brow. "So I'd advise you to fall in line, or there will be hell to pay."

That got a laugh, and he crossed his arms over his beautiful chest, ruining her view. "I feel a distinct need to challenge that."

In response, she crawled onto the bed, snagging his arms and spreading them wide on the mattress as she settled astride his hips. With so much Val stretching out between her legs, she scarcely knew where to start. Seemed as if *he* knew. His powerful thighs flexed, pushing into her crevices with such beautiful, encompassing friction that she gasped.

"You were saying?" he murmured.

"Shut up, I forgot what I was talking about," she muttered and let it all go in favor of drowning in the renewed fire Val had easily stoked a second time. "You've created a monster. I hope you're happy with yourself."

"Supremely." He sat up, capturing her in his tight embrace, and the position slayed her as his hardness abraded her center. "But I haven't created anything. I'm simply letting you be your true self and reaping the benefits. Win-win."

That was…spot-on. It resonated through her as easily as he'd invoked desire. Val was her conduit to her true self, and she had free rein to be greedy with it. They were a much better team than she'd ever anticipated.

Twelve

Val had a naked Sabrina in his lap, her delectable legs wrapped around his waist and, for some unknown reason, he'd started a conversation.

He was clearly doing it wrong.

He rolled with her still in his arms and got her situated under him. Better. Capturing her smart mouth in a long searing kiss, he shut her up with one long stroke of his tongue. Better still.

Not that he hated it when she talked. It was only that he had so many other more important things he wanted to do with her mouth. Like taste her heat. He lapped it up with great, greedy gulps, sliding deep into the notches of her body in order to nest them tighter together. Her body welcomed him, exactly as he'd imagined so many times.

No. This was far, far better than his imagination. Sabrina burned like a bright flame, her iciness as far away as the east from the west. He'd done that, melted her with a carefully applied seduction campaign, and the victory tasted so sweet.

Frankly, he'd almost given up hope that he'd be with her like this, and he recognized it as the gift that it was. Her long, cinnamon-colored hair spread out on the comforter, begging for his fingers, so he indulged himself with a handful of it. The strands wound up through his fingers, and he pulled gently, exposing her neck to his lips. Fitting them to the hollow at her throat, he nibbled his way down, reveling in her soft gasps.

This was every bit an extended culmination of their courtship, and he could not get enough of her throaty sounds of pleasure as he dipped farther down, exploring her in the way he couldn't have in the kitchen. She'd been too hot, too needy, and he'd had to wholly concentrate on her pleasure to take the edge off.

Now it was his turn to bring himself pleasure. That ridge at her hip—it was so tempting that he had to run his tongue along it, just to taste. Fire and woman erupted beneath him as he licked, and that was so arousing that he swirled his tongue along the line of bone that arrowed straight to her core.

Pushing her thighs wide, he took the next lick between her folds. Her hips bucked, driving her deeper against his lips, which put her closer to where he wanted to be anyway. More of her silk gathered along his tongue as he explored that part of her thoroughly. She liked it best when he circled her pleasure center with little teasing strokes and then flattened his tongue for a longer taste. Her cries emboldened him, and he worked her faster until she bowed up, coming apart a second time.

That's when he sheathed himself with a condom and slid into place to notch himself at her heated entrance.

As he pushed inside, he slowed down, savoring the sense of completion that washed over him the deeper he slid.

She watched him, her hair tangled around her head in a halo, her lids at a slumberous half-mast in the wake of her orgasm. The smug sense of satisfaction seeping through his chest couldn't be helped. He'd hoped to unleash her—he'd gotten his wish.

Moving to the internal beat of his heart, he lost himself in the pleasure that was joining with Sabrina. He couldn't lie. Part of it was so sweet because she'd been such a puzzle to unravel, so challenging at every turn. Making love to her was icing on that cake.

But as she rose to meet each thrust, he began to drift into another world where nothing existed but the two of them, and he had to revise that. Sabrina was the whole cake. She filled him to the brim with her energy. Nothing could have prepared him for the glory of being with her when she let her guard down. It was humbling, exciting, fulfilling. Not feelings he'd ever associated with sex before.

But this was far from just sex. Maybe it never could have been between the two of them. Their dynamic had been off-kilter from the first, and he'd never fully recovered. He looked down into her molten gaze and saw a universe of things he scarcely understood—but wanted to.

Faster now, he chased his pleasure until the tight, sweet rhythm clamped over his whole body, and he came with a long shudder. Gathering her close, he held her in his arms through the aftermath, both of them quaking. This was so far beyond what he'd hoped this night would bring and, as he breathed in her scent, he blessed the fact that she'd gotten into his car after all.

And, if he had his way, she wouldn't be leaving. All weekend. How he'd talk her into that he didn't know yet, but there was so much more between them he wanted to explore that he couldn't fathom getting to all of it in one night.

"Now I'm ready to eat," she said brightly with a lusty sigh.

"Really?" He didn't bother to hide a smile. "I was thinking I never wanted to move again."

"Don't be silly." She sat up, taking all her delicious heat with her, and his arms got cold so fast that he blindly scouted around for her hand with the sole intent of yanking her back to the mattress. "That was better than the best workout, don't you think? Energizing. I could run a marathon. Probably."

She easily pulled her hand from his loose grip, and he groaned good-naturedly. "You're not natural, woman. That was supposed to be relaxing to the point where we can drift off to sleep in each other's arms."

"Can't help it," she told him primly and bounded from the bed. "I didn't get dinner, and you're the least relaxing man I've ever met. Get over it."

Blearily, he watched her buzz over to his dresser uninvited and open all of the drawers until she found what she was looking for—a T-shirt and gym shorts with a tie waist. They hung on her lissome body like those After pictures of people who had lost a lot of weight. She'd never been more beautiful, and he wanted her all over again.

Perhaps there was something to her point about being energized. He sat up and found that he could in fact move his body if he really applied himself. But when he reached for her, she danced out of his way.

"Oh, no," she said, wagging her finger. "Judging by the look on your face, pasta is not in my future if I let you get your hands on me."

"Smart girl," he muttered and had no shot at hiding his disappointment as she shooed him out of the bed.

Getting dressed presented a whole new set of challenges as she laughingly tried to help, her fast hands smoothing over his flesh in deliberate little teases that were not overly conducive to introducing clothing to his body. Somehow, they both wound up covered, but how she wasn't hot and bothered like he was he'd never know.

They ate the spaghetti at the island, both perched on stools swiveled toward each other, legs intertwined, and it was the best meal he'd had in a long time. Sabrina's eyes sparkled in a way he'd never seen before. Almost as if she had carried around this layer of frost that had shaded everything and, with it removed, her vibrancy shone through undimmed. It was breathtaking.

"Stay the weekend," he said impulsively, but quickly warmed up to the idea the longer he thought about it.

She blinked. "Like overnight? I didn't bring anything with me."

"That's not an objection. Or rather it's not a reasonable one," he amended. "I'll take you home to pack whatever you want. Better yet, I'll take you shopping."

Dubiously, she eyed him. "Isn't that moving a little fast?"

Not really. Maybe. He didn't care. "You took me shopping on our first date. I'm only returning the favor."

"You know what I mean. And that was not a date."

"I paid for the snow cones and kissed you. How is that not a date?" The label mattered not at all, but he liked riling her and, as a reward, he got twin stains of pink blooming in her cheeks.

"Do you always deflect when you don't want to talk about the real issue?"

That was not the kind of riled he'd been shooting for.

Sobering, he took in her serious expression. "I'm not deflecting."

"Staying over implies things. What, I don't know yet. I need to before I can answer."

"How about: Don't overanalyze, and stay because you like the idea of sleeping in my bed. Waking up to me. Eating the fantastic breakfast I'll make for you in the morning. Pancakes," he promised with an eyebrow waggle. "If you're lucky."

Twirling in her seat, she untangled their legs and faced him. Normally, he'd call that her no-nonsense pose, but she was so cute in his gray T-shirt that he almost couldn't take it.

"Val. I'm trying to have an honest conversation here."

"What do you want me to say?" He swallowed. "That this thing between us is bigger, deeper and/or stronger than what I'd expected? That I want to be with you 24/7?"

Something akin to shock darted through her expression. *Too much. Too soon.* His conscience was screaming at him to backpedal.

"Not even close," she mumbled, her voice thick with... what? Distaste? Panic?

He had no experience with this kind of conversation. Or with this kind of uncertainly swirling through his chest.

"Good, because that's not what's going on here." She bought that lie. Her spine relaxed and, conversely, his stiffened.

Was it so bad to talk about the things going on inside him? Was she really not okay with knowing the truth about how he felt? Because that was crap. While he might have origgally pursued her strictly to best his brother, she'd come to mean something much bigger than that to him.

They were a team. He liked that. Whatever else that meant he didn't know yet, but how the hell was he supposed to figure it out if she took off?

"What is going on here then?" she asked.

A reasonable question. It shouldn't make him itchy. But all of a sudden, he was afraid of the answer. "Lots of sex. All weekend long. We haven't yet begun to exhaust the limits of pleasure I have in mind for you."

Intrigue slowly filtered through her demeanor, replacing whatever she'd had going on before. "I do like the sound of that."

"It's settled then. I'll drive you home to get your things."

It was only after he'd parked in her driveway to sit idle while she dashed inside that it occurred to him that he'd edged out Jada Ness in favor of Sabrina. Drinks with Jada tomorrow night had gone by the wayside, which was not a good thing.

That's when he panicked. He'd never blown off a date with a woman, especially not one that held such monumental importance to him. He had to fix this or it might mess up his inheritance. What was wrong with him?

And then he began to wonder whether he'd subconsciously forgotten about the designer because he'd started falling for Sabrina.

The weekend did indeed end up being a smorgasbord of sex, and Sabrina couldn't find a thing wrong with that. Val brought new meaning to the terms *sensual* and *passionate,* and when he aimed all of his considerable charms at her, she pretty much spent every moment in a giant puddle of pleasure.

She scarcely knew whether to go with the flow or bring up what was going on between them again. The first time hadn't gone so well. All she'd sought was some kind of clarification. This was all new and different for her. She'd never been with a man like Val, one she could imagine trusting. One she could envision laying out some kind of long-term agreement with. One she could...well, anything more than that was too much to contemplate, especially since he'd been so clear that she shouldn't expect him to take their relationship seriously.

Sex. That's what he wanted. What he'd sweet-talked her into. Sure, she'd wanted it too. What breathing woman wouldn't be ecstatic to have Valentino LeBlanc at her service?

Except...it felt like there were still unsaid things between them. As if she should press him on it. But probably that was her paranoia talking. She didn't do secrets well, and neither could she accuse him of having some without coming off as possessive at best. Crazy would be more on point of how he'd view it if she started demanding he tell her everything about his every move.

Not that she intended to. But still. She didn't like the uneasy, skittery feeling that she left his house with Sunday night. Probably, things would settle naturally once they moved back into a working relationship Monday morning.

That's not what happened. The moment she stepped into Val's office at LeBlanc for their normal 7:00 a.m. session, he cornered her up against the door.

"Hello, gorgeous," he murmured and dropped her into a searing kiss that got out of control instantly.

Her passions had been unleashed, oh yes they had, and the hot, slick curl of his tongue on hers enflamed her to the point of irrationality. The uneasiness melted away under his onslaught. Ravenous, she sucked him in, her back scraping the door as his clever hands skimmed under her skirt. Questing fingers slid beneath her soaked panties, and she gasped as those fingers twisted into her core. Bursts of light exploded behind her eyelids, and she came while riding his hand.

Within half a second, he'd freed himself from his pants and rolled on a condom, then boosted her up. Right before he pierced her, he caught her gaze and held it as he lowered her down onto his length until they were joined. Val was wearing one of his, oh, so sexy suits *while he made love to her,* and it was so hot she nearly asked him to stop so she could take a picture.

But then he began to move inside her, and she lost every last marble in her head.

Slowly, so achingly slow, he levered them both to a higher plane and, five minutes after she'd crossed the threshold, he had her panting through a second spectacular climax without even undressing her. That was *talent*.

He groaned through his own release and let his head tip forward against hers as they both went boneless. If that's how things were going to go from now on, she was a fan.

Finally, he released her, helped her get her clothing set to rights, and then they dove into work. The secret smiles he shot her did nothing to erase the memory of his hot hands on her body. Not that she tried very hard. He'd broken down her barriers in more ways than one.

At five to eight, the witching hour when she had to leave, she yanked her mind out of Val's slim cut charcoal pants and remembered to ask about the designer he had been trying to land.

"Have you spoken to Jada Ness?"

"No." Val's gaze flickered. "I need to talk to Legal about drawing up a contract that I can present to her. Thanks for the reminder."

"You're welcome." The flicker grew some shadows, and she searched his face for some explanation of what had tripped her radar. There was nothing there but Val and the slight smile that seemed a permanent part of his expression lately. The vague sense of having waded into quicksand didn't ease.

She dropped it. A first. In the past, if a man gave her the slightest hint that he'd been keeping things from her, she bailed. Instantly. No second chances, no explanations. Her heart wasn't available for shredding.

The next morning, Val greeted her much the same way as yesterday—hot sex, mostly dressed, this time on his desk. On Thursday, she learned exactly how little room there was for two people in his chair and how that allowed for some very inventive moves. By the weekend, she'd long since given up the idea of the two of them returning to a business-only relationship. And she'd yet to exhaust her craving for Val.

LeBlanc's quarterly reports came out, showing a nice month-over-month increase that may have been more attributable to Xavier than Val, but the will didn't specify any caveats—an increase was an increase. Val celebrated by taking her to a five-star restaurant and ordering the most expensive champagne on the menu. They spent nearly every night together, and she'd started to practice what she would say if he asked her to move in with him.

Though not out loud. They'd yet to revisit the conversation he'd cut short that first Friday night when she'd asked what they were doing. The time for that question had come and gone. They were still having a lot of sex, but the way he looked at her sometimes while in the throes hooked her in the chest and would not let go.

She was falling for him. So much so that she found herself daydreaming about him at odd moments, imagining his smile or the way he'd seamlessly incorporated her into his life. They giggled at each other's jokes in bed long into the night when they should have been sleeping, and then capped that with more long, languorous love-making sessions. As a result, she grew more and more exhausted. Less able to concentrate.

It frustrated her to be so scattered. Instead of coaching Val, she'd turned into his lover who occasionally talked to him about his day and offered advice about a sticky situation that had happened at the office. That wasn't working for her either, especially since she was still getting paid for a job that she wasn't doing. Not fully.

Okay, it was *working*. Her life had taken an unexpected, amazing turn that she still hadn't fully reconciled. But still, there was room to have both a man and a career, right?

"We have to talk," she told Val one night when he met her at the door of his house, as was his custom lately because he couldn't wait for her to use the key he'd given her.

"All right." He stepped back and let her through the door instead of sweeping her into his arms for yet another delirious and amazing session of being the sole center of Val's attention. "That sounds ominous."

But before she could unstick her tongue from the roof of her mouth to explain that she needed some time to get her feet under her, to figure out what she was doing with her coaching, her stomach rebelled.

Dashing past him, she barely made it to the bathroom before expelling the contents of her stomach. And then some. *Ugh*. She flushed the toilet and lay her burning cheek on the counter, heaving in great big gulps of air.

Stomach flu. Where had she got that? Or was it something she'd eaten?

Val's face reflected his concern when she emerged, but he didn't bat an eye, just hustled her into bed and made her chicken noodle soup from scratch with little corkscrew noodles that melted in her mouth. It tasted like something more than soup, but she was afraid to ask if he'd made it with love because what if the answer was *no*?

He settled onto the coverlet next to her in bed, but made no moves other than to stroke her hair as she finished the soup. "So the talking we have to do. Does it involve the reason you're sick?"

With a short laugh, she lifted a hand in a half shrug. "I don't know. Maybe. I've been tired a lot lately, so probably that's why I caught this whatever-it-is. My defenses are down. But yeah. I was going to mention that we've been a whole lot crazy lately, and maybe we can slow down. Take stock."

Val grew quiet for a long beat and then cleared his throat. "I thought you were going to tell me you were pregnant."

Heat then cold bloomed in her chest at the same time, and she shuddered with the dual sensations that shouldn't exist together. Oh, dear God. She couldn't even think that word, let alone say it out loud. How he had she'd never know. "What? *No*. We haven't even been sleeping together that long. Plus, we've used protection."

Except for that one time the condom had broken that first weekend. They'd immediately ripped open another one and they'd been careful since then. She hadn't even thought about it since.

He flashed a brief, not very amused, smile. "Hence the talking. I was bracing to hear it wasn't mine."

Wow. Were both of them on the lookout for secrets the other had been keeping? It was a bit of a revelation that he'd think of that. And care, apparently. "That would be so horrible, I don't even know how to respond."

A thousand emotions warred through his expression. "Does that mean you'd be okay with it if it *was* mine?"

"Geez, Val." Her head started spinning and there was a real possibility that she might lose the chicken noodle soup if this conversation kept up. Mostly because the answer was a resounding *yes*. She could picture that baby perfectly, with his father's dark hair and gorgeous smile. But they weren't that serious. Were they? "Can we pick this up in the morning, maybe? I want to talk, I really do. But I'm not feeling so hot. I just want to sleep for a million years."

"Sure."

Val took her bowl and set it aside, then stroked her head until she fell asleep. Or so she assumed since, when she woke, it was dark and he lay next to her, snoozing, with his hand still tangled in her hair. She extracted herself carefully so she didn't disturb him and wandered to the bathroom, happy at least that she didn't feel like death warmed over so much at the moment.

Probably, she shouldn't have taken a three-hour nap because now she was wide awake. Taking her phone in hand, she checked her email, while fetching a glass of orange juice from Val's fridge. Fresh squeezed, it tasted divine on her parched throat, and she drank every drop as she scrolled through the emails. Most of them could be instantly deleted, but she filed the notification from her bank that LeBlanc had paid her monthly invoice. That was one of the benefits of sleeping with the boss: she always got paid on time.

That's when her analytical brain kicked in and started doing the math. Dual hot–cold sensations exploded in her chest as she instantly recalled the date of the last time she'd been paid, which, naturally, was a month ago. And the same day as that Friday night Tina had canceled on her, allowing her to say yes to Val, spaghetti and the start of an affair that had led to this moment.

A month ago. Plenty of time for her to have gotten pregnant. There was no way. No way.

And yet…there was a way. Funny how she'd never have thought of pregnancy in a million years if Val hadn't suggested it first.

She snagged her keys and let herself out of the house, then drove to the store wearing leggings and an old T-shirt that she'd dug out of one of the bags she'd left at Val's house.

The whole process took less than fifteen minutes and, suddenly numb, she slid to the floor of his bathroom to await the results, slim white stick in hand. That's where Val found her some indeterminate period of time later, long after the two pink lines had appeared.

As he crouched next to her, his expression grave, she waved the stick. "Guess we're going to have that conversation after all."

Thirteen

Sabrina held a positive pregnancy test *in her hand*. A positive pregnancy test. Sabrina was *pregnant*.

The swamp of emotions blasting through Val's gut could not be quantified. Hope, panic, joy, uncertainty. No one thing jumped to the forefront as he sank to the floor to sit next to her.

"I'd dismissed the possibility of pregnancy from my mind after..." He swallowed as he recalled the exact point at which they'd cut off the conversation, once he'd stuck his foot in his mouth by bringing up the point that he might not be the one celebrating this news with her.

And now he had to wedge his foot firmly into his mouth.

"Sabrina." He blew out a breath and forged ahead. "We can't skip that part this time. Is there the remotest possibility that the baby is Xavier's?"

She shook her head. "We never slept together."

Then everything else was manageable. Hope and joy

won out, flooding his heart with so much raw emotion that it pushed upward, leaking out through his eyes. "That's…great."

His voice stopped working, and he swallowed a few more times to no avail. Looked like he had no choice but to greet the news that he was going to be a father with happy tears.

"Is it?" She didn't so much as glance at him in favor of staring at the white plastic stick clutched in her fingers. "I would have thought you'd be the last in line for a complication like this. I hate to force it, but this is the part where you have to tell me where our relationship stands."

Last in line? Wait, she thought he was unhappy about this?

"Sabrina, look at me." To help that along since she didn't seem inclined to move, he cupped her jaw and brought her chin up, unable to keep a tender smile from curving his mouth upward. "We're building a family. That's what we're doing. Unexpectedly, sure. But that doesn't dilute the fact that we're having a *baby*. Together. We're a team. Nothing has changed."

The rightness of it inundated him and, suddenly, it all clicked into place. The terms of the will had been difficult, challenging, archaic and unfair—but his father had unwittingly introduced the first step in the rest of Val's life. This was hands down the best thing that had ever happened to him.

"Everything has changed," she countered, her eyes huge and troubled as she nestled her cheek against one of his palms without even seeming to realize that she'd sought the comfort of his touch. "We don't even live in the same house."

He snorted. That was her concern? "Please. You sleep

here ninety percent of the time. The address on your driver's license is simply a formality. Change it. Today."

"Are you asking me to move in with you?" A line appeared between her eyebrows as she processed that. "Because I was expecting something a little more...*more* to accompany that question."

"Hell, no, I'm not asking you to move in." He was botching this, likely because he'd never done anything remotely like this before, and of course Sabrina wasn't going to hesitate to call him on it. That was one of her best qualities. "I'm asking you to marry me."

Shock made her mouth drop open, and that's when she pulled away from his hands. "*Marry* you? Val, that's insane. No one gets married after dating for a month."

His hands fell into his lap, and he let her go because what was he supposed to do, force her to let him touch her? Force her to feel the same way about him that he felt about her? "Yet we're having a baby after dating for a month. Facts are facts. I don't want my child raised anywhere but in my ancestral home. Call me old-fashioned, but I'd also like to be married to my kid's mother."

Sabrina slumped against the bathroom wall. Yeah, not the most ideal place for life-changing decisions, but he had to work with what he had. He'd like to tell her how much she meant to him, but she wasn't giving him a whole lot of encouragement to continue spilling his heart all over her.

"Think about it," he encouraged her. "We have eight months to get this worked out."

She nodded, and the tight bands that had been squeezing his chest loosened somewhat. As long as Sabrina wasn't going to run screaming into the night with his baby along for the ride, he could handle anything else she threw at him.

"I'm having a hard time imagining you in a long-term relationship," she said.

Except that. Uncomfortable all at once, he shifted, and his own back hit the wall. Yeah, okay, so he'd never been in a long-term relationship. He'd never been the CEO of LeBlanc either, but he hadn't burned the place down yet.

Somehow he didn't think mentioning that was going to wipe away her very real concerns about an untried concept like Val being tied to one woman for the whole of his life. The fact that the concept filled him with a warm glow instead of panic was proof enough for him. He just had to figure out how to convince her of that.

"We have time to work through that too. Just don't give up on the idea before then, okay?" She nodded again, and he pulled her into a long hug, burying his lips in her hair. "It's going to be great, you'll see."

His mind spun as he contemplated all the ducks he had to line up in a row come sunrise. Engagement ring, first and foremost. Would it be out of line to combine that with a trip to Botswana? He'd love to present Sabrina with a diamond he'd pulled from the earth himself. Or was he overdoing it again?

Before he could even think about proposing to Sabrina for real, he had a very important meeting with Jada Ness to initiate. He owed it to his future wife and the mother of his child to draw a very firm line in the sand where other women were concerned. The handsy designer was the number-one place to start.

Getting Jada to agree to an appointment ended up being harder than Val had anticipated. He contemplated leaving her a voice mail, but he did have a thin thread of hope that he could firmly convince the woman to sign with LeBlanc regardless of whether she got side benefits or not.

The deal he'd worked up with Legal had pizzazz, and she'd get the winning hand out of the agreement. Val had made sure of that.

But she made him cool his heels for two days before she finally strolled through the door of his office, coolness cloaking her from the moment she appeared. No problem. He had lots of practice melting Sabrina's ice. Jada wouldn't be too tough a nut to crack.

"I've decided to forgive you," she announced with fanfare, flinging a long vintage ermine scarf around her neck as she waltzed toward his desk. "For standing me up. But just this once."

And the Oscar goes to… Val bit that back. But come on. Drama queen much? To be fair, he had been the one to cancel drinks with almost no notice and then busied them both with emails and options rather than using the personal touch she responded to. He should be thanking her for gracing him with her presence at all. "You're too kind, Ms. Ness."

"Jada," she murmured and slid into the closest chair, crossing her legs carefully for maximum exposure. "I do hope we're still friends."

"We can do business together," he told her, his voice steady as he slid the sheaf of papers toward her. "But that's the extent. This contract is a bit more generous than we discussed, but I think you're worth it."

"There you go again, being charming." She pursed her lips into the practiced pout that she seemed to favor. "It hardly seems fair that you then turn around and soundly dismiss the idea of being more than business associates. I have a fair amount of talent in certain—shall we say—*areas*. You don't know what you're missing."

"I'm missing your signature on this contract. I'm recently engaged, so there's no chance of anything more than a mutually beneficial business venture between parties."

Jada snagged the contract, her sleeves rising to reveal sapphire-encrusted cuff bracelets on both arms, and stuffed it into her giant alligator bag. "You're the most slippery male I've ever come across, Valentino LeBlanc. I'll read over the contract, but don't hold your breath. I'm still hoping you'll honor our original agreement." She rose and held out her hand, but to her side, forcing Val to skirt the desk in order to shake it.

He could afford to bend in this one instance. But the moment he clasped her hand, she pulled him closer, catching him in her embrace. The quick movement knocked them both off balance, and his arms came up around her automatically. Before he could correct his stance, she lifted her lips to his, almost connecting, but he turned his head at the last microsecond.

That's when he realized they weren't alone.

Sabrina was standing at the door of his office, her face devoid of color.

"Sabrina. Slow down."

Val had followed her down four flights of stairs, God knew why. Sabrina had told him in no uncertain terms to leave her alone. Had he listened? No. Just like every other time she'd tried to tell him how she felt about something.

Except this time, her heart had cracked in two and fallen out of her chest to land in a heap on the carpet of his office. Every other time, she'd still cared somewhat. Now she didn't. She'd known this was coming. *Known.* The fact that it was *Val* who'd betrayed hurt worse than anything she ever imagined.

Whirling at the base of the next flight of stairs, she confronted him, her index finger flying up to stab him in the chest. "I don't want to hear what you have to say. Back off!"

"You do want to hear what I have to say," he countered hotly, their voices echoing in the enclosed concrete stairwell. "Because what you saw is not what it looked like."

Her laugh sounded hysterical even to her own ears. "Oh, my God. Do men pass around an excuse jar? Next time you need a good one, just pull out a slip of paper and use that?"

"It's not an excuse—"

"Okay, I'll bite, only to get you to stop following me. Please, Val. Tell me whatever lies you'd like me to believe about what was going on in your office. You had a beautiful woman in your arms. With the door closed. She was kissing you, and you avoided it by turning your head. Stop me when I get to the part where it wasn't what it looked like."

Oh, God. Another woman had put her hands on Val. If she'd had any question about how she felt about him, that scene had answered it. She was in love with him. Otherwise it wouldn't hurt so much.

He scowled. "That's exactly what was happening. If you know I wasn't actively engaged in that kiss, then what is the problem? You're clearly upset and—"

"You had a beautiful woman in your office with the door closed!" She pinched the bridge of her nose, furious with herself for even bothering to get emotional. "What if I hadn't walked in? Would you have broken down and eventually kissed her? What about next time?"

"No!" he shot back. "And thanks for the trust, by the way. I specifically met with her to make it clear that I would never be interested in her. I did that for you."

"Oh, no, don't push this on me. We've been dating for a month. One would hope that you'd already made it clear that you wouldn't be interested in her." Some of the unease from earlier conversations about Jada filtered through her beleaguered senses. "But you hadn't, had you? I overheard her mention an original agreement. I'm not daft, Val. I know what I saw, and she was disappointed that you weren't coming on to her. What was the original agreement?"

Guilt flickered through his gaze and arrowed right through her heart. Funny, she'd have said there was nothing there to hurt. She'd be wrong.

Why was it always the same? She'd known going in that he wasn't a one-woman man. But somehow she'd convinced herself that it was okay because they hadn't made any promises. Until she'd gotten pregnant and he'd spilled all of those pretty words about getting married. That was a hell of a promise.

And she'd fallen for it. Actually believed that he'd done a complete turnaround because something momentous and unprecedented had happened. Was she destined to always fall for the same kind of man? Her stupid hormonal brain had actually convinced itself that marrying Val was a great idea, that it would all work out if she willed it hard enough to be so.

"There was no original agreement," he snapped, his face like granite with no give. "She thought there was. But I never told her that was happening. I cannot believe that you're upset I was having a business meeting with someone you'd pushed me to sign an agreement with. You weren't even supposed to be here right now."

That tipped her over the edge. Raw, sheer fury coursed through her blood, tightening her hands into fists. If he kept talking, she might drive one into his mouth. "Oh, my mistake. You're right. This is all my fault. I'm too clingy and expect too much from the man who just proposed to me. Like propriety, even when there's no chance of being caught. You can't believe I'm upset? That proves that we're not meant to be together."

In spades. He didn't get it. At all.

Val sighed and shut his eyes for a beat, his shoulders sagging. "That wasn't what I meant. You're not to blame. I am. I'm sorry."

It was her turn to blink. "What did you say? Did you apologize?"

He lifted his hands in confusion. "Yeah. Is that not allowed either?"

"It's allowed." And for some reason, it deflated her anger. A little. She had no experience with a man who apologized. What was she supposed to do with that? "Tell me what I don't know, Val. I'm pregnant, and my emotions are running high. I need you to be honest with me."

"I'm trying to be." His face had softened somewhat. "I know you have a history of men who are less than honest with you, and I'm trying not to be angry that you're lumping me into the same category," he returned tightly. "And I did not cheat on you."

This time. "So, this was all one-hundred-percent Jada Ness barking up the wrong tree. You've given her zero encouragement."

"That's exactly right. I had asked her to have drinks before we got involved—at your instence by the way—and once you and I started seeing each other, I canceled. I can't help the fact that she took one last shot. Or that you walked in on it."

A chill invaded her chest, and she had just enough energy left to be surprised that she could feel it. "You were interested in her at one point."

Bingo. It was written all over his face. But he shook his head, firmly in the denial zone. "As a business associate. Only."

"You were stringing her along. Making her think there was something going on so she'd sign with LeBlanc. Weren't you?" Oh, dear God. It was all so clear. He'd been playing Jada. And thus also playing Sabrina. If not overtly, then subconsciously, especially since this was the first she'd heard of it. "You were stringing us *both* along."

Val had the nerve to bristle at that, and that's how she knew she'd hit a nerve.

"I wasn't stringing you along."

She jerked her chin. "But you were stringing Jada along?"

"God, Sabrina." He stared at the ceiling for a long time, his knee jiggling as tension vibrated through his whole frame. "This is you with your emotions running high? I'm glad you told me, or I wouldn't have recognized it."

"What's that supposed to mean?" Stung, she took a step back.

"You've barely even raised your voice. This is all so matter of fact to you, as if you were just waiting for this opportunity to accuse me of unforgivable things so you could be done. I want to marry you. My stomach is churning over the possibility that something I have no control over will prevent that. And yet, you don't even seem particularly bothered by the fact that we're having a very difficult discussion."

Because letting him see how this was affecting her was *not happening*. Being vulnerable gave a man ammunition to gouge out even more flesh, to continue twisting that knife until the gutting was complete. Better that he never realize how this conversation was killing her.

At least she'd gotten that part right.

The chill in her chest spread to take over pretty much everything. Numb, she stared at him, a little shocked that it had come down to this after all. "You're not far off. I have been waiting for you to show your true colors, and you just did. I'm allowed to be upset in my own way, and it doesn't erase the fact that you're the one who is in the wrong here. An apology doesn't make it go away. I need to be able to trust you, and I don't."

That was the bottom line. He'd failed the test. She couldn't marry him and subject her child to the same thing she'd gone through. To willingly sign up for more heartache as he pushed the envelope further and further with the next woman who came on to him. It was better to be alone. She should have realized that long ago and saved them both the heartache.

Pain etched his expression, and he shoved his hands into his pockets. "So, this whole time, I've been falling for you, and you've been looking for an excuse not to trust me."

"Val." She shook her head, damping the tug on her heart—and a confession in kind. "I've been desperately looking for a way to trust you. I started to, or I never would have let you kiss me over snow cones. The rest never would have happened."

She'd broken her own rules time and time again for him. That was probably the hardest thing to swallow. She'd known better and done it anyway.

"If you'd really started to trust me, you'd be able to see that I was trying to do the right thing for our relationship. Since you can't, our romance is doomed anyway."

His dark blue eyes dimmed, and she almost took it all back just to see him light up again, just to hear him say he was falling for her. But that wasn't going to work. Not now. He was absolutely correct. Their romance had likely always been doomed, simply because of her history.

This was more her fault than she'd been able to admit. "Actually, I see more than you're giving me credit for. This is my issue. You probably did do what you think is the right thing, and that's the fundamental problem. I'm sorry. This was all a mistake. I shouldn't be in a relationship with anyone."

Least of all a sensual, gorgeous man, who had his pick of women. They'd always seek him out like moths to a flame and, eventually, one would break through his marriage vows.

Doomed. It was as good a word as any to describe the nature of her feelings for Val. This was her cross to bear, and she couldn't crumble in the face of so many conflicting emotions. Val deserved better.

Fourteen

"So that's it?"

Val couldn't keep the incredulity from his voice. Didn't want to. This was an unprecedented situation, in which the mother of his child was handing him his hat, cool as a cucumber. Scarcely affected by the fact that she'd ripped his soul from its moorings.

"I'm not sure what else you want me to say."

Of course she didn't have a clue—she hadn't bothered to even try to get one. She'd conveniently given herself an out by claiming that this was all her fault because she shouldn't be in a relationship. That was crap. A cop-out. "I have an entire list of things I'd like you to say, but it seems I'm not being given a choice but to let you walk away."

She lifted her hands with another shrug, as if to say *win some, lose some.* "I think it's best. Now you're free to call Jada and get her on board by whatever means possible."

"Free to call—" Val held in an extremely profane word that had sprung to his lips and controlled his temper for the hundredth time. This was not the place to let his emotions off the leash, or he'd say something he regretted.

Actually he'd already said several things he regretted, not the least of which was telling Sabrina that he was falling for her. She'd accepted that news without blinking, as if learning that he'd selected the ripest melon at the grocery store.

Well, it was huge to Val. First time he'd ever said that to a woman. First time he'd ever *felt* that for a woman. Sabrina had no idea how difficult it was to confess something of that magnitude and get nothing in return.

"I don't want to call Jada," he informed her tightly. "I never did. That's what's so frustrating about all of this. You're crucifying me over something that isn't even a thing."

She nodded. "I get that you'd see it that way. But I'm trying to make it clear that I'm the one with the issue. Not you. This is my problem, and I should work on it before I can be with someone long-term."

Val shook his head. Didn't help. He could still hear the roaring in his ears as one truth became self-evident. This was nothing close to her fault. It was his. For letting his emotions get in the way of doing the task his father had laid out for him. For letting himself fall for the person who was supposed to be helping him get there.

He'd completely taken his eye off the ball, letting his need for acceptance and love cloud his judgment. Instead of embracing her, he should be pushing her away. Also known as the most difficult, necessary task he'd ever been faced with in his life.

"You're absolutely right. You've averted a disaster in

the making. We have no business getting involved. I'm the one who made that mistake."

And now the evisceration was complete. Sabrina didn't feel like a mistake, and he'd just lied to her. She was the best thing that had ever happened to him. He cursed his father for creating such an impossible situation, cursed the fact that Sabrina was forcing him to learn the lessons she'd been trying to teach him after all.

He wasn't supposed to feel *anything*. CEOs ruthlessly cut people out, easily divorcing the action from their emotions without a backward glance. This was his singular opportunity to practice that.

The paradox swirled through his chest, riling his temper, despite all his efforts to keep it under tabs. "So what now? You're still pregnant."

Sabrina stood there, coolly contemplating him, her emotional center nice and unaffected behind her frosty walls. "I don't know. I guess we still have eight months to figure that out."

He nodded once. "I'll consider the options, and let you know what I think will work best."

She didn't argue. Likely because she was ready to be done. So was he. He couldn't stand to be so close to her and not have the luxury of touching her, talking to her. Telling her all of the things in his heart, none of which reflected what had just come out of his mouth.

He skirted her without another word and descended the rest of the stairs to the ground floor—the opposite direction of where he should be headed. He'd lost more than the woman he'd hoped to spend his life with. He'd lost his coach, his teammate. The one person he'd counted on to help him push the needle to the billion dollar mark at LeBlanc, and he couldn't even take her excellent advice to pick things up with Jada again.

Heartsick, he drove until he had no idea where he'd ended up. The problem was that he wanted to go to LBC, where he understood everything and the people wore their hearts on their sleeves. Caring was encouraged, not lambasted, and every move he made at his food bank helped someone.

But that was Xavier's domain now and would be for months still. Instead of bemoaning the reality, Val's time would be well spent doing his job with the chair he'd been given behind the CEO's desk at LeBlanc Jewelers. Thus far, he'd failed nearly every task he'd been given, and he needed to turn that around. Earning his inheritance would help LBC the most, which had always been his first priority.

The cure for his heart didn't exist.

Sabrina was nowhere to be seen when he returned to LeBlanc. Just as well. The hollow feeling in his chest would serve as all the reminder he needed of his brief, bright time with her. He'd never gotten around to asking her why she'd come by earlier, not that it mattered. But he did have a warped curiosity about what had prompted the visit that had brought about the end of their relationship.

The mining contracts served as a great distraction from the miserable events of the day thus far. Or rather, they should have. He found his attention drifting. The verbiage read like a dry law textbook, and Val wished for nothing more than an excuse to heave the entire binder out the window.

Now would be a great time for a coach. Or a mentor. Someone. Anyone who knew the slightest bit about the pitfalls he should look for on these printed pages or, barring that, the ins and outs of the government of Botswana.

A crash jolted his attention from a contract, and he

glanced up sharply. One of the framed pictures had fallen from the bookcase across the room. It lay on the carpet, face down. Val swiveled out of his seat to retrieve it.

As he picked it up, he examined it, mostly to ensure the glass hadn't broken. Xavier's face stared at him. It was a photo of his brother with a dark-skinned man, both of them grinning at the camera as they held a large pair of scissors, poised to cut a red ribbon. The banner behind them read *Gwajanca Mine*.

Xavier. There was no stipulation in the will that said he couldn't ask an expert to help him through this contract, even if the person was his brother. He set the picture on the shelf. A ghost in the machine perhaps?

Val called Xavier and left a voice mail, wondering if he should have combined this request with a trip to LBC, just to check on things. Xavier might not even respond to his message, deleting it as a matter of course without even listening to it. But within fifteen minutes, he had his answer in the form of a knock at the open door.

"You rang?" His brother eyed him. "Holy hell on a horse. Are you wearing a suit?"

"Yeah." Val scarcely noticed it anymore unless Sabrina commented on how hot he looked. Maybe he had changed more during his stint in the chair than he'd credited. He stood and crossed the room to hold his hand out to Xavier, who shook it cautiously.

How horrible was it that a simple handshake between brothers put such a suspicious glint in Xavier's gaze?

"I wasn't expecting you so soon," Val said.

The handshake broke the odd tension, strangely enough. That was the first time Val could remember extending anything approaching a warm welcome to Xavier.

"I wasn't expecting to get your call." Xavier glanced

around the office, taking it all in. "You haven't changed anything."

Except for the potato plant which had started outgrowing the pot Val had planted it in, that was true. He shrugged. "This is still your office. It's only on loan. There's no reason to put my stamp on it."

"I hope you'll forgive me that I didn't take the same approach with LBC. I've…struggled, to put it mildly. It helped to do some redecorating."

A little shocked that Xavier would admit such a thing, Val ushered his brother into the office and bit back the questions. Not the least of which was what his former office looked like with Xavier's taste directing the decor. It was probably fine.

On that note…

"I'm struggling too," Val admitted and let out the breath he'd been holding. "That's why I called. Why are we keeping our struggles to ourselves? It makes no sense, and Dad's will doesn't say we have to do this alone. Let me help you. I'd be happy to. In return, you help me."

Xavier perched on the chair Sabrina had always favored. The couple were more alike than Val had fully recognized, both emotionless, unfeeling. Or so it seemed. Once he'd dug through Sabrina's layers, he'd found a warm, wonderful woman.

What would he find if he took the time to do the same kind of excavation with his own flesh and blood?

"I'm surprised you'd offer." Xavier ran a hand over his closely cropped hair. "You've never cared about anything that had my name on it."

In years past, Val would have let his own hurts rule his heart, to the point of saying things that he shouldn't. Things he couldn't unsay. Case in point, it would be easy to turn that back on Xavier, illuminate how Val had been the one cut out from the LeBlanc Men's Club, not the other way around. "Let's say that I'm learning there are two sides to every story. I want to hear yours."

Astonishment played about Xavier's expression, but he was too well schooled in keeping his cards close to the vest to let it take over. Val would have missed it if he hadn't been paying specific attention to his brother. Did Sabrina do the same—haul her frostiness out in order to keep more hurt at bay? After all, she'd been hurt repeatedly by people who should have cared for her. Val included.

Fine time to be working on how to relate to the woman who had just cast him off.

But the unsettling realizations wouldn't leave him be. How well had he really known how to read Sabrina? How much credit had he given her very opposite personality type when attempting to build a relationship with her? Not much. His conscience convicted him of another forty-seven sins in the span of seconds.

"Marjorie quit," Xavier said flatly. "I was hoping you might help me hire someone to take her place. I had no idea that she basically ran LBC, and I'm pretty much dead in the water."

Val blinked. That was a hell of story. "Marjorie quit? What did you do to her?"

Oh, God. This was a disaster. Why hadn't she called to talk to Val first? Xavier must have gotten crossways with her something fierce if she'd just up and quit. Marjorie loved LBC almost as much as Val. He made a mental note to reach out to her and get the lay of the land before he blasted Xavier for losing the glue that had held the charity together.

"It's a long story," Xavier said bleakly. "I'm sorry, okay? Losing Marjorie is huge. I get that. I've made a lot of mistakes. I'm making mistakes as we speak, such as hanging out here instead of at LBC where I should be."

Val nodded and dredged up some grace from God knew where, though he could hardly cast stones. They both still had several months left to get their respective tasks wrong. "I refused to let the CFO close the New England division."

It was Xavier's turn to let thunderclouds gather across his face but, to his credit, he took a page from Val's book and left off the rant. "That's a tough call. I'm sure you made the decision that seemed best to you at the time."

What was this conversation they were having? It was civil, productive. Not like their normal interaction at all. Was it possible they were both learning valuable lessons, thanks to this ridiculous inheritance business?

"Regardless, I've hit a wall with the contracts. This is a long-term relationship with another country, and I don't want to take the chance of screwing it up. I need help."

Thanks to the insights he'd gained recently, he could say that out loud. He had little experience to draw from when it came to anything long-term. Even food, his first love, was ephemeral. Cooked and consumed in such a short period of time.

How much of his life had been built on the same concept? And how sad to figure out that he pretty much expected things to slip through his fingers. Which had led him to never tighten his grip for fear of that loss.

He'd let Sabrina go, perhaps because he'd always been braced for it. But nothing felt settled with her. It didn't feel *over*. On hold, if anything.

Xavier leaned forward, bracing his elbows on the desk. While Val had somehow transitioned into a suit-wearing executive while he wasn't looking, Xavier wore a simple T-shirt and jeans. Frankly, it might be the first time in recent memory that Val could recall his brother being clad in something other than capitalism.

"The idea of wading through contracts makes me weep with joy," Xavier said so calmly that Val had to laugh.

"I'm guessing that wasn't actually a joke, which means today is my lucky day." Pushing the binder across the desk, Val waved at it. "Be my guest. Tell me what I need to know."

Together, they poured over the contract. At 7:00 p.m., Val ordered delivery from a Chinese restaurant around the corner, and they ate kung pao chicken while slashing and burning through the non-beneficial clauses the legal team in Botswana had snuck into the verbiage. It was the first meal he'd eaten with his brother since their mother had forced them to the table together at Christmas.

Val much preferred this one.

And maybe that meant it was time to clear the air about something that had been scraping at his consciousness. "You didn't really have anything serious with Sabrina, right?"

Xavier glanced up, his expression open, a testament to the fragile bonds they were weaving here.

"I heard you were dating her. It's fine. I struck out with her and you didn't. I was over it a long time ago."

Oddly, that made Val feel a lot better than if Xavier had said he hated the idea. Somewhere along the way, besting Xavier had faded as a goal. If he did manage to find a way to resume his relationship with her, it would be because he still loved her.

The brothers slid back into the contract easily. It was nice.

When they'd reached a suitable place to stop in the document, he clapped his brother on the shoulder. "Call me once you get some passable applicants for Marjorie's position. I'll swing by and interview them with you, if you want."

It was a gamble. Xavier could reject that idea out of hand and insist on doing things his own way, which was perfectly within his rights. But, instead, relief spread through his gaze. "That would be great."

Val's brother left LeBlanc after a few parting instructions on how to deliver the revised contract to the company's liaison in the Botswanan government office, citing a probable one-to two-month turnaround on the response. Disappointed that he had to wait to see if things shook out as they'd hoped, Val sat in his chair, at a loss as to his next move when this corporation moved at the speed of a glacier.

An empty house greeted him, which shouldn't have been such a shock, considering that it had always been that way from the moment he'd moved in. But lately, it had been filled with Sabrina, and he missed her keenly all at once.

In the short time since he'd become aware of her pregnancy, he'd imagined his own child following Val's mother's footsteps around the property. Sure, he could and would share custody, but that wasn't the same. It was too entrenched a vision to erase, and sadness crowded into his chest all over again. That dream would never be a reality now, not with the categorical rejection Sabrina had dished out over something as trivial as a woman making a pass at him.

Except it wasn't trivial to Sabrina. That had been her point all along—a man who cared about her would have been extra cautious about potential triggers and, instead of honoring that about her, he'd blown it off as no big deal when she called him on it. Like an idiot. Then to top it all off, she'd readily accepted that it was her issue. And that was that. Val had kissed their relationship goodbye without a fight because being passed over due to his inherent flaws was par for the course.

The silence of his big empty house condemned him further. Val's father was dead, and thus he couldn't confront the old man about the legacy of crap he'd left in his son's head. If he could, what would he say?

What he should say was *Thanks*. A good old-fashioned, sincere thank-you. Val had formed his own place at LBC and, having seen the other side through his own eyes, he'd have hated feeling like he had to follow his father into LeBlanc. Why was he still holding on to that hurt?

Ironic—that was the one thing he'd kept a tight grip on.

There in the dark, he let it go. And vowed to find a way to get back everything else he'd failed to hold close.

Sabrina pried her eyes open and went over her résumé again. If third time was the charm, what was number 403? The round of insanity?

Her résumé still felt thin. She didn't have enough experience for the director job, even for a small office-supply company like Penultimate. The headhunter she was working with had convinced Sabrina she should submit her résumé, that her experience as the CEO of her own company went a long way. She had to take this shot, since it would give her the experience needed for a higher level executive job. Walking away from Val two weeks ago had destroyed her, and only reaching toward something else, something positive, would build her up again.

If she was better off alone, then she'd have to raise this baby by herself too, and things like health insurance were expensive for self-employed people. Of course Val would pay child support, but this was all new and she had no idea how to provide for a child other than to ensure all her ducks were in a row. Finally, Sabrina was making smart decisions.

Which didn't explain at all why she answered her phone when Val's name popped up on the screen. She should hang up. Pretend she'd lost her phone. Throw it in the freezer. Something. Anything other than say hello.

"Sabrina. Don't hang up."

Too late. His voice bled through her like a soothing balm over all the places inside that had been scraped raw. Instantly. Two weeks of hell, and all it took to make it vanish was four words from the man she'd been unable to forget.

"I wasn't sure you'd answer," he said in the long pause.

"I shouldn't have," she muttered. But she shouldn't have done a lot of things and, much like her entire history with Val, she couldn't take this back either. "It's almost midnight. I could have been asleep."

"Yeah, about that. I'm standing on your front porch. I, um, saw you sitting at your desk through the curtains, or I wouldn't have called."

Val was *here*? She rocketed to the door and flung it open, completely ashamed of how the sight of him punched her in the gut in the very best way. Oh God, had she missed him. The days apart melted away.

But not the hurt and anger.

"What do you want?" she said into the phone that she still held to her ear like an imbecile. Lowering it to her side, she stared at the slightly disheveled man on her doorstep.

His hair hung over one eye, giving him a rakish, one-eyed pirate look that slayed her. With his suit jacket discarded somewhere and his shirt sleeves rolled to mid-forearm, she'd be hard-pressed to call him anything other than devastatingly handsome.

She shouldn't be calling him anything.

"I want you," he said simply and, in continuation of the craziness, he knelt on one knee, his hand outstretched.

That's when she saw the enormous diamond set in platinum clutched between his fingers. Her hand flew to her mouth, but it didn't stanch the squeak that leaked out anyway.

"I did it all wrong last time," he explained. "So I'm starting over. Sabrina, first and foremost, I love you. I don't know how it happened or when, but it's almost like it was always there from the first moment. I love the way you eat snow cones, the way you analyze the crap out of every last thing I say, even the way you announce that I've screwed up. And I screwed up. A lot. You had every right to be upset about Jada because I didn't get it. But now I do. I've spent the past weeks figuring out how to be in love with someone who needs me to take extra care with something so fragile and precious as trust."

"That's an engagement ring," she said inanely because her brain was still on the fact that Valentino LeBlanc was on one knee asking her again to marry him. Wasn't he? "So you've figured it all out?"

He nodded, his gaze turning tender. "My life…it was pretty hollow before you came along, and I never realized it until you were gone. If you can forgive me for getting it all wrong so far, I'd like to spend a very long time getting it right. Marry me. Let me prove I can be monogamous, now that I've found the only woman I want to be with forever."

That pretty much covered all of her questions. But

wasn't an answer at all. "You have a talent for pretty words, I'll give you that, Val."

"They're heartfelt." He rubbed a thumb over the diamond, drawing her reluctant eye to the fire contained within it. "I went to Botswana. Like you suggested. It was glorious. The president of Botswana appreciated the personal visit so much he granted us the exploration contract right then and there with no revisions."

"Us?" It was a revelation to hear him speak in such inclusive terms about a company he'd only begun to helm and would give up again eventually.

"Xavier went with me. We're working together. It's the best of both worlds, the combined power of the LeBlanc brothers."

He was talking about his brother. Xavier was the *we*. Sabrina's knees almost gave out. "You traveled with Xavier? On purpose?"

He hated his brother. Or at least he disliked him strongly. Every time Xavier's name had come up, she felt like she'd been dropped on eggshells and then told to walk without cracking one.

"It was time to grow up." Val shrugged, a difficult task indeed with a diamond that had to weigh umpteen pounds still gripped in his fingers. "I let my emotions rule me and excuse it by calling myself passionate. I'm learning a lot by taking a step back and paying attention to others instead of my own agenda. That's the only way I could have realized how deeply I hurt you by sabotaging our relationship. And I've done a lot of soul-searching about that. Jada was my subconscious way of ensuring that you didn't get too close. I'm sorry, sweetheart. That will never happen again."

The quiet humbleness in his voice hooked something inside and wouldn't let go. She shouldn't keep listening to this. It was making her doubt everything, especially what she knew to be true: that she and Val didn't belong together. They didn't work. They shouldn't work.

All at once, she was so tired of *shoulds*.

Sinking to the ground, she knelt before him. "Your arm must be tired of holding up that ring."

He smiled. "Then let me put it on you."

In true Val fashion, he didn't wait for her to hold out her hand but caught it up in his and slipped the ring on her third finger. It had enormous weight and not just the physical kind. The stone was gorgeous, full of fire and ice.

"I mined that myself," he told her quietly. "With the help of some very nice miners who are probably still laughing at me to this day."

Curling her fingers around it, she held it close to her heart. "I'll never take it off."

"See that you don't. There's not another one like it in the world. I had our names lasered onto the diamond's girdle when it was being cut."

Awe and disbelief went to war in her heart. Staring at the diamond, she tried to see the names, but that was silly. Surely they were too small. But she'd always know they were there. "That's a huge step. What if I'd said no?"

"I wasn't going to give up. Ever."

Her eyes filled with tears. Dear God, where had Val been all her life? She didn't have any words for how he'd healed her heart with that one bit of confidence. That was the only way she could admit her own failings. After all, she'd hurt him too, by refusing to have conversations they should have had much earlier but hadn't because she'd been too afraid of the answers she'd get.

"I have my own problems. I shouldn't be wearing this ring right now. Are you sure you want to put up with a woman who is constantly looking over your shoulder, constantly braced for signs of deceit? I don't know that I'll ever completely lose that."

Oh, but she wanted to. She wanted to believe that it could be different this time. What if that was the only thing it took to make it so?

"I hope you don't. Put me to the test over and over. My eyes are fixed on you and you only. I want to show you that I can pass your trust detector for the rest of my life."

There must've been something fundamentally wrong with her because all she could say was *Yes*.

Yes to Val, yes to forever, yes to him passing all her tests with flying colors. Instead of only feeling safe and secure in a relationship, Val was giving her the opportunity to be brave. Passionate. To *feel*. And she wasn't giving that up for anything.

That's when he pulled her into his arms and, as they knelt on the porch of her house, he kissed her, murmuring *I love you* in between. She said it back with all of her heart.

Epilogue

Sabrina moved into Val's house, and it finally became the home he'd always envisioned. Funny how he'd thought the ghosts of his mother's childhood had created a homey feeling already, but the pale shadows of the past could not begin to compare with the future that Val had fought for—and won.

The current Mrs. LeBlanc became fast friends with the future Mrs. LeBlanc, and his fiancée spent an enormous amount of time with his mother putting the nursery together. He'd have thought the wedding plans would dominate both women, but they scarcely gave him a nod when he brought it up. What, was he the only one around here who cared about the *I do*s?

A few weeks later, he got Sabrina into a white dress and gifted his bride with heirloom earrings from the LeBlanc vault. She wore both when she married Val in front of the fireplace at the palatial LeBlanc estate, with only close friends and family in attendance. He wasn't the slightest bit ashamed to be the first one to shed a tear as he recited his vows, though Sabrina gave him a run for his money now that her pregnancy hormones had turned her into an emotional faucet. She sobbed through her vows defiantly, letting Val and everyone else see exactly how she felt about him.

Val loved that almost as much as he loved her. What better way to keep his wife's frosty attitude at bay than to make sure she stayed pregnant for the next twenty years or so? He'd be thrilled with nineteen more kids. Sabrina laughed and told him to let her get through the first child before he started making plans to knock her up again.

A few promising résumés had trickled in and, three days after Val and Sabrina returned from a honeymoon in Fiji, he and Xavier started the process of interviewing a replacement for Marjorie. It turned out that she'd quit not because of his brother's dictatorial style but due to her mother's failing health. Bad timing, which she profusely apologized to Val for at least four times when he finally got her on the phone.

Val and Xavier talked nearly every day, bouncing ideas off each other and working through issues together. Sabrina was still a part of his team, but she'd taken the job with Penultimate and, more often than not, she was asking Val for advice on how to handle a distribution snafu or what qualities he'd value most in an HR manager. Every answer helped him solidify his own strategy with LeBlanc.

Neither brother had quite met their inheritance goals, but they still had three more months to get it in the bag. Val had a whole new perspective on the will and, frankly, each night as he lay in bed listening to Sabrina breathe, he felt like he'd already won.

How could money possibly compare with having the love of his life by his side forever? It didn't. Couldn't. Val wasn't his father's favorite and, finally, he was at peace with it. Love was the real inheritance lesson.

* * * * *

LET'S TALK
Romance

For exclusive extracts, competitions
and special offers, find us online:

f facebook.com/millsandboon

⊙ @millsandboonuk

𝕏 @millsandboon

Or get in touch on 0844 844 1351*

For all the latest titles coming soon, visit
millsandboon.co.uk/nextmonth